THE FLYWEI

GUY THOMSON

LONGCROSS PRESS

The Flyweight
Copyright © Guy Thomson 2014
Longcross Press

ISBN 978-0-9560983-2-0

THE FLYWEIGHT

To Louigi
(she knows who she is)

Acknowledgements

I would like to extend my heartfelt thanks to the many people who have assisted me with the creation of this novel, in particular, Caroline Mitchell-Innes for typing the original drafts with such patience; Henry von Blumenthal of Longcross Press whose experience in the book world proved invaluable as *de facto* editor and publisher; Louise Grant for her help correcting and finessing the final manuscript; Claire Forster and Cascade Group for their able assistance in printing the working drafts; Sean de Burgh for supplying material for the back cover; John Graham, managing director of the aptly named AD Creative for his time, input, expertise and execution of the overall cover design and finally, in this context, Lynn Curtis for the thoroughness of her work as correctional editor and content advisor .

Also, I would like to mention the following people for their assessment, encouragement, criticism and suggestions for the book, in no particular order but with equal thanks: Marc Burca, Jane and Hugo Charlton, Mark Glowery, Amanda Hermitage, David Bennet, Claire Clay, Maryan Milanes, Claire and Charles Pelham, Patricia Madden, David Sutton, Nicholas Monson, Jane Cooler and Mark Ryder.

CONTENTS

Chapter 1: Confusion

The duvet smelt of old socks. There was nothing new about that. I felt many sorts of awful. There was nothing new about that either. The bedside clock read 7.05 am. I had to see my probation officer that morning, which was always a laugh. I threw back the duvet and got out of bed. My head was still running the Cole Porter song 'Anything Goes' that had been driving me mad for the last two days. The Harpers Bizarre version from 1967. I couldn't get rid of it. I must have picked it up from an advertisement or something. My slippers were nowhere. The room was a mess. There was half a month's worth of newspapers on the floor. I peered in a mirror. Yech. I turned back to the bed. There was an empty wine bottle on the side table, but no glass. Good. One less item to wash up.

I shuffled to the kitchen and looked in the fridge. There was nothing there except for a can of beer and some stuff I wouldn't have eaten in a nuclear winter. Food was not important; it never was with me. It was the hair of the dog that I was after. Coat of the dog, more like. I grabbed the can, pulled the ring and gulped it back with the passion of a legionnaire. The shock of the cold liquid hitting my throat gave me a bracing jolt. I saw a packet of smokes and shook one out. I sparked it up as I filled the kettle and then returned to the bedroom, clutching my beer and cigarette.

I ran a bath. More mirrors. As if I needed to know what I looked like: a tense, middle-aged man holding a can of beer and a fag first thing in the morning before a nine thirty appointment at the local probation centre. I turned off the taps and lobbed the rest of the cigarette into the loo. I got into the bath and put my head under the water. The bliss. After all my years in prison I still hadn't got used to the peace of living in my own home. To talk in my own voice. To think my own thoughts. Heaven. I lifted my head out of the water and folded a flannel over my eyes.

There didn't seem to be anything exciting or auspicious about that particular spring morning, and yet somehow it marked the start of a chain of events that were to take me on an unexpected journey to an unanticipated destination. If a butterfly's wing was fluttering to some climatic consequence elsewhere or fortune's feathers were being ruffled by an incoming breeze, I was not aware, at that point, of anything other than my normal routine.

I removed the flannel, washed, finished the beer and gently got out of the bath. I dried my bits, dressed becomingly and went back to the kitchen. I hit the kettle switch and waited for the water to boil. The previous night's entertainment had been a solitary affair, as usual. I was contemplating my lack of a social life just as the kettle was reaching orgasm, when I remembered I had a party to go to that evening. It was the first communal event I'd been invited to since my release from jail. My hosts, Wally Barker and his French wife Anne-Marie, didn't live far away. We'd only spoken on the phone since I'd been let out. Wally and I had worked together many years before and Anne-Marie had written some uplifting letters of encouragement to me while I'd been in the clink. I wasn't too concerned about the evening, in fact I was now looking forward to it, but I wasn't sure what to expect. There had been considerable outcry about my transgression at the time. Although it had all happened more than a dozen years before, not everyone had forgotten, even if my release had mercifully, until now anyway, passed largely unnoticed. Culturally, I was coming in from a pretty low base. To have gone to prison might be mildly interesting. To have gone to prison for murder might, at a push, be considered thought-provoking. But to have gone to prison for murdering one's own girlfriend, however well intended, was, I found, just a downright conversation-stopper.

I looked at my watch. Shit! If I were to walk to the probation service's offices, I'd have to leave soon. I poured out half a cup of coffee, adding a large dash of whisky to cool it down and knocked it back in one. I grabbed my jacket and hastily made my exit. There was a letter for me in the previous day's post at the bottom of the main stairs. Yippee! It was a giro cheque from the benefits agency. I slipped it into my pocket and closed the front door behind me.

I sauntered towards Kensington High Street, stopping briefly to look in the shop windows. Everything was *so* expensive. I made it to the probation service's building just off the main drag in good time. I announced the miracle of my existence and the beauty of my objective to the woman on reception and was told to take a seat. I thumbed idly through a copy of *Probation Today* before Mrs Balakrishna, my pleasantly plumpish probation officer, greeted me and ushered me into to her office.

"How are you, Mr Mallet?" she enquired with cursory indulgence as we took our respective positions at her desk.

Mr Mallet. That was me: James Mallet, former bank employee and now ex-jailbird.

"I'm fine, thank you," I replied vapidly, looking with suspicion at the clipboard in front of her.

"And how have you been keeping?" she asked, warming up to something more specific.

"Fine," I repeated, knowing from the form on her clipboard that there would be several boxes to tick before I could walk away as a free man.

"So how is the job situation?" she questioned, picking up a pen.

"Not brilliant at the moment, Mrs Balakrishna," I replied, shiftily.

"No job yet?" she probed, shifting her clipboard before getting down to business.

"I've been to a few recruitment agencies and the Jobcentre, of course," I responded, truthfully.

"What did they say?" she asked, starting to tick a box.

"The recruitment agencies were pretty down about me ever working for a bank again, and I was turned down for the two positions that the Jobcentre put me up for."

"What sort of positions were they?" Mrs Balakrishna queried, growing worryingly inquisitive.

"One was to be a security guard and the other was for a night watchman's job."

"So what did they say?" she quizzed, sounding hopeful.

"They went a bit philosophical when I said I'd just got out of prison and never called me back," I replied, attempting not to look too unsurprised.

Mrs Balakrishna regarded her clipboard forlornly.

"I'll have a word with the council and see if they might have something that you would like."

"Thank you, Mrs Balakrishna," I said, having heard her mention the council on previous occasions, "but I must warn you that they are an equal opportunities employer."

"What's wrong with that?" she challenged.

"I'm English," I replied, casually.

"Mr Mallet, are you saying that by being a British citizen you cannot have a job with the council?" she demanded.

"No, Mrs Balakrishna, that's not what I said," I returned, trying to sound reasonable. "It's just that I'm not, at the moment at least, in a social minority. This puts me at a disadvantage with an equal opportunities employer."

"What nonsense you talk!" she protested, giving me a withering look. "I think you're the one who's prejudiced; you have the problem, not the council. Anyway, I have taken the precaution of making enquiries on your behalf with the Jobcentre. They have the Jobclub that I think you will find most useful. I have taken the initiative to arrange a meeting with them for you at two o'clock tomorrow afternoon."

"But… Mrs Balakrishna," I spluttered, struggling to think of an excuse not to go. But she wasn't taking any prisoners.

"Mr Mallet, you cannot go on receiving unemployment benefits forever," she explained, patiently. "You must take all the necessary measures to obtain a job. The Jobclub has the excellent 'Restart' program which they will discuss with you and if it is suitable they will arrange to enrol you for the excellent one week 'Restart' course. Then all your problems will fly away!"

Arbeit macht frei! And rejoin the sausage machine of life. She proceeded to tick all the remaining boxes with a flourish and then looked at me with a smile as wide as the Ganges.

"Two o'clock tomorrow, Mr Mallet," she reminded me. "At the Jobcentre. Ask for Mrs Huang. She is expecting you."

"Anything goes," I sighed, before I had time to check myself. Stop it!

I got up to leave, but not before Mrs Balakrishna seized the chance to cram a leaflet about overcoming post-natal depression into my fist.

Although Mrs Balakrishna's command of English was excellent and her conversation all the more interesting for it, there were times when I couldn't help wondering whether something was amiss. Perhaps she'd confused 'post-coital' with 'post-custodial'. It was an easy mistake to make.

I left the building feeling annoyed that I hadn't thwarted Mrs Balakrishna's attempts to turn me into a model citizen. I couldn't understand why she'd become so uptight about my unemployment benefits when she'd been the one who'd put me up for them in the first place. It wasn't my idea. Was it my fault that she'd been in such a hurry to write 'a few mortgage arrears' when what I had in fact said was that I had very few budgetary considerations beyond 'a few more beers'? After that there'd been no stopping her.

Thinking about it reminded me that I needed to go to a bank to pay in my giro and buy some money. I headed towards the high street to look for a PABS sign with its inevitable ever-assuming tag: "Your friendly Bank". I didn't have to look far. They were everywhere. I was surprised they hadn't set up a branch in my lavatory. ('Do come in, Mr Mallet! Take a seat!') But gone were the glory days when I was in its employ when it had traded under the mighty moniker of

'The Pan Asian Banking System'. For the staff members it was simply 'The Bank'; always with a holistic big 'T' and 'B'. Capital letters were encouraged wherever possible.

I found myself in front of a large branch. I pulled out a hundred pounds from the machine outside, knowing full well they wouldn't last a hundred hours. I went inside to the stately banking hall and joined a queue to pay in my giro. Only one till was open. Half a dozen floorwalkers were wandering about, looking helpful but useless with their hands behind their backs. I glanced around. There was an assortment of promotional literature on display, including a pile of The Bank's annual accounts. I picked up a copy and glimpsed at the figures. They were too big to make any sense. I moved onto the Chairman's statement. It had a familiar blend of corporate self-congratulation and big company irreproachability. There were pictures of the members of the board of directors, all looking faintly embarrassed in their PABS logo ties. One of the faces rang a bell. It was Leonard Fawcett. *Leonard Fawcett?* What was that dink doing there? I used to share a house with him when we were colleagues in Saudi Arabia, some twenty five years earlier. What had he done right? I remembered him as a bully and a bullshitter who was heavily into trafficking his own homemade hooch to the locals and expats. I grudgingly recalled he'd been quite good at his job, albeit in a somewhat bombastic fashion. It had obviously worked for him. I put the report down when it was my turn to pay in my cheque and left.

I wandered outside again. I looked at my watch. Great! It was bang on opening time! I walked along the street until I spotted the cheery tell-tale hanging flower baskets of a pub further up the road, which from a distance appeared to be called The Angry Masturbator, but on closer acquaintance was, in fact, The Ancient Mariner. Except for the barman, the pub was empty. I ordered a pint and had a go on the one-armed bandit machine lurking behind some nautical kitsch in the corner. I didn't know how it worked, so I gave up after going through a pocket's worth of change and finished my drink in resentful silence.

I stepped back out onto the street and went for a mooch around the shops. I was in no hurry; there was nothing to go home for. I dropped in on a glass-and-concrete retail cathedral specialising in electronic gadgetry and marvelled at all the wizardry on display which had been either miniaturised beyond my comprehension or supersized beyond my wallet. I abandoned the shop and made my way to a Pret a Tentious to purchase an overpriced ham and cheese baguette, then ambled along to Weirdbins to inspect their wine racks. I selected a sensible bottle of Australian screw top to complement my baguette for when I got home and then bought some breakfast beers for future use. I continued to wander down the street until I came across a turd-spangled alleyway I'd forgotten about, which took me back home in less than ten minutes.

I looked at the day's post as I let myself in through the main door and sifted through the various envelopes. Who'd have thunk it? Two letters for little me!

Emigrates Tours had thoughtfully sent me a copy of their latest brochure of holiday breaks in Dubai at either the five-star Al Sharmouta Hotel or the six-star Manyouk Palace, all for a shade under three thousand pounds for five days, if I promised to fly in their 'Fakir Class'. How nice. Better watch out for those hotel mini-bars, I forewarned no one. Touch those and it could double the cost of the holiday. I didn't know where they'd found my name. They must have mistaken me for a high roller, but I wasn't that sort of high roller. I opened the other envelope. It was a mailshot with some 'exciting opportunities' from a recruitment agency I'd been obliged to contact. I tossed both letters into the communal bin and carried on up the stairs.

I dumped the nutrition on the sideboard. The flat was depressingly quiet. I put on a tape to liven things up. I still hadn't made the technological leap from tapes to CDs yet alone downloads. The tape got caught in the machine and went *'zift'*. Naughty Mr Hitachi. Mr Sony would never have done that. I switched on the TV and set my princely banquet on a tray. I found the squeezy under a cushion and clicked through the festival of afternoon television. There was a soap with some shouty teenagers having a go at each other in Australia. I switched over to a fifties safari saga with an assortment of people running around in panic, then a programme about a boring couple trying to buy a prefab in Spain, then some fat slag telling me how to ice a cake on Five, and finally another kids' soap on Freeview with yet more adolescents getting worked up over nothing, this time shot in the millionaires' paradise of Romford. And of course there was always *Friends* to be found somewhere. They were the only friends I had that afternoon but there were only so many reruns a grown man could take, so I plumped for the fifties safari number. This was living!

I'd missed most of the first half, but I knew the form. I took two large gulps of wine straight from the bottle and tore wildly at my baguette to get in step with the mood of the movie, while menservants darted about in wide-eyed consternation as a lion looking like its arse was on fire sprang out of nowhere. I chewed my way through the rest of the baguette and took another swig of wine. Eventually an English geezer turned up with a rifle, shot the lion and everything was all right. I looked at the wine bottle and wondered whether I should have gone for the Cabernet rather than the Shiraz. I reminded myself of my social obligations that evening and screwed the cap back on the bottle. I felt tired all of a sudden and decided I owed myself a siesta. I went to the bedroom and fell on the bed, fully clothed.

The phone woke me up two hours later. It was Pete Divis, an old friend from my pre-prison days who was in the recruitment business. He was offering me a lift to the Barker gathering as he was going too. I accepted willingly. He told me to be ready at seven. I went into the kitchen, fixed myself a stiff whisky and felt, for a moment, a sense of misgiving. I'd tried to put my doubts about the event to one side, but they were now more of the lingering kind.

Chapter 2: Confrontation

Pete came at seven and we drove on to Wally and Anne-Marie's house in Fulham, only ten minutes away. I'd seen Pete at his office a few times since I'd been released back into the world, ostensibly to discuss my job situation but more often than not we just ended up getting trolleyed in the pub next door. We parked near the house. Wally was waiting at the door.

"Ah! Messrs Divis and Mallet: welcome!" he pronounced with exaggerated decorum. "Do come in. How good to see you again – especially you James, at last. We must have a chat once I'm through with this ridiculous door-keeping business."

He showed us to the drawing room and passed us over to a generously over-lacquered Anne-Marie, who promptly went into a state of near vapour.

"Boys! How lovely to see you!" she gushed. "You look marvellous – both of you. And, James... it's so wonderful to have you back in circulation!"

We expressed our thanks and returned plaudits.

"Help yourself to anything," she instructed, steering us towards the drinks table.

"I'd better go easy as I'm driving," Pete declared self-righteously, as he helped himself to a large glass of red wine.

I was a bit off wine and opted for a beer instead. I looked round the room while Pete chatted to Anne-Marie. The Barkers had been in the same house for as long as I'd known them. Little had changed in the time I'd been away. Their two infants were now somewhat bored-looking adolescents, grudgingly passing round canapés to breathlessly over-appreciative guests, but otherwise the Barker household was much the same. I'd forgotten that Wally, against Anne-Marie's own inclinations, was a stickler for continuity and reviled modernity in almost any form. The celebration of chintz and hand-me-down Edwardiana created an air of jaded gentility which somehow had been uncomfortably shoe-horned into the modest confines of a mid-terrace dwelling. Family portraiture and mismatched hunting scenes in chipped frames jockeyed for attention as bygone invitations the colour of stained teeth gazed on in weary gilt from the mantelpiece. It gave me the creeps.

The unseasonably mild spring weather had allowed the guests to congregate on the patio outside. I did a quick stocktake. There must have been thirty or so people; not so many as to startle a probationer in my position, but not so few as to exclude the possibility of an interesting evening. I felt a bit awkward at first as the only social yardstick I'd had for the last twelve years had itself been in a yard, of the prison variety, for half an hour's stroll before lunch each day. Anne-Marie snapped me out of my daydream.

"Come on, you two," she enthused. "Let me introduce you to some of the others!"

She grasped Pete and me by the arm and marched us outside. I gulped. There were one or two faces I recognised and one or two I detected who I thought recognised mine. For me, the last twelve years had been an eternity but for others, I suspected, it had been no time at all. She presented us to an odd-looking couple whose names I didn't catch and left us. He was chunky, red-faced and in suit with a stripe that seemed to emphasise his portliness. She on the other hand, was stick-thin and hawkish with her hair fiercely scraped back into an incongruous girlish chignon. We started talking. He was a broker, and a senior one from what he was saying. They were married and she stayed at home to look after their three children, which killed her part in the conversation. Eventually Mr Broker asked me what I did. I said I was 'between opportunities' but had been in banking. There was no point elaborating. Pete managed to get things going with Mrs Broker and we became separated in our respective dialogues. Mr Broker seemed a nice chap and asked me what I wanted to do. I said I hoped to get back into a job in finance.

"How old are you? Forty-five?" he asked, bluntly.

"Plus VAT," I muttered, morosely.

"Knocking on a bit; difficult... difficult," he opined. "You're at the wrong age. If you haven't made it by now you probably never will; and if you're out you'll probably never get back in. You're no longer part of the cabal... added to which you'll be yesterday's newspapers against all the young bucks in today's environment I'm afraid, old boy."

I was a bit taken aback. I knew that. I didn't need him to tell me quite so candidly. We were only making what I thought was polite conversation.

"But on the other hand," he continued reflectively, "you could be quite useful in something where your experience and contact base would be more handy than, say, that of a twenty-five year old. Have you ever considered trying recruitment, or in another word, 'headhunting'?"

My heart sank. I'd never been particularly bowled over by the recruitment business or headhunting. They were service industries to a service industry. It was not the way I wanted to make a living. But my hopes lifted a little as he went on.

"My brother-in-law happens to have been in the trade for a while and he's done pretty well... in fact, so much so that he's started his own company. I know he wants to develop a banking arm and he might be looking for someone like you. I can find out, if you like."

"That's very decent of you," I said in surprised disbelief, vaguely warming to the idea. "Although I must confess, I'm a little bit ring-rusty with the telephone and my contact base isn't what it was."

"It doesn't pay to be bashful," he advised, gravely. "I was once 'between opportunities', so I know what it's like. If I'd shouted my inadequacies from the rooftops, I wouldn't have the job I have now."

"I just wanted to be honest."

"Well, don't be," he harrumphed. "No one else is. And besides, I own the company in question. My brother-in-law may have started it, but I financed the venture, so I do have some say in what's what. I think you'd get on with him. He's pretty easy-going. It's no picnic by any means, but for the right person it's a good business... and perfect for people with wishy-washy career histories."

I didn't know what to say. I was dumbstruck. I didn't know whether this was a stroke of luck or just cocktail party chit-chat, but if it was the former it was worth listening to.

"Well, I'm up for it if you think I'm viable," I said, tentatively. "Anything goes."

Stop it! Stop it!

"Good. It can't do any harm," he said, taking a business card out of his wallet. "Give me a call next week; the earlier the better. In the meantime I'll have a word with my brother-in-law."

He handed me the card. I looked at it.

Martin Letts
Managing Director
Emerging Markets
UltraCapital Brokers Ltd.

"Impressive," I mumbled.

"Don't worry about that," he remarked, dismissively. "We'll have lunch; nothing formal. Bring Wally with you. His office is just round the corner from mine."

"Thanks Martin," I said, still feeling a bit dazed.

"Think nothing of it. And remember: don't be bashful."

"I certainly won't be, Martin. I'll call you early next week without fail," I said, hoping I didn't sound too desperate.

"Excellent!" he commended, changing his tune. "Now, if you'll excuse us, we have another engagement to go to."

With that he touched his wife's elbow as she was just finishing what she was saying to Pete and said they had to go. She smiled and apologised for having to leave so soon. They turned and left to say goodbye to Wally and Anne-Marie.

"Extraordinary!" I said, looking in bemusement at the business card.

"Extraordinary what?" Pete echoed.

"A bloke talks to me for five minutes, gives me his business card and then tells me he'll put me up for a job," I marvelled. "It's bit pat, isn't it, or are all recruitment jobs like that?"

"You dork!" Pete growled, unimpressed. "If I'd known you were that hard up, I'd have told you to work for my lot, but you were so snooty about headhunting I didn't bother."

"But this is Martin Letts," I said importantly, as if Martin was my new best friend, which at that moment he was.

"It doesn't matter. Headhunters are all the same," he said, disparagingly. "Some work in smart offices, some operate from kitchen tables, but we're all just commission grifters in the end."

"Isn't everyone?" I challenged, trying to justify my change of perspective. "I need all the help I can get at the moment, so I wasn't going to be rude to him."

We fell quiet for a moment.

"How was Mrs Letts?" I asked, as an aside.

"You mean Jar Jar Binks?" Pete questioned.

"Was that her name?"

"Nice girl, but nae tits," he retorted, ignoring my gullibility, but adding, as if to emphasise his own indifference, "Just an ironing board with a beak, really."

I looked mournfully at our empty glasses.

"Time for another drink?" I suggested.

We returned to the drawing room. Several other guests had arrived since we'd been on the patio and the room was now full. Despite my recent flicker of what I took to be good luck, I felt agitated. We made our way to the drinks table. I straightened my collar as we passed a mirror and caught a glimpse of three women watching me in the reflection. I did a double take. I knew them and had a pretty good idea why they were looking at me. It was little wonder that I'd felt peculiar. They hadn't forgotten me, nor had they forgotten what I'd done. The last time I'd seen them, they'd all been working in media-related jobs.

I turned to the drinks table and decided I needed something stronger than a beer. There was an unopened bottle of whisky just out of easy reach, standing like a fire extinguisher, in case of emergency. I leant over, seized it and skilfully broke the seal as I grabbed the only tumbler on the table. I poured a large measure and carefully nudged the bottle behind a flower arrangement. Not carefully enough. The girls were still looking at me. It was as if the whole procedure had been caught on camera. I grinned sheepishly and was just about to address Pete as a diversion, when I saw that he'd moved on. He was talking to a sultry female at the far end of the drinks table who was quite clearly pleased with the effect her tight leather trousers were having on him. So was Pete. I didn't want to spoil their moment, so I faced the three women.

There was nothing in their demeanour to suggest that I was particularly welcome, and yet they had a look of anticipation that indicated that I was expected to say something to them. Of the three I knew Katie Church the best, having once shared a drunken embrace with her at a party when we were considerably younger. I looked at her as she drew angrily on her cigarette and noticed how her once kissable lips were now etched in a cock-starved rictus.

In the few seconds I had, I considered the girl nearest to me, Lucy Edwards with her immaculate coiffure and make-up, set as if to compensate for her unremarkable face, and wondered if she'd ever had a boyfriend. I briefly captured the image of the third girl, Sarah Beckett, standing to one side, and remembered how she'd always stood in Lucy's shadow. Her chocolate-box looks had started to melt, but I knew the centre would be as hard as ever. From their air of disdain I sensed that their estimation of me was probably just as toxic.

"Hello girls!" I said with hollow enthusiasm, as I approached.

"Hello, James," Katie acknowledged, with a distinct absence of delight.

I tried smiling but I was at a loss.

"So what have you all been up to since we last met?" I asked.

"We're still in the communications industry, but we're at the top of our game now," Katie crowed, taking the lead.

"That's good!" I said, sensing trouble. "So where does that put you all at this juncture?"

"Lucy's Head of Religious Affairs at *Sloane About Town*; Sarah's Head of Logistics at Howard Spanks Communications, and I'm

Political Editor of *Glitter* magazine in Windsor," Katie continued, authoritatively.

"How majestic!" I acclaimed, feeling my confidence ebbing away. "Congratulations all round. You all seem to be doing well, by the sounds of it."

"We are, Alcatraz Boy," Katie bit back, unexpectedly.

Ouch! Queen to Rook four. Katie was wasting no time showing her fangs, which I noticed, just happened to be the colour of bygone invitations.

There was a slight pause before she resumed the initiative.

"What about you?"

"Well, my career's been slightly on the back-burner for the last few years, so I've got a bit of catching up to do – ha, ha!" I burbled, trying to make light of her comment.

"So when did they let you out?" Lucy cut in listlessly, clearly not giving a damn.

"A couple of months ago," I said, feeling relieved the conversation was opening to a quorum.

"So, Dr Lecter," Katie continued, not wanting to relinquish her assault, "what's cooking? Or rather, who?"

Nasty; not even clever, but what to do? Absorb or abort? Shoot or scoot?

"Katie, *please*," I said, more in fatigue than as a plea for clemency. "It was an accident."

"Some accident!" she scoffed. "I'm glad my boyfriend doesn't try to mash my face into a Picasso every time he comes back from the pub. How come you got your sentence reduced?"

"It just happened; good behaviour or something," I said, hoping against hope that the conversation might move on. Fat chance! Not with Katie.

"*Good behaviour?* That's disgraceful!" she snapped. "What you did was despicable. You should've been locked away for good."

Half of me agreed with her. I'd never compromised on remorse, or shame for that matter, but in this case what use was either? Neither could turn back the clock. It was a mistake; an alcohol-fuelled mistake; a loss of control, but the deed was now done.

"Thank you, Katie," I said, feeling my face start to sweat. "I had no say in the penal aspect of the case. It was the parole board's decision, not mine."

"Bollocks!" Katie barked, crossly. "Your parents had the money; they had lawyers."

"That's nonsense, Katie," I cried, exasperated. "My release was the result of an independent inquiry. It had nothing to do with my parents. They had no influence or authority over the ruling, or money for that matter."

"But they've got friends who've got both," she hammered on.

"I don't think so," I said, thinking enough was enough. "Can we perhaps talk about something else?"

"Like what?" Sarah demanded, brave enough now to join in the fray. "Kabuki theatre? The astral plane? Cabaret Voltaire? Existentialism within the spatial context of twenty-first century incontrovertibility? Or how about your career prospects?"

"Very clever, Sarah," I said, now feeling played out. "It hasn't been easy for me or my family, and yes, I would agree my job prospects aren't particularly flamboyant, but it's unsettling having to fend off all these brickbats at what would otherwise pass for a normal Fulham drinks party. I'm not courting sympathy, but I wasn't expecting grief."

"Well, you should've been," Sarah cooed, with noxious satisfaction. "Everyone knows what you did. You'll never get another job. Not with your history, honey."

"Thank you for your generous assessment, Sarah. Charmed, I'm sure. As it happens, I'm going to the Department of Employment tomorrow for an aptitude test, so perhaps I'll have the benefit of a less partisan view of my employment perspective," I said, casting around for a seemly means of escape.

From the expression on her face Lucy was about to say something unpleasant, but I moved in before she had the chance.

"Right, girls, I'm done. It's been lovely seeing you again. It's good to know that nothing's changed, whatever you say, but we must circulate with the other guests, surely?"

"Yes, we must," Lucy said, trying to make the best of the final moment. "But I suggest you don't address us as 'girls'."

"Will 'spinsters' suffice?" I said, turning to leave

"Oh, that really hurt, Borstal Boy," Katie said, as a closing riposte.

"Get a life, Katie," I shot back, over my shoulder.

"No, James, you're the one who should have got that," Lucy caterwauled, getting in one last pop for herself.

Pete appeared with hapless timing, unaware of any affray.

"Hello, girls!" he said, jauntily.

"Don't you start," Lucy seethed.

"What's the problem?" he enquired, still cheerful. "Got the monthlies?!"

"Not now, Pete," I said, pulling him away and announcing with a disarming smile, "It's time to take our leave. And on that note, *dahlings,* may I wish you all a very warm and pleasant menopause."

We made our getaway before the trio had time to assimilate and retaliate.

"That could have gone better," I murmured.

"What was it all about?" Pete asked, looking puzzled. "Amateur night over at the Charm Academy?"

"Just the prison thing," I said with a sigh. "Or maybe just me."

"Well, it's good to see you haven't lost your touch," he commended, approvingly. "And nice to see you using real bullets, however unsporting. Life's all about these little victories, is it not, dear boy?"

"Whatever. They weren't exactly firing blanks," I said, feeling relieved that the confrontation was over. "In fact every time I opened my mouth I felt as though I tripping over a Claymore. I hope I don't have to put up with that sort of crap everywhere I go."

"You won't," Pete assured me. "Look at them – they're pathetic. Lucy Edwards looks as though she's on day release from the Clarins counter at Boots, not to mention having the same daft hairstyle as my mum. Katie Church is just vile and has the teeth of a Hydra to go with it. And as for Sarah Beckett... she is so devoid of personality she actually sucks in light. That's when she's not in the gym trying to find a shag off some rich beefcake."

"How do you know?" I cross-examined.

"Because I shagged her," he answered, without a flicker.

"But you just said she only shagged fitness freaks with loads of money?"

"I told her I was a rich Pilates instructor," Pete explained, his face still not moving a muscle.

"I'm impressed: you have a dark gift," I enthused. "I can't claim to have gone as far as carnal knowledge, but I did once have some tonsil hockey with Katie Church, many moons ago, almost before she was a virgin, but we were both very pissed."

"You certainly must have been!" Pete cried, in disgust. "She's got a mouth like a burnt-out fuse box. It must have been horrific."

"I can't remember much," I said, wistfully, "although oddly enough I can remember the scent she was wearing; it reminded me of lemons."

"That's probably why she's such a bitter twat now," he theorised. "Kissing her must've been like licking a mortuary drain."

"*Jesus!* I'm glad you're haven't lost *your* touch."

"I'm available for children's parties and weddings,' he imparted, modestly. "But my advice to you is never, ever, take shit from a woman. Unless you have to. Those girls have too much money and too little love in their lives; it's a tragic combination."

"Talking of tragic combinations," I said, feeling more my normal self, "who was that girl with the leather incontinence trousers you were talking to? She looked quite glam."

"She is," Pete conceded. "Her name's Francine... Francine Meffre. She's one of Anne-Marie's French compadres."

"Any chance, do you think? A bit of *Boursin* on the foreskin?" I enquired encouragingly, suddenly aware that the whisky was having an interesting effect.

"Nah, not a prayer. She wouldn't have me even if I came with a nest of tables," Pete replied, morosely. "She's only interested in rich cock; it's her natural default setting."

"That's not exclusive to Francine, surely" I queried, looking admiringly at her glossy backside as she stood talking to another spellbound male guest across the room.

"Yeah, but women like her can spot a loser from a hundred yards, however smart the jacket."

"I'd knob it," I sighed, hazily.

"Don't even go there. She's a bread-head and not about to alter her terms of business for the likes of you and me."

"Neither of us has much of a balance sheet, which leaves a bit of a gap," I conceded. "And people do like to trade up."

"Mostly," Pete considered, pensively. "Money does tend to keep the score."

Then he brightened up and pronounced, "Let's find Wally!"

Wally was sitting alone in the kitchen, licking out what looked like the remains of the guacamole dip from a mixing bowl, and had a beer mug full of wine by his elbow. He didn't look happy.

"Hi, Wally!" Pete chipped in cheerfully, once again trying to lighten the occasion. "How's tricks?"

"Not good... some arsehole's swiped the only bottle of whisky in the house, leaving me with this gunk." He gestured towards the pint of wine by his side.

I was about to explain.

"It's that bloody wife of mine," he muttered, adding, without any sense of seriousness, "I've never liked her."

I quickly closed my mouth and put my other hand over the tumbler I was still holding.

"Anyway, are you guys having a killer time?" he sighed, borrowing, I suspected, from his children's vernacular.

"Having a great time!" Pete whooped, determined to remain upbeat, but then pausing for a second to reconsider. "Although I don't think Francine Meffre and I will be making sweet music together later tonight. Or any other night for that matter."

"Ah, Francine," Wally said, conjuring an image. "Pity about her. She's one of Anne-Marie's press-up playmates from the gym and also French, of course. Don't take it personally, but she's unreceptive to anyone but the mythical and completely fictional knight in shining armour, which is why she's always on her own. She came to England hoping to find her *patron* and would have no dealings with the *concierges* of the world... an *impasse*, I fear, that befalls many a modern damsel. Francine's been holding out for something better for a while now, but so far nothing's turned up. It's been all sizzle, but no steak. So I'm afraid you're probably right Pete... you'll be nil-by-mouth with Francine for the foreseeable future, unless, of course, your immediate fortunes turn for the better. Instead I expect Mr Nasty with a Porsche will eventually appear one day and whisk her off into the sunset, but until then we can only hope for her. What about you, James? Have you spoken to anyone pleasant?"

"Yes and no," I replied, ambivalently. "I talked to Martin Letts who was more than helpful about my job situation. He said he might have something in the headhunting world. I'm to call him next week to meet for lunch and he suggested you come too, if you want. It sounded informal but the end game is to set me up with his brother-in-law who's just started a new recruitment company."

"That's good," Wally adduced, "as is Martin. He's a client of mine, and a decent enough soul. I'm not saying that he has an undeveloped sense of his own importance but in reality he's just a natural born ten-percenter, always looking out for the BBD."

"BBD?" I quizzed, unknowingly.

"The Bigger, Better Deal," Wally explained apologetically, as if my ignorance was his fault. "And if his signet ring is a tad too large to mark him out as a true gent, it doesn't matter; if he says he's going to do something, he'll do it if he can."

"Martin may be OK," Pete interjected, "but his brother-in-law's a real pain in the butt. I had dealings with him a few weeks ago and found him a right pushy bastard, but I don't want to put James off at this stage."

"Put me off?" I asked, askance. "As if I can pick and choose! Martin did indicate that the company weren't no country club, but he'll probably find out about my past in the next couple of days anyway. Once he's put that together he'll cancel lunch, sure as eggs is eggs."

"You can keep your eggs," Wally insisted. "I said, if Martin says he'll do something, he'll damn' well give it a crack. As for your past, that's a bit of a stumper, but it may work to your advantage. In a perverse way he might even get a kick out of having someone like you on payroll. Besides, for all his bullishness, Martin's not exactly perfect himself."

"Really?" I quizzed, thinking it might just be my lucky day to meet a fellow murderer. "Like how?"

"He's said to have a major wandering eye problem," Wally ventured.

"Is that all? Doesn't everyone?" I questioned, pausing a little to think of Jar Jar Binks. "It's hardly in the same league as my history though, is it?"

"It's still a bit of dirt," Wally said, trying to be encouraging.

"James: tell Wally about the three harpies we were just with," Pete addressed me, not seeming to share the same preoccupation with Martin Letts as Wally and I.

"Is this the 'no' side of your encountering experience?" Wally enquired.

"It was nothing," I said, trying to play things down.

"OK, but was it anything to do with Kate Church, Lucy Edwards and Sarah Beckett by any chance?" he speculated.

"How did you guess?" I replied, relieved that they came to him as no surprise. "They gave me quite a roasting, but I've known them a while. Have you?"

"Sort of," Wally answered, ruefully. "They're another group of Anne-Marie's barbell buddies from the health club. All three are quite successful, but they seem to think they're exempt from making any effort to mix with other people outside their own group. Katie's a little vicious and there's a slight reek of the open casket about Lucy in the way she trowels on the yacht varnish... and Sarah Beckett: now there's a face I'd never get tired of slapping! But that's enough misogyny for one night. How are things going for you, James? What's your take, now that you've been out in the free world for a bit, on twenty-first century Britain?"

"Pretty awful," I said, quietly. "Whatever it is, it's the opposite of good. It's an odder world than I was expecting. I see great sadness. The chocolate bars have got smaller. There's more of a dog-eat-dog mentality than before and common decency is definitely a thing of the past. What's happened to everybody? There must be a common belief system beyond merely making money. Anyway, what passes for prosperity is just froth floating on a sea of ridiculous government policies and statistics, riding on the back of pork-barrel spending of public funds to ensure a protected electorate. This is not a sustainable business model. Weak government has been followed by weak government for far too long. Rome isn't burning: it's burnt."

"Are you finished yet?" Pete appealed, looking confused.

"Sorry," I said, guiltily. "I was just paraphrasing something I read in *The Telegraph* yesterday. I hope I haven't bored everyone shitless."

"Not a bit of it," Wally declared supportively, wiping some avocado excess off his chin. "Never use a scalpel where a sledgehammer will do. It's all very Hell-in-a-handcart stuff, but there is an odd dichotomy in the way the government has effectively become the enemy of the state. And yet there seems to be a sense of innocence in the way they grind the country to dust. Tax this, tax that and spend, spend, spend. There'll come a day when they'll tax us on how many times we use the lavatory!"

"It's already got to the white paper stage," Pete put in, earnestly. "But seriously, folks, we could go on all night and we haven't started on immigration or the slow-motion train wreck that is the EU. However at this moment the most important thing is that our glasses are beginning to look a bit sorry for themselves."

Wally looked at his beer mug and drained the last of its contents in one swallow.

Pete picked up a rogue bottle of Saint Emilion that was standing by the fridge and started to peel back the foil.

"Pete! You can't open that!" Wally cried out anxiously, passing him a corkscrew. "Anne-Marie will kill me! One of the guests must have brought it and she's obviously kept it to one side."

Too late! Wally and I put our glasses forward to be filled. Wally noticed my whisky tumbler and was about to utter an expletive when we heard the angry goosesteps of an irate wife approaching the kitchen.

"Lord!" Wally whispered, as he tried to hide his beer mug behind a blender. Pete quickly re-corked the wine bottle and slipped it into the swingbin.

Anne-Marie stomped in.

"Oh, you lot... Wally... you're always in the kitchen at parties. It's your show as much as mine, you know."

"I'm sorry, Anne-Marie," he mumbled, subserviently. "We'll come out straightaway. James and Pete were just catching up on old times."

"Don't try to blame them, you… you… you *wally!*" she screeched, seeming cross with herself that she couldn't come up with a stronger epithet.

We shuffled out guiltily as she eyed the kitchen with deep suspicion.

The party was starting to thin out. The three media witches were nowhere to be seen. Wally was trying to make up for his absence with a last minute show of man-about-town conviviality, oozing hostly effervescence, except that as an effect his shirt tail was hanging out and he had guacamole dip all over his trousers. Pete and I looked around. Francine Meffre was not about either, which was disappointing as I would have liked to have inspected her leather pantaloons at closer quarters. Pete looked at his watch.

"It's not late, James. Fancy finishing off somewhere tavernward?" he asked, hopefully. "I'll drop you home either way."

"No tavern tonight, thanks Pete," I said, suddenly feeling tired. "I'm completely bushed. I'm not used to all this excitement. We'll do it another time, but I'll take you up on your lift, if it's not out of the way."

It was our turn to say goodbye.

"Let me know if Martin Letts still wants me to come to lunch with you after you've spoken to him," Wally reminded me.

Pete dropped me home and I climbed the stairs up to the flat for the last time that day. I removed my jacket once I was in the bedroom and turned on the bedside TV. Hugh Grant was doing some low-level naughty and trying to make a fist of a not very good script. I took the rest of my clothes off, brushed my teeth and got into bed. It had been an interesting day. I'd certainly learnt who took exception to me and who was OK. At least I'd got rid of that blasted song that had been ruling my brain for the last three days. It had been replaced by South Pacific's 'There Is Nothing Like a Dame', which didn't seem so bad. The film version. The dreck on the TV was becoming eye-wateringly awful, so I put it out of its misery and switched off the light.

Chapter 3: Revelation

I awoke next morning with the sneakingly familiar feelings of worthlessness, joblessness and now resentment, as I recollected some of the hostility from the night before. Most of the evening had been fine, especially my chance encounter with Martin Letts and his offer of a possible ticket back into Jobland. Whether it was merely cocktail-party showmanship on his part or something more substantial, only time would tell. Was Martin Letts a man of success or a man of value? Dude or dud? What was the dealio? I was mulling over these matters and the concept of employment when I reminded myself that I had my Restart appointment with Mrs Huang at the Jobcentre that afternoon. Two o'clock was not my favourite time of day to be sober however, I reasoned to myself, now that I was armed with the prospect of an actual job interview the following week, there might be a chance of making short shrift of Mrs Huang.

I wandered without thinking into the kitchen and found myself in front of the fridge. As if on autopilot I reached in, snatched one of the beers I'd thoughtfully bought the day before and ambled back to the bedroom. I re-considered the previous night's events and reflected on the three girls again. On the basis that I shouldn't have treated fucked with fucked, perhaps I had been a bit naughty with my parting adieu, but what the heck? They had a point, of course. I had accidentally killed my girlfriend by pulping her face into a purée after we'd had a particularly drunken and brutal 'domestic' one evening. My lawyers had pleaded manslaughter on the grounds of diminished responsibility, but the court wasn't having it and I got life. Which turned out to be twelve years, as it happened, and I had the feeling it was this that vexed the girls more than the actual heinousness of the crime itself.

But the important issue was Martin. I could already see myself sitting at a desk, making calls and looking cool. I wanted to phone him there and then to fix a date for lunch but I knew I had to hold off until next week, as he'd instructed. That was four days away. I looked at my watch. It was nine o'clock. My appointment was five hours away.

I ran the bath and got in with my beer. As there was nothing worth eating in the kitchen I resolved to take a walk on the wild side and go to a cabbie's sandwich bar in South Ken for breakfast. I finished my beer, got out of the bath and contemplated my wardrobe. I didn't want to run the risk of appearing too employable, but nor I did I want to look like a full-time loafer. I opted for the relative anonymity of a tatty blazer and an old pair of Debenhams Casual Club chinos. I looked out of the window. The weather wasn't being helpful and didn't look as though it knew what to do. I seized a mac and brolley from the cupboard and headed out to whatever the elements had to offer.

The gunmetal palette of the sky made me think of my prison days. I was glad that I'd abandoned my preconceived ideas, formulated while I was doing my time inside, of what I would and wouldn't do once I was outside. Now I had no ideas. Except for chasing up Martin. I stopped at an off-licence and bought a cold can of pre-mixed gin and tonic. I popped the can open outside, had a quick slurp and hid the rest of it in my pocket as I walked along. I looked at the other pedestrians around me. Chinese students, doubtless on their way to Imperial College, marched in huddled unison, clutching their Styrofoam cups of Costa coffee. Students? Costa lot of money. What was wrong with a kettle? And the other people? Where were they were going? Shopping? To pick up their dry cleaning? To work? I wasn't going anywhere, figuratively. It started to rain. I was glad I had brought an umbrella.

I saw the sandwich bar and bought a paper outside. A waitress, perhaps of Balkan extraction, directed me to a table and I sat down with my drinks can up my sleeve. I looked at the other customers as I fiddled with the menu. They sounded as though they were mainly English language conscripts or young French dudes from the Lycée nearby. The girls looked animated and laughed a lot. The young men appeared chilled and reserved. The waitress came back lethargically to take my order, her head seemingly back in her homeland or boyfriend-land, a thousand miles away. I favoured the bacon and eggs on white toast and told her so. I looked at the newspaper as she went away and started to read about events over which I had no concern or influence. I took a surreptitious swig from the can and then hid it under the table between my thighs. I skipped past the demeaning jobs section and moved onto the business part, quietly discarding the condescending MBA supplement that came with it in the process. I gazed idly at the statistics, forecasts and company results, wondering whether I'd ever used, directly or indirectly, any of their products. The only thing that I'd ever produced was some rather unsavoury newsprint twelve years before. Who said there was no such thing as bad ink? Suddenly the idea of the Restart interview didn't seem so pointless.

The waitress came back with my order. I looked at the group of students as I started to eat and noticed that one of the young men wasn't talking or listening to the others. He looked a bit miserable. I knew the feeling. Even being in a crowd could be lonely. I turned my attention back to the paper and read, right next to a routine item about the head of the Provisional Assurance's socking great bonus, a piece about the Latin American debt market. *"This is an area to which we are totally committed," Leonard Fawcett, Director of Group Finance for PABS said in Geneva, yesterday.* That dork? Again? *In Geneva?* And another picture of him, this time looking all authoritative and jowly. A vision of chauffeured limousines, luxury hotels and pampered air travel enveloped me like a warm towel. Talk about the prince and the pauper! Why was anyone giving that fraud the time of day? I could have said the same thing just as well if I'd played my cards differently. For ten million bucks a year plus share options there were a lot of things I could have done differently, but how could anyone of such vague value command so much with a straight face?

I finished my plate and swished the remains of the gin and tonic around my mouth, then slowly and bitterly crushed the can before returning it to my pocket. I paid the bill and looked at the lonely man with his friends as I got up. He'd started talking to someone, which was a relief.

I stepped back into the rain and looked at my watch again. It was still only eleven o'clock. What was wrong with the day? It just wasn't moving and yet there was little point going back to the flat. I put the umbrella up and lit a cigarette. At least it was pub opening time. Or so I thought. I gave myself a two-pint drinking limit for the sake of the Restart interview, but I knew it wouldn't be enough to kill the two hours before I had to make my journey over to the Jobcentre. I looked at the shops but I didn't really need anything, and then I saw a pub, but it wasn't open. The bastards! I continued down the street in the hope of finding an alternative drinking venue when a passing smudge stopped suddenly beside me and turned.

"James Mallet?"

I looked. At first I didn't recognise the face. It had changed. I vaguely recollected a Hongkong connection.

"Jerry Jansen?" I ventured, in question rather than greeting.

"From the root to the fruit, old boy! How the devil are you?"

Normally this would have been a simple, straightforward enquiry requiring nothing more than a simple, straightforward reply, but in my case it always depended on how much a person knew about my past.

"Fine, Jerry," I said selecting a simple response in the hope that he might be ignorant of my latter-day goings-on. "How about you?"

"Oh topping, old boy!" he replied, in the faux neo-colonial jargon that we had all affected as émigrés all those years ago.

I scrabbled around for something sensible to say, but I couldn't think of anything. I had seen Jerry at various parties in Hongkong, but beyond small talk we had never known each other well. He had worked for Jardine Matheson but had been transferred to their Tokyo office before we'd had a chance to get better acquainted.

"It would be good to catch up," I proposed, thinking that it was unlikely that we ever would.

"Yes, it would," he agreed. "Are you doing anything at the moment?"

"What? Right now or in general?"

"I was thinking more about now," he answered, looking around shiftily.

"I've got an appointment this afternoon, but apart from that I'm just wandering about," I replied, unambitiously.

"So am I," he said abstractedly, before fixing me with a stony stare. "But I am a little thirsty. Do you fancy a snifter, then we can really catch up?"

Bingo! The standard expat clarion call! That would help fill in the time.

"What an excellent idea!" I said, as if the thought hadn't crossed my mind, then spoilt it by adding, "But is anywhere open? The last pub I passed was closed."

He looked around, gimlet-eyed.

"Bollocks to that," he declared, authoritatively. "I know just the place!"

With that he spun on his heel and started to head purposefully across the street to a hotel on the other side, leaving me trailing in his wake.

"*This* is Civilisation!" he proclaimed imperiously as we negotiated our way through the revolving doors. We made our way to the bar area, which looked threateningly empty.

"Are you sure they're open?" I asked, timidly.

"They're always open when I'm around," he decreed with the assurance of a man who knew his territory.

I cast my mind back to my time in Asia and remembered that the Jardines boys had always had a certain panache that had set them apart from the other expatriate employees. A waiter greeted Jerry with familiar servility and showed us to a spot with two armchairs and a coffee table in between. We were the only customers. The place was ours. The waiter took our order.

"The usual for me, please, Captain, and what about you, James?" Jerry asked, expansively.

I was relieved to notice two beer taps at the bar, one for lager and the other for bitter, thus obviating the need for trifling and expensive bottles.

"I'd like a pint of house lager," I said temperately, but feeling hugely relieved that Jerry had managed to clock me, of all people, amongst the faceless swarf drifting along the pavement.

"Right, James, what are you up to now? You don't look as though you're still with the Pan Asian."

"Is it *that* obvious?" I said looking at my badly pressed turn-ups. "Actually, I left The Bank more than twenty years ago."

I gave him a brief résumé of what I'd been doing since we'd last met, mindful that he might not be aware of my prison interlude, which I touched on briefly without embellishment.

"Sounds most interesting," Jerry remarked, distractedly. The waiter returned with our drinks, a bowl of cocktail nuts and some napkinettes. This was the life! I *was* Leonard Fawcett! I threw the question back.

"So what's your story, Jerry?" I enquired, before sucking in my first deep draft of lager.

Jerry considered the question and then his drink. If it was a Bloody Mary, it was as pink as an albino's eye. He picked up the glass, dispensed with the straw and held the glass up to the light.

"What a gyp," he snarled disgustedly, downing half the contents at once.

"That's better," he declared, wiping his mouth with a wad of napkinettes. "For a moment I was worried that they'd skimped on the voddie. Now where were we?"

What followed was the not unusual tale of expatriate woe, of returning to the UK and having to readjust to a life without sun and servants. In Jerry's case it involved numerous job changes, divorce and near penury, but he'd managed to pick up some of the pieces. He was now working for a rough-and-ready group of South African property speculators and living, as he put it, in 'born-again bachelor splendour' in Earl's Court.

"What works overseas doesn't always work back at home," he remarked ruefully, referring, I assumed, to the number of people we would have both known whose marriages had failed since coming back to the UK.

We talked about Hongkong as if it had been the days of wine and roses, which to an extent, it was. I consoled Jerry that at least he'd got his life back together. I said I still had some way to go before I could claim to have made *that* transformation. We'd finished our drinks. The waiter asked if we'd like some more.

"Same again, please, Captain," Jerry said wearily, without referring to me.

"Funny how life takes a left or a right," I said, apropos of nothing.

"It certainly does, Bagpuss," Jerry said with a sigh. "And none so more than with your old boss, eh?"

"Sorry?" I said, vaguely wondering who he was talking about.

"You know who I mean... Alec Dunhill, your former Chairman at The Pan Asian."

"He was hardly *my* Chairman," I said, almost with a shudder. "I was only a peon in the organisation; I only met the man once, and that was in a lift. Anyway what of dear old Sir Alec, or rather my 'old boss' as you call him?"

"That's the point, James, I thought you'd know. He's not called 'Sir Alec' any more. He's now 'Lord Dunhill of Egham'."

"Blimey," I said, unmoved. "You must be confusing me with someone who gives a shit, although I must admit it slipped my radar; the newspapers available at my last port of call didn't quite stretch to the Court Circular. When did this happen?"

"Fairly recently, old boy," Jerry replied, reverting to his colonial patter. "It was done very quickly, very quietly."

"That's odd," I remarked, reassessing the scenario a little more carefully. "I mean, he was an adequate Chairman from what I gather, but not *that* good."

"Lack of talent never stopped anyone," Jerry noted archly, suddenly sounding serious. "There is a feeling among those who know that he might have been ennobled for not entirely noble reasons. It is evident that a certain quantity of silver crossed palms to lubricate the process."

"You don't say!" I exclaimed, exaggeratedly. "You're not suggesting a former Chairman of The Pan Asian Banking System and the House of Lords selection committee, both cornerstones of the establishment and guardians of the common good, have been complicit in something untoward?"

"They don't spoil a pair," Jerry observed, perniciously. "Not for nothing is it called the 'House of Frauds'. But moving on: you were in Hongkong when the Thorn Bay Investment crisis finally came to a head, weren't you?"

"Yes I was. I remember it all too well. Who wouldn't if they'd been there?" I posed, recalling the utter chaos that had followed the company's demise in the early-1980s and the disastrous effect it had had on other firms in the region. Thorn Bay Investments had once been quite the wonder company of Hongkong, with fingers in nearly every pie, but by 1982 it had run out of steam and imploded with such spectacular force that the local stock markets of the area hardly dared move for the next two years.

"There was a bit of bad blood about it at the time, as I recall," Jerry commented, blandly.

"A bit of bad blood?" I cried. "The entire colony nearly fell into the sea!"

"I suppose it did rather," Jerry continued, with apparent lack of concern. "Quite a lot of people were stung pretty badly, if memory serves me right."

I smelt a rat.

"Yes, quite a lot of people were, Jerry," I said, waiting for him to get to the point.

"Quite a lot of money and credibility went down the Swanee with that little lark," he reminisced, nonchalantly scratching his chin for effect. "Who were their bankers?"

Now I knew what he was getting at.

"They had lots of them," I said, thinking back, "but The Pan Asian was normally the lead manager, as far as I was aware."

"The Pan Asian Banking System," he intoned, relishing every syllable. "Registered in Hongkong as a Public Limited Company."

"What of it?" I demanded, suddenly feeling strangely loyal towards my former employers.

"Nothing," Jerry said hastily, as if it was silly of him to have mentioned anything at all. "Except the Pan Asian didn't get particularly burnt, as far as I recollect; it lived to fight and win another day, which is more than can be said for a lot of other companies at the time."

"I suppose it did," I mumbled. "There was a court case, some people were tried, some were found guilty and someone went to prison in Hongkong, as far as I'm aware."

"Who went to prison?" Jerry challenged, almost accusingly.

"It happened such a long time ago," I answered, hesitantly. "I think it was a chap called Tony Mander."

"And what was he?" Jerry needled.

"He was head of the investment banking division."

"Of what?" Jerry persisted.

"The Pan Asian Bank."

"Precisely!" Jerry trumped, with a slightly sour smile.

"Precisely what?" I begged, mildly at a loss.

"Oh, dear!" he cried. "You really don't get it, do you? Can't you see? Tony Mander was the fall guy paid to carry the can when The Bank was caught up to its conkers in hookey loans and shady shenanigans with Thorn Bay. Why else would he have been sent to jail? For unpaid speeding tickets? In Hongkong? For two years?"

"That's one possible way of looking at it," I discerned, still not convinced.

"It's the *only* way of looking at it," Jerry insisted, reprovingly. "Once it became clear that there wasn't going to be any financial redemption, people started wanting their pound of flesh. And not just Tony Mander's. They wanted more meat from further up the bone."

"Like whose?" I asked thinking enough was enough.

"Try Tony Mander's boss, for one."

"You're not referring to Alec Dunhill again?"

"I might be," he replied, primly. "Amongst others."

"But as I said before," I retorted, aware that I was beginning to sound like a stuck record, "this all happened years ago, so why the fuss now?"

"That would have been a good point," Jerry intoned, earnestly. "Thorn Bay was already a busted flush by the end of 1982, but the court case wasn't. It didn't actually get going for another couple of years and then went on for another twelve, not that it was ever properly concluded to many minds, including mine. So you see it's not such ancient history after all."

Now I definitely got it. Jerry must have had some of his own money tied up with Thorn Bay.

"But this sort of insider dealing wasn't considered a crime in those days. The term didn't even exist in Hongkong then. It was the way things were done; it was normal practice," I said, making what I thought was a valid point.

"It might have been normal practice then, but not now," Jerry said, closing in on something else.

"But the system can't retrospectively penalise people for doing what was then a legitimate way of doing business," I reasoned, quite plausibly to my mind.

"It can if bribery was involved, especially on the scale and scope that was going on at Thorn Bay," he countered, belligerently.

"That was never proved from The Bank's standpoint. And again, even that was standard practice at the time." I was becoming a trifle truculent myself.

"That's it!" Jerry jumped in. "At the time there was a whole box of frogs about to open up, which everyone now seems conveniently to have forgotten. I'm not talking simple bribery here, I'm talking about murder, boyo - many times over."

"Now you're just being silly, Jerry," I said, feeling sure of my ground at last. Or sounding like Penelope Keith in 'The Good Life'.

"Oh, yeah?" he rounded on me. "Think back: all sorts of dead bodies turning up in odd places; one taking a dirt nap in a Malaysian mangrove swamp, another discovered tied to a manhole cover at the bottom of a swimming pool in Hongkong, and even a Vatican financier's found swinging lifeless by a London bridge of a cold winter's morn - all suicides, apparently, but none of them ever properly investigated or resolved."

"There's no need to exaggerate," I grumbled. "There was only one victim in each case. And anyway, what in God's name has the Vatican to do with it all?"

"You've done it again!" he trilled. "In God's name – that was another point. Think back to Hongkong once more. Think about all the funny money that was going through the place and the funny places it came from. How much of it was coming out of mainland China? How much of it was laundered? And Mafia money? Mafia money versus Chinese money? No contest! I might be just spit-balling here, but don't you see the conflict of interest? The Vatican dude at the end of the rope was a gibbet... a warning from China to the Mafia that not even God was going to fuck with their gravy."

"I think you might be getting a little carried away with this thing, Jerry," I said, questioning his sanity. "I mean, going back to Alec Dunhill... I can't believe that the powers-that-be made him a peer of the realm just to ensure that he didn't have to walk the plank all the way back to the Far East two and a half decades after the event, or to shut him up about some dodgy dosh that he was busy pretending not to be warehousing in his bank in Hongkong."

"OK, James," Jerry said, relenting a little. "I'll admit most of this is conjecture rather than statement, but it's not all fiction. Making Alec Dunhill a peer wouldn't have exempted him from prosecution, but it would have had the effect of entering the exclusion zone of parliamentary privilege, and made extradition procedures, shall we say, 'awkward'. What I *do* know is that Alec Dunhill was sufficiently motivated to have paid a pretty penny for the privilege of taking ermine, whatever his reasons. But there are pointers to some rum goings-on in the timing of events. For instance, take 1982: the Pan Asian Bank made an abortive attempt to take over the Sovereign Bank of Scotland, which was duly turned down by the Bank of England because it 'didn't smell right'. Move on ten years when the smell's gone away, as had A. Dunhill Esq as he was at the time, and, here's the capper, the Bank of England practically hands PABS the keys on a plate to an even larger bank, the Midshires, and it's all smiles. So what was the bad smell in 1982? My guess, for what it's worth, was The Bank's involvement with Thorn Bay."

"And it *is* a guess," I scoffed, before reminiscing irrelevantly, "It was a great shame because the Sovereign Bank of Scotland would have been a much better fit."

"That's not the point," Jerry said, sounding as if he was beginning to tire of the subject. "The fact is the whole system is rigged and most of the time people don't even notice or care, not that they could do much about it if they did."

I looked at my watch. It was nearly time to go.

"I think I'd better call it a day, Jerry," I said, with some sense of regret. "It's been good seeing you after so long and you've been most informative, but my appointment's at two o'clock, so I'd better bounce. Shall we get the bill?"

There was a little time left before I had to go to my appointment but I'd had enough conspiracy theories to chew over for the time being. I didn't quite know what to make of them but there were a few things Jerry had said that seemed worth considering. Jerry motioned to the waiter for the bill. We sat back and I congratulated Jerry for having recognised me in the street. The waiter returned with the bill in an imitation leather pochette and presented it to Jerry.

"I'll do this one Jerry. You can do the next one another time," I said, thinking that he'd earned it, but also imagining that our next encounter would need to be equally fortuitous if we were ever going to see each other again.

"Are you sure, James?" he asked, perking up as he quickly passed me the leatherette sleeve. And then I remembered. That was another thing that set the Jardines boys apart from the rest.

I paid cash, slightly wincing at the cost of Jerry's cocktails, and we got up to leave. I stopped at the loo for a pee as Jerry went on his way. I peered in the mirror. I looked a bit pissed, but I didn't feel it. In fact, I could have done with another drink but thought better of it.

I made my way to South Kensington tube station and fought through half the tourist population of Tokyo, armed with their Pacamacs and folding umbrellas, as they milled around waiting for their tour guides to take them to the museums. What possessed them?

Didn't they have any museums of their own? The platform was heaving with excited, damp schoolchildren making a racket. I watched the sprinkling of teachers looking on helplessly and decided perhaps my situation wasn't quite so bad after all.

The train took me to Hammersmith. I noticed the weeds sprouting from behind the antsy graffiti on the station-cutting walls. Now *there* was a job for me! I left the station and negotiated my way through the labyrinth of underpasses to the Fulham Palace Road. I walked along the pavement past the bookmakers, kebab shops, tired estate agents and mini-cab ranks, and wondered at what a difference four short tube stops made in a town.

I took a right at the lights and found myself outside the Jobcentre. I joined a small queue at the front desk and gazed at the determined underclass of unemployed punky folk and stalwart idlers sitting around, some of whom would have been working for cash on a lucrative mixture of wits and car boot earnings but for this unfortunate fortnightly imposition of having to prove that they were still at a loose end.

I got to the front of the queue and told the she-pluke on the other side of the desk that I had an appointment with Mrs Huang at two o'clock.

"There's a presentation in the conference room down the corridor, second on the left," she directed, through her gritted teeth straighteners.

"But I thought it was an interview," I said, feeling slightly short-changed that I wasn't being accorded a papal one-to-one.

"'Restart?' Nah, dahlin', it's a presentation. It's just to tell yer what's 'appening. Nufink to be afraid of. Now 'urry up or you'll miss ver beginning."

I went to the conference room and gave a perfunctory knock on the door. There was no response so I let myself in. There were eleven men sitting austerely in a circle, with a pile of undisturbed Jobseeker leaflets on a table in the middle. I took the last seat and studied my fellow conferencees. They seemed to be a cross section of gum-chewing white van men and down-on-their-luck corduroy-jacketed supply teacher-types, the latter looking indignant at having to rub shoulders with the very same stubble-chinned scum whom they would much rather have been marking sociology papers about.

Mrs Huang walked in with a female under-colleague ten minutes late and introduced herself as our 'client manager' and her assistant as our 'client support officer'. She did a quick roll-call of her flock and got down to work.

She started by outlining the purpose of the meeting. It was a precursor to the Restart week that we would be allocated in due course according to the availability of places on the schedule. She prattled on for a bit about Jobclubs, Jobplans and Jobsearch programs as the assistant undermouse passed around the Jobseeker leaflets. A man opposite with building site-hardened hands gazed uncomprehendingly at a pamphlet inviting him to learn all about data processing.

When Mrs Huang had finished, we watched a chirpy black and white training video which demonstrated interview techniques for occupations that had long since been massacred by time and technology. After that the underslug handed out a mental workout sheet to everyone, apparently designed for those with IQs only marginally higher than sea plankton, before we were treated to a discussion on inappropriate professions including nursing, air stewarding and secretarial work as possible changes in direction.

One of the 'clients' touched on the pitiful and malevolent world of the Child Support Agency and the benefit trap of being financially even more worse off on the sort of income that the Restart program was proposing. The rest sat in simmering silence, only holding their displeasure in check out of respect for their fortnightly incentive-destroying giros.

The meeting came to an end without coming to any conclusion, except that we would be advised of our actual Restart week assignments shortly. I walked past the crisp-eating malcontents in the reception area again whose destiny would seem, in pool-room parlance, to "dot on" until retirement age. I came to the conclusion that the whole ethos of the Restart program was an elaborate hoax to distort unemployment figures and act as another statistical massage, like the Youth Training Schemes and Community Action Programs already in force.

It had stopped raining. I wandered back to Hammersmith tube station. The trains were starting to fill with returning office workers unaware of the existence of the vast waste of human potential of the long-term unemployed, still waiting their call in the very building the trains were passing. I wondered whether people with steady jobs ever thought or cared about the unemployed or whether they regarded unemployment as just another statistic.

I got back home and checked the mail. There was yet another letter from PABS trying to get me to open an internet account. It must've been the tenth they'd sent me on the subject that month. It was kind of them but I didn't have a computer. I chucked it in the bin. I'd had enough of PABS for one day. I climbed the stairs to the flat, let myself in and headed for the drinks cabinet. I poured out half a glass of whisky and drank it in one. It felt good. I flopped on the sofa and switched on the TV. There was some herbert in a sunny faraway place trying to get matey with some unsmiling cannibals. I wanted to be with him. I didn't care if I was eaten. Just as long as I was somewhere else.

Chapter 4: Instruction

The weekend was tedious.   I couldn't work out whether the apprehension of calling Martin Letts the following week or my general level of freakish agitation was the cause, but time weighed heavy. Saturday seemed to cling to every passing second like a needy child, while Sunday only appeared to be going through the motions of temporal advance out of a grudging deference to the etiquette expected of the space-time continuum. The phone didn't ring once. Not even the honey-throated lovebirds from the call centres of Bangalore thought to say 'Hello' and rhapsodise over their magnificent life insurance policies, thus robbing me of the autoerotic opportunity of asking them to repeat each succulent clause again and again and again, until the final master stroke.

I thought about calling Pete Divis on Saturday evening to see if he was on for hitting the town but I didn't want to drink too much, so I opened a bottle of wine instead. I didn't know anyone else. Most of my friends had either disappeared into the woodwork or settled down to wedded adequacy or were shy about finding themselves in my company since I'd re-emerged from disgrace. I'd spent most of the morning trying to be normal and involved myself with non-essential domestica, but by mid-afternoon I was bored with re-ironing my handkerchief collection, so I settled down to read some magazines about other people's accomplishments. I got out of the chair, ate something, watered a plant, looked in a mirror, switched on the radio then switched it off again before yielding to my inner nihilism and turning on the TV. There was a film about some people playing cards with Steve McQueen looking a bit constipated, followed by a game show with some ill-matched couples being introduced to each other amid great hilarity. I watched it to the end and then went to bed with a book, but I couldn't read or sleep. It was still daylight.

Sunday proved to be equally uninspiring, so I decided to go to a morning church service nearby. There were a few Filipinas sitting in the front row and a man in a sweater at the back. The sermon wasn't particularly interesting and I felt that the pound that I had cautiously slipped onto the collection plate could have been better spent on a newspaper. I walked home broodingly and contemplated calling my parents, more to show willing than out of any feeling of filial affection, if I could still use the term 'parents' in the usual sense. My father had died shortly after I'd been sent to prison and my mother had been a bit off me ever since the 'incident'.   She'd subsequently married a genial septuagenarian chancer who played off six with an eye for a free ride and a widow's pension, who didn't see me from a paternal perspective. Also in phoning them there was the worry that they might initiate some sort of meeting procedure, which although not dispiriting in itself, invariably meant having to tread carefully around any references to my 'problem'. 'Problem' and 'incident' were the seldom mentioned, but always palpable code words for my drinking and killing activity that were never far from all our minds.

That was another matter that stuck in my craw. Having murdered once, it was difficult to be considered an 'ex-murderer'; I was always going to be a 'murderer'. Of course I only had myself to blame, even if I wasn't, to my mind, murderous by nature. But the passage of time just seemed to exacerbate my feelings of guilt and remorse, to the point where there was hardly a waking moment when I didn't hate myself. Unless I was drunk and oblivious to it all.

It was a good time to call, just before lunch when my mother would be at her own boiling point and my stepfather pulling at the only thing he really loved between his legs, namely a bottle of £4.99 supermarket claret, the cork from which he would probably be drawing at that very moment. The thought of it sent me into an almost diabetic thirst and I had to reach for a sanative glass of whisky in order to calm myself down before dialling the number. It rang three times.

"Mum!" I exclaimed, knowing that she hated the word, but thinking 'Mummy', at my age, was no longer an appropriate form of address.

"Hello, darling," she retorted, her voice striking a discordant note somewhere between despair and despondency. It was perfect.

"Is it a good time?" I asked, hearing the rewarding sound of dropped cookware on kitchen flooring.

"Not right now, blossom," she cried loudly, leaving me feeling as welcome as a trick cyclist at a pogrom. *Blossom?* What kind of term of affection was that for a murderer?

"Oh, I'm sorry," I shouted back, as if we were now under mortar fire, "I've just come back from Church. They didn't have a clock." I thought she'd like the Church bit.

"Can you call after lunch?" she pleaded, sounding as if she'd taken a direct hit as an egg-timer exploded in the background.

"I'll try," I screamed desperately, as if I was about to run for cover. "I'm going to a museum with some friends."

I put the phone down and let out a whistle. That was close. I reloaded my glass of whisky and raised it to my temporary escape, laughing to myself at the concept of 'museum' and 'friends'. As if.

The afternoon seemed to be wearing lead marching boots for all the momentum it could muster. I flicked on the TV to catch the afternoon film on Three. It was *Out of Africa*, and out of boredom I switched it off. I resumed my attack on the whisky bottle and then retreated unsteadily to the bedroom for a snooze.

The phone went a few hours later. It was Mother.

"How was the museum?" she enquired, sounding slightly more composed than she had at lunchtime.

"I didn't go in the end, Mummy," I said, employing her preferred term of veneration. "It was closed or something."

"Oh dear," she remarked, unconvinced. "What we really need to discuss is whether you're free for lunch next Sunday."

It was bound to happen. I tried to think of something quickly.

"I must go to Church, Mummy," I said, self-righteously.

"Can't you go to Evensong?" she suggested, doubtingly. "Elspeth has the children and it would be nice if you could join us. We haven't had a proper family re-union since you were released from..." She stopped suddenly, before she strayed into 'incident' territory.

Elspeth was my elder sister, whose disapproval towards me was aimed, perceptively, more at my drinking than the criminality of my 'incident'. She was ten years older than me, and in an insidious way had never let me forget it, to the point that she'd almost become a mother substitute or surrogate above me and had developed, over the years, an indefinable yet overwhelming hold on my psyche.

"I'll see what I can do, Ma. It should be OK," I said, trying to hide my anguish. I had six days to think of an excuse not to go.

Monday arrived at last and I was in good spirits as I emptied the remains of the previous day's whisky into my first cup of coffee. I decided to show some restraint and delayed my call to Martin Letts until eleven o'clock in order to give him time to get his feet under his desk. I skipped down to the shops to buy a newspaper and read the business section when I got home as if I was Warren Buffett. It was important, if I was going to be a key constituent of the financial world, to be *au fait*.

I rang Martin at one minute past eleven. He seemed happy to hear from me.

"James, I'm pretty busy this week," he said after our perfunctory exchange, "but I can squeeze you in tomorrow at a pinch, if it's not too short notice."

"Martin," I said, casting aside any notions of restraint, "if you wanted to see me the morning before my own funeral, I'd make time."

"Point taken, James," he said, chuckling a little. "I like a positive attitude. Make sure you bring Wally; he owes me lunch. We'll have it on him! He knows where I like to go. He'll make time."

I called Wally a few minutes later to see if Martin's dictates squared with his own arrangements.

"I suppose they'll have to," he replied in resigned tones: "He's my client and I make more money out of him than he does out of me, or so he keeps telling me, so I do whatever he wants. Besides, we're friends. The place he likes isn't particularly flash and it's not far from either of our offices, so I don't see a problem; tomorrow will be fine."

"I still don't get why you have to be there for what is after all, essentially a two-man event."

"I agree," Wally concurred. "But Martin is one of those people who will insist on making a party out of a séance."

We left it at that, with Wally suggesting that I popped into his office at midday before we went to meet Martin.

I had trouble deciding what to wear the next day. None of my suits fitted me with quite the élan that they had on their original purchase, and the only shirt that tolerated having its top button tampered with was a gingham nightmare that simply wasn't up to the occasion. The only viable option was a beguiling beige jacket and trouser combination which, together with an open-necked blue shirt, I hoped would strike a casual but worldly chord with Martin.

I found Wally's office in the catacombs of the old financial district, just within the shadow of the Morgan building. Someone buzzed me in. Wally was sitting with his feet on his desk and a newspaper on his lap.

"Ah, James: welcome to The House of Fun," he beckoned witheringly, without moving. "Come and take a seat."

I sat next to him in a swivel chair that didn't and peered brainlessly into a dealing screen. There were half a dozen other men, well into middle age, reposed in various states of languor with their lunchtime sandwiches and crosswords. If there was a cleaning woman, it must have been her week off. The wastepaper baskets were full to bursting and there was a republic of unwashed coffee mugs stacked by the sink in the makeshift kitchen. The three time zone clocks on the wall had either stopped or given up any pretence of monitoring the material world's pulse with any semblance of responsibility. The company had been formed a few years earlier by a group of disenchanted associates who'd subsequently carved a niche for themselves as specialists in 'value impaired debt', which appeared to be a polite term or a close relation to the former 'junk bond' market.

"You're looking very Saga holiday today," Wally observed, referring to my choice of outfit.

I started to explain the dilemma surrounding my old suits but he cut me short.

"It matters not one jot," he said, looking at a hole in his sweater the size of a tennis ball.

He took his feet off the desk and threw his newspaper to the floor.

"Right!" he said, drawing his chair closer to mine. "Let's talk about Martin Letts."

"Let's!" I parroted, tritely.

"I don't need to go over Martin's credentials in miniature," he began, side-stepping my inanity, "but suffice to say he's done pretty well at Ultrafinance and you don't do well with a company like that without at least a modicum of ruthlessness."

Wally paused for a moment as if to assess his assessment.

"So what's there to expect?" he continued. "To put it frankly, Martin's a bit of a prick and there's no bigger prick than a successful prick, but he's loyal and jovial up to a point, beyond which his ruthlessness starts to kick in."

"I think I'm getting the picture," I said, conjuring an image.

"Good," Wally went on. "He certainly likes the sound of his own voice. There's nothing unusual about that, but my advice in Martin's case is to make a friend and shut up; just listen to what he has to say."

"That suits me fine," I commented, grateful for Wally's depiction, "because I don't know much about anything at the moment."

The briefing was over. Wally stood up.

"Now let me introduce you to the scum," he trumpeted, provocatively referring to the others sitting around us.

I shook some hands and was pleased to note that no one seemed to be put out by the momentary intrusion on their schedule. I knew one or two of them by name from my own time as a bond broker, but I was relieved that no one knew mine. The company seemed to be more of a rest home for disaffected trader-folk of a certain age than a financial powerhouse of much consequence. It was the sort of firm I would have liked to have worked for, if I'd been able to get a banking licence.

We left them and headed for our rendezvous with Martin. The venue turned out to be more of an old-fashioned drinking den than a dining establishment, with tables hardly large enough for glasses let alone food, and silly little milking stools to sit on. We couldn't see Martin to start with, so we edged our way towards the bar.

"Two pints of 'Nasty' please," Wally said to the mildly anomalous spiky-haired youth behind the bar, and then turned to me to explain. "It's Martin's favourite tipple, so we all have to like it."

"I'm always eager to broaden my horizons," I remarked with alcoholic worldliness, although I was pretty sure I had sampled the brand somewhere before.

Martin hovered into view just as the barman was putting our two pewter tankards of foaming sludge in front of us.

"Could you make that three?" Wally asked the barman without looking as he waved to Martin. "And could you run a tab for me?"

The barman shot me, for some reason, a look of utter disdain and proceeded to pour another pint.

"Wally! Glad you could come!" Martin exclaimed, and then, as an afterthought, "And good to see you again, James," as he extended his hand towards me.

I took his baseball mitt of a hand into my puppy-like paw. He was dressed in a suit with a wider stripe than when we'd last met and looked even more gangsterly.

"Hello, Martin. It's good of you to spare the time," I said, obsequiously.

"Nonsense! We're here to talk business!" he intoned heartily, before adding in a stage whisper, "Although there is another matter that might amuse you."

"How interesting," I remarked, looking at his face for clues.

"I've heard a lot about you since we last met," he said, with the curl of a naughty smile preparing to embark on the short journey across his lips.

"All good, I hope," I said, instantly regretting the banality of my riposte.

"We have someone very much in common," he said, brushing aside my platitude, as his smile altered course from mischief to menace.

"What a coincidence!" I trilled, not quite through with my frippery as I gathered the guts to ask, "And who would that be?"

"I believe Christine Hale needs no introduction to *you*, James," he replied, putting me out of one misery and into another.

Christine Hale? No! No! No! *Not now, please!* Christine was a long-gone but much-remembered former passion of mine who dumped me with such force that I became convinced she'd put a jinx on me in the process. A series of misadventures had followed that eventually led to my downward spiral into penal servitude, which I put down entirely to what I referred to as 'Christine's Curse'. But what did she want now? Surely she wasn't back to haunt me again?

"You believe right, Martin: I used to know her well, but a very long time ago," I said, as if I was alluding to the Sung dynasty. "And may I ask your connection?"

"She works for me," he replied, as if there were very few people in London who didn't. "She joined me about six months ago. She's turned out to be quite a good bookie," he added, giving me a hooded wink, as if it wasn't the only thing that she was good at.

"Wonderful!" I enthused, with an expression that probably said otherwise. God only knew what she'd said to Martin about me. The fact that she was still in my orbit was, to me, a curse in itself.

"I told her to drop by and see us a bit later," Martin put in casually, his tone reverting to its naughty mode. "She said she was dying to see you again."

Not if I died first.

"OK, gentlemen," Wally announced, either noticing my discomfort or wanting to get on with things. "Shall we have some lunch?"

We moved away from the bar and managed to secure a table in a quiet corner, where we solemnly took our places on the diminutive milking stools. Martin looked as if he was sitting on a potty.

A waitress with a decorative safety pin through her nose came to our table to deliver some dog-eared menus and stood by in pelvic petulance waiting for our order. There were only six items on offer.

"The Belgian Duck's Liver pâté is always excellent here," Martin declared, authoritatively.

"I agree," Wally said with equal scholarship, "except it's not from Belgium."

"Yes, it is," Martin asserted, indignantly. "It says so on the menu."

"Yes, but not on the great big tubs of the stuff I happened to chance upon being delivered the last time I was here," Wally insisted, obstinately. "It's from Gateshead."

"I don't mind where it's from, I'm happy with it," I said cheerfully, trying to deflect any hard feelings.

"I suppose I'll have to make do," Martin mumbled, dejectedly.

"As will I!" Wally concluded piquantly, and then, as if offering Martin a sop, "Why don't you choose the wine."

Martin turned to the wine list at the back of the menu. There was only red or white house wine. He looked at the waitress.

"It looks as though we'll be having three *Terrine du Canar*d au Truffes and a bottle of your *Macon Rouge au Village*."

"The duck and the red," the waitress recited impassively as she picked up our empty tankards and turned to leave.

We started talking on general matters before Martin changed the subject to my employment. Wally assumed observer status and withdrew from the foreground.

"James, although Christine speaks highly of you, I gather you've had a leave of absence for quite some while now," he said, in gentle understatement.

I heard a warning bell. Why would Christine be speaking highly of me?

"Yes. There's no getting away from that," I admitted, trying to keep to the time-related aspect of my sabbatical rather than its actual cause. "But I'm a conscientious worker with a desire to do well."

"I can see that," he responded, looking warily at my jacket. "And Wally speaks well of you too, so out of the two people canvassed that makes a one hundred percent approval rating! And we won't worry about your time away. It'll disappear in the news cycle, like everything else. Your name's in chalk, not lights, friendo. But do you think you could handle a job that requires endless charm and patience before you even begin to see the emergence of a business relationship?"

"I must concede that I am a bit out of touch with my clients, but from past experience I don't see, with the right product, talking to the right people with the right knowledge, why some sort of business overlap can't be achieved on an equal footing," I said, wondering what on earth I was talking about.

"Sounds good," Martin commended, without any obvious signs of excitement. "So if you were initiating a business plan, which would come first: the client or the product?"

"As one can't exist without the other within a business scenario, it would be difficult to apportion priority without foreknowledge of the other integers involved," I dribbled, hoping Martin could make sense of my narrative. I couldn't.

"However," I continued, "if I could single out 'initiating' as a key word, I would say that 'product' has to be the foundation of a proper client relationship, otherwise what else would a person have to offer?"

"What if no one was interested in what you had to offer?" he questioned, starting to be difficult.

"Then I would have to find out what would be of interest," I said, realising too late that I'd set my own trap.

"But shouldn't you have done that in the first place?" Martin taunted.

"I was assuming that this was a hypothetical situation, and for argument's sake the vendor would have known the vendee's requirements," I replied, knowing at this stage anything I said would be wrong.

"To assume is to make an 'ass' out of 'u' and 'me'," Martin quipped, much to his own amusement.

"Nice one," I said, as if I hadn't heard it before.

Fortunately the waitress reappeared at that moment with our order, temporarily robbing Martin of the chance to trip me up again. She cleverly negotiated our plates on to what little table space that was available. Her presence was enough to provide a distraction for Martin and a diversion for me, but it was the sight of her miserly cleavage as she stooped over to attend to the cruet caddy that saved the moment. Martin looked at her as if sizing up a balance sheet, and grunted. She poured some wine into his glass and waited indifferently for him to try it. He raised the glass to the light, sniffed it and then boldly sluiced the wine round his mouth before swallowing it with a grimace.

"It'll suffice," he declared gruffly, as if he'd had plenty better.

The waitress proceeded to fill our glasses with a trembling hand as she struggled to contain her giggles. Martin ignored her and inspected his plate. He looked at the pâté as if it were an imposition. The waitress left before he had time to say anything else.

"Gentlemen, if I may interject for just a second," Wally said, looking at both of us, but primarily clarifying matters for my benefit. "I think the point is that recruitment is not the same cold-call schlep that can be found at some of the other broking jobs we've all done before; there's a bit more to it than that. In this instance research is every inch as important as delivery."

"Exactly!" Martin commended as he broke a piece of crust off his bread roll. "And William Davidson's the best in the business for both!"

"William Davidson?" I quizzed, unprimed.

"My brother-in-law I was talking about when we met at the party," Martin explained, looking at me as if I should have known. "Research indeed! You've had a four day head start!"

"I'm sorry," I mumbled. "I thought that was what today was for."

"It's Ok: you're a little ring-rusty," he said, without bothering to inflect any invective.

He shovelled some pâté onto his bread. Wally was already eating. I was damned if I was volunteering any more conversation.

"Look," Martin said, in a slightly more conciliatory tone, "it's not the best job in the world and in many senses it can be a thankless task, but when it works, it's money for old rope. However, in order to get there you have to learn the basics and acquire some technique. William can help you with that to get you going, but in return he's not going to pay you a lot; not to start with. You'll be like a trainee. He'll give you a small, token salary which will be drawn from the commission pool, to which you will contribute and benefit according to the amount of business you generate. It's a crude but efficient way of finding out whether a person's up to the job. If, in your case it is, you'll never look back; if not, you'll have to think of something else. You'll know either way soon enough. What do you think, James? Do you see this as an opportunity or a firing squad?"

"Well, Martin," I started, uneasily. "I can't accuse you of giving me any soft sell, so I'll try not to give you any soft soap. I need a job and a living. I think I've got the gumption and determination to make this sort of thing work, but I won't know for sure till I get there."

"James, I'm not hearing a real salesman here," he retorted, to my annoyance. "Are you really hungry for this sort of work or are you going to be stuck with being 'ring- rusty' for the rest of your life? There's no law against it; it doesn't make you a bad person. But don't go chasing waterfalls if you're not up for it. Try a charity shop. They're always looking for people. Or were."

I gulped. What did he want?

"I'm one hundred percent sure I should give it a shot," I said, grittily. "But how can I ever be more than ninety percent sure that I can pull it off?"

"That's not enough, James," he retorted, without irony.

"OK. A hundred percent then," I offered, against my better judgement.

"That's better," he said, knowing I was lying. "I'll just have a word with William... but only if you truly want me to?"

"I want! I want! I want, Martin!" I yelped, despairingly.

"Good," he growled. "And you'd better be good. In the meantime I'll put William in the frame and we'll take it from there."

Bastard! He'd got me begging for a job that repulsed me.

I let the other two do the talking when, through the crowd of suited nondescripts, Christine appeared. Time didn't stand still. There were no thunderbolts. It wasn't the 'Holy cow!' moment I was expecting. If my stomach took a turn or my heart missed a beat, both organs quickly regained their composure. I was disappointed by my stunted reaction. It was an anticlimax. My years of accumulated bile had been for nothing and all that was left was an empty bud of stale resentment, now withering under the gaze of Christine's masterly indifference.

"Hello, boys!" she said, announcing her arrival with measured buoyancy.

"Hello Chrissy!" Martin chimed, gleefully. "Let's find you a chair and get some more wine going."

Chrissy? New one on me.

Wally and I exchanged glances and jumped to it. Wally motioned to the waitress for another bottle and an extra glass and I purloined a spare stool from a table nearby.

"Thank you, James," Christine said, before I had the chance to acknowledge her properly.

"My pleasure, Christine," I replied, partly because it was. I took in her appearance. She looked nice in her dark suit with her hair tied efficiently in a half bun, but the eyes weren't right. And then I remembered. She'd been involved in an accident and been thrown through a car windscreen just before I'd been put away. She'd undergone ophthalmic surgery and been obliged to wear corrective glasses for a while.

"Laser treatment, James, in case you were wondering," she said, reading my mind. That was the problem. She always could.

"You'd never know," I said, more in solace than candour.

"Thank you," she said again, surveying me coolly. "You're looking very Oscar de la Renta today."

"Really?" I said, not realising in time that she was taking the piss.

"Funny you should mention it, Chrissy," Martin said, joining in the disco, "but I was thinking more Ted Lapidus, ha ha!"

I'd lost the will to explain.

"Either way," she said, suppressing a snigger, "I like the blue shirt, but it must be strange not having any numbers on the front – eh, James?!"

"Chrissy! That's outrageous!" Martin guffawed, approvingly.

I had to let it ride. I had no choice.

The waitress reappeared with clement timing and a glass and bottle. She was getting good at it. Martin grandly declined his right to try the wine but went on to introduce Wally to Christine. Wally extended his hand across the table and smiled without offering much else.

"So what's happening upstairs, Chrissy?" Martin asked, for conversation's sake, referring, I assumed, to his office.

"Nobody's particularly worried about Friday's non-farm payroll," she replied precociously, alluding to some sub-genre of US employment data that I vaguely recalled from the past.

"They'd better not be," Martin said gruffly. "I want that Banco do Brasil deal to go through without a hitch."

"It'll be a breeze," she remarked, as if she knew what she was on about.

I didn't. They were talking nonsense.

"Your bonus depends on it, my dear," Martin said, with a slight hint of intimidation.

"My bonus is in your hands, oh master," Christine responded, with sham servility.

Bonus? For what? Playing pass the parcel? One man's bonus was another man's loss, surely?

"Funny time of year for bonuses," I remarked, pretending to be knowledgeable on the subject.

"They're paid pro-rata at Utrafinance," Wally explained, rejoining the conversation.

"That's right, Wally," Christine said, willing to give him an opening. "And where do you sit on the bonus tree, James?"

She must have known perfectly well that I didn't have a job, but perhaps she didn't know why I was there with Martin.

"That too may be in Martin's hands," I said, feeling faintly awkward under his watchful eye.

Christine had the sense to not push the matter further and held her tongue.

The conversation had run its course and anyway it was time for us to go our various ways. Martin made a point of stiffing Wally for the bill, but Wally didn't care. It wasn't much and he could claim on expenses. As we went outside Martin pulled out a cigar the size of a workman's turd from his breast pocket and snapped his fingers.

"Chrissy old bean? Have you got a light, my dear?" he asked, in what could have passed for a well-rehearsed routine.

Christine had a match at the ready and held it to Martin's cigar with the indulgence of a priestess anointing a pharaoh.

"Thank you, Chrissy dearest," he said, with the noblesse of a nabob as he turned to speak to me.

"OK, James," he said, enveloping my head in a cloud of brown smoke. "Leave it to me; I'll get you sorted with William Davidson."

"That's very good of you Martin. I'll try not to let you down."

"Nonsense!" he barked. "You won't be letting me down; you don't have to worry about me. Just get on with it. *Comprende?*"

"Of course," I said, duly chastened. "What should I do now? Call you?"

"No, we're done for the time being; call Wally in a day or two. I'll tell him what's going on."

Wally looked surprised, but shrugged his shoulders compliantly.

With that we said our goodbyes, leaving Wally and I watching the other two as they walked away, if not arm-in-arm, certainly in a manner that indicated a distinct intimacy.

"Phew!" I said, breathing a sigh of relief. "I'm glad that's over."

"You didn't do too badly; you seemed to pass muster as far as Martin was concerned," Wally remarked, encouragingly.

"As long as he didn't spot too many wormholes in my bullshit, I should be Ok," I affirmed, cautiously.

"I wouldn't worry about that," he assured me. "Martin's a matador to his own brand of bullshit, so I doubt if he would have picked up on too much of yours."

"I hope not," I mused, "but I wasn't expecting Christine to be in on the occasion."

"Yes," Wally concurred, "you did get a bit of a double dose. I thought I detected a mild *froideur* between you... some unfinished business from the past maybe, or am I way off track?"

"You're way on track, I'm afraid, Wally," I said, ruminatively, "although our little film went to DVD a long time ago."

"And that DVD looks a teensy bit turgid to me" Wally discerned, insightfully,

"Yes, and now when she laughs an angel dies in heaven, but it was not always thus," I said, casting my mind back ten thousand midnights before. "Unfortunately the love we once shared so ardently wilted as suddenly as a petrol station carnation, but now's probably not the time to expand on the subject."

We shook hands. I thanked Wally for his time and support. We agreed that I'd phone him in a day or two as Martin had instructed, by which time Martin would have discussed with William Davidson whether they wanted to take matters further. I suggested that it would be nice if he and Anne-Marie could come to supper one evening soon, if they didn't mind bachelor cooking.

"The cooking's not important, James, not to me at least. It's what's in your drinks cupboard that counts: I'm sure you won't disappoint in that respect."

I smiled and turned to go home.

Chapter 5: Preparation

The phone was unusually lively the next morning. I was by the drinks cabinet applying the finishing touches to an Irish coffee when I heard the first call. I cursed but dashed across the room in case it was something important. It was worse than that. It was Elspeth, not sounding her sisterly best. I recoiled, initially thinking that she must have some sinister sibling telepathic insight into my alcoholic timetable, but the real purpose for her call was far more disturbing. It was about Sunday lunch. Gadzooks! I had completely forgotten to dream up a reason not to go. There was no way I could blag my way out of it now. Not with Elspeth.

"Of course I'd love to come," I said, dully. "I can't think of anything nicer." Except pancreatic cancer.

She gave me instructions for the best train to near where she lived at Arndale (twinned with Birkenau) and said she'd be there to pick me up from the station. She even extended the invitation by proposing that I spend the night. No way! Not in the home of on-tap disapproval. And that would be the only thing that was on-tap. I made my excuses and politely passed on the offer of accommodation.

I put the phone down dispiritedly and got back to my liquid handiwork, but it had gone cold. I was just toying with the idea of adding another shot of whisky and treating the whole thing as a poor man's Whisky Alexander when the phone rang again. This time it was Wally, who I wasn't expecting to call quite so soon.

"Wally?" I questioned, a little surprised.

"Ah, James, I thought I'd spare you the agony of waiting; I've just received a message from Martin Letts. It's good news, if that's what you want to call it. He's given William Davidson the go-ahead to see you next week. Monday at eleven o'clock, if that suits."

"Stone the crows!" I said in mild bewilderment. "It suits all right. They must be desperate! It's either an amazingly crap job or they must be under the impression I've got something to offer."

"I'm sure the job's not that bad, added to which it's based just on the other side of the Morgan building, so you'll be close to your mates."

"All two of them," I sighed, ruefully. "And I haven't got the job yet."

"If Martin's put his seal on it, you're probably as good as halfway in."

"If that's the case it's in no small part down to you."

"It's in *very* small part down to me," Wally corrected, kindly. "Your availability played a far greater role, I'm sure."

He told me where to go and wished me well. I reiterated my suggestion that he and Anne-Marie should come over to supper one evening.

"Perhaps once I've gone through the routine with William Davidson," I continued, short of committing to a firm date, "although I've got precious few friends to make it much of an event."

"Don't worry about that. If you want I can ask Anne-Marie to bring one of her girls from her gym."

"That sounds an excellent idea," I said, taking to the suggestion. "So long as it's not one of the media women from your party. What about the French lass you were so rude about?"

"You mean Francine Meffre?" Wally questioned, indignantly. "I wasn't rude about her. I was merely expressing an opinion about her conjugal aspirations."

"Whatever," I said. "She was certainly decorative enough, so see what you can do."

"I'll mention it to Anne-Marie and we can fix a date when you're ready," he said, as if he too was warming to the prospect of seeing what Anne-Marie might have in mind. "But talking of being decorative, James, do you think it might be wise if you invested in a suit before your meeting with William Davidson? You never know, you might need it even if you get don't get picked for the job. Or were you thinking of dieting in time to squeeze into one of your old ones?"

"Thank you, Wally," I said, inured to his ribbing. "I think I get your point."

We rang off and I went back to my coffee. It now looked grey and undrinkable. I was deliberating whether to throw it into the sink and starting again, when I caught my reflection in the lid of the ice bucket next to the drinks cabinet. Although the effect was conically comical, there was something disconcerting about the colour of my face. It was bright pink. I looked like a full-blown alcoholic. How had that happened? I hadn't been like that since before I'd gone to prison. Perhaps I was allergic to something – duck pâté, possibly? Whatever it was there were only a few days for it to clear before I had to meet Elspeth and William Davidson. I was debating whether a large glass of white wine might provide an antidote, on the basis that at least it was 'white', when the blessed phone went yet again. Thankfully it was Peregrine Blücher, a friend I'd originally met through Wally before I'd been put away. We'd hadn't spoken since.

"Peregrine!" I exclaimed, joyously.

"James," he responded, as if we'd only been talking the day before. "I gather you may be coming back to the typing pool."

"Hold on!" I retorted. "I haven't made it to the water cooler yet. But I must say word gets round quickly. Did Wally tell you about my situation?"

"He might have mentioned it," Peregrine acknowledged. "But don't let's concern ourselves with who said what. The important thing is that you're going for an interview on Monday."

"What of it?" I challenged, warily.

"I just wondered whether you'd like to meet afterwards. To celebrate or commiserate. Over a drink, perhaps?"

A drink! A drink! Always a drink! But who was I to complain? I agreed to give him a call once I was through with William Davidson and then we'd decide on a venue.

"And we shall administer sacraments as necessary," he intoned, solicitously.

We rang off. I smiled. There was hope. I reluctantly abandoned my current drinking project and resolved to buy a suit instead. I thought I'd start with the King's Road and work my way towards a pub I used to frequent before 'the incident' changed everything.

I didn't have much luck. They weren't quite the right shops for me. They were mainly fashion chains for younger men and all the suits made me look like a chauffeur. I gave up after an hour and made my way to The Artist, the pub I used to inhabit all those years ago. It was lunchtime but still quite empty. There was a small group of devotees at one end of the bar and a solitary figure standing at the other. He turned to look at me.

"James Mallet? Back from the dead? Where have you been, you old tosser?"

It was Mike Dexter, a similarly disposed down-and-out, propped in more or less the same position as I had left him twelve years before.

"In prison, you dozy prick," I muttered.

"Oh, yeah, I think I heard about that," he said, distantly. "But you're not there now?"

"Evidently not," I said, not wanting to leave the abstract and yet pleased to talk.

"How's romance?" he enquired, routinely.

"Ever tried wanking with a noose round your neck?" I answered, dismissively.

His beer glass was empty and judging from the sud-crud on the inside it had been lacking contents for quite a while. I put a fictive ha'penny into the slot and asked him if he'd like another one. He was not the sort to refuse. I ordered two beers and asked about his news.

"Same shit, smaller shovel," he began, edgily. "Ain't nothing going on but the rent, James. I'm broke; the other day I was so hungry I could've eaten my granny's arse through a wicker chair, but I ate my watch instead. Same goes for the others. Most of the geezers who used to hang around here have moved on or sold up and gone sensible. Or divorced. Whatever, there's not enough money floating around for guys like us to spend all day in a pub."

"Guys like us?" I quizzed, interested in his definition.

"Sure. You know: the guys caught in the middle. The guys who haven't quite made it but are too proud to beg," he explained, taking a gulp of beer. "The working world as we knew it doesn't belong to us anymore. From the international financier to the humble office cleaner or the lass who's just served us drinks, employment, as we knew it, is now the preserve of youth or the foreigner. The red squirrels have been driven out by the grey. There's no in-between. Not for us deadbeats; we're obsolete, destined to wallow in the mire of dead-end jobs as estate agents or recruitment consultants or something just as piffling. There's no work at the coalmine anymore."

I winced but didn't want to say anything. I was getting my ha'pence worth and I wanted to keep him going.

"Because there is no coal?" I asked, hoping he would elaborate.

"Exactly!" he enthused. "The country's completely fucked and it's the government that's doing most of the fucking. It's no longer about wilful negligence - it's about criminal intent. They're just a bunch of tea-guzzling, biscuit-dunking wimps, woefully out of their depth, subbing out contracts to any of their mates who'll give them a kickback to fuck up whatever they've been paid to do. It's jobs for the boys, pure and simple. Except it's all gone horribly wrong; it's out of control. Crime's a joke. Single mums spit out kids every time they sneeze; the kids grow up nuts so nothing gets done to the extent the place is crawling with immigrants, leading the whole thing to a demographic meltdown without a pension plan. Where's the money coming from? Not from me, buddy! We're on the brink of infrastructure collapse, James. This is the perfect storm, baby. This is scary biscuits."

We sipped our drinks in silence for a moment, as if to draw breath. But not for long.

"And you know what, James?" he asked rhetorically, not looking for a reply. "There are still thousands of people out there making millions out of what can only be described as a daisy chain of bullshit."

"Of course there are. There always were. All wealth is suspect," I said grandly, safe in the knowledge that my financial situation spared me that indignity.

"Fuck global warming," Mike blathered on, tangentially, oblivious of my meagre input. "That's the least of our problems. There won't be a country left to sink by the time *this lot* are through with us. It'll be each man for his self, mark my words."

I looked at him for a moment. The hair was thinner but the rant was as magnificent as ever. But I was bored.

"I just want to find a nice, undemanding lass to shag," I said, wistfully, thinking that a change of subject would do no harm.

"In this town?!" Mike protested, practically spluttering his drink through his nose. "You'd have more luck finding a life partner down a well than living in London. I can't even get the girls I don't want. I have even less sex than married people. There's no romance without finance and having two bob and an old condom at the bottom of your pocket doesn't quite cut it. Not with London girls. Funny that. When the money runs out, the gusset runs dry. And the foreign sluts are no better. They're only out to skank you for your wallet, if you've got one, that is."

"Foreign sluts? Really?" I asked notionally, just seeing my last dying hope of Francine Meffre drift elegantly past the window.

"Well, they're not here just to pick the daisies," Mike declared, reprovingly.

"That's a shame; it doesn't look as though either of us is going to be getting the Queen's Award for leg-over this year, whichever way we look."

"You're not wrong there," Mike rallied. "Jesus! I can count on one hand the number of times I've had sex in the last decade."

"You're lucky." I matched him, listlessly. "I've had to count on one hand for *any* sex I've had in the last decade."

We'd nearly finished our drinks but from the timbre of Mike's conversation it didn't seem likely that he'd be offering to buy the next round, so I decided to leave it there and make a quick exit.

"It's been good seeing you again, Mike," I said, more or less truthfully, and then I realised I hadn't asked him how he was actually keeping his body and soul together, so I enquired, partly out of curiosity, partly out of courtesy.

"Don't ask, James, you don't want to know," he answered with a reticence that belied a void. "Everyfink and nuffink these days, mate. Everyfink for cash; nuffink for the taxman."

It sounded like a lot of nuffink to me.

"Appears most commendable," I said, turning to go. "Keep up the good work."

"I will, mate. Don't worry too much. If you're the tramp, I'm the dog at the end of the piece of string," he said, sounding relieved that he'd been spared the ignominy of not buying a drink. "My round next time!"

I stepped out into the fresh air, amused by what Mike had had to say. It was nothing I hadn't heard from a hundred other mouths, but I was touched by the way he'd taken it upon himself to educate me in his personal perception of the world.

I hadn't found a suit and I was still parched. I decided to give up on the suit and returned home to slake my thirst.

I spent the next few days composing myself for my assignments with Elspeth and William Davidson and tempered my drinking accordingly. If all went well with William, not only would I have solved the problem of getting a job, but it would get Mrs Balakrishna, Mrs Huang, and above all Elspeth off my back. That would be good. From prison inmate to full-time employee in two easy months, but I still had to find a suit.

I left it until Saturday before I resumed my suit pursuit. It was the last day I had; I had to buy *something*. I decided Marks and Spots in the High Street would be my best bet. I moderated my normal morning drinks routine and was heading for the shop by ten. I wandered around the men's department for an hour and eventually found something that didn't look too ridiculous. I took the plunge and bought it, thinking that as I was there, a pair of new shoes wouldn't be a bad idea either. I was just making up my mind about some black brogues when I felt a tap on my shoulder. I turned around. It was Richard Hartley, who I'd worked with on several occasions during our excursions with The Pan Asian Bank. Indeed it was Richard who'd taken over from me on my last, unhappy posting in Taiwan, some twenty years earlier. We hadn't seen each other since, but here he was with his Chinese wife, Patty, by his side.

"Richard! Patty!" I exclaimed. "What brings you to this neck of the woods? You should be out cracking the whip in somewhere absurd like Kota Kinabalu or Bandar Seri Begawan"

"I'm afraid not," he said, ruefully. "All the action's here in Blighty at the moment."

They were holding their recent purchases in carrier bags and looked as though they were on their way out.

"We're done with our shopping here," Richard said, confirming my assumption. "We were just thinking of resting our feet somewhere and having a drink. Would you care to come along? We were wondering where would be a good place."

A drink! The expatriate clarion call struck again! I decided to abandon my shoe-buying impulses to join them.

"I think I know just the one," I said, recalling The Angry Masturbator only slightly further down the street. "It's not very far."

We trundled into the pub with our shopping and despite the hubbub of other Saturday morning customers, managed to find a table to ourselves. Richard bought the drinks and we settled down.

"So what job has The Bank palmed you off with in the UK?" I asked, addressing both of them, but Richard specifically.

"I've been put in charge of the so-called 'special projects' for the new headquarters being built in the Docklands, but quite frankly I'm just a bloke in a yellow hat shouting on a building site at present and I'd much rather be doing something else."

Richard was one of the few people I knew who actually understood and enjoyed banking, so the Pan Asian had made a point of involving him with as many projects as possible that had absolutely nothing to do with finance.

We chatted about other people we knew, where they were living and whether they'd been promoted. I referred to Leonard Fawcett's remarkable rise to the top.

"Yes. It's extraordinary," Richard agreed. "You were with him in Saudi Arabia, weren't you? What was he like?"

"At work? A bit of a stop-at-nothing cunt, if I remember rightly," I assessed, instantly regretting my vocabulary in front of Richard's wife. "But to give him his due, he was good at his job." Patty didn't mind. She was a Bank wife and used to it.

"Well, he's managed to cock-slap his way up to the top," Richard remarked, cheerlessly.

"That was the problem, as I think back: he was the sort of man who knew all about up and down, but nothing about left and right," I opined, wondering quite what I meant.

"Wasn't he a bit of a naughty boy in Saudi?" Richard followed, looking at me intently. "Importing illegal booze in a big way?"

"He wasn't importing it!" I railed. "He was making it in a big way! In fact, if he'd made one more drop of ethyl alcohol he would have put Saudi Aramco out of business, but I expect everyone's forgotten that by now."

"You haven't," Richard observed, sharply.

"So what? I don't work for The Bank. This all happened over quarter of a century ago," I protested. "What's more scandalous, to my mind, is a rumour I've heard concerning Alec Dunhill's promotion, if one could call it that, since *he* left The Bank."

Patty Hartley had finished her drink and asked to be excused for a few minutes to look at the shop next door.

"See what you've done!" Richard said jokingly, as she disappeared.

"What do you mean?" I responded, confused.

He stopped smiling.

"Alec Dunhill isn't really discussed in The Bank anymore," Richard said, looking serious. "It's all a bit *sub judice*."

"Sorry," I said, abashed. "It seems to pass for general conversation in other pastures."

"Well, it's something that The Bank's trying to draw a veil over, and we've been asked not to discuss the matter," Richard said, looking pained.

We went quiet for a moment. This was unlike Richard. We'd often shared confidences together in the past and he'd always had a healthy disrespect for Bank protocol. It was obviously a thorny issue.

"Look, James," he said, marshalling his thoughts. "It's a little complicated to explain here, but in a funny sort of way we're all involved. Why don't you give me your number and we can meet somewhere to discuss the matter in greater detail? I have to be careful. It's become a touchy subject and now's not the time to take it further."

"I understand," I said, failing to. "But don't leave it too long or you'll be promoted beyond my jurisdiction."

"Kind words, James," he reflected, sadly, "but I don't think that will ever be a problem. I'll tell you more about that too."

Patty returned a few moments later, empty-handed.

"That's a relief!" Richard said, with bluff husbandly humour. They had to go and I had some lunch ready at home. We said our goodbyes.

"I'll call you sooner than you think," Richard assured me.

"Don't be a stranger," I endorsed.

"I won't," he reassured.

"My round next time!" I called, as they left.

I bought a weekend newspaper with the obligatory free Paul Weller CD and walked back to the flat in thought. Why had Richard been so cagey? To be cagey was one thing, but to be officially cagey was something else. And what did he mean by 'we're all involved'? Did that include me? Impossible! I'd been out of The Bank for over two decades, and even when I was there I'd been a nobody. I'd been current accounts manager in two or three of the overseas branches and did a stint as an audit officer in the Head Office in Hongkong, before shouldering the mighty title of 'Manager Accounting and Foreign Exchange' in Taiwan, which I was hopeless at. So I left The Bank, of my own volition, and joined Parker Barrow Brothers in London, but I'd been too unimportant during my Bank days to have made a dent, good or bad. It didn't make sense, surely?

I pushed these thoughts to the back of my mind once I was home with a decent drink in my hand and the newspaper on my lap. I looked at the TV page. There wasn't much on. I was stuck between a clunker and a stinker for the two main movies of the evening. I threw the paper down and switched on the radio. I went to the bedroom to try on my new suit in front of the full-length mirror. It looked OK. There was some wailing noises from The Drips on the radio in the background. I knew the words all too well. They seemed strangely appropriate.

And goodness knows I'm miserable now.

I looked back at myself in the mirror and thought about my interview on Monday. Mr Hitachi might have had a point, but was I miserable? I wasn't sure. I hadn't had the interview yet.

The visit to Elspeth's the following day was not a great success. In order to get myself in the mood I'd taken the precaution of bringing a few cans of pre-mixed gin and tonic for the journey, and arrived at the other end in what I considered to be fine form. Elspeth thought otherwise. Unfortunately I fell over a paving stone just as we spotted each other in the car park, and the box of chocolates I had so lovingly bought for her at the station in London tragically became instrumental in breaking my fall. I picked myself up, dusted off my coat and presented my wounded offerings to her with a smile.

"Good trip... obviously," she dismissed scornfully, ignoring my chocolate philanthropy.

"Which one?" I quipped, quite wittily to my mind, but Elspeth was having none of it.

"Get in," she snarled, opening my door.

We left the station in silence. The house wasn't far but Elspeth's disdain made it seem like a million miles.

"How could you?" she barked, finally breaking the silence.

"How could I what?" I whimpered, aggrieved.

"How could you arrive so drunk, today of all days?" she spat, white with anger.

"I'm not drunk," I protested, defensively. "I stumbled on a flagstone, that's all. It happens sometimes."

"You stink of it," she seethed, unmoved by my piffle.

"It's mouthwash," I insisted, plaintively.

Elspeth, now mute with rage, bit her lip. The house eventually hove into view. It spoke of money unimaginatively spent. We swept past the garden centre stone lions and stopped by the front door. My parents' car was already there. I lurched unsteadily into the hallway and hung up my coat. I proceeded to the drawing room with Elspeth just behind. They were all there: my parents, my brother-in-law and my nephew and niece. My mother seemed tiny.

They all looked at me expectantly. I said 'Hello' as cheerfully as possible. My brother-in-law handed me a glass of fake champagne before Elspeth had time to stop him and I edged myself towards my parents. My mother was asking the youngsters about their recent skiing holiday. She turned to address my brother-in-law.

"It's so important that the children keep their skiing up to a good standard," she assessed, knowledgeably. New one on me. The closest I'd come to skiing as a child was watching holiday programmes on telly.

Elspeth stomped off to check the vegetables. My brother-in-law took the opportunity to top up my glass. I think he was in on the wheeze. The others continued talking. I listened benignly without saying anything.

Elspeth returned and announced that lunch was ready. We shuffled into the dining room and helped ourselves from the hotplate on the sideboard. I managed to negotiate a place between my nephew and niece. Elspeth pointedly filled my water glass as I sat down, but my brother-in-law had beaten her to it and there was a lovely big glass of red waiting right in front of me.

We started to eat. My nephew had just returned from his ghat year in Ethiopia, which we discussed and I spoke to my niece about her finals at Reading University. It was like talking to mud. The food was really rich. I wasn't used to it. The conversation became more general and we moved on to discussing other relatives, now long gone; how Uncle Gussie had been such a laugh and how dear old Aunt Grace had kept a duck in a hatbox. Elspeth looked on disapprovingly, her small, efficient lips that had made her the darling of the local charity circuit, now pursed at the ready, livid and vivid. I noticed she'd put on a bit of timber since we'd last met. Too many cream buns at all those village fêtes she was obliged to attend, I wondered.

We finished the main course and passed our plates for stacking. My brother-in-law leapt up to recharge my wine glass the moment Elspeth took the luncheon debris out to the kitchen. I liked him a lot.

The pudding was apple strudel and cream. More rich food. I wanted to fart. We got up to help ourselves from the sideboard again. My brother-in-law opened a bottle of Sauternes. *Dessert wine?* The man was a genius! Much against my wishes the conversation started to veer in my direction. I obliged everyone by talking some cack about my Restart course but inadvertently let slip that I had an interview the next day for the headhunting job. Elspeth looked most put out. The others appeared concerned, as if tomorrow was too close for comfort. I hadn't touched my water glass.

Lunch was over. We filed back into the drawing room. My brother-in-law had thoughtfully lit the fire and the room now had a nocuous, sleep-inducing fug. Elspeth wheeled in a trolley with various coffee accoutrements aboard and a silver dish with my mangled chocolates artfully arranged to hide their injuries.

"These were from James," she pronounced, tonelessly.

"Oh! Velvet Miracles! *Mon préféré!*" my mother purred, as a morsel promptly disintegrated *en jet* between the plate and her *bouche*.

"Anyone for some port or brandy?" my brother-in-law chirped, hospitably.

"No!" Elspeth shrieked, sounding so irritated I thought she was going to hit something.

There was a delicate hush. My stepfather made a considered remark about the weather in Portugal. My sister passed me some coffee in a thimble and offered me a chocolate. I wanted to puke.

My parents made noises about wanting to return home before it started to get dark in spite of the sun being indecently high in the sky.

"You couldn't give me a lift to the station?" I put in quickly, not wanting to be caught on my own with Elspeth.

"Of course, darling," my mother assured me, accommodatingly. "What time is your train due?"

"In about half an hour," I said, off the top of my head, praying that my conjecture wasn't hopelessly at odds with Elspeth's familiarity with the local train schedule.

Everyone got up, but in the excitement Elspeth was able to take me to one side as the others were leaving the room.

"James, we need to have a word."

"What, now?" I whispered in exasperation.

"You know what it's about," she hissed, her face a study of impending torment. "It's obvious. You look like a drunk; you smell like a drunk and you act like a drunk, *because you are a drunk*. You have to get a grip on yourself, but I know you won't, so I've done my research."

"What do you mean?" I asked, desperately.

"If you don't stop drinking right now, you'll be dead within a year, that I guarantee. I've got the details," she said, pointing to a file on a table. "All the counsellors I've spoken to are one hundred percent convinced you're a terminal alcoholic."

I gulped.

"Just look at yourself. Look!"

She turned me round to face a mirror. I peered at my reflection. I did look a bit peeky.

"Is this what you want?" she persisted. "It's frightful. Look at that pathetic drunk. What happened to the nice young man everyone found so attractive? All gone. For what? Tell me, what?"

"I think you're being a bit harsh, Elspeth," I said, feeling slightly hurt. "We're all growing older; I'm still a nice chap."

"Says who?" she demanded. "You don't have any friends. You spend every weekend alone. God knows what you do during the week. Drinking by yourself in the pub all day, I'll bet. And what about this job? Are you going to be drunk tomorrow like you are today? Even if they do offer you a position, do you think you'll be able to hold it down for more than five minutes once they discover exactly what you are? Or are you just going to let everything go, like you did before until you run out of money and really hit the gutter for good? If you don't do something about it, I will. Very soon. Do you understand?"

"Look, Elspeth," I said, trying to muster some form of defence. "You're born, you walk around for a bit and then you die. End of. What you do in your walk-around period is up to you. And to me."

"Darling, we're ready!" my mother called from the hallway, mercifully relieving me of the need to comment any further on what looked like an ultimatum on Elspeth's part. Thank heavens for mothers. Elspeth let me go, reluctantly.

I hobbled out to the hallway and unhooked my coat. I braved a smile to my brother-in-law and the children and stumbled towards my parents' car.

"James, are you all right?" my mother asked, anxiously. "You look as though you've seen a ghost."

"No Mummy, I just feel a bit full. I think I was a bit piggy and ate too much," I answered, in a language she could understand.

But I had seen a ghost. The ghost I had become just prior to the murder, over twelve years earlier. Thin, round-shouldered, shabbily-dressed and that look of desperation.

My head was spinning and in my haste to leave I hadn't given myself the chance to have a pee. I needed to get back to London badly, safe in my own private Idaho, wrapped in a duvet with a glass of dry white at my side.

We drove off.

"Isn't Elspeth wonderful?" my mother enthused, out of the blue.

"Isn't she just?" my stepfather chanted, dutifully. "Absolutely wonderful."

I let my parents talk without me for the short journey to the station. I got out shakily once we were there and said goodbye.

"Oh, James," my mother started, as if something had escaped her mind. When I heard what it was, I wished it had. "I've just sent five hundred pounds in your name towards the Guatemalan earthquake relief fund. I thought you'd like that!"

No! No! No! Not more of the pitiful Mallet inheritance getting pissed against the wall for yet another bilious cause a million miles away that happened to catch my mother's fancy? She must have thought we were made of it! It was my turn to do some lip-biting. I grimaced pleasantly, as if I'd just sipped a Whisky Sour without ice, and wished them well.

There was an hour's wait till the next train. The station was cold and empty. I went behind a shed and peed. I zipped up and put my hands in my coat pockets. I felt something unfamiliar in one. It was a can of pre-mixed I'd forgotten to drink on the way down. I felt something familiar in the other. It was a packet of cigarettes. I shivered and smiled. Let the party begin! There was a God.

Chapter 6: Negotiation

Alas, events the following day proved to be just as unsettling as the previous day's regrettable display. I was up with the lark, but also with a major sense of apprehension about my impending meeting with William Davidson later that morning. In an attempt to dispel my unease I was perhaps unusually liberal with the whisky dosage in my first cup of coffee, but by the time I'd had a bath some of my anxiety had, as if by magic, disappeared into a top hat. I put on the new suit and while the effect looked pleasing enough in the mirror, I felt uncomfortable wearing something quite so ceremonial after such a long time without. I helped myself to another measure of whisky in my second cup and once again the day ahead didn't seem quite so daunting.

I was almost unethically early for the interview. The receptionist told me to take a seat and called William Davidson to let him know that I had arrived. I looked around. It was very much an 'outfit' rather than an 'organisation' in the way I would have used the words. There were four or so working rooms staffed by what appeared to be half a dozen almost uninterestingly young women going energetically about their business between the various desks and chunks of business machinery linking each office.

A man, pretty obviously William Davidson, came into the reception area and stopped in front of me with an acidic smile.

"James? I'm William Davidson," he said, shaking my hand heartily as I got up. "I see you're nice and early. I like that! Do come this way."

He escorted me down the small corridor and showed me into a room set apart from the others. There were two desks, one with a computer and a stack of files piled high and the other in a corner, bare and untenanted. He pulled up a chair for me in front of what was clearly his desk and we sat down. He was younger than I had expected, a good fifteen years younger than I, with the rosy-cheeked assurance of someone who had yet to experience proper failure. The room smelt odd. It was either his feet or something unpleasant had got caught in the air conditioner.

"Right," he started. "I haven't had the benefit of seeing your CV, if indeed you possess such a jewel, but Martin briefed me on your history and background. I gather you used to work for the Pan Asian Bank and Barrow Brothers in the course of your exploits?"

"Amongst others," I replied modestly, feeling slightly alarmed by the elaboration in his phrasing.

"I'm sure," he mused. "But they're an interesting cross-over in terms of corporate culture, wouldn't you say?"

"They were very different," I remarked, wondering where he was heading.

"Do you still keep in contact with either company?" he interposed, congenially.

Aha! Now I knew where he was heading.

"I used to share a house with a chap who's now on the board at The Pan Asian Bank," I replied, trying to keep it vague. "But as far as Barrow Brothers are concerned, a career there would be seen as hot-desking in any other company, so it's difficult to keep tabs on what's happening."

"I see," he said, glassy-eyed with calculation. "They would be very good accounts to know, if you can see what I'm getting at."

I could see exactly what he was getting at.

"It would take a bit of work," I said, trying to distance myself from any preconceptions he might have had about the strength of my connections with either firm.

"Perhaps it would be worth stirring some old coals," he said, not to be put off.

"I could certainly try," I responded, anxious not to spoil his day.

"I expect you'd like to know a little about this company," he proposed, expansively.

"That would be nice," I said, relieved that the onus of conversation would temporarily be his. It was his feet.

He proceeded to tell me something about the firm, the business, the people, and then quite a lot about himself. I was by now getting skittish about re-entering the dreaded world of employment, especially the sort of smile-and-dial garbage that William appeared to have on offer. The idea of kissing-up to various venal scrotes half my age on ten times my likely salary seemed distinctly underwhelming. Also, the more William spoke, the more I doubted our chances of working well together. He was too much of a good thing. So were his feet.

"So, James, what do you make of it so far?" he asked, bringing me back to earth.

"It sounds most impressive, William," I replied, for want of anything better to say.

"Good, James. I see we talk the same language. I see potential!" he declared, unaware of the whimsy in his presumption.

I wasn't quite so sure. He seemed to be shirking the issue of my prison internship, which was fine, but struck me as a little odd if he was seriously considering me for a position. Or perhaps he was just being polite.

However there was nothing polite about the salary he was proposing. It was a very rude little stipend indeed, even by my beggarly standards. In fact, it was almost less than the sum total of my unemployment benefits, but alas some sort of occupation was expected of me and watching daytime TV was not on the list. And even I was getting tired of endless reruns of *Friends*. Evidently neither of us was in a position to be choosy. I would have to take what I was offered and make the best of it. One word would decide it.

"Net?" I ventured, not that it made a major difference to the sort of money I would take home in the end, but there was a principle at stake.

William looked at me. Those feet! I could hardly think.

"When can you start?" he growled gruffly, in what could have been conditional assent or a disgruntled 'maybe'.

"In about three weeks?" I volunteered, not wanting to sound unwilling but at the same time wanting to put some distance between now and when I'd be put out to kebab in the real world.

"No way!" he howled. Then, after a slight pause, muttered grudgingly, "One week and you've got yourself a deal."

Why the rush?

"Two weeks and *you've* got yourself a deal!" I parried roguishly, hoping I wasn't pissing him off at such an early stage of the game, but desperate to delay the day of reckoning.

"Monday after next then?" he grunted, just in case there might have been some misunderstanding.

"Sure. It's a deal," I shrugged, thinking I really needed some fresh air.

"Yo! We have lift-off!" he whooped, as if we'd just struck oil.

I didn't know what to say.

"And *voilà!*" he rasped, with ringmasterly relish, sweeping his arms majestically towards the empty desk in the corner. "Your new home!"

"Fantastic!" I rejoiced with commensurate brio, not to disappoint him.

"So bring in your crayons and pencils," he continued, with a Heepish twinkle, "and we'll see you Monday week. Eight o'clock sharp!"

That spoilt it. I managed a pukish smile and that was it. It was over. It was a wonder how small companies could move so much faster than large ones. If this had been The Pan Asian now, I would have had to produce the world and a stool sample before I had a hope of getting even close to the starting blocks, yet alone 'lift-off'.

William walked me to the door, one hand resting paternally on my shoulder, the other pumping my arm like a piston rod. Fortunately his phone rang before he had time to do anything silly like kiss me, and he went to pick it up prior to waving me off distractedly.

I let myself out into the corridor and made my way to the reception area. As agreed I gave Peregrine a call to let him know that I'd finished the interview. He told me to meet him at The White Sock, a watering hole nearby which we used to frequent in the past, where he said Wally Barker and Pete Divis would join us later. Just like old times. I said goodbye to the receptionist, no mean beast herself, and smiled at two girls I happened to pass on the way out. Little did they know I would soon be one of their colleagues.

It was good to be outside. William's feet were quite something but so too were the girls in the office. That would be a perk. But no. They wouldn't be interested in me. I was too old. I'd lost my touch, my spark, my mojo, but it would be good discipline for other things. I rounded a corner into a side road and saw The White Sock. Just looking at the word 'Sock' made me feel ill.

Peregrine was already sitting *à table* with a pint of 'Neverhards' waiting for me.

"How'd it go?" he asked, as if our twelve years apart had been twelve minutes. Some friendships were like that.

"All right... sort of," I moped, as I took my seat. "I think it's a job marked 'shite' and the geezer seems a bit of a four-letter man. He's offered me a position and I've accepted, but I'm not so sure. I don't know whether I can be arsed."

"None of us can be arsed," Peregrine remarked glumly, "but someone's got to pay the rent, boy."

I looked at him. We both laughed.

"You twat!" I said, feeling glad to be back. There would definitely be some perks in returning to work.

"And where do you see yourself in five years time?" he asked with a straight face, adopting standard HR department claptrap for chucklesome effect.

"No! No! No!" I squawked. "I haven't started there yet!"

At least Peregrine hadn't changed his tune since I'd been away. His face was redder and fuller but his suit appeared to be the same as the one he'd worn every day a dozen years before. He was still resolutely broke; a victim of the aspirations of his station in life without the means of support. His life was no worse than many others. It was a medley of school fees, mortgage payments, credit-card arrears, problems with the council, wifely disappointments and the loathsome 'Joneses' next door. I had none of these problems and yet, when Peregrine talked about them, they became mine too. Some friendships were, indeed, like that.

And then, just as he was finishing some tale of woe about his son getting up to not much good at school, some other friendships walked in through the door.

"Comrades! Forward with the revolution!"

It was Wally, with Pete Divis right behind him.

"Whose round is it?" Wally called, matily.

"I'm in the chair," Peregrine said, getting up from his own without umbrage.

"I'll get them," I said, thinking that the cost of Peregrine's children's education took precedence over any macho drink-buying protocol.

"Don't be silly! Nobody has to get them," Wally said, backtracking on his previous flippancy as he slipped Pete a twenty-pound note, uttering, "I think four of the same should do it."

"I think Pete's a bit narked that James didn't come to him first about this recruitment thing," Wally elucidated after Pete had disappeared to the bar.

"So it's my fault?" I protested, defensively.

"It's nobody's fault, you tit," Wally assured me. Then, as an afterthought, asked, "How did it go?"

"Fine," I answered, unenthusiastically. "Apart from having a major hygiene problem in the foot department, William seemed tolerable."

"But did he offer you the job?" Wally pressed, beginning to sound agitated.

"Oh, yes," I said, perhaps sounding a little flippant myself. "But that's the easy part. It's like double glazing... anyone can get the job, but trying to shift the stuff is a completely different matter."

Pete returned with the drinks and gave Wally back his change. I didn't need to apologise for anything, but felt some sort of explanation might put Pete in a better frame of mind.

"Thanks, Pete, and you, Wally," I said, taking my drink. "Pete, I think you know why I'm up here."

"I do *now*, you pillock!" he replied, bolshily. "If I'd known what you were doing I would have told you to look at my mob first."

Wasn't I the popular one?

"The remorse is mutual, Pete," I said soothingly, hoping a public apology might shake him out of his peevish funk. "But I can't understand what the fuss is about. It's not as if I'm hot property."

"You're right, James," he concurred, getting a sense of perspective. "It's not the most important thing in the world."

"That's for sure," I said. "It happened quite suddenly. One moment I was unemployed, having a casual conversation at Wally's party with Martin Letts, who I'd never met before, and ten days later he's referred me to another unknown, who promptly offers me a job. How strange is that?"

"OK," Pete conceded. "But watch yourself. William Davidson doesn't have the friendliest reputation in the industry. I'm not saying that he isn't good at what he does, but he's been looking for a wingman for quite a while and nobody in the know wants to go near him because he's such a pushy bastard. But it's all right now: he's got you."

"Thanks, Pete, you're a great comfort!" I said, feeling a slight knot in my stomach. "I have my reservations too, but I have to start *somewhere*."

"Sure you do," he said, consolingly. "But call me if you need to talk."

"Well done, chaps!" Peregrine commended. "You see, even in Hell you need friends."

We drifted onto other things; what we'd done before and where we were now. I got up to buy some more drinks. By the time I'd got back the conversation had settled into the familiar territory of a middle-aged compare and despair. It seemed as though we'd all painted ourselves into our respective corners. For Peregrine and Wally it was the burdens of wedlock and parenthood that seemed to outweigh the relative freedom of Pete's and my absence of attachments. But they didn't know that the ennui of their Volvo-in-the-garage existence was a soft option compared to the loneliness of the long distance bachelors that Pete and I had become.

Drinks came and went but by the fifth pint we'd all had enough. The others were senior enough in their companies to dictate their own lunchtimes, but even they had to go back sometime. We wobbled out of the pub and said our goodbyes. I was going in the same direction as Peregrine so we walked together.

"So when do you start?" he asked.

"In two weeks."

"What are you going to do for clients? Apart from us losers here, is there anyone else you know in the City?" Peregrine quizzed, perceptively.

"No one of consequence," I acknowledged. "Except some big swinger I used to work with at The Pan Asian who's probably forgotten my existence, so I must admit it looks like slim pickings."

I didn't particularly want to dwell on the subject, but in my attempt to divert the conversation in another direction, I remembered that Peregrine had a passing interest in things to do with nobility and heraldic research. As I had been discussing The Pan Asian, I mentioned Alec Dunhill the former chairman's appointment to the House of Lords.

"It seems strange that someone should receive a peerage for no apparent reason," I remarked, hoping to elicit Peregrine's opinion on the matter.

"No, there's nothing strange about that at all," he asserted, knowledgeably. "The fact the reason is not apparent doesn't mean it's not there; it's always there. We may not know the rationale, but they do."

"And ours not to reason why," I pronounced, inanely.

"Quite," Peregrine agreed, picking up his pace a step. I left him by his office and walked to the tube station, feeling none the wiser for my foray into the thinking behind Lord Dunhill's ennoblement. And perhaps that was where things should have stayed.

There was a call I didn't want to make hanging over me. At some point I had to speak to Elspeth, even if it was just to thank her for Sunday lunch. The longer I left it, the more difficult it would become and I did not want to be caught unawares by her calling me.

I was busting to go to the loo by the time I got home. I pissed like a horse and then went to check the answer machine. To my relief there was nothing from Elspeth.

I removed my tie and looked in the mirror. My face had reassuringly regained its florid tinge. I looked tired. I felt tired. I disconnected the phone, took off my jacket and shoes and slipped into bed.

I woke up a few hours later feeling groggy. I found a dressing gown and went to get a beer from the fridge. I hadn't eaten all day, but felt too on edge to be hungry. I went back to the bedroom and gingerly put the phone jack back into its socket. The phone went almost immediately. I had to pick it up. I knew it would be Elspeth. At least I was sober. Ish.

"What happened to your phone?" she demanded, accusingly.

"I took it off the hook for a while."

"Why?" she probed.

"Does it matter? I wanted a rest after my interview," I said, trying to draw the fire from what I knew was the main purpose of her call.

"How did it go?" she asked, allowing me a momentary stay of execution from whatever thrashing she had in store.

"Fine," I reported, casually. "Nice guy; good job. Not much money to start with, but it should be OK once I get going."

"What?" she gasped. "You mean he actually offered you a job?"

"Well, yes... I think that was the idea," I replied. "Why shouldn't he? It was no big deal."

"But you were so drunk yesterday... you must have been in a complete state this morning."

"I wasn't drunk..."

"Bit touchy about it, are we? Have you had time to consider our discussion?"

"What discussion?" I challenged, knowing full well what she was talking about.

"Oh, my! We must have been a bit pissed," she needled, needlessly. "Our discussion about what we're going to do about your drinking."

"Elspeth," I said, squaring up, "I'm embarking on a major new leg in the journey that is *my* life and all you can do is bang on about whether I like a drink or two."

"Balls!" she exploded. "If only it *were* a drink or two. I've been in contact with your local alcohol dependency centre and they want to see you immediately."

"My local alcohol dependency centre? *Dependency!*" I cried. "Elspeth, just what the fuck are you on?"

"Not the same as you, that's for sure," she shot back, bitchily. "They can see you tomorrow at ten so I've booked you in."

"Well, that just ain't going to happen. I've got to see the probation officer about my new job," I rallied bravely, flailing about for anything that might get me off the hook.

"Not tomorrow you don't; you're going nowhere. I've checked with Mrs Balakrishna," Elspeth returned effortlessly, trouncing my ruse in one fell swoop. "She and I have become quite good friends, you know."

"What?" I yelped. "Why did you have to bring her into the equation?"

"Because she's an 'able witness', for one thing," Elspeth explained, unsettlingly.

"To what?" I wailed.

"To a restraining order perhaps, or, more to the point, as counter signatory in the event that you need to be sectioned."

That was just lovely. Now I was totally screwed.

"You can't be serious?" I choked.

"Put it this way, James: I'm not in this for the laughs. "Let's be honest: your psychiatric record is not your strongest suit. You're treading a very fine line here."

That hit a nerve.

"And it won't be helped by *you* shoving me into some back-street dependency clinic to assuage your own amateur, half-baked prognosis on my life-style," I bawled.

"I'm not letting you make the same mistakes as last time."

"So instead you want to stand right in the way of my so-called life, just when I'm getting to the vinegar stroke!" I spluttered, wondering where I'd heard the phrase before, or if it even existed. It didn't matter.

"Whatever," Elspeth exhaled impassively. "Just be ready at ten tomorrow."

She clicked off. She wasn't threatening me. She didn't need to. She knew she had a hold over me... especially when I was enfeebled by my addiction.

I let the phone hang for a moment. I needed to think. I was stuffed. I put the receiver slowly back onto its rest and went to the bathroom. I ran the taps. I *had* to think. Short of booking into a hotel there was not a lot I could do to get out of tomorrow's fandango, especially now that Mrs Balakrishna was in on the act. I couldn't move without her consent. I would have to go with the flow. I needed my P45 and National Insurance stuff if I was going to start work in a fortnight's time, and for that I had to be nice to Mrs Balakrishna. And to be nice to Mrs Balakrishna, I had to be nice to my sister. And to be nice to my sister, I'd have to be nice to the dependency clinic. And to be nice to the dependency clinic, I'd have to stop drinking. For a while anyway. Shit! I switched off the taps, my thoughts already wandering towards the drinks cabinet.

Elspeth came to the flat at ten. I was ready. She'd brought some food she'd prepared, soups and casseroles that she put in my freezer. I couldn't bring myself to thank her. Greeks bearing gifts stuff. We drove off in her car to the dependency centre. It didn't take long. We found a space and walked up to the entrance. I sat in the reception area while Elspeth talked to someone at the desk. My life was a reception area. A woman came over to speak to her. They looked at me. The woman was a counsellor. Elspeth signalled to me to get up and follow her. The woman introduced herself. I didn't quite catch her name. There were so many women on government service. She was composed, of African-Caribbean extraction, and looked far too cool to have ever bothered with a drink, ever.

We went into a room with some chairs and a coffee-like table with a small tape recorder on it. The counsellor asked if I was OK with Elspeth sitting in on the meeting and whether I minded the tape recorder, just for the first session. The *first*? I said I didn't care in either instance but I regretted my laissez-faire disposition once she got going. She pushed the tit. I took a breath. It was simple at first. She just asked me about how much I drank and when. I gave her a brief rundown of my regime. I wasn't concerned with the truth. There were certain things I didn't want to say. Not then. Not in front of Elspeth.

"Do you drink in the morning?" she asked, staring at me as if she cared, which perhaps she did.

"Hell, no!" I fibbed.

"When do you start then?"

"At about lunchtime."

"What do you drink?"

"Mostly beer."

"Do you eat anything?"

"I usually have a sandwich in the afternoon."

She was quiet for a moment.

"Do you drink in the afternoon?"

"It depends what you call 'afternoon'."

"Do you have a break from drinking between lunchtime and the evening?"

"Of course," I replied, indignantly.

"When do you start drinking again?"

"When everyone else does - at about six o'clock."

"You don't have to drink just because everyone else does."

"What does that mean?"

"Mr Mallet, I think you might have a problem."

"I feel OK. I'm just a bit bored at the moment. I'm starting a job in two weeks' time. Once I've established a regular routine, I'll be fine. I mean, I've hardly been drinking for the last twelve years. I don't think a momentary period of indulgence before I take off on the next stage of my existence warrants this level of criticism."

"James... I mean... Mr Mallet..."

"You can call me James."

"James. We're here to help, not criticise. And we can help. But we need a partnership. First you must accept that you need help."

"And what if I don't?"

"That's called 'denial'. We cannot help you unless you admit you need help."

"I never said I did. My sister pistol-whipped me into this place and it just makes me... "

"Restless, irritable and discontent?" she suggested.

"Yes... yes... that's exactly it," I said, feeling as if she had somehow got it sussed.

"And wanting a drink?"

How did she know?

"It might help," I said, feeling very restless, irritable and discontent.

"Look, James," she continued patiently, "you need to take one step at a time. We don't expect you to stop drinking *just like that*. That would be unrealistic; even dangerous. All you need to do is to agree that you will at least *listen* to our suggestions, nothing more. You are under no obligation to alter your lifestyle. You need not feel that your privacy is being invaded. You don't have to take part in anything against your wishes. This is a National Health facility. The procedure is the same as, say, going to your GP with a sore throat. If you were prescribed any medication there, it would be up to you whether you took it or not. It's the same here, except our prescription is advice. There are no tricks."

"Well you said 'one step at a time'. What's the first step?" I asked, mistrustfully.

"You've just taken it."

"No I haven't," I vetoed, heatedly.

"OK, you haven't then. But you did ask me a question."

"Well, answer it!"

"All right. I would like you to have a blood test so that we can see where you are. You may have some signs of jaundice or liver damage. Sometimes there's a loss of bone density as a result of vitamin deficiencies. We can give you food supplements. Vitamin B is often helpful."

"Is that all?" I said feeling relieved.

"To start with. I would like to see you again after we've run the tests and we can suggest a program that suits you."

I didn't like the word 'program'.

"What does that involve?" I asked, feeling cagey again.

"Maybe a weekly or fortnightly consultation or some outpatient care."

"But I'm starting a new job. I can't say I'm on some alcohol reform program just as I'm about to begin working."

"That will be up to you, but we do counselling outside office hours and we work in conjunction with the AA twelve-step program, which we would also urge you to seriously consider," she proposed, passing me her card details in the process. "You can call any time and I or one of my colleagues will talk to you and listen."

I thought for a moment. At least it would get Elspeth off my back. Or so I thought.

"OK," I said reluctantly. "I'll take the blood test."

"That's great," she said, encouragingly. "If you go to reception they'll give an appointment form. Just sign it to indicate that you have agreed to our care, and we can take it from there."

It was too easy. I'd been duped. I didn't see any way out. It didn't sound as if it would kill me. Maybe it would help. If I needed help. She switched off the tape. We were through.

We shook hands and then she saw us out. I filled in the form at reception and was given a chit to take to the hospital for a blood test.

"Please do it immediately so that we can get back to you as soon as possible," the receptionist instructed.

Elspeth and I left the clinic.

"That wasn't too bad, was it?" she said, airily.

"I feel as though my life doesn't belong to me anymore," I said, sapped of joy.

"Nonsense. It's just the start of your new one," Elspeth said, buoyed by the apparent success of her mission.

It wasn't the time for small talk. We parted at the end of the street as Elspeth wanted to go shopping and I had a few things I wanted to do nearer home. Like find a pub.

I called Mrs Balakrishna the following day. She spoke first.

"Your sister called again and told me about your decision. I'm happy for you."

"Did she tell you about my new job?" I enquired, trying to get to the main purpose of my call.

"Yes, I've heard about that too," she replied equably. "Congratulations are in order: you won't be needing the Restart course after all! Well done, Mr Mallet, and good luck to you."

"Thank you, Mrs Balakrishna," I said, feeling a brief sense of end-of-term respite. "You've been most understanding, given the circumstances."

"That is kind of you, Mr Mallet," she reciprocated, with a slightly more restrained sense of elation. "But you will have to keep in regular contact with me and keep me informed of your progress or change of circumstances."

"Of course, Mrs Balakrishna," I said, in the full knowledge that my 'Get Out of Jail' card did not come without its encumbrances.

"I regret the inconvenience, Mr Mallet, but as I'm sure you are well aware, you will remain on probation at the prison service's discretion," she explained, without rancour. "I will send you the necessary documentation and conditions as soon as everything has been collated, but in the meantime you are now free to work!"

"I'm looking forward to it!" I fibbed, ruefully aware that my social security benefits would no longer be part of my new found 'freedom'.

I spent the next few days attending to various tasks, including my blood test, and attempting to prepare myself for the upcoming job. I made some tentative enquiries as to how best to approach my new vocation, but for the most part I drew a blank. I didn't know the right people and I was loath to ask Pete Divis for advice just as I was about to join a competitor. I didn't know what to expect. I began to count down the last remaining days of my liberty until there were none left.

And then that Monday took over.

Chapter 7: Realisation

It wasn't very pleasant. In fact, it was a nightmare. And it wasn't because I hadn't worked for twelve years. I had. Prison was hardly a holiday, but nothing had prepared me for *this*.

My first trip in as a commuter took me less time than I had expected and I was indecently early, again. The doorman let me in. I sat down at my assigned desk and read my paper while I waited for William to arrive. He came in at eight o'clock on the dot, gave me a brisk welcome and then disappeared into the kitchen. He returned with a cup of coffee just as I was finishing an article I'd been reading on the train.

He rapped his knuckles on my desk as he was passing and remarked, "The only part of a newspaper we read in this office after eight o' clock is the jobs section."

Good to know, especially as there was no jobs section in my newspaper till the Wednesday edition.

"I'm sorry," I said, folding the paper and putting it to one side. "How would you like me to start?"

"I'll tell you in a minute," he replied, inspecting his own paper earnestly. It must have had a jobs section.

I waited in silence as William sipped his coffee. I moved a pencil quietly from the top drawer to the middle one and repositioned my telephone a centimetre to the left. His feet seemed OK.

"Right!" William announced when he'd finished his cup. "You'll be needing a computer!"

I looked around.

"There's a spare in the girls' office," he continued. "Come on, you can lend a hand."

We went to the other room. The girls were at their desks, looking occupied but depressed.

"Morning team!" he declared, with proprietorial abandon. "This is James. He's come to work with us."

"Hi, James!" they meowed, in kittenish unison.

"Oh, Hello," I replied, mousily.

They were gorgeous. Or young. Or maybe it was because I'd just got out of prison and wasn't accustomed to youthful females. William briefly introduced me one by one, till he came to the last and most seraphic of the assembled angels.

"And this is my sister Chantal, who's responsible for the well-being and decorum of these virtuous maidens."

My jaw dropped an inch. She was *something*. And then, just for the briefest of instants, I wondered about her feet.

Between us we hoofed an old computer and the accompanying paraphernalia out from a corner to my desk in the other office. One of the girls fiddled with some plugs at the back and the machine blinked to life.

"Shazzam!" William exclaimed, with wizardly glee.

"Great!" I said, trying to join in the fun. "What do I do now?"

His face became a microclimate, going from sunshine to thunder in less time than it would have taken to count to three.

"James," he said, quivering. "I know you've had a bit of a career break, but have you ever worked with a computer?"

"Of course," I said affronted, thinking back fondly to my word-processor years. "But it would help if I knew where to start."

"Silly me," he remarked, frowning. "Let's go through it to refresh your memory. This is a computer. Each day you log in your calls and register any relevant points that may be of benefit in the future. That's how you make a database. You build a database in order to amass information that may be of use in securing contracts. Without contracts you cannot make money, and if you cannot make money, this company is not the place for you. Do you understand?"

I nodded, dry-mouthed, and sat down.

"So you'd better start phoning around for your database," he instructed, raising his watch exaggeratedly to his face, "right now!"

Super. I'd been with him less than half an hour and already I wanted to hammer his head to a wallchart.

I couldn't think of anyone I'd dare call at 8.30 in the morning, not even my parents. There was no way that Wally Barker would be in at that time of the morning. He hadn't set up his own company just to keep office hours. My only hope was Peregrine Blücher. I dialled and begged providence that he'd be at his desk. He was, thank God.

"Ah, Mr Blücher," I yodelled, hysterically. "Good morning to you! It's James Mallet from William Davidson Search and Selection. I was just calling you to re-establish our acquaintance and perhaps update our respective business circumstances."

"And your Mr Davidson has told you to start making calls and is listening to you right as we speak," Peregrine chuckled.

"Exactly, Mr Blücher!" I guffawed, gratified but not surprised by Peregrine's immediate grasp of the situation.

"Bad luck!" he commiserated, now openly laughing. "Feel free to call me anytime you need to look busy."

"Thank you, Mr Blücher, that's very kind of you," I said, trying to keep up the act. "Would you like me to give you a brief outline of our service?"

"Must you?" Peregrine pleaded, as if it was far too early to listen to anything to do with business. "You don't mind if I read my newspaper?"

"Not at all, Mr Blücher," I said, aware that William was now staring at me intently. "If I can begin by telling you that our primary purpose is to match our clients' needs in respect of their staffing requirements."

"Is that it?" Peregrine giggled, mercilessly, before regaining his composure. "Good God. This is serious, isn't it? Say something! Ask me what my star sign is."

"What's your…" I blurted, before I had time to check myself. "I mean, in order to achieve these objectives, we research and source suitable candidates for each particular vacan…"

"What about lunch?" Peregrine cut in, rudely. "I'm already thirsty. We can go over this shit then and discuss alternative tactics."

"I'm afraid that won't be possible today, Mr Blücher," I responded politely, thinking I wouldn't be able to blag any time out of the office past William for the foreseeable future. "But perhaps another day, soon."

"No lunch means no business, Mr Mallet," Peregrine taunted.

William was now looking far too interested.

"I understand, Mr Blücher," I said, wondering whether William was beginning to smell a rat. "I shall try to make alternative arrangements."

"I'd better let you go, James," Peregrine said, sensing that our ruse was about to be rumbled.

"Of course, Mr Blücher," I replied. "I shall look into what we've been discussing. Thank you for your attention."

I put the phone down delicately. I thought I hadn't done too badly for a first call. William was watching me. He didn't appear to have the same opinion.

"What was that about?" he demanded, tersely.

"I was calling an old business colleague to let him know where I was and what we were about," I explained, guiltlessly.

"And what does Mr Blücher do, exactly?" William enquired, quietly.

"He's head of syndication at KFB," I answered, confidently.

"What's KFB? A chicken restaurant?" he jibed derisively, seemingly unaware of the obviousness of his analogy.

"KFB? Korea First Bank," I clarified, as if those in the know would know.

"Korea what?" he scoffed.

"First Bank."

"Do they have a second bank? Or a third? How many banks do they need in Korea?" he goaded, much to my confusion.

"I don't quite get your point, William. It was my first call as a headhunter. I didn't think I did too badly. Jesus! Milton Keynes wasn't built in a day. I was just calling someone I know who works in a bank."

"Well it's hardly the Bank of flippin' America, is it?"

"I beg your pardon?" I said, hanging on to my professional calm. Just. "I mean, what do you want, William? I'm not entirely up to date with the market at the moment, but give me a chance to get stuck in, please! Besides, what were you expecting on your budget? Henry flippin' Kissinger?"

"James, it's not about budget, it's about results," he remonstrated. "Martin said you were up close and personal with some nob-end at the Pan Asian. *That's* the sort of person you should be talking to. That's why I hired you. I didn't employ you just to talk to some poop in the coop at the Korean Chicken Bank. Are you with me?"

"Sure," I acknowledged. "But I left the Pan Asian over twenty years ago. Martin's information is way out of date. I used to share a flat with a guy called Leonard Fawcett who's now quite high in the PABS organisation, but he was more a colleague than a friend."

"That's just what we want!" William exclaimed, as if I was missing the point. "Friends are two-a-penny, but colleagues, ex or otherwise, are worth their weight in gold, so get on the case!"

"But I haven't spoken to him since I left The Bank..."

"So now's the time to get sociable!" William enthused, ignoring my discomfort.

"This is crazy!" I cried in horror. "I don't think he actually liked me that much. I'm not even sure what he does now. The way things are going, I'm not even sure what we do."

"We hunt heads James," William said, calmly. "So call him and see what he wants."

"I don't know his number."

"You don't have to be Max Planck to find it out," he said, lobbing a bank directory the size of a Greek lexicon in my direction.

I missed the catch and it fell to the floor. William shook his head. I picked it up and started to leaf through, knowing that if Leonard Fawcett were an executive director, his name would be up in bright lights. But I was damned if I was going to call any direct lines, so I called the main switchboard and was put through to his secretary.

"I'm afraid Mr Fawcett's not in the country at the moment, sir."

Whew! The relief! Then she went and spoilt it.

"But he's easily contactable if you wish."

"No, no, no! That's fine. I'll call him when he's not busy."

"He's due back in the office at the end of the week. Can I say who called?"

"No, I'll leave it there. I'll track him down when he's available. I'm just a friend."

I put the phone down. I could taste the sweat on my upper lip.

"That wasn't very good, was it?" William remarked, casually.

"What do you want?" I begged, looking in vain for a shred of humanity. "He wasn't in, for crying out loud!"

"Well, don't look so happy about it!"

William stopped for a minute to consider and then started to speak, very slowly.

"Look, James, you went to the trouble of making the call. You may even have got yourself a little psyched up for it. You were using probably the most important lead you're ever likely to have, and you blew it. You wasted the call."

"In what way? I can't help it if he's not there," I objected.

"What about the secretary? What was wrong with her?" he persisted. "Why didn't you get her name? Even secretaries have identities. Nothing wrong with getting familiar. They like it. She wasn't doing anything; not with your mate away. She's probably looking out of the window as we speak, filing her nails, wondering at this very moment who that smoothie with the nice voice was who just called."

"What?" I asked, in disbelief. "Are you suggesting I proposition her?"

I wanted to slash my wrists.

"I could be," William replied, matter-of-factly. "Why not? People don't hire ugly secretaries unless they have to. Especially at director level. She might be hot."

"No, William, no!" I said, getting up from my desk.

"Hold on, James! Cool your jets!" he instructed. "But you get what I'm driving at, don't you?"

"No, William, I don't. Tell me."

"Well, you could have said to her, 'OK, I'm James Mallet from blah blah fishcakes; do you know who would be the best person to talk to in your blah blah fishcakes department?' Or better still, you could have asked, as this Fawcett chappie wasn't around, who would be available for a meeting to discuss the Pan Asian's direction and hiring emphasis and could she be so kind as to arrange an appointment for you to meet said wonder-bollocks? Thank you very much, Miss Secretary. End of. Simple, isn't it?"

"I suppose so," I whispered, wanting to weep.

"So call her back," William urged, gently, as if he was only trying to help.

"I can't. Not today," I said, feeling roundly beaten. "I need to think it out. I haven't got your balls yet. You do it if you want to."

"She's your friend, James," he reminded me. "Or could be."

I put my face in my hands.

"OK, we'll leave her for today," he murmured. "Who's your next call?"

"I don't know," I answered, miserably.

"Make sure you log it in the computer when you do, James."

That was the theme, the tempo more or less, for the rest of the week. William's feet started to go at around midday on Wednesday and went from mildly putrid to downright gopping throughout Thursday. By close of play on Friday they'd gone seriously off menu. It was some consolation that this and his general demeanour seemed to have the same effect on the others in the company. I felt a wave of sympathy roll over me every time I passed the outer office. Another comfort I found was that, for all William's bombast, he never really stuck to anything for very long. That or he knew when not to flog a dead horse.

I never did call Leonard Fawcett or his secretary again because by the following day William had moved on to some other act of tomfoolery to bludgeon me into doing against my milder inclinations.

After a while I got used to his feet and his funny ways, although his brooding presence, his persistent eavesdropping and relentless castigation were never far from the fore. I got the hang of the computer and built, bit by bit, a navigable database as I nibbled at the outer fringes of the banking fraternity. I even managed, more by accident than design, to arrange an interview for a graduate trainee at a small Italian bank. The candidate in question, a woman, was herself Italian, that was why I did it, but she had originally phoned under the assumption that we, as a 'search and selection' company, had something to do with her qualifications in genetic research. I managed to persuade her that, in an oblique way, this was exactly our field, and she happily sent me her CV. I made light of the matter, but when Peregrine Blücher happened to mention that there was a junior vacancy at Banca Monte dei Paschi di Lavazza's London office, I saw no harm in contacting them to tell them that I had a possible applicant who might fit. To William's exasperation the ensuing meeting went surprisingly well.

Towards the end of that week I received another unsolicited call, this time from Ian Smiley, an old broking friend who'd phoned to say he was having problems with his boss at Probonds & Company, and could I keep my eyes open for other opportunities. Also by chance I'd recently re-introduced myself to a dealer at Norinmunchkin Bank, who I'd once got horribly drunk with after a seminar we'd both been obliged to attend concerning the deregulation of the Djibouti Stock Exchange. He remembered me well and likewise disclosed that he was looking for a bond dealer to work with his money market team. I told Ian Smiley to send me his CV immediately.

Easy breezy! At last my job was beginning to make some sense! Unfortunately William didn't see it that way.

"James, this is not quality business," he complained, waving his arms about. "It's all arse gravy! It's no good relying on your no-hoper friends to do you favours, and what's with this Monty de Python bank that you've been talking about? It's rubbish!"

"It's actually the oldest bank in Europe, William," I informed him eruditely, remembering something I'd read.

"Well, Mrs Harris is the oldest woman in our village but that doesn't mean I want to fuck her every night, does it?"

He went quiet. I bent a paper clip into a thing and then turned it back into a paper clip. Was this the eye of the storm? I decided to say something.

"OK: I still might be able to do something with a call I've just received from a senior broker who's looking to move out of Probonds. I've got an idea. Things may look up next week."

"They'd better," he retorted, looking at me menacingly, "because I'm not going to be here next week."

What? A reprieve?

"That's a shame," I said, confident that he would probably think I meant it. "What gives?"

"I've been invited on a fortnight's free fishing in Scotland," he said, his face going from thunder to sunshine. Then back to thunder. "And you know what that means, don't you, James?"

"I do?" I asked, still taking things in.

"Yes, James, you do," he intoned. "That means you've got two weeks to make things happen. I want proper live situations cooking when I get back, OK? None of this Delmonte di Peaches in Cinzano Bank nonsense. It's my holiday, not yours, so use your time wisely. And no sliding out for drinky-poos with your loser mates like Mr Blobby at the Fried Chicken Bank, goddit?"

I bowed my head, humbly.

I went home that evening with a spring in my step. A whole fortnight without William! I was going to have lots of drinky-poos with my loser mates with William out of the way.

The weekend was fun. I received the results of my blood test from the hospital in the Saturday post. From what I could little I could decipher, they weren't fantastic. In fact they were terrible. The way they were looking at it, I was only 24 hours from ulcer. I got drunk and made some plans. With William away for two weeks there were plenty of things I could do. I might even do some work. I could also get my head round having Wally and Anne-Marie for supper sometime and thus better my acquaintance with Francine Meffre, perhaps.

The atmosphere in the office was different the following Monday. It was as if a cloud had lifted. The girls were happy. I was happy. Even the part-time admin guy who I never usually saw, said 'Hello' with a cheery smile. The mood was so convivial I almost felt sorry for Chantal who must have realised that the change in everyone's temperament was almost entirely down to her brother's absence.

I saw her in the kitchen later in the morning while I was looking for a biscuit. She was standing by the window, smoking. She looked sensational. She always did, but today she was on a rocket. The alabaster cool of her complexion, the swatch of blond hair hiding her cobalt blue eyes teasingly, and the cruel red streak of lipstick across her mouth, all came together to perfection. And yet she wasn't wearing anything special; just a plain white shirt and a pair of jeans that were too big for her, probably a boyfriend's, but the overall effect was endearingly cute: half farm-girl virgin, half line-dance vamp.

I couldn't just stand there.

"Hi!" I effused, in a reckless attempt at conversation.

"How's it going?"

"Fine... today at least... for some reason," I croaked, unsure of my ground.

"Funny that," she acknowledged.

"How about you?" I enquired, uncertain what to make of her insinuation.

"It's tough," she said, drawing languidly on her cigarette.

"For you? I thought I was the only one," I said, sensing a vague feeling of shared subterfuge.

"You must be joking!"

She blew out a long plume of smoke.

"But you all look so busy... so involved... like a family business."

"Some family!" she scoffed.

"In what sense?"

"For a start there's no family," she informed me, to my puzzlement. "William's not my brother; he's my stepbrother. There's no bloodline or, for that matter, love lost between us. He called on me to set up the secretarial division here. I had no experience of recruitment prior to this. He said it would be as easy as falling off a log."

"Do you feel as though he sold you a pup?" I asked, empathising madly.

"You bet I do! And I sold it to the others, for my sins," she declared, angrily grinding her cigarette into a saucer.

"Well, you could have fooled me," I said, trying to present a more cheerful aspect. "You all look as though you're doing something."

"Oh yeah... the girls are great but the clients just aren't biting," she lamented.

"At least you've got some clients; I've hardly got any," I grumbled.

"You've got your 'no-hoper' friends," she threw in, with a faint tinge of mischief.

I gave her a double take.

"You know?" I gulped.

"I heard... I am William's stepsister."

"I suppose you should know him quite well."

"Right from the top of his pointy little head down to the tip of his stinky little toes," she endorsed, with perverse pride.

I gave her a triple take.

"Chantal... you're magnificent!" I cheered.

"I know," she rallied, with model conceit. "But all that glisters... come on; we'd better get back to work."

"Talking of work," I said, regretting that the show was over, "I need to see some of my... "

"'No-hoper' friends for drinky-poos?" she cut in, knowingly.

"Exactly," I said, once more taken aback. "If it's OK with you and doesn't cross the demarcation of... "

"My association with William?" she presupposed, second-guessing me yet again. "It's fine. You can do what you want. Just don't be too long and don't come back drunk. The little creep could call in anytime."

What a woman! I bounced back to my desk, biscuit-less but thrilled. I looked at my computer. Ian Smiley had sent me his CV. It was fine. All it needed was a few tweaks and it would be ready for onward transmission to my fellow inebriate at Norinmunchkin Bank. Today had been a good day so far and now was as good a time as any to call Peregrine Blücher out for a drink. I felt I owed him one for tipping me the wink about the vacancy at the Italian bank, and besides, any reason to have a drink was good enough for me. Unfortunately Peregrine seemed to have beaten me to the cup. It wasn't yet twelve o'clock.

"Where's William?" he asked, suspiciously.

"Gone fishing," I quipped, pleased with the literality in my statement.

"Well, he's a good soul," Peregrine pronounced, bizarrely.

"What do you mean?" I queried, sensing something unhinged.

"I don't want to carp on about it," he carried on, blithely.

"Stop it, Peregrine!" I ordered, realising that he was about to engage in an aimless series of fish references. "Save it for when we're having a drink."

"I'll have a pint of Bass, if you don't mind."

"Peregrine; don't be silly."

"What'eel you be having? A bottle of Kingfisher, perhaps?"

"Please, Peregrine!"

But it was too late.

"I'll be perched at the bar. It might be teeming. They pack you in like sardines these days."

"Peregrine, this is getting tedious."

"Don't talk such codswallop!"

"Peregrine, I'm going to hang up."

"Where shall we go? We could skate along to a nice little plaice near Fishmongers' Hall. You could wear your mullet hairstyle again, just for the halibut!"

"Stop it! Stop it! Stop it!"

"We've got to swing our hook somewhere."

"Peregrine, I know you've been drinking..."

"Yes, like a fish, dear buoy. It doesn't manta, although I'm beginning to flounder."

"Peregrine, you're completely wankered. You can't drink anymore; you'll be sacked! Let's do it tomorrow instead. I'll call you."

"That would be brill. We'll have a whale of a time and maybe we could do a conger or see a film with Lawrence Fishburne in it. Directed by Ken Loach."

"I'm going now."

"Sorry if it's all been a bit of a red herring. I didn't mean to sell you down the river. It's all pollocks, really."

"Goodbye, Peregrine."

"Are you leaving me to the sharks?"

"Yes, I am. You make sure you behave yourself for the rest of the day."

"Otherwise salmon will get cross."

"You're damn' right, Peregrine."

I put the phone down. The state of the man! At this time of day! It was a worry but I was comforted that he had not matured one jot in the time we'd been apart. It meant I didn't feel so bad about myself. But I still wanted to make use of William's absence, so I called Wally Barker to see if he could come out to play. Unusually for him, he couldn't leave his desk because he had to wait for a business call, but he said there were a few beers in the dealing-room fridge if I cared to join him. I wanted to plug him on the state of the money market in advance of entering into any dialogue with Norinmunchkin Bank about Ian Smiley, and also to ask him when would be a good night for him and Anne-Marie to come round for supper. And Francine Meffre, of course.

I got to Wally's office ten minutes later. He was idly thumbing through a small sheaf of tickets to something. He passed them to me. I looked at them. They were for an open-air gig in Hyde Park that coming Thursday. There must have been twenty or so acts listed, the typeface bold at the top and diminishing in descending order according to the popularity of each band. None of names made any sense. Top billing seemed to be 'Sooty's on Drugs Again' with 'Spastic Patrick and the Creepoids' as support and 'Simply Ill-Bred' as '*very* special guests', followed by 'Alvin and the Pervs', 'Subutex Sandwich', 'The Feeble Hand Driers' and so on.

"Why?" I asked in stupefaction.

"It's the children's half-term," Wally explained, fatalistically. "All the kids are crazy about 'Sooty's on Drugs Again' and the organisers have kindly put on 'Simply Ill-Bred' for the grown-ups. Anne-Marie has a thing about Rick Cooper, their tousle-haired love-god lead singer, so that settled it. I don't know about 'Spastic Patrick' but we have to go. The children are too brattish to be left on their own, so much as they hate us, we're determined to make a family day of it."

"The joys of parenthood!" I eulogised, without envy.

"It has its moments," Wally conceded, getting up to fetch a couple of beers from the fridge. "Someone's got to do it, but you're not here to talk about that. You wanted to discuss the present money market conditions?"

He put a can of beer in front of me and sat down again. The money market stuff was old hat but the accompanying world of derivatives and credit default swaps was another universe. Wally tried to give me a thumbnail sketch of what they were all about, but I didn't get it. It all seemed too contrived, just dealing for dealing's sake. Wally could see I'd lost the thread, so he stopped. I perked up and mentioned my long-standing supper invitation.

"Any day that suits," I prompted. "Preferably while William's away."

"Next week looks busy," Wally murmured, peering at his desk diary. "And Thursday's out because we'll be too knackered after the concert. Friday would be good, if that's not too short notice?"

"No, that would be fine," I said, suddenly panicked by the prospect of having to provide. "And Francine Meffre?"

"I'll get Anne-Marie on to her," he affirmed, airily. "If not Francine, she'll find someone else; we won't come empty-handed. And going from what I've seen of Anne-Marie's gym club cuties, you won't either.

Friday came. Anne-Marie had called to say that Francine was away in Paris but she had another girl, an American from her club called Suzy Summers, who was free and happy to tag along in place of Francine. It was time to wash that duvet!

I had gone to considerable lengths to prepare for the event. Regardless of how small the gathering, it was the first social occasion I had hosted for a long, long time and I wanted to do it properly. I could have used one of Elspeth's casseroles that she'd left for me in the freezer, but they were cursed. Or poisoned. Instead I chose the finest microwavable beef stroganoff that Waitmore had on offer, then some flowers, a few scented candles and a packet of exotic paper napkins that were so expensive they should have come framed. I hoovered, dusted, polished and wiped every visible surface visible until I was fully satisfied. I wandered around the flat to inspect the overall effect. It looked like a flat.

I was just adding the finishing touches to the candle display when the doorbell rang. I flicked on some ambient music, checked my reflection approvingly in the hallway looking glass (never dust mirrors) and went to answer the door. The Barkers were all a-twinkle, but it wasn't them that I was so interested in. Anne-Marie sensed my agitation and turned to introduce me to Suzy. We eyed each other cautiously as we shook hands, I searching Suzy's face for any signs of disappointment; she assessing me for I knew not what. There wasn't much to assess, but from my perspective Suzy was *not* a disappointment. Not physically. Her gym-hardened body couldn't conceal her womanly curvature, and if her face hid the merest suggestion of a double chin, the effect only added to her allure. A pudding in the making perhaps, but with some time to go, and no less delicious for it.

I took their coats and showed them to the drawing room. They settled down while I fiddled around with the drinks. I asked the Barkers about the concert the day before, thinking that Wally would vent some amusing invective about the experience, but he was tight-lipped.

"It was cold, wet and looless."

"What utter nonsense!" Anne-Marie interjected, forcefully. "It was a lovely day and 'Simply Ill-Bred' were fantastic!"

"Just because you've got the hots for the flaxen-haired yobbo at the front doesn't mean they're particularly good musicians," he retorted, fogeyishly.

I left them to argue about it with Suzy looking on in bemusement, as I went about mobilising kitchen operations. There wasn't much I needed to do beyond turning on the microwave, so I took the opportunity quickly to guzzle a glass of wine, wiped my mouth and gingerly slipped back into the drawing room. The conversation had turned to other things. Anne-Marie was explaining to Suzy how Wally and I had originally met as colleagues in the same firm. Suzy looked at me.

"What do you do now, James?" she asked, with an inquisitive smile.

I took a breath, paused and smiled back. There was no point bigging up my place of employment, and since we were both smiling I decided to play it for laughs. I told her about my recent introduction to the world of headhunting and regaled them all with what I thought was an amusing account of William's over-zealous behaviour. Wally laughed and Anne-Marie tittered obligingly, but Suzy couldn't see the funny side.

"I think this guy sounds really cool," she commented, definitely wide of the intended effect. "In fact I think you're extremely fortunate to have such a go-getter as a boss... someone who's willing to lead by example and share his technique. Such leadership should be applauded, not ridiculed. It's easy for you to laugh, James, but he's the one doing the work. I don't think you realise how lucky you are."

Oh, dear. This did not bode well. Wally did his best to suppress a giggle as I snorted, but it was Anne-Marie who turned on us.

"You two never take anything seriously. Everything's a joke to you. Neither of you will ever make it into the big league with that sort of attitude."

This was not the way I wanted the conversation to go for the rest of the evening, but the die was cast. The microwave pinged conveniently, albeit giving the gastronomic game away, but at least it got me out of discussing my work issues with Suzy any further. I asked my guests to take their places à table and retreated into the kitchen to set about serving the food and wine. I warily installed myself next to Suzy and decided, for the moment, to let the others do the talking. The girls transported themselves into a socio-economic fantasy involving debate about the merits and price comparisons of various department stores in central London. Wally listened grumpily as their fantasia transmogrified into a never-never land until he couldn't take any more.

"Whatever happened to the dignity of simple necessity? Can't you see that you don't need any of this stuff? It's pure self-indulgence."

It was Wally's turn to face Suzy's sharp tongue.

"And your Mercedes isn't?" she challenged.

"That's hardly a bauble," he objected, wincing.

Suzy looked at him doubtfully before launching into an oddly tangential Anglophile assault on Wally's ingratitude for the benefits of his position in life. Suzy's picture-postcard image of the British way of life jarred with Wally's notion that the country had long gone to the dogs.

"How can you say that?" she remonstrated, incredulously. "You have your culture, your history, your museums, your theatres, your parks..."

"And a nasty little government which, but for its own incompetence, would behave as if it was the inverse cousin of the Third Reich, that's Hell-bent on sucking the lifeblood out of the normal population while having no intention of delivering anything of any consequence in return," Wally declared, with unequivocal conviction.

"All headed up by a particularly slimy self-serving cabinet that seems to be running the country solely for its own benefit," I said, adding my well-worn tuppence-worth as if it was anything new, just in case Suzy had any illusions about the male sentiment around the table.

She cast her eyes dolefully down towards her plate.

"Would anyone like some more or shall we move on to the next course?" I asked, brightly.

The rest of the evening passed more smoothly. With Suzy knocked into a box, the conversation became more easy-going and genial as we flitted from subject to subject, with gentle banter replacing blunt acrimony. Suzy and I eventually warmed to each other, but from what little I was able to glean about her position in life, it became increasingly obvious that I was not the sort of person ever to form part of her 'to do' list.

It was getting late. The Barkers had a babysitter to consider and Anne-Marie had stopped drinking several hours before because she was driving. I offered to order Suzy a taxi but she accepted the Barkers' offer of a lift home.

"See: the bauble has its uses," Wally uttered darkly, as I handed him his coat.

We exchanged goodbyes and thank-yous, and as I closed the door behind them, I concluded that the evening had been a qualified success. Seven out of ten perhaps, but not bad for a first attempt. I mulled over my impressions of Suzy and what sort of impression I might have made on her. Her American 'get-to' attitude was at odds with my general inertia, but that was probably not the only block to a likely liaison.

The weekend was unexceptionally unexceptional. After executing the pleasurable task of clearing away the previous evening's hoopla and polishing off the leftover contents of the wineglasses and half-empty bottles, I settled down to relax with a drink. My reverie was only briefly interrupted by Anne-Marie calling to thank me for the evening's jollification and to say that they all enjoyed themselves. I didn't want to push, but I called on her feminine insight to advise me as to the likelihood of getting any mileage out of Suzy.

"I think there's someone in the background," she said, non-committedly. "But I'm not sure how serious it is. You might know him: Matthew Howard? He owns a small chain of French pastry parlours... 'Comme une Tarte'... does that ring bells?"

My heart sank. I hadn't heard of either, but already I felt defeated. Mathew Howard smacked of entrepreneurialism. I didn't. I knew which one of us Suzy would prefer. There would be no contest. I thanked Anne-Marie for the information and we rang off.

There was another call about an hour later, before I had the chance get properly smashed. This time it was Richard Hartley, my former colleague from PABS, sounding ill at ease. He asked if I was free for a drink after work on Monday and suggested meeting at Raider Nick's Polynesian bar under the Poor Reasons Hotel on Park Lane. I was intrigued to know quite what it was all about, but he said it would have to wait till we met.

"About 6.30?" he suggested.

"I'll be there."

Chapter 8: Accusation

I was on time, but Richard wasn't. I didn't mind. I hadn't been to Raider Nick's for so long I was surprised it was still in business and was interested to see if it had changed. It hadn't much. It had never screamed of good taste, but it was unusual. There was the same profusion of plastic palm trees and mains-operated waterfalls, all adding to the illusion of being in an air-conditioned swamp. I settled myself at the bar. The drinks menu was more or less the same too, even if the prices were now more eye-watering than the cocktails themselves. I ordered, for frugality's sake, a simple bottle of beer. I looked around again. If anything had changed, it was the clientele. Gone were the Lebanese gangsters and their molls of yore. In their place sat their Slavic equivalents and *their* friends of the night, speaking in murmured tongues, unintelligible to all but their own.

It had been another good day. Banca Monte dei Peschi di Lavazza seemed poised to offer my Italian girl a permanent position and Norinmunchkin Bank had expressed interest in seeing Ian Smiley. Furthermore, I had managed to establish diplomatic ties with two new banks and had made inroads with another brokerage company. All without William's help! Was it time to buy another suit? Admittedly the two new banks in question were not what he would have considered 'premier league', but at least they'd taken my call. I liked the smaller banks. They were polite. Big banks weren't quite so easy.

I saw Richard as he was entering the club. He waved at me to indicate that he'd spotted an empty table. I finished my beer and got up to join him. We shook hands and sat down.

"I'm glad you were free to come this evening, James," he said, with unexpected earnestness.

"Always a pleasure, never a chore seeing you, Richard," I responded, pertly. "So what's kickin', chicken?"

"Thank you James, for letting me get straight to the point," he said, relaxing a little. "There's nothing too alarming on the face of it, but there are two or three things that have arisen in the course of business recently that I think you should be aware of."

That surprised me. I couldn't think of anything that Richard and I would have in common, business-wise, having not worked together for such a long time, but I was interested to know.

"I'm intrigued," I said, not without sincerity.

"Good; then perhaps I should explain the circumstances," he continued.

"Tell me do," I effervesced, expectantly.

A sarong-ed waitress floated towards our table before Richard had the chance to elucidate and asked in a Mancunian accent what we'd like to drink. Richard considered the question thoughtfully and then, ignoring the cocktail menu, ordered a mixed Martini, giving a lavish description of what would constitute the ideal balance of ingredients. I hadn't the energy or inclination to order anything complicated, so I opted for the simplicity of a double gin and tonic.

I watched Richard eyeing the waitress as she swished her way back to the bar.

"You were saying?" I reminded him.

"Oh, yes," he said, regaining his thoughts. "I had a very strange call from Leonard Fawcett last week, asking me to pop in and see him. I don't report to him directly, but he is a director so I dropped everything I was doing and was outside his office within ten minutes."

"Pant sniffer!" I sniped unfairly, knowing full well he would have had little choice to do otherwise.

"You have to kiss the ring... you know how it is," he admitted, without umbrage. "I assumed he'd summoned me in to discuss some aspect or other of the new building, but it was nothing of the sort: all he wanted to talk about was you! He wanted to know what you were up to, whether you kept in contact with anyone else at The Bank... that sort of stuff."

"Why?" I asked, disconcerted. "And why was he asking you?"

"Walls have ears, I suppose," Richard speculated, with a shrug. "Patty or I may have mentioned that we'd seen you that day at the shops to someone who may have passed it on to someone else... you know what The Bank's like. It's very parochial for such a large organisation."

"I remember all too well," I said, with a shudder. "But I can't understand why he was interested. I would've thought he had better things to think about."

"Well, he knew that you'd tried to contact him a few weeks before," Richard divulged, to my consternation.

"How? I didn't leave my name."

"It's not difficult to trace a number. His secretary didn't have a problem. She thought there was something suspicious about your call."

"Well, there wasn't," I snapped.

"How were they to know?" Richard countered. "Besides there was something else."

"Like what?"

"Someone called The Bank's archive department, asking about Alec Dunhill. He said he was from the Heraldic Association and claimed to be a friend of yours."

"For the love of fuck!" I cried plaintively, remembering the last conversation I'd had with Peregrine Blücher. "That would have been one of my idiot friends. He should have known better... but then he doesn't know The Bank."

The waitress returned with our drinks and perhaps sensing, wrongly as it happened, that we might be in for the long haul, had thoughtfully procured some salted cashew nuts to help propel our thirst and *ergo* our bill into the stratosphere.

Richard looked at the waitress again as she shimmied away. He loved that arse.

"And Fawcett knew about *that*?" I asked incredulously, trying to capture Richard's attention.

"Apparently so," he answered, sipping his drink distractedly. "The archive department, for what it's worth, is a Head Office function and thus technically falls under Leonard's remit. There must have been something in the daily excepion report that caught his eye and it turned out to be linked to you. You know The Bank's attitude to snoopers: it's paranoid, especially about outside snoopers. And I warned you that anything to do with Alec Dunhill is strictly *verboten*. Your idiot friend couldn't have done a better job of stirring up a hornet's nest."

"Or a storm in a teacup, more like," I remarked, dismissively.

"Not to The Bank, it ain't," Richard certified, stiffly. "Not when you're involved, James."

"What do you mean? What makes me so special?" I asked, askance and mystified.

Richard sat back and twiddled with the swizzle stick in his drink while I leant over and helped myself to a nut.

"James, you're going to have to cast your mind back on this one," he forewarned, putting his drink down carefully.

"Try me," I said, unfazed.

"OK. Strap yourself in. Can you remember what you were doing in or around May 1983?"

I thought back for a moment.

"Yes, I can, actually. I was working for The Bank's audit department. I had been doing local audits in Hongkong for the better part of nine months when they finally entrusted me with an overseas assignment."

"And you remember where you went?"

"Of course," I said, wondering where the conversation was leading. "I was part of the team that went to inspect the Jakarta Office."

"And the inspection went well?"

"Yes, I enjoyed it. It was hard work but Jakarta was interesting. We were put up in the Hilton, which was nice."

"I expect it was," Richard commented. "Did you find anything unusual when you were conducting the audit?"

"To an extent; the operation wasn't quite as slick as you'd find in Hongkong, but local conditions were different. More rudimentary perhaps."

"But everything balanced at the end of the day?"

"Yes. We wouldn't have signed off the books if they hadn't."

"But you did notice one thing that wasn't quite right, didn't you, James?"

"I did?" I quizzed, beginning to suspect that Richard was angling for something more particular.

"I think so. As the junior auditor on the team you were charged with the tedious task of counting all the cash and foreign exchange, weren't you?" he questioned, ambiguously.

"Yes, among other things."

"And everything balanced?"

"Sure. Everything was fine."

"Even the travellers' cheques?"

Shit. He knew something. He was on to me.

"Hmm… there was a bit of a glitch, now you mention it, but they were OK in the end."

"How long was 'in the end', in this instance?"

Now he was there: he knew that I knew that he knew.

"The next day," I replied, uncomfortably.

"Can you remember the amount involved, by any chance?"

"Yes. It wasn't very much; only two thousand Hongkong dollars, if I remember correctly."

"You do remember correctly, James, though the amount is immaterial. The important thing was that they were all present and correct *the next day*."

"They balanced, if that's what you mean?"

"Not quite, James, but never mind. Do you remember the name of the clerk who was responsible for the travellers' cheques?"

"Yes," I said, irritably. "She was called Joy Wathen."

"Correct again, James. Your memory serves you well; you must have been a very astute junior auditor."

"Look, Richard," I said, getting a little fed up with his game. "Can *you* get to the point?"

"All right, James. Just hold on for two more minutes and I'll be done and you can have your go. Now these travellers' cheques were all brand new, weren't they?"

"Of course. You can't sell used travellers' cheques to an unsuspecting public, can you? Not at a bank; it wouldn't be polite."

"OK. So if they were all brand new they would have been numbered in sequence, wouldn't they?"

"Yes, Richard, they would."

"So the next day, *in the end*, when they all balanced and everything was fine and dandy, were their numbers all in sequence?"

"No. The last two thousand Hongkong dollars' worth were not from the same batch; they were in a different sequence," I admitted, sheepishly.

"Didn't that strike you as a little odd?"

"They could have been leftover stock from a previous consignment."

"But they were newer numbers so they wouldn't have come from a previous set. They would've had to come from elsewhere."

"Look, Richard, I don't know where you've got all this shit from but, as a junior auditor, as far as I was concerned the physical stock was all there so I signed it off accordingly."

"Bollocks! And I'll tell you where I got all this shit from in a moment. It was your duty to report anything untoward to the senior member of the audit team and let *him* decide whether or not to pursue the matter; at the very least a record of the anomaly should have been noted, and you knew that."

"Of course I did," I said, wondering why I was bothering to bother about matters that were safely tucked away in another millennium.

But Richard was by no means finished.

"So when you first noticed something didn't quite balance you went off to have a cigarette and a think, didn't you? A little contemplation, perhaps? There you were, a humble junior auditor on your first-ever international assignment, feeling mildly miffed, but nothing major at that point; nothing that wouldn't sort itself out in the fullness of time. There had to be an obvious explanation: a mix-up between the stock in treasury and the stock on hand or in the counter float or something. Anyway the amount was so small, it wouldn't have occurred to anyone that there was something incongruous about the anomaly, least of all a junior auditor, eh?"

"Cut the crap, Richard," I said. "What exactly do you know?"

"Not as much as you, James, at least in certain respects. So if we are to form any sort of coherent picture I'll need your help to fill the gaps. Are you prepared to do that?"

"You mean, you'd like me to take over the narrative for the time being?"

"You'll have to," he replied, bluntly. "I wasn't there. I'm only going by hearsay; the devil is in the detail, so the stage is yours, should you would wish to make an entrance."

I hesitated for a moment. What had I to lose? Not much, I assumed, and besides I was curious about any ripples I might have caused by what could be construed as mere oversight.

"OK," I said, drawing breath, "I'll continue where you left off. Everything you've said so far is true, but I'm trusting you to tell me the source of your information."

"I'll tell you, but let me hear your story first," he insisted.

I moved my chair back an inch and leant forward.

"I did go for a cigarette, upstairs in a corridor leading to the staff lavatories as it happened, and yes, I was slightly perplexed that some of the travellers' cheques stock didn't stack up. But at that point I thought it was my inexperience that was at fault, not the branch counter system. I wasn't too worried because I could always ask one of the more senior auditors for help, but I had quite a lot of other things to check before the day was done and I wanted to sort out the problem on my own initiative. As it was getting late, I decided to catch up with the other stuff and attack the travellers' cheques conundrum the following day."

I paused again. I was coming to the difficult part.

"As luck would have it, one of the desk clerks that I'd just been asking to help explain the counter shortage to me came up the stairs just as I was finishing my cigarette... I assumed to go to the loo."

"Who didn't happen to be Ms Joy Wathen, by any chance?" Richard cross-examined, looking as though he was beginning to enjoy himself.

"Yes, yes, yes," I admitted, defensively.

"And did she?" Richard solicited, disconcertingly.

"Did she what?"

"Go to the loo?" he pressed, as if it was of material significance.

"I don't know," I answered, confused. "I can't remember, but she did stop to say 'Hello' and we had a chat."

"Go on."

"She asked me how I found living in Jakarta and where was I staying. I told her I'd been billeted at the Hilton and found it very pleasant. She said she went ten pin bowling there every so often with her women's club and asked if I bowled at all. I said I'd never tried it properly. She asked if I'd like a lesson and I said wouldn't mind. She enquired if I was doing anything that evening. I said I wasn't, so she suggested coming round. She was eating an apple, as I recollect."

"I think I can feel a trouser twitch coming on," Richard interrupted, crudely, "with you playing Adam to her Eve – eh?! So what happened?"

"She came to the Hilton at seven and we went bowling," I replied, succinctly.

"Or balling. Was that all?"

"Not quite," I said, uneasily. "We had some supper afterwards in the hotel coffee shop."

"Nothing but the best for madame," Richard observed, patronisingly.

"Hang on!" I protested. "We went for some very smart cocktails in the piano lounge afterwards."

"You spoilt her!" Richard cried, sarcastically. "And?"

"And we got a bit merry and I proposed that we continue with some champagne on the balcony outside my bedroom."

"Sounds a reasonable idea; very convenient; very cosy. I can just picture the scene: Oh, to spread a little Joy!" he goaded.

"All right, all right," I griped, guiltily. "We got down to it. I was pissed; she was pretty and willing. It didn't happen to me every day, even then. I was doing the talking and my balls did the walking. She left at dawn and the next time I saw her was when I went into The Bank in the morning. That was it."

"No, it wasn't!" Richard declared, adamantly. "It was just the beginning, dear boy. Was it merely circumstantial that the travellers' cheques happened to balance, all of a sudden, of their own accord, the following day?"

"I re-counted all the stock and everything was fine," I said, knowing that I was in for a panning.

"*Everything was fine?*" Richard contested, incredulously. "Just like that? One day it was fucked; next day it was un-fucked. Didn't that strike you as odd? Didn't you think to check the serial-number register?"

"I also had to count over fifteen million dollars' worth of very soiled Indonesian Rupiah notes, one by one," I answered, without answering. "Do you think I had time to go through every register? My job was to make sure the physical stock of cash and foreign exchange was present and correct, according to the pertinent balance sheet at the time of the audit."

"James, I've never heard you talk such rubbish!" Richard banged on, pitilessly. "It might have been 'present', but it certainly wasn't 'correct'. And you knew it."

"Of course I fucking did! But what could I do? They had me over a barrel."

"They?" Richard quizzed, continuing his inquisitional act.

"The foreign exchange department or whoever bought the travellers' cheques fresh and unsigned from outside to cover the shortfall, if it wasn't actually Joy herself," I explained, superfluously. "They were all in on the act. And I'd just fucked one of their number the night before, which as you should know is strictly against Bank rules; it could leave a man open to all sorts of blackmail. Like this, for example. *Quis custodiet ipsos Custodes?* and all that crap. Those counter clerks or whoever was part of the stunt knew that too. That was the whole point of the boogie."

"Well, that was easy," Richard murmured, coming off his high horse at last. "I'm glad you came clean, to me at least."

"Fine," I said, feeling beaten and confused. "But you did say you were going to tell me how you came by all this stuff."

"I did, didn't I?" he conceded, reclining comfortably back in his chair. "You were lucky; you got away with it. Joy Wathen didn't in the end, which is the amusing part. You see, you'd conveniently left The Bank by the time the ruse was rumbled. Joy managed to sit on the fishy travellers' cheques without selling them to the unsuspecting public, as you call it, for as long she could, but eventually she was transferred to another department and her replacement inadvertently sold them in the course of normal business to, you guessed it, a customer. The cheques went through the system but were never reconciled with the stock manifest, because they weren't issued or registered by The Bank in the first place. The funny thing is there'd been another audit in the meantime and they hadn't picked up on it either, so no one knew who to was to blame when it all came out. But eventually Joy got the rap."

"Oh, yeah? How?" I asked, my attention beginning to flag somewhat.

"You weren't the only member of the international staff she availed herself of, over the years," Richard informed me. "She was quite a flighty piece of goods, as it turned out. She'd gone through two managers, a sub-manager and the head of documentary credits by the time she got to you, James."

"And I thought I was special."

"She'd gone through lots of things by the time she'd finished, including half the branch's petty cash, not to mention numerous suspense accounts," he added, with growing relish. "But no one could touch her for a while because she had too much shit on the right people and her father was a very rich and influential client of The Bank's indeed."

"So when did it all come out about me?"

"When the hooky travellers' cheques were finally traced back to their original point of sale, at some backstreet money-lending outfit," Richard replied, matter-of-factly. "The purchase was made under an assumed name and the cheques were, of course, sold un-countersigned. Joy 'fessed up once it became obvious that the net was closing around her, but not without a fight, using you in particular as a very blunt sword in every sense."

"How?" I questioned again, warily.

"She blamed the entire travellers' cheques misappropriation on you, old dude, and then she claimed that the subsequent cover-up was at your instigation."

"She never!" I cried, in disbelief.

"Stitched you up like a kipper, old pal, or at least tried to," Richard chuckled, to his own merriment. "She did you proud all right, apparently referring to you all along as her 'lover' and saying you met every night, dining practically buckshee at her father's various restaurants around town, before retiring back to the Hilton to, in her words, 'make passionate love'."

"I don't know about 'passionate'," I protested, adamantly, "and I wouldn't have described her father's establishments as 'restaurants' in the usual sense; 'clip joints', maybe. Opium dens of sorts, but without the opium. We tried to be discreet. Neither of us, for obvious reasons, exactly wanted to go all 'Hello!' magazine about the liaison."

"Whatever," Richard whistled, apparently uninterested. "By the time the subsequent investigating team found what was going on, they'd long ceased to believe a word she was saying, so in effect you were exonerated *in absentia* and consigned, in this instance, to the dustbin of Bank history."

"Except, in this instance, I obviously wasn't," I said, wanting to get to the nub.

"History, of course, is made for reading," Richard opined. "And this is where I make an entrance."

"About time!" I grunted, ungraciously. "How much of this was common knowledge anyway?"

"Not much, I think," he surmised. "Only a few of the big cocks would have been informed, or cared for that matter by the time we're talking about, and they've long since retired."

I'd forgotten my gin and tonic. I made up for lost time and drained half of it in one gulp.

"So how come you were in on it?" I asked, suppressing a burp. "You were no more senior than I was. There was nothing 'need-to-know' for someone at your level."

"You're right, James, I was no more than a pebble in the stream back then," Richard started to explain. "Evidently I'm more senior now, but that's not how this came about. I'll never be a proper big cock myself but I've stumbled across a number of well-documented surprises since being put in charge of The Bank's new building project."

"Really?" I quizzed as I knocked back the other half of my drink.

"Yes, *really*," Richard emphasised, as he polished off the remains of his glass. "Perhaps not to you, but to a Bank nerd such as myself, some of the old stuff was fascinating. You see, part of my role is to oversee the shifting of tons of this bulldust... filing cabinets and countless reams of meaningless information... from their old premises to wherever they are required in their new locations. Thank God most of The Bank's documentation is stored on the database, but, depending on the department, a fair amount still remains on hard copy or microfiche. One place in particular, the Personnel Department, has crates of old files dating back from the quill pen, including various records of long-gone international staff. It was in the course of sifting through the DOD section that I happened to come across your paperwork, which to my surprise and delight had a separate typed addendum detailing your Jakarta adventure. It was even headed: 'Jakarta Incident'.

"Sorry, DOD?" I quizzed, out of practice with The Bank's terminology.

"Documents Out of Date," Richard reminded me. "It's when they decide whether to shred the stuff or send it off to die in the archive department."

"Which, don't tell me, is a Head Office function that would technically come under Fawcett's dictate?"

"You're as sharp as a tack, James," Richard commended, with the merest hint of sarcasm.

"So he may have seen my file," I continued, undeterred. "I wonder who wrote the attachment, if indeed it wasn't Fawcett himself?"

"Well, it wasn't signed, or dated for that matter, but that doesn't detract from its legitimacy. The fact that it appears on file at all must mean that it came from on high. Only someone from on high would have had access to it. Files like those don't get tampered with easily."

The waitress made another appearance before I could consider Richard's guesswork and asked if we would like some more to drink.

"Enough for one night?" he asked, looking at me rather than the waitress for a change, and referring, I assumed, to our conversation rather than the relatively modest quantity that we'd drunk.

"I think we've covered enough to be getting on with," I said, thinking longingly of the whisky bottle back at home.

Richard smiled at the waitress and asked for the bill. I quickly jumped in with another question before his concentration was lost on the waitress's retreating posterior.

"I don't suppose you photocopied the attachment?" I asked, thinking he would have already told me if he had.

"No, I didn't need to. I got the gist."

"Sounds like it," I remarked, testily. "But I'd still kill to know who the author was and what impact it would have had on me, had I still been in The Bank."

"We could speculate on either count," Richard ventured, unsurely. "The mystery is partly in the timing: we don't know the instigator of the add-on and, without a date we can't narrow it down to whether it was officially inserted at the time of discovery or placed there at a later date by an amateur chronicler. If it wasn't Fawcett himself, of course. Either way you would have been for the high jump once it all came out, if you'd still been at The Bank."

The waitress came back with the bill. I didn't fight for it; I knew Richard would pick it up, regardless of it being my turn. I glanced around again at the surroundings while he administered his credit card and noticed how similar they were to the plasticine rainforest at the Hilton piano bar where I'd taken Joy all those years ago. I quivered, either from the memory of a bygone wet dream or at the thought of how close I'd been to becoming embroiled in Joy's embezzlement.

We got up and walked out of the bar together, Richard to get a taxi, me to get the tube home. We shook hands as we parted and agreed that we would keep in touch. Although we hadn't been talking for long it had felt like quite a session. I was glad it was over, not out of any feelings of remorse, so much as a sense of regret for the passing of more exciting times.

I wandered slowly towards Hyde Park Corner and watched the Park Lane devotchkas as they went about their business outside the hotel lobbies in preparation for their night's possibilities. I stopped for a moment to reflect on what Richard had disclosed. Had he been a touch melodramatic in his delivery or was he right to be paranoid on my behalf, for something I'd always assumed I'd got away with? It seemed to be chewing him up. I continued walking. I would have to tell Peregrine Blücher to mind his own business regarding Alec Dunhill's peerage. Reports, archives, documents, files... there were more immediate matters to attend to, I pondered, thinking once again about the whisky bottle nestled in my drinks cabinet.

There were two letters on the front doormat when I got home. One was from the Provisional Assurance Company, and the other had the regular, slightly looped handwriting of American penmanship, probably Suzy Summers'. I opened them as I trudged up the stairs.

The letter from the Provisional was the annual update on my mortgage endowment plan. It said there was likely to be a shortfall on my total payment cover, which rather defeated the object. The plan had been to cover the mortgage. It had been sold to me as 'with profits'. There had been no mention of losses. There was a booklet enclosed called *Money Made Clear*, which I couldn't understand. The letter was signed with an unapologetic flourish by the chairman, Sir Peter Young. (Why are they always called 'Sir Peter Young'?) I remembered I'd read about his calculator-defying bonus in the newspaper a short while ago. Why? I didn't get it. He had failed and deceived his customers. I got to the top of the stairs and looked at the other one. It was from Suzy, as I'd expected.

Dear James

Thank you so much for not only a lovely evening but also a delicious dinner – you are a wonderful cook. It was interesting hearing everyone's views about England – it certainly opened my eyes!

I hope to get you over to supper here when the weather is nice. I am rather reliant on my terrace – maybe next month.

Very many thanks again and be in touch.

Suzy

Yeah, right: 'maybe next month.' As if. As if English weather was sufficiently dependable that she could plan a dinner party round it. And she'd sent the beastly thing by second class post. I thrust both letters angrily into my breast pocket, opened my front door and headed straight for the drinks cabinet.

A surprise was waiting for me on my desk the next day. My business cards had arrived. At last I had a corporate identity. Admittedly, they'd spelt 'Mallet' with two 't's, but who'd know? I got a call from Banca Monte dei Paschi di Lavazza informing me that they wished to make a formal job offer to my Italian woman. Bingo! My first placement! Then Norinmunchkin Bank asked me to fix a time to interview Ian Smiley, and finally one of my new clients, in this case the Bank of Butterworth, expressed interest in one of the CVs I'd sent them for a German sales position. I was winning! I was cooking on gas! I called Ian Smiley to fix a time for him to see Norinmunchkin. He said Friday noontime would suit him best and we agreed to meet for a debriefing drink afterwards. Friday would be my last day of freedom before William came back. And it had all been going so well.

The days sped by. I was busy. I interviewed potential candidates, corrected several CVs and made various introductory calls to prospective clients. Peregrine was suitably chastened when I took him to task about his intrusive incursion on the PABS archive department. He promised not to do it again, but the cat was already out of the bag. And then it was Friday.

Ian Smiley called me after he'd finished his interview with Norinmunchkin Bank. By way of a change we decided not to meet at The White Sock and instead agreed on a wine bar near Ian's offices by London Bridge. To my surprise and delight he was with Wally Barker and, judging from the champagne in the bucket beside them, something was being celebrated.

"Meet my new client!" Ian announced, gesturing to Wally as he passed me a glass.

"I take it that the interview went well," I remarked, as Ian poured me some champagne.

"Very. Unless they know something I don't," he relayed, with cautious optimism. "They practically offered me the job there and then. They need to discuss a few things such as the overall package and definition before they submit the proposal to their Tokyo office, but it looks very positive. Wally and I were just debating how best to develop our prospective business relationship, should I be taken on board."

"Sounds all to the good," I commended, relieved that things had gone smoothly. "The next bottle's on me."

"Thank you for moving so quickly on my case," Ian complemented, raising his glass. "There may be a few other people I know who could use your services; I have a few names you may like to have."

"If I'm not interrupting, I'll take them down now," I said hastily, feeling my pockets for something to write on. I found the two letters I'd picked up from the mat the night before still in my breast pocket. "I hope Wally doesn't mind, but I need all the protective armour I can get before the boss comes back on Monday."

"Wally doesn't mind at all," Wally said, unassumingly. "In fact, Wally may have a few names for you himself in the fullness of time."

I started to jot down a few details on the back of my letter from the Provisional as Ian rattled off half a dozen malcontents who would look at alternative employers if properly approached.

"I got a thank you letter from Suzy Summers," I mentioned to Wally as I was writing, and passed it over. "Alas, I can't detect a hidden agenda."

He looked at it briefly. It was a brief letter, after all.

"What do you expect? It's a 'thank you' letter, although I'll admit there's a distinct absence of romantic grit to make a pearl in this oyster," he conceded, as he handed the letter back. "But she does have a loose attachment to the owner of a very secure bank balance."

"So Anne-Marie said," I acknowledged, putting my pen down moodily.

"Oh, she told you about Matthew Howard then? He's just sold 'Comme une Tarte' to the Serviette Restaurant Group for a cool forty mil, which can only add to a young woman's fancy. You know what the delicate little things are like."

"A matter of Rolex versus Timex in my case," I sighed. "So what's he doing now?"

"I think he's contemplating a move into media," Wally answered, blithely. "With that sort of money, he can do what he likes. Success breeds success; it's malignant. Forty million gives a man a certain confidence, a confidence that's not lost on Ms Summers, I'm sure. I've seen other sandwich bar and health juice millionaires just like him. Everyone thinks they're wonderful, because making sandwiches is just about the outer limit of British innovation these days."

I looked at the list of names that Ian had just reeled off for me.

"Thanks for this, Ian," I said gratefully, folding the reverse of the Provisional letter back into place. The logo caught my eye.

"By the way, have either of you had a shortfall on your mortgage endowment policy?" I asked.

"Is there anyone who hasn't?" Ian replied, gruffly. "They're a con."

"Isn't there any recourse?"

"You might be able to cite mis-selling, if you're lucky," Wally advised. "Who sold you the policy?"

"The Pan Asian, when I took out my mortgage."

"You can try, but they'll oil their way out of it; they always do," Ian cut in.

"I didn't need the flippin' mortgage in the first place," I grumbled. "I only took it out because they said it was tax-efficient."

"Which they were, for five minutes," Wally observed. "Then the government moved the goalposts, as per. It's the system. It's what we vote for."

"Surely there's an ombudsman or regulatory body one can appeal to?"

"They're all a load of tissues," Ian spat in disgust. "Industry watchdogs have about as much substance as a low-fat yoghurt. They're completely toothless and in cahoots with the organisations they purport to regulate anyway, so you won't get any joy there. The fact that companies have been getting away with it for so long just proves it. The financial sector has shown time and time again that it can't be trusted, but still it gets the government's blessing. Financiers' greed has completely knackered the economy. Basically, the country's run on the Nigerian business model, the only difference being that at least in Nigeria they're honest about their dishonesty. So raise a glass next time you obediently lower your trousers to be gently spanked by your local, friendly mortgage adviser... it's all in a good cause. Without people like us there would be no fat cats. It's Joe versus the Volcano, I'm afraid. You can't win."

"Joe did win and don't forget we're bankers," Wally pointed out to Ian. "We both work for banks, of sorts, and James makes a living out of them. However insignificant we think we are, other people may see us as part of the Volcano."

"But we're on pretty poxy salaries," Ian objected.

"That's the way the cookie crumbles. But we have a chance that things may change; others don't," Wally moralised.

It was typical of Wally to make a self-defeating ethical declaration out of the blue, but it was his love of debate rather than any ideology that spurred him on. Ian didn't look in a debating mood.

I ordered the other bottle of champagne I'd suggested earlier, in an attempt to recapture the celebratory mood. Ian poured it out.

"To Sodomy and the Pirate Tradition!" Wally proposed, raising his glass.

"The Pirate Tradition!" Ian and I reprised, raising ours.

I stayed for only one more glass as I had things to attend to before William's return on Monday. I told Ian that I'd get back to him once I'd ascertained Norinmunchkin's plan of action, bade them both farewell and skulked back to the office.

Chantal was writing something at my desk when I got back.

"James, I was about to leave you a message," she said, sounding flustered. "William's just called. He wanted to speak to you."

I looked at my watch. It was nearly three o'clock.

"I hope you told him that I was out with a client?"

"Of course. I tried to make everything sound bright and sunny," she offered, plaintively, "but he wasn't having it."

I could imagine. In William's world three o'clock on a Friday afternoon was not a good time for an employee to be out of the office, whatever the reason. Monday looked as though it was going be interesting. It was.

Chapter 9: Variation

I left for the office early that Monday. William hadn't arrived, but his presence was already evident. The girls were fluttering around like crows before a storm; they squawked for a bit and then they fell silent. The admin wallah looked as though he wished he'd chosen a different day to make one of his intermittent visits and I was overcome with an utterly rational desire to hide in the stationery cupboard. For ever.

William eventually appeared, looking mildly volcanic. The words 'happy' and 'bunny' appeared to be living on different continents as far as his planet was concerned. The girls became even more subdued, either out of apprehension at William's stony demeanour or because he was just a complete dickhead.

My weekend had been OK. Masturbation, Italian table wine and toffee-flavoured ice cream provided the basic joys, but in-between I had rehearsed my lines for every possible eventuality in the wake of William's return. I had a sneaking suspicion that he might not be quite so taken with my achievements as I was.

My sneaking suspicion was right. I averted my gaze as he swept in, but by dint of good manners felt obliged to say *something* once he'd settled into his chair.

"How was your holiday?" I asked, hairdresser-like.

"Fine," he said with a grimace. "How was it here?"

"Good. Very good in fact," I replied, knowing that whatever I said, he would think otherwise. "One placement in the bag and another one about to exchange."

"Not bad," he conceded, reluctantly. "Who with?"

"The placement's with the Delmonte Bank as you like to call it," I replied, wanting to get in there first. "And the other's with Norinmunchkin Bank, which is looking very positive."

"Says you," he remarked, dryly. "Anything else?"

"I've got a mandate from Bank of Butterworth to look for a sales position to cover Germany," I specified matter-of-factly, to dispel any doubts. "And I've made some good progress with one or two of the broking companies."

William did his pausing trick for a moment then pounced.

"James, these banks: I'm still not hearing any household names. I mean, what in fuck's name is the 'Gnawing Chicken Bank?' What is it with you and your chicken banks? And what is this Bank of Butterflies nonsense? Are these the sort of banks that are going to give you repeat business on a routine basis? Or are they just going to take one of your bed-wetting friends off you once every five years, if the mood takes them? You can waste your time talking to these chicken banks, but not on my time. You need to get some proper banks on side, but your problem is you're too chicken. Whatever happened to your friend Mr Leyland Forklift at The Pan Asian Bank?"

It didn't take a huge leap of imagination to work out to whom he was referring, but I was determined not to go there. I'd done nothing, of course.

"I don't know," I mumbled, remorsefully, praying that he wouldn't press me. "But I have it on good authority that Leonard Fawcett's a very busy man."

"I bet he is," William surmised, derisively. "Look, James, you need banks like The Pan Asian. They're the ones with the big trading floors. They're the ones who'll take on a quants geek, a swaps trader and an institutional salesperson, all on the same day. On big salaries. Which means more for me and more for you. There's no point chasing butterflies with the Bank of Buttercups, or running around the hen coop after your stupid chicken banks. You're just sucking wind."

He tossed his biro onto his desk, indicating that the conversation was over, and turned his attention to opening the post.

I followed William's instructions for the next few days and phoned most of the 'proper banks'. The line managers I spoke to were polite enough, but they hadn't the time for introductions and explanations. More often than not they referred me to their Human Resources departments where I'd have to talk to some woman who didn't want to know either. The main bone of contention was the 'PSL' – the dreaded 'Preferred Suppliers List' – which I was never on. Without that I couldn't do anything, and to get on board I had to jump through more hoops than the dog at the circus. It was OK for William; he could make a handsome living off the business that Martin Letts, as his brother-in-law and benefactor, referred his way. That left me as the unwitting *de facto* business development manager, and from where William was sitting I wasn't doing much *de facto*. One day soon afterwards I couldn't stand it any longer. I called Pete Divis.

"It's getting hot in the kitchen," I said, speaking quietly into the mouthpiece while William was out of the room.

"And you can't stand the heat?" Pete suggested, perceptively.

"Affirmative."

"I think this might call for a drink after work," he proposed.

"I think you call well," I saluted.

We met at the Airport Lounge, a large, impersonal wine bar near Pete's offices that celebrated its aeronautical credentials by saucily costuming its bar staff as cabin crew minions. The crowd was young off-the-peg Eurotrash, probably working at the Commerzbank headquarters next door, but there was plenty of room. Pete bought a bottle of Pinot Blanc and we sat down in an alcove close to the bar.

"So: you're in a bit of jam," Pete began, as he poured the wine.

"More like a total plum duff."

"Well, there's a surprise," Pete noted, unsympathetically.

"Thanks. What to do?"

Pete took a long sip of his drink, as if deep in thought.

"Do you think you're ready for our gaff?" he asked, unhurriedly.

"Put it this way, I'm not proud."

"Nor are we, particularly," he advised, draining the last of his glass. "And why not? You've cut your teeth with William Davidson; now may be the perfect time to join a company like ours. You've got nothing to lose... and besides, what other options do you have? Not many, I bet. I'm afraid we've both left it too late to jump on to the corporate gravy train at this stage of our lives. And there's no point having ambition: it's obsolete at our age. We have to take what we're offered, because there's nothing else. That's our lot, so why not join *our lot*?"

"Well, that's cheered me up," I remarked, knocking back all contents of my glass in despair.

Pete refilled the glasses. The bottle was going down nicely, even if nothing else was.

"But it's the truth," he said, looking at the wine label serenely. "When do you want to come and see us?"

"As soon as possible," I replied, uncomfortably.

"OK, but don't change your mind; I'd hate anyone to think that you were only using us as a last resort," he warned referring, I assumed, to his boss, Fred Armitage.

"It could be sooner than you expect," I said, thinking of William's short fuse.

"Whatever. Let me know and I'll fix something up."

Two young women appeared at the bar. I practically choked. *Holy Rohypnol!* One was a bit of a minger but the other was an absolute stonker: a gazelle in a ponytail.

"It's my turn to do the drinks," I said briskly, getting up from my seat.

I didn't know quite what I was doing but I placed myself behind the two girls and listened to their conversation. They both sounded and looked Scandinavian but seemed to be using English as a common language. They weren't aware of me. That had been happening a lot recently. They got their drinks and moved to the other end of the bar. I caught the barman's eye, bought a bottle of Pinot and got back to the table.

"What was that about?" Pete asked, looking a bit puzzled.

"I was just getting another bottle," I replied, virtuously.

"Bollocks!" he declared, looking at the two girls, curiously. "You're such a prick, Mallet. What do you think you were going to do? Talk to them?"

"Perhaps," I answered, tartly. "I have an idea."

I reached into my wallet and fished out one of my shiny new business cards. I turned it over and scrawled on the back:

I think you're absolutely gorgeous.

I inspected my workmanship. It wasn't very good. It looked as though I'd written 'I think you're absolutely grisly'. I got out a second card and had another go, putting the old card back into my wallet. This time was much better.

"What now?" Pete enquired, monitoring my progress ambivalently.

I looked at the girls. The pretty one had her back to me.

"Identify prey: kill and eat," I replied, with precision.

I made my way across the floor. I stopped just before I got to the girls and asked the barman if I could have an extra glass. The pretty one still had her back turned. As the barman went to fetch the glass, I slipped the card next to pretty one's elbow. She didn't notice. I retreated with the empty glass back to a stupefied-looking Pete in the alcove and sat down to survey the proceedings.

"You wanker! What are you going to do?" he asked, mouth agape.

"I don't know. Wait and see, I suppose," I replied, suddenly realising I was a bit pissed. I hadn't had much lunch and the wine was now beginning to take a hold. I refilled our glasses. We sat watching in silence. Eventually the pretty one took the hook. She saw the card, picked it up and read the message. Good girl. She looked around. I caught her eye and manfully wiggled my little finger at her. She held her hand to her mouth and started to laugh.

"Warm up the choppers: I'm moving in. Thunderbirds are go!" I announced, gleefully, as I launched myself out of my chair again to amble coolly over to the bar area. But I was practically sick with embarrassment. Her friend wasn't getting the joke. She wanted pretty one to herself. I kept my shit-eating smile on high till I got to them and introduced myself. Pretty one was something. She was cute with a capital 'Q' and seemed amused by my antics. Her friend was spitting feathers. She could have been spitting A-bombs for all I cared. She didn't exist. I zeroed in on pretty one. She made Chantal look like an old trout by comparison, or maybe it was just the wine. The blueness of her eyes didn't belong to this dimension, and her face was beyond the idle dreams of even soft-core pornography. And what had I to offer in return, beyond my own imbecilic brand of impudence? She was Swedish, which came as no great surprise. Her bus-ugly friend said she was Finnish, which seemed apt. They both worked for Commerzbank. Blue Eyes was called Pia. Ugly was called Helga. I didn't have much time. Something was expected of me. I didn't have a lot. I looked at Pia.

"You've got my card, obviously. Do you have one?" I asked confidently, while quietly bricking it.

"I'm out," she said, perhaps in truth. "But I can give you my e-mail."

Result! I decided to quit while I was ahead.

"That's cool," I said, jotting down her details as casually as possible. "I'll drop you a line. I don't want to get in the way, so why don't I let you ladies get on with your evening and we can meet another time."

Ladies? Yech. I turned and sauntered back to the alcove. I didn't know who was more flabbergasted, Pete, the girls or me.

"Outstanding, soldier!" he commended. "Get her number?"

"E-mail," I said, as if I could have done better.

A friend of Pete's came to our table just as I was sitting down. Pete introduced us and suggested he pull up a chair. Pete poured some wine into the spare glass and we began to talk. The friend was a financial journalist who'd just lost his job at a news agency he'd been working for.

"Any ideas, James?" Pete asked, looking at me hopefully.

"I don't know of anyone in financial journalism per se," I said, expansively, "but I may have some leads in something related."

I didn't, but I was feeling very much the trousers after my little mazurka with the Scandinavian girls and confident I could turn my hand to anything.

"Why don't you give me a call in a couple of days' time?" I continued smoothly, leafing through my wallet litter for a business card. "I'll see what I can rustle up."

He thanked me with the alacrity that could only have been born out of desperation, and put the card carefully into his pocket. A couple of days would give me enough time to think of an excuse to get him off my back. We chatted for a bit and then the wine ran out. The journalist offered to buy another bottle but Pete and I declined. We'd had enough. The girls had left and it was our time to make tracks. We got up and Pinoted our way to exit. We stood outside for a while. The journalist had to go his own way, but Pete was all of a fidget.

"Shall we try somewhere else?" he suggested, cautiously.

"I don't think I can face another wine bar," I answered, jadedly. "I might go home."

"Or you might come back to my place, why not?" he countered, with a slight note of hesitation. "I've got a bottle of whisky and I'm only a bus ride away."

I was curious. Neither I, nor anyone else I knew had been to Pete's flat before and the whisky sounded interesting.

"Hang the bus!" I scoffed, still riding my wave of glory. "I'll do us a taxi and we'll mete out justice on your whisky accordingly!"

We found a cab and headed towards Pete's flat across the river. Suddenly I was struck by a horrible thought.

"Pete!" I squawked in despair. "That card I gave the journo… it had the first message I tried to write out to that girl on the back!"

Pete gulped.

"Oh my gawd!" he cried, realising the implications. "If he calls... get the Hell out of town!"

Pete's place turned out to be a prole-hole at the fag-end of Battersea and the ride cost more than I'd bargained for. But the real reality check was the state of Pete's flat. It was no wonder he'd never invited anyone back. It was a dump and three-dimensional proof that nature abhors a vacuum cleaner. There was a large box TV in the drawing room and several dozen one-handed video cassettes strewn over the carpet. I bent down and took a closer look. They all had silly pseudo-erotic film titles: 'Ice Hard in Alex'; 'This Sporting Wife'; 'Lord of the Rims'; 'The Damp Busters'. There was a theme.

"Why tapes rather than DVDs?" I asked, out of interest. "Seems a bit outdated for a starship trouper like you."

"Better for slo-mo," he explained, without elaborating.

"Really?" I queried dubiously, suspecting financial considerations might also have been a factor, but I needed to go for a pee rather than discuss the pros and cons of contemporary technology.

"Khazi's down the hall," Pete directed, as he picked up two whisky tumblers from a shelf.

I went down the dimly lit hallway and entered the bathroom from Hell. The sink was encrusted with toothpaste gunk and the bath looked as though it hadn't been rinsed out for a century. To cap it all there was a turd lurking like a naughty Kursk behind the U-bend in the loo. I tried to flush it. It didn't want to play. I took a piss anyway and looked away. There was no soap. I ran a tap and then wiped my hands on the mankiest towel in the world. I didn't know how Pete could live like this. He seemed so normal on the outside. I felt a chill. This was not something I wanted to turn into. I returned to the drawing room feeling a bit green around the gills. Pete could sense all was not well.

"Something rotten in the state of Skidmark?" he asked, anxiously.

"Slightly," I gasped.

"Fuck! Don't tell me someone's left a night watchman in the chodbin!" he yelped, as if I didn't know he lived alone.

"Perhaps it belonged to a workman," I suggested vaguely, slowly regaining my composure. "That, or the poo fairy's had a real day at the races."

"Sorry about that," he muttered, repentantly. "That bog hasn't got the best swallow; I'll see to it that it gets coat-hangered immediately. Help yourself to a drink."

He went off to attend to his task and I poured myself a life-reviving shot of whisky. I'd rather gone off the idea of a drink, but I thought it would be rude to leave so soon after having just got there.

I heard a flush. Pete came back, beaming.

"Sorted!" he announced, cheerfully. "Now what shall we watch? There's 'Good Willy Humping' or 'Titty Titty Bang Bang', if you want."

I picked up a couple of videos lying at my feet.

"How about '*Down and Out in Beverly*' or '*Backside Story*'?" I suggested, more out of curiosity than a genuine desire to watch anything in particular.

"I'll tell you what is good," Pete said, not wanting to appear impolite, but quite definitely having something special in mind, "and that's '*The Taking of Ellen 123*'."

I saw no reason to object, although I liked the look of '*Eternal Sunshine of the Spotless Dick*', that caught my eye as Pete was loading '*Ellen*' into the slot.

He pressed 'play' and retired with his drink to the sofa.

"Isn't she great?" he enthused, as Ellen disrobed.

She was, but I couldn't get into it. The picture above the bed where she was writhing was askew and there was the sound of traffic going on in the background. Pornography is too often the victim of low production values, which spoil it. Another woman came in, stripped and sat on the end of the bed watching her. Pete gave an appreciative wolf whistle as Ellen did something stupendous with her stupendous breasts, but the spell was broken when three hairy-arsed German gentlemen came into shot and blocked the view.

Ellen grabbed a semi-erect penis and, in her best porno English, declared: "I love this caark!" as the other two dudes went plural with the shazza at the other end of the bed.

"*Das iz gut!*" grunted the slightly round-shouldered owner of a 'caark', which even in its half-state was the size of a wholemeal baguette.

"Go on, Ellen! It won't suck itself!" Pete cried excitedly, as if he'd never seen the scene before.

I sipped my whisky. It made me feel sick on top of all the wine. It was an effort to concentrate on the video. I didn't like their choice of curtains and the soundtrack was driving me round the twist. Ellen, Pia, William Davidson, the U-boat by the U-bend in the lavatory... it was all too much. I started to get an attack of the helicopters. Suddenly all the Germans turned and started entering Ellen from every angle at great speed. Ellen was making noises I'd never heard before. It was a stranger world than I'd thought. I wanted to vom but I couldn't go back to that loo.

"I've got to go, buddy," I said, slapping Pete on the knee.

"Really? It's just getting to the good bit," he bleated.

"Nah. I need some fresh air. I'll get a taxi on the street," I said, trying to sound lucid.

"Are you sure? We can change the video if you want?" he offered apologetically, in case I was gay, or worse, asexual.

"No. It's been a big day. I'll be fine."

I limped towards the door and turned to say goodnight. One of the German funsters was about to blow his load over Ellen's face. Pete caught my gaze, then looked back at the telly, but the explosion had now gone well beyond detonation.

"Shit! We missed the money shot!" he cried forlornly, forgetting the existence of the 'rewind' button. But it wasn't for me.

"Gotta go, dude," I insisted desperately, and immediately stumbled out of the door.

I waited till I rounded the corner before I puked the biggest puke I'd ever puked. I didn't think I had anything to throw up, but I was blowing chunks, fair and square. It felt good. I was crying like a wolf. And there was nobody around! I wiped away a tear and steadied myself. No harm done. I slipped some gum into my mouth and continued down the road. I saw a taxi and waved it down. It had been a very big day.

I didn't have the energy to do anything about Pia when I got into the office the next morning. What was the point? True, I had gone to the trouble of making the initial move and affecting an introduction, but did the audacity or unconventional nature of my approach – however excruciating – warrant any particular reward? On the basis of 'faint heart never won the fair lady' I supposed the answer could have been a justifiable 'yes'. But on the likelihood of my ever having the personal resources to make the thing work, the conclusion had to be an unequivocal 'no'. The effort-to-reward ratio simply wasn't there. No, the point at stake was not the boldness of my opening move but the fact that I ever had the gall to go through with the whole procedure in the first place. That, however drink-fuelled, had been a success. The fact that I, as a middle-aged poop and average in every sense of the word, had even considered that I might get away with it, was reward enough. That showed self-respect. The lad done well.

But that was another point: I had forgotten how old I was in relation to the sort of woman I thought I had a right to pursue. That was the dilemma. The classic middle-aged man's dilemma. The best years had all been taken. I very much doubted that she'd get in contact with me. Why should she? What could possibly make her want to squander her good looks on a seriously middle-aged and totally unremarkable sap such as myself? What was so special about *me* that would lead her to think she'd won the DNA jackpot? The answer was 'nothing', whereas *she* had the world at her feet.

So I let Pia off the hook. I let her go. She was not going to form part of a five year plan. Not with me. Besides, apart from sex, what right had youth to command such a premium? Most of the time the premium was a pain in the neck.

I had other work to do. Aside from dodging William's routine expletives I wasn't happy with my mortgage endowment plan. Ian Smiley's comments had added to my angry suspicions that I had been mis-sold the policy. I decided to give the PABS mortgage centre a call. I did the usual thing of waiting till William was out of the office then dialled. I was put through to a woman in the mortgage department. I explained my situation and said that at no time when I had originally taken out the plan had 'with profits' been explained to me as also meaning 'with losses'. The mortgage adviser listened to me stoically but gave me a 'computer says no' response. I said that wasn't good enough. She said she'd get back to me. I received an e-mail that afternoon.

I had several conversations with my Endowments Complaints Department. They have told me that you have a right to appeal against our final decision and take it to the Ombudsman within six months. When this term expires, both the PABS and the Ombudsman will treat this complaint as having been dealt with, and that you were satisfied with the outcome or accepted the outcome.

I have been told that unless you have a new point to make, which would class as a new complaint, there would be no further action to be taken by the Bank.

I am sorry if this is not what you wanted to hear, but if you feel dissatisfied and have new points to make, please put your complaint in writing and send it to Endowments Complaints Department. Please enclose a copy of the latest correspondence so that they can cross reference.

Regards.

Regards? Was that it? Was that the best they could do? To invite me to take issue with them? On their terms? So much for helpfulness! I thought back to their television advertisement. 'PABS: Your Friendly Bank.' 'Your Friendly Crank', more like. I started to draft a letter to the Ombudsdman but gave up halfway through and threw it in the bin. What was the point?

The Italian woman began her job at the Monte Dei Paschi Bank the following week and Ian Smiley started working at Norinmunchkin the week after. The commission cheques came through, addressed to William and once they'd cleared he fired me. It was more of a relief than a surprise. We weren't each other's type. It wasn't a question of Christine's Curse or misadventure at work on this occasion. I wasn't sorry to go. I wouldn't miss William. Or his feet. But I'd miss his stepsister.

I called Pete Divis to tell him the news.

"Well, well, well!" he chortled. "You'll *have* to join us now!"

He fixed a time for me to come over to his office to meet the boss, Fred Armitage and, as he put it, 'the rest of the motley crew'. It seemed a *fait accompli* that I would be working there. I didn't mind. Anything would be better than William Davidson.

I started to clear my desk. The admin geezer gave me my final payslip. It had all been drawn up. I noticed it didn't include any of the commission I'd earned. I mentioned it.

"Yeah, I saw that" he said, scratching his head. "To be honest, it wouldn't have made much difference. Your basic salary absorbed most of the fees. You didn't have a written contract and so any commission paid was on a discretionary basis. William's discretion, that is. You can take it up with him if you want. I didn't, for obvious reasons. You know what he's like."

I left it, either out of cowardice or from an aversion to being at close quarters with William any longer than I needed to be. I saw Chantal on the way out. It was lunchtime.

"Fancy a drink?" I suggested, unsuggestively.

"Why not?" she said, tilting her head.

She fetched her scarf and handbag. We went to The White Sock because it was easy. I bought the drinks and joined her at a table.

"Well, you survived for nearly three months!" she said, raising her glass. "I envy you: there's a beautiful world out there."

"You can leave too if you want, can't you?" I queried, thinking that if she left it might precipitate a mass exodus for the good.

"I can't," she replied, remorsefully. "There are family ties and I was the one who got the other girls into this situation in the first place."

I told her about William short-changing my commission.

"That's him all over!" she snorted. "He always has to have the last laugh. There'd be no point arguing with him; he'd find some excuse and probably end up saying you owed him money!"

"I've already let it go," I said, gallantly. "Anyway, he taught me a lot in a short space of time. At least I feel I learnt something. Someone else said they might take me on, so it's not the end of the world."

"I'm sure you'll be fine, James. Why shouldn't you be? You're a decent guy," she said, knowing I wouldn't take the compliment the wrong way.

"Thanks, Chantal," I said, wishing all the same that she was mine. "You're terrific. You've got it all, except the other day you mentioned 'all that glisters isn't gold'. What was that about?"

"OK, James," she said, straightening up. "What do you see before you?"

"A beautiful young woman with everything going for her," I said without hesitation.

"That's what you *see*, James, but it's what you can't see that I have to live with."

"Like what?" I enquired, suddenly thinking it was none of my business.

"Like, I haven't had a period for over ten months," she said, looking me straight in the eye. "And I'm not pregnant. The doctors don't know what's going on. I certainly don't. That's one thing. Another is that I'm engaged to a complete twat who likes whoring around with anything that'll take a credit card."

"Why? That doesn't figure. I mean a beautiful fiancée... it's a bit like Hugh Gr..."

"Exactly," she interjected, pleased with my analogy. "Plus I live in a shitty flat that keeps getting burgled; I have no money, no car, and the way I'm going, no friends. Oh, and, of course, I work for William."

"When you put it like that..."

"... it's not all roses. It never really was," she sighed, finishing her drink. "And now I've got to go back to the office. Honey, I hope to see you around. Good luck."

She got up to leave. I watched her as she walked out of the door. She was ten times better than Pia. She existed.

I met up with Pete Divis's mob later in the week and was introduced to Fred Armitage, the boss man. He took me into his office and we talked about this and that. He had no problem with my lurid past and offered me the job with a handshake across the table. There was to be no salary. Like the others in the company, it was to be a commission-only appointment. Fred was quick to explain the benefits of self-employment. By not offering a salary he was able to afford a higher commission pay-out. Provided I generated the necessary fees, my take-home pay would, pro rata, exceed anything that the other headhunters could provide. How much I earned was down to me and circumstance. There would be no other pressure. It sounded so unlike William Davidson's set-up. It seemed fair. Or so I thought.

We agreed a starting date and shook hands again as I left his office. Pete was outside. He introduced me to 'the motley crew'; half a dozen former marketeers who I'd either met or knew of from my pre-custodial existence. They were perfunctory in their welcome; they had seen people come and go. They had stayed. They had nowhere else to go.

And so began a period of relative calm. I acquired a tenant, a man of unexciting manners who'd been put forward as a suggestion by a mutual friend. He wasn't quite the sort of person I had in mind when I'd decided I needed someone to help with the bills, but we got on well enough. I met a woman I liked who, to my surprise and delight, liked me in return. It wasn't love, but it was what suited us. It was as if we were too grown-up for passion. Her name was Jane and more about her later. I still drank a lot, but so did most of the people I associated with, and those who didn't, I didn't see. I started my alcohol reform program in earnest, and earnestly lied once a fortnight to my counsellor about how much I'd drunk.

I managed to evade Elspeth's invasive snooping by being otherwise engaged whenever she wanted to see me, and politely declined any lunch invitations to Arndale with a series of spurious excuses, until she gave up. As for my parents, we kept in respectful but infrequent radio contact. I knew they would always be there for me, but to my shame I was seldom there for them, especially now that they'd reached an age when I could have been of use. To my credit, if that was the right word, I sensed that they didn't want to know what they already knew.

My new colleagues tolerated me guardedly at first but gradually, if sceptically, accepted me as bona fide and more than just a passing ship. I was sufficiently preoccupied with trying to make a go of the job that I temporarily forgot about Richard Hartley and all The Pan Asian Bank issues we'd discussed. But for the merciless repetitive, smug advertising, omnipresent and indiscriminate in its abundance, and occasionally having to cosy up to members of staff in the course of business, The Bank had all but faded from my consciousness. Christine's Curse was nowhere to be felt and the past became a thing of the past. Life began to assume an aura of normality. Or so it seemed.

Chapter 10: Satisfaction

I was lucky. It didn't take long to get the hang of things. After William Davidson's regime, working at Fred Armitage's place was just a fart in the park. It certainly made a change from being reamed by William every five minutes. I now had the luxury of only having to make calls when I was ready, willing and able. That suited me much better. I could goof off whenever the mood took me and office conviviality at the bar across the road was actively encouraged. After only two weeks I already had some tangible work in progress and the future seemed not without hope. I even managed to squeeze a big swinger in to see The Pan Asian without any of their higher executives batting an eyelid, so I assumed Richard Hartley's warning about my being on The Bank's shit-list had, perhaps, been over-stated.

It was early one morning near the start of my third week in the office that I found myself chuckling over the newspaper I'd just brought in. Pete Divis was the only other person around. He was eating a bread roll. There was an item about The Pan Asian's purchase of the Stronghold Finance Corporation of New York, a major player in the American sub-prime mortgage market, together with a picture of Leonard Fawcett looking slightly banjaxed.

"Here, Pete, take a look at this," I said, reaching across and passing him the newspaper. "I used to share a house with that geezer when we worked for The Pan Asian in Sordid Arabia, about twenty-five years ago."

"No bull? I'm impressed," he remarked, sounding anything but, as he glanced over the article.

"He's done well," I said, with a mixture of envy and melancholia. "Although I'm not so sure about this American sub-prime nonsense."

"Nor is he, by the looks of it," Pete said, tossing the newspaper back to me. "Anyone who has anything to do with that crap must be out to lunch."

"People have to be seen to be doing something, I suppose," I reasoned, abstractly.

"Yes, but that doesn't mean they have to be seen to be buying toxic debris like Stronghold to justify their existence, does it?" he retaliated crossly through his bread roll.

"Maybe they know something we don't."

"Maybe they do," Pete said, wiping some crud from the corner of his mouth. "Otherwise why the Hell didn't The Pan Asian snap up J.P.Morgan while *that* was up for grabs? If The Pan Asian seriously wanted to get involved with the North American debt market, they should have gone for quality, not this rubbish. The Brits *always* fuck up in the States. What they never learn is, if the Americans won't touch something, it's because it'll never work. The Pan Asian is buying a dog; you'll see. Never buy a pair of shoes just because they're cheap."

It was my turn to be impressed.

"It's still not ours to reason why. Besides, I don't think my guy was on the board at the time the decision was made," I said, referring to Leonard Fawcett.

"Somebody must've got something out of it; they always do," he lamented, as he flung his roll wrapper into a nearby wastepaper bin.

"You mean... kickbacks? I don't think that's in The Pan Asian Bank's dynamic."

"I didn't say it was," he retorted. "But do me a favour: don't mention the words 'bank' and 'dynamic' in the same breath; it hurts my ears."

The others slowly trickled into the office. I wondered what had made Pete so irascible that morning, but he told me later it was just a hangover. Apart from the two part-time secretaries, Pete, Fred Armitage and me, there were three others who made up the team: Craig who liked his drugs, Mike a former forex dealer and Andy, an older chap who'd been in insurance. We were just enough to form the necessary critical mass to operate as a unit, but occasionally we clashed.

After my time at The Pan Asian, I'd worked for a stint at Parker Barrow Brothers investment bank as a bond salesman, before being fired for daring to question the wisdom of their involvement in the collateralised mortgage obligation market. The company now was just called 'Barrow Brothers', 'Parker' having been unceremoniously wheeled off and dumped from the letterhead several years earlier, but I still had one contact there who'd become surprisingly senior in my absence. He was happy to act as a link when I endeavoured to introduce various candidates to the company, and it wasn't long before I had a bite. It was a very big fish who I hooked up with a very senior line manager and the catch involved a lot of money. Suddenly Craig became extremely interested. He claimed that Barrow Brothers were his account and therefore he should be handling the deal – and the bait, of course. As he had no connections in the company and had never done any business with them before, I objected, naturally. We came to blows and I referred the matter to Fred. Fred didn't care, as long as he got his full slice when the cheque came through, so he left it to Craig and me to sort things out.

The problem festered as Craig grumbled and I tried to operate as normal. Eventually the fish was landed and the deal went through. It was only at that point that Fred intervened, suggesting in no uncertain terms that I should share my commission with Craig. I demurred initially, maintaining that Craig had ingratiated himself into the deal on false pretences and, beyond souring the atmosphere, had added nothing of value, but my protestations were met with silence. I looked at Fred's unblinking, obsidian stare and saw a blank wall of obduracy. His suggestion was an order. The charm had gone. He had found my weak spot. He knew I wouldn't stand up to him. I had too much to lose. He didn't need to give me a choice.

I wondered, correctly as it happened, whether this was the shape of things to come. As it was the first deal I'd completed for the company and the largest since I'd started headhunting, I backed off in case things turned nasty, but I didn't hear much gratitude. It left a bad taste for a while but I had other things to think about. Business was good and booze was flowing.

Outside the office, people came and people went, but the one that stayed, for a while at least, was Jane Shackleton, whose life I started to share with her family of two small children. Jane was a divorcee, similar in age to me and we got on well. She was attractive in an undernourished way, and easy-going. Her house, nicely decorated in flea market chic, reflected her character. I told her about my past and my time 'on the naughty step', as she called it and that's how she treated it. To my surprise and relief she put it down to a momentary aberration and didn't appear to have a problem dealing with the matter. Perhaps we were both in denial, but we got on with things and I was as grateful for her comfort as she was for having me around. We soon slipped into a manner of living with meals *en famille* and long strolls across the common with her dogs. I had forgotten the sanity of waking up next to another person, of sharing stuff, arguing over little things and the joy of making up. I had forgotten what it was to be an adult and yet it was as natural as sex, which now that it was there, seemed as routine as life itself. And yet something, I couldn't put my finger on it at the time, was missing. It was as though I was acting a role, which however well performed, was still just an act. And it wasn't one I could keep up forever.

I contemplated the situation as I helped Jane prepare for an informal supper gathering one evening, and wondered quite where I fitted in. Most of her friends, to their credit, took me as I was in good faith and I had done likewise with them, but there were times when I was at a loss as to what they had in common with me beyond Jane herself. That evening was a case in point.

There were eight of us around the table. The talk meandered, as it tended to at Jane's gatherings, between issues concerning children, schooling, childcare and suchlike. The only divergence on this occasion was the presence of a younger, newly married couple who'd recently returned from their honeymoon. I listened attentively to whatever was said, commented appropriately and generally tried to go through the motions of what would be expected of a boyfriend co-host, but my attention started to wander as the evening wore on. I turned to the bottle for amusement and let the others do the talking. The younger couple were being encouraged to eulogise about their honeymoon. The others listened indulgently, but the babble was too much for me and I drifted in and out of consciousness. One of the guests, a woman of certain bearing, spotted my torpor and, in a playful attempt to draw me into the conversation, decided to shake me out of my trance by asking me where, should the situation arise, I would like to take my bride on honeymoon?

"Up the arse, of course!" I blurted out, before I had a chance to stop myself.

Oh, no! What had I done?!

There was a hush and then a cough.

"Gosh! Is that the time?" one of the guests asked, looking accusingly at his watch.

"It is getting a bit late, isn't it?" observed another.

They all got up and shuffled around, saying what a good evening it had been. It was only 10.30. Two of the men shook me firmly by the hand and said how interesting it was to have met me, while the women remained at a cautious distance.

"Well, that was clever!" Jane said, laughing as she closed the door on the last guest out. "At least the children weren't around!"

"I'm so sorry," I bleated, feeling a total idiot. "I was completely caught off guard. It just slipped out of my mouth. I didn't mean to let you down."

"You haven't, you noodle!" she said, pulling me close. "I'm more concerned about what slips in your mouth than what slips out. Anyway, do you like that arse thing?"

"Certainly not!" I censured, primly. "It's against nature and the Bible says 'no'."

Whatever our conversational diversion, there was no escaping the fact that I'd made an ill-considered remark at an inappropriate moment. How could I expect Jane to trust me in a social situation when I couldn't trust myself? It didn't help that she'd clearly considered the notion that I might be a drinker. I'd tried to be discreet but obviously my conduct was giving the game away. It wasn't as though errant behaviour and excessive alcohol consumption were mutually exclusive, as my sister had so doggedly observed.

It was at around that time that I received another call from Richard Hartley. It was night-time. I thought he might be calling about my recent attempts to do some headhunting business with The Pan Asian, but it wasn't about that. It wasn't about anything at that point, other than he wanted to see me very soon.

"How about tomorrow, after work?" he suggested, anxiously.

"Sure... whatever you want," I said, wondering why the panic. We hadn't spoken since the night we'd met at Raider Nick's.

"I hope I'm not interrupting your schedule?"

"What schedule?" I retorted, self-deprecatingly. "I'm sure I can fit you in somewhere. Where would you like to meet?"

"Your place; 6.30?" he proposed.

"Don't you have an expense account that can take us somewhere more exotic?" I protested.

"I'll bring something exotic to drink," he promised.

He was waiting outside the flat when I got back that evening.

"You're early," I remarked tartly, without saying 'Hello'.

"My itinerary's obviously not as exacting as yours," he returned, knowing full well this would not have been the case.

He had a carrier bag hanging bewitchingly by his side.

"What have we here?" I enquired.

He opened the bag without saying anything.

There were half a dozen Cokes, a packet of crisps and a bottle of something interesting. I pulled out the something interesting.

"Hmm... Mount Gay rum; very nice," I commended, approvingly. "Exotic indeed. We must commence research immediately!"

I didn't really care what it was, as long as it did the trick. We trudged up the stairs and entered the flat. Richard took off his jacket and looked around. He'd been there before, but not for some time.

"You've hardly changed a thing since the last time I was here," he remarked, looking at an old calendar of Hongkong harbour that I still kept on the kitchen wall.

"Sentimental value; spacious days. I can't seem to chuck out anything from my old life," I said, getting an ice tray out of the freezer compartment.

"I don't suppose they do calendars of famous prisons," he interjected.

"Now, now," I cautioned. "You didn't come here just to be rude, did you?"

"Not exactly," he conceded, watching me making a balls of the old aluminium ice tray. "But I may have some other stuff on your 'old life' that's of interest."

"Not again? That *is* rude!" I muttered, mainly to myself as the stupid handle on the ice dispenser bent out of shape, referring to both Richard's comment and the ice dispenser, adding, "Fucking parents! Why do they only pass down shit that doesn't work?"

I gave up on the ice tray and ran it under the tap. The ice fell obligingly into the sink. I scooped up a few cubes and put them into a couple of tumblers before adding the rum and Coke.

"I haven't had a Cuba Libre since I was at school," I pronounced as I passed Richard his drink.

"The goat is strapped to the altar; let the sacrifice commence!" Richard exhorted, raising his glass. "To Fidel!"

"To Raúl," I countered glibly, raising mine, neither of us actually drinking.

I put the crisps into a bowl and we went into the drawing room.

"So: why are we here?" I asked, sitting down and savouring my first sip.

"Why do you think? There appears to be another peculiarity in our little saga that I want to run past you."

"What now?" I sighed.

"Fawcett summoned me to his office again last week," Richard replied quietly, taking the chair opposite. "He's still interested in you."

"Can't he find something useful to do?" I queried, testily.

"Obviously not," Richard affirmed. "He was aware that we'd met at Raider Nick's, and from the way he was carrying on he seemed to know what we were talking about. The only thing I can think of is that the tables were bugged and we were on camera."

"Come off it, Richard! We're not *that* fascinating."

"No? But consider who owns The Poor Reasons Hotel," he challenged, as if I should know.

"Consider I have no idea," I offered, uncooperatively.

"How about The Hongkong and Canton Land Company for one thing," he informed me, as if it was unsporting of me not to have had even a stab at guessing.

"So?" I demanded, unimpressed.

"And Alec Dunhill being on their board, for the other," he embroidered, as if these were both conclusive revelations. "He might not be Chairman of the Pan Asian anymore, but he's still got his fingers in just about every other prawn dumpling in the area."

"But as if he'd be interested in us!" I cried out, in exasperation. "I only met the bleeder once in my entire stretch at The Pan Asian, and even then it was in a lift. And don't pretend you were on his social calendar every waking moment either. I suppose you think he was manning the security cameras the night we walked into Raider Nick's."

"Don't be a prick, James," Richard snapped back, irritably. "Bugging devices these days pick up key words. It's not rocket surgery. It's the only way Leonard Fawcett could have had access to our conversation. That's why I wanted to meet here. Walls have ears."

"It's all sounds fantastically silly, but I'll go with it, for amusement's sake," I said, truculently. "*C'est trop pour moi.* But there must be more..."

"There'd better be: Che Guevara is thirsty!" Richard declared, rattling the remains of his ice in his tumbler. I finished my own on cue and went to the kitchen for refills.

"So what was Fawcett's reaction to our purported conversation?" I asked, returning with the drinks.

"Nothing much, except he knew about the travellers cheque incident in Jakarta and your little sideshow with Joy Wathen. He was curious, as usual, to know what you were currently up to, but that's not the whole story."

"What is the *whole* story, Richard?" I demanded, impatiently.

"I don't know yet," he replied, looking distracted. "But there was something I didn't bring up when we met at Raider Nick's, mainly because I didn't think it was particularly important."

"I did wonder," I said, thinking back. "What was it?"

"My personal file was attached to yours in the archive department," he answered, with more than a hint of apprehension in his voice.

"Surely that's not the end of the world," I said, wondering what all the fuss was about.

"You might not think so," he interposed. "But what I want to know is what it was doing in 'Documents Out of Date'? As you now understand, that particular privilege is normally restricted to records of staff who've actually left The Bank."

"You're just being paranoid. It's just an ordinary filing cock-up."

"Perhaps," he said, sounding unconvinced. "I hate to say it, James, but I don't particularly like being tarred with the same brush. That and back in the day being sent to the same resignation-friendly assignment immediately after you'd just chucked yourself out of your job in Taiwan... I just wonder... was it deliberate? Was the same expected of me? I'm seeing too many coincidences."

"I'm certain you're worrying for nothing," I said, trying to reassure him. "There's nothing exceptional here. There'll always be company idiocy that scares the snot out of us, but nine times out of ten it turns out to be completely baseless."

"Thanks, James, but I'm a one in ten kind of guy," he said. "I'm worried about being on the shit-list too. I don't feel safe anymore."

"Don't be so stupid," I said, trying a tougher approach. "What have you done wrong? You're doing a great job in a difficult situation, like you always do. They can't take that away from you now."

"They can do what they want. That company is run totally on the whim of those from on high," he said, starting to get fractious.

"Name me a company that isn't! You're just going to have to get over this one, sweetheart."

He said he had to go. He still didn't seem very happy. I was. There was two-thirds of a bottle of rum sitting in the kitchen.

I saw him to the door. We said we'd be in touch. Poor sod. He was really wound up about his job or what was left of his career, but there was nothing more I could say. It wasn't my sort of problem. It was too abstract; too corporate. I closed the door and went back to the kitchen. Even I couldn't kill the rest of the bottle, but I had a go. I had an appointment with the Drug and Alcohol Dependency Unit the following day. If they were so adamant that I was an alcoholic, it was not my place to deny them their right.

I didn't feel particularly bright the next morning. I heard the new tenant in the bathroom. I hadn't noticed him come in the night before. I hid in my bedroom till he left for work and then headed straight for the refrigerator. There was a four-pack of beers to buck me up. Rum, I decided, was definitely not going my regular tipple. I thanked my lucky stars that I didn't have to be at the alcohol centre till eleven. I sat in the bath, guzzling my way through the beers for half an hour, trying to steam the rum out of my system. I caught my reflection in the mirror as I dried myself. It was shocking. My eyes were like discharged waste pipes and my face was a pink balloon. It wasn't a good look.

I still had some time to kill before the meeting. I'd run out of smokes, so I decided to make a detour via Insanesbury's before the meeting. I joined the young and not so young pram-faced mothers out on their only thrill of the day, namely the endless quest to buy anything, and listened to them loudly addressing their infant offspring for all to hear, as if they were addressing sentient adults. I hadn't been to this particular Insanesbury's since I'd been released from the hole. The shelf-stackers and check-out staff were the same as before I'd been sent away. I picked up a can of pre-mixed vodka and cranberry, some gum and paid for them when I went to buy some fags at the cigarette counter. Some jerk was creating a rumpus about his lottery ticket while another insisted on paying for a tube of pastilles with a credit card that wouldn't go through. Then the woman in front of me tried to return an item without a receipt. I hadn't that much time. Why did they always have just one member of staff, and invariably the most retarded, working the busiest till in the shop? I looked back at the happy misery in the queue. Busy, busy, busy. Finally it was my turn. I got my fags, paid my bit and popped open the vodka mix outside. I downed it in one, belched and chucked the empty into the bin. At least I was beginning to feel human. The counsellor was going to get a run for her money.

She was waiting for me when I got to the centre. She showed me to the meeting room. I handed over the drinks diary I'd been asked to keep. She examined it with a frown.

"There doesn't seem to be much improvement, does there, James?" she said, putting it to one side.

Bitch. And I'd been lying. At least she'd had the courtesy to ditch the tape machine.

"You're still drinking more than eighty units a week," she continued. "That's over three times the maximum recommended limit. And that's not counting the ones you've forgotten to write down."

"It's pretty accurate," I fibbed.

"And you look pretty rough, James."

"I'll admit I tied one on last night."

"It's not mentioned in your drinks diary."

"It was business," I said, irrelevantly.

"You look dreadful. And you stink!"

"Sorry. We were drinking rum. I don't think it agrees with me. It wasn't my choice."

"You don't have a choice, James. You've got to quit."

"That's out of the question. It's part of my life; my work; my environment. It's what people *do*. No drink means no friends. Anyway I can't understand how I can be classified as 'an alcoholic' in the space of just six months. I hardly had a drop while I was in the slammer. I think the whole thing's an exaggeration."

"You think you're not living in a prison now? The difference is that your misery doesn't have to be obligatory. Your sister said you were displaying alcoholic behaviour long before you were sent away. Your habit's just been hibernating, lying in wait for the last twelve years. Now it's out and wants to mess up your life. That's what happens."

"OK, I am aware that drink is a factor in my life."

"James, it's not a factor; it's a problem, that's for sure, and being aware of it is not the same as being in control. Your addiction is controlling you. It's letting you *think* you're in charge when all you're doing is feeding it. That's how it is with alcoholism."

"That's ridiculous. That means everyone who drinks is a practising alcoholic."

"James, don't be boring. We're not here to talk about other people and you know that's not what I'm getting at. I'm getting at you."

"You're not wrong there."

She smiled at last.

"You're so obstinate! I'm here to work *with you*. That's what I do. I meet lots of good people who've lost their way, but there's always a way back; there is a solution, but it needs work. Very few people can do this sort of thing on their own; particularly not in your state. That's why we need to decide on a course of action."

"*We?*"

"Yes, *we*! You, me, other people. There's a whole support structure out there and a whole new existence for you. Life doesn't have to revolve around booze. Millions have done away with it to lead lives they never thought they'd see again. All it takes is belief, and with belief comes decision. And with decision comes action, and with action comes results."

"Oh, come off it! If only it were that simple."

"*It is simple!* It's a simple solution for complicated people, you'll see. But you'll see it sooner if you get help now."

"What do you mean?"

"I mean rehabilitation. I can set the wheels in motion straightaway."

"Whoa! You're way out of line! You're jumping to some very odd conclusions."

"Where would you like to jump then, James?"

"Nowhere. My life's fine. I've got a new relationship; a new job; it's all working out. I can't afford to just drop everything and go to a rehab. Anyway I don't want to. Why should I? I want things as they are. My circumstances are pretty OK at the moment."

"They won't be for much longer; not the way you're going. Things are going to have to change if you want them to stay the same. You need to get real otherwise you're just fooling yourself, which is exactly what your disease wants you to do."

"Disease?"

"That's what they call it."

"They?"

"Alcoholics Anonymous; doctors; experts. If you won't consider treatment, perhaps you should consider AA? It's the program we use because we know it works."

"Look, maybe I should cut back a bit, but I don't think AA is quite my thing."

"You haven't cut back so far. Have you ever been to an AA meeting?"

"No, but I've heard…"

"You've heard what? Alcoholics only hear what they want to hear. How do you know if you've never been?"

"It's a bit preachy, isn't it?"

"No, not at all. It's a discussion group where people share their experience, strength and hope. There are no requirements for membership except a genuine desire to stop drinking; you're pushing against an open door, James."

"But I don't want to *stop* drinking. I just want to stick to normal drinking."

"James, there's nothing normal about your drinking so I wouldn't advise you to stick to it... not that you're in any shape to stick to anything at the moment from what I see."

"That's not very nice."

"There's nothing very nice about your situation, certainly not in the alcoholic sense."

"Now I'm the one who's getting bored."

"Bored or avoiding the issue?"

"Oh please! *This* is obstinacy."

"On whose part?"

"Stop it or I'll go mad!"

"Maybe it'll be an improvement. It can't be much worse than the way you looked when you walked in this morning. Nothing changes if nothing changes. We're talking about the courage to change."

"Are we? I'm totally lost."

"You can say that again."

"*Please!* Can't you cut out the smart-arse comments?"

She didn't answer. Instead she got up to go to a bookshelf and pulled out what looked like dictionary.

"Read this. Just the first part to start with. It should make sense. It explains a lot. You might even like it."

It was the AA 'Big Book'. It looked big.

"It's hardly Robert Ludlum."

"It's about the same size, and if you give it a chance, you'll find it's an easier read."

"When do you want it back?"

"I don't. It's yours to keep. But please read a bit. It could be the start of your new life."

"Now *you're* going mad."

"I told you: we're in this together."

Crafty old cow! She had me eating out of her fucking hand! It was bullshit. She'd been trained for it and was clearly a practiced practitioner. I was just another punter. I'd had enough. I left the building quickly and headed for the nearest pub, for a palliative pint. I flicked through the AA tome she'd just given me. It seemed a bit old-fashioned but the message was simple enough. I wasn't alone. It described my symptoms to a tee. I wondered whether I should consider trying a meeting. I finished my pint, closed the book and quietly dumped the dust jacket. If I couldn't disguise my condition, at least I could refrain from advertising it.

I arrived at the office in the early afternoon. It was good to be back among fellow boozers. Here I was free: a freak among freaks.

The cheque from Barrow Brothers had come through. We all went across the road after work to celebrate. There had been enough in the cheque to keep everyone happy. The boys wanted to hear how my meeting at the alcohol centre had gone. I told them what the counsellor had said. They said she was an arsehole and I just needed to cut back a bit, to keep my family happy. That was what I wanted to hear.

I went back to the office to turn off my computer and collect my stuff. I couldn't find the AA book. I must have left it on the train. So much for my new start in life.

Chapter 11: Termination

Every silver lining has a cloud and none more so than mine by that autumn. I'd had a good run until then. In business I'd been in the right place at the right time. The whole world seemed to be Hell bent on hiring itself and I was part of the process. The Pan Asian deal came through hot on the heels of my Barrow Brothers triumph and although the cheque wasn't quite as magnificent as the Barrow Brothers' masterpiece, it was still large enough to buy a half-decent car had I wanted one, which I didn't. Not with my blood-alcohol level permanently on four times over. However for a brief, glorious moment I was the office pin-up. But it was brief. Whether it was beginner's luck or just two bright flashes in the pan I never knew, but once my winning streak had tired of me, I was back on my own.

Things outside the office were also coming to a head. My involvement with Jane was beginning to lose its lustre. It wasn't a surprise. Neither of us had ever pretended it was an *affaire de coeur*. That sort of liaison didn't happen anymore. Not with me at least. Or so I thought. Jane's gradual grasp of the extent of my drinking began to revolt her. I wasn't up to the mark. I certainly wasn't stepfather material. In spite of this we remained fond of each other and I endeavoured to return her warmth with consideration, but it wasn't enough. The problem manifested itself once again at a *soirée* she had organised for two of her cousins and their husbands. I wasn't expecting much: "Feta cheese tartlet, anyone?" and the usual child-related drivel, spiced up perhaps with some cousinly banter, but it wasn't until I met one of the husbands that I experienced the true meaning of monotony. We were introduced. He was a golf nut and had all the toys that went with it. It wasn't my subject, but that didn't stop him going the whole nine yards with endless blarney about birdies, bogeys and bunkers. I made an effort to appear interested, but the more I listened the more I hated him for inflicting his private Idaho on me. He seemed to be being deliberately dull.

Jane announced that supper was ready and asked me to help with the serving. The guests were sitting down as I returned from the kitchen with the vegetable dishes. Jane was behind me with the casserole. I put the serving dishes in the centre of the table. One of the cousins, Amanda, the golf nutter's wife, remarked with matronly surrender:

"Mmm... I love vegetables."

"I know," I said, pleasantly. "You married one."

Shit! *Not again!* What had I done?! The room went still. I could hear the clock ticking. I had to think. *Serving spoons!* Thank God. Thank God. Thank God and *Deo Gratias*!

"How silly of me, I've forgotten the serving spoons!" I shrieked in maniacal desperation. I dashed back to the kitchen and wrenched open a cupboard where I'd clocked a bottle of cooking sherry earlier. I skulled two large gulps from the neck before Jane barged in, on fire.

"*How could you?*" she hissed. "Once was funny but this time you've really blown it. For fuck's sake, grow up. Now go back and behave."

I crept back, serving-spoonless, sat down and hardly dared utter another word all evening.

"You idiot," Jane said quietly once the guests had left. "Amanda's my cousin. I know her husband isn't exactly sex on a stick, but did you have to make it so obvious? You weren't nice. I want to be proud of you but, boy, you don't make it easy. And we *know* what causes *that*, don't we?"

"Angel, I hardly drank anything," I pleaded. "I only meant to be funny. There was no target. It was just an off-the-cuff remark that came out wrong. Does the rest of the family know he's a dork?"

Jane didn't answer. She'd switched off. I tried to make it up to her over the next few days but she wasn't having it. She'd lost interest. Humouring her was like re-heating an omelette. It didn't work.

It was Jane's ex-husband's turn to have the children the following weekend. In an attempt at appeasement I suggested that we got out of London for a change. I had nowhere special in mind. I didn't know anywhere. The only place I could vaguely think of was Elspeth's. She wasn't top of the list of people I wanted to see at that moment, but I thought Jane and she would get on and I could disappear under the mist of their mutual admiration.

They got on like a house on fire. They practically wore the same clothes. I watched them as they loaded the dishwasher together after supper. They were definitely bonding. My brother-in-law tried to slip me as many drinks as possible without Elspeth noticing, but Jane did.

"Can't you leave it alone for just five minutes?" she bitched when we went to bed that night. Elspeth had automatically put us in the same room, but we might as well have been at opposite ends of the house for all the intimacy we were able to muster once the lights were out.

My brother-in-law and I went to the pub the next day while the girls set about preparing lunch. We discussed Elspeth's concern over my drinking.

"She's clearly got it in for you, I'm afraid," he commiserated, "which takes the heat off me, but must make life very difficult for you. The only way you'll get her off your back is either to give up drinking completely or emigrate to somewhere she can't find you. Tasmania's quite nice, or so I'm told."

He wasn't joking on either count.

The weekend had served its purpose. Jane gave our relationship a temporary reprieve and Elspeth stopped bothering me for a while. I had a pretty good idea what they'd been talking about while they'd been making lunch, but there was nothing I could do about it. Not then.

Meanwhile my social Siberia, now that I'd been out of prison for a while, was beginning to show some signs of thawing. Part of my post-custodial initiation was other people's lack of awareness that I was no longer in the clink. However, slowly old acquaintances I'd given up for lost started to crawl out of their caves and began to re-associate with me. One such, a former drinking buddy I hadn't seen since his wedding nearly twenty years before, actually had the temerity to send me an invitation to his fiftieth birthday party. It was a black tie affair being held at The Royal Roehampton Golf Club the following month. It said 'James Mallet and Partner'. I looked at it carefully, wondering who else would be there. It was a sign of the times that members of my peer group were now entering their sixth decade. I supposed it was naturally assumed that I would have some sort of 'partner'. I did, of course, in Jane, but on this occasion I wanted to travel light. Without an appendage I could be invisible; incognito; inebriated. I could, if necessary, retreat into the shadows or vanish at will into the night. I had learned lots of tricks in my time alone. I reached for my grown-up fountain pen and accepted on my own behalf only.

I bought what I thought was an appropriate present and when the day came, organised a taxi to Roehampton. My dinner jacket was a tad tight and the dress shirt a shade too frilly to suggest a recent purchase, but at least I could do up the top button.

I contemplated the forthcoming revelry on the journey over with increasing apprehension. If the dude could hire out the Royal Roehampton I suspected he'd done pretty well since we'd last met, which to my mind meant there'd probably be plenty of other success stories in attendance. I had no doubt that middle age would be a uniting factor, *ergo* almost everyone would have a spouse or significant other and doubtless there'd be a separate table for the sad individuals without.

I arrived at the front entrance, deposited my present by the pile in the lobby and made my way past the main reception. There was a ballroom that was starting to fill up. I nodded to one or two bemused faces who vaguely recognised me as I looked around for the host. My assumption about the sum and substance of my co-invitees was more or less correct. Behind the over-stuffed cummerbunds, the rotten apple cleavages and party-weary smiles lay an aura of pervading acceptance that whatever our various stations in life, no one was time-exempt. Yesterday's young rips had become today's sensible parents. The previous decade's nightclubs had become this decade's pony clubs. PDA had become PTA.

My host and his spouse were in the centre of the room, grinning slightly self-consciously, snow-blinded by all the well-wishing and congratulation. I decided to postpone adding to their bewilderment and headed for the drinks table. I saw a bottle of Speckie and surreptitiously doused it with some whisky from the trusty hip-flask I had brought along in case of a *crise*. I weighed up the vibes. The club was garnished to the highest golfing metaphor. Cups and trophies glistened, sacrosanct in the magnificence of their display cabinets. Portraits of past captains and presidents snarled malevolently behind their owners' carefully pruned moustaches, all blending to within an ace to a perfect caricature of self-importance. And the cornucopia of tartan bunting bejewelling the entire club? What was that about? We were nowhere near Scotland. What was it with golf?

Some people were already sitting and chatting *à table*. The glitterball lighting of the nearby dance floor picked out every line and fissure on their eager faces, rendering them as pantomime grotesques at a freak show. I inspected the seating plan close by and saw, as I predicted, that I was on an outer table with what appeared to be nine other singletons. There must have been nearly two hundred names listed. The host must indeed have done well to demonstrate such largesse. Maybe that was the point of the party. I knew some of the names on the board and identified one or two whom I considered to be safe. I decided to look for them before dinner was announced.

I mingled, minister without portfolio, vainly trying to establish some sort of secure recognition, but with little success. I spotted Graham Ruddock and his pretty but now not so young wife in the crowd and did a body swerve. I had once been unspeakably rude to both of them, more out of envy of their seemingly charmed life than any tangible rancour, paradoxically on the same night that I committed the final act of abomination that had led to my twelve years of penal servitude. There was something about Graham's composure that suggested that he wasn't quite so pleased with himself as when I'd last seen him. Had he received a reality check perhaps, or a little learning? The master of ceremonies announced that supper was being served before I had the chance to explore further and the waiters started to usher the throng to their places.

I didn't know anyone on my table but they seemed well-disposed and set for a good night out. I introduced myself to the women on either side of me and we formed a conversational troika that lasted comfortably into the second course. There was a pudding buffet after that. People started to drift between tables. The two women got up to help themselves at the buffet but I didn't join them. I was full. I'd had enough. I slipped some whisky into my water glass under the table without anyone noticing and sat back to enjoy the scenery. Graham Ruddock caught my eye and waved at me to join him. That was strange. I got up awkwardly and walked over to his table.

"Hello, Mallet!" he said genially, without any indication of any former upset. "Is everything OK?"

What was it to him? This was weird.

"Fine, thanks," I answered, confused. "How about you? Still making grillions?"

I didn't care, except I wondered what he was playing at. Graham had all his melons in a row in the fruit machine of life. The last time I'd seen him he'd been head of derivatives at Goldbergs.

"Why don't you take a seat?" he said, pointing to the chair next to him. "And in answer to your question: not grillions, but enough."

"Really?" I said, sitting down. "What happened?"

"I had my moment in the sun at Goldbergs," he answered, filling a wine glass for me. "But I cashed in my chips a few years ago and now I'm running a small hedge fund."

"Isn't everyone?" I said, attempting to be conversant with the subject, but with no real wish to belittle him.

"You could say that," he admitted, self-effacingly. "But it pays the rent. What are you up to now?"

"I'm headhunting," I said, still feeling confused by his interest. "Suity people and pointy heads. But it pays the rent."

"Different from what you've been doing for a while prior to that, eh?" he shot in, unexpectedly.

"Slightly! I've been very lucky recently, but I had a pretty grim twelve years."

"That's the same time I've been married; different sort of sentence, I suppose," he assessed, as he looked dreamily across the table at his wife.

"That's a sentence I could tolerate," I said, following his gaze.

"You've met Simone, haven't you?" he enquired, as if our evening of pyrotechnics all those years ago had never happened. "She's in headhunting too. I'll get her over."

"Don't do it for my sake," I said, recoiling from the prospect of making more small talk in what were already somewhat uncomfortable circumstances.

"Nonsense, James! Honey? Come over here!" he called over bossily, as if he was used to being obeyed.

Simone rose almost immediately and came to his side.

"You remember James, don't you, darling?" Graham prompted with a treacly smile.

How *embarrassing*! How could she have forgotten? Why was he doing this to me? Or her?

"Oh, yes! I can't think why!" she said perkily, sparing my blushes. "Pleased to meet you!"

Yech. I stood up to shake her hand.

"I gather we're both in the headhunting game," I said, as a diversion.

"You too! Isn't the market brilliant?" she gushed, ebulliently.

Not particularly, I thought, but perhaps if I was a pretty girl with an influential husband, things might be different.

Graham moved up a chair and we sat down again.

"James," he said, looking mildly disappointed with his wife's inability to pinpoint me. "Have you heard of 'The Old Faithfuls' luncheon club?"

"No," I said, surprised by the abrupt change of subject. "Unless you're referring to a load of old geysers spouting a lot of hot air from time to time."

"Ha-ha - not far off! We're a group of ex-Hongkong hands who get together every so often, for old times' sake," he explained, lowering his voice to a masonic undertone. "I'm one of the founding members and we normally have a Christmas lunch in the second or third week of December. Would you like to come as my guest?"

"I'd love to," I said, again completely taken aback.

Was this the same man I'd last exchanged expletives with all those years ago? Was he insane?

"Excellent!" he enthused, as if he'd just sold me some life insurance. "It's eighty pounds, which includes a champagne reception and a superb three-course lunch."

I blanched but couldn't back out now. I'd forgotten that Graham too had a Hongkong connection. His father had been quite high-up in the colonial government. I sipped my wine as Graham went on to tell me who else would be attending. Their names rang bells but they hadn't been my group. They'd been too important. I wanted to return to my table, but just as I was about to make a move, the master of ceremonies called for silence for the birthday host to give a speech. I had to sit back in my chair. He kept it brief, but wanted to thank various people who'd helped him along the way in life. There was some clapping and then suddenly the disco kicked in. The DJ clearly loved his job.

"Good evening groovers! And what a groovy evening it is too, so to get the ball rolling – geddit? – let's do some rocking with an old favourite from Tony Orlando and Dawn!"

The obscene plinkety plonk of 'Tie a Yellow Ribbon' began just as I was about to make a break for my table, but Simone stopped me in my tracks.

"Come on, James! I love this number! Let's have a bop!"

No! No! No!

"Go on, James!" Graham insisted, pitilessly. "Simone's tired of dancing with me at parties. You have a go. Throw some shapes! She's wild!"

I dragged my feet reluctantly onto the dance floor and had a shot at some syncopated darting movements. Simone started gyrating like a flywheel out of control.

"This is really great!" she gurgled, as I broke into a sweat. "You dance really well!"

I wasn't so sure. The rest of the crowd were having fun hopping from foot to foot, but I was out of practice. Simone was miles taller than me, and I felt like a cider-fuelled Morris dancer prancing around a village maypole. And the music wouldn't stop. It must have been the twelve-inch disco mix. Simone was going at it like she was climbing a Stairmaster on max, when, finally, the hundredth yellow ribbon was tied round the old oak tree. I was exhausted, as much by embarrassment as exertion. It had been three long years. I declined Simone's wheedling to stay for the next dance and limped back to my table as Bachman-Turner Overdrive struck up a lusty refrain to further hysteria. The DJ had assessed his congregation well.

I flopped into my chair and wiped my brow. The two girls were glad to have me back. I was glad to be back with them, but it was difficult to talk. The music was too loud, although I could hear my hipflask screaming in my pocket. I pretended I needed a piss and hobbled to the loo. I peered into the mirror above the basins. I was fucked. My bow tie looked like a broken propeller and my hair was stuck to my head. I looked like a stoned bingo ball caller. I unscrewed the top of the hip flask and drowned a mouthful, grateful for the momentary paradise of an empty washroom. I straightened my tie. It was time to go home, either to quit while I was ahead or to cut my losses. I slipped out of the washroom and skirted past the ballroom towards the reception desk. I asked the woman if she could call a taxi and waited outside behind a pillar. I hadn't even said 'hello' to my host, yet alone 'goodbye' to the girls. I didn't care. The host wouldn't notice. I'd write him a nice letter and the girls would live on without me.

I still had enough in my hipflask for the journey home. It had been a passable evening with no harm done. It had justified the taxi fares. But the astonishing phenomenon had been Graham and Simone Ruddock's almost amnesic absolution of events from the time when we'd crossed swords before. And what was just as amazing was Graham asking me to something quite so comradely as the Hongkong gathering in December. It was bizarre.

On the home front however, a once sublime delight was beginning to turn sour. I was starting to get on my flatmate's nerves. It was impossible even for a fool not to notice. The elegance of his reserve that had at first seemed such an admirable trait, had now turned to lofty disdain. I resented the glum reflection of my unworldliness against the image of his urbanity, which became even more opaque when bathed under the floodlight of my intoxication. I knew I bored him. The garrulousness of my conversation irritated him beyond distraction, and more often than not he would retire early to bed, leaving me to howl at the moon on my own. For my part, his steadfast refusal to help with the household chores or enter into the normal spirit of flat-sharing left me in no further doubt of his contempt. It was only a matter of time before one of us was going to go off-scale.

These and some of the other obvious factors finally convinced me that it might be a good idea to be more proactive in trying to address my drinking problem. Almost out of curiosity I decided to set in motion the counsellor's suggestion of seeking help from Alcoholics Anonymous. Alas, it wasn't for me. I found the meetings doctrinaire and the AA dictums formulistic: 'Take it easy', 'One Day at a Time' and 'Keep it Simple'. Keep it 'Dimple', more like. And the people were weird. Or I was, but I couldn't see the purpose of listening to other fellow sufferers talking about booze for an hour. It didn't make sense. It just made me want to drink more, so I stopped going; there was no point. But that was the point, although I didn't know it at the time. I wanted to remove the problems surrounding my drinking but I had no intention, conscious or otherwise, of actually abstaining from drink itself.

Back at work things weren't looking too wonderful either. My deal with Barrow Brothers was a one-off. They didn't need me for anything else. Ditto The Pan Asian. Both were polite, but adamant. That was it. I didn't know what to do. I was back where I'd started, not knowing anyone who could be of use. In desperation I cast my mind back twenty years and tried to think of some of the people I'd known in Hongkong who'd re-settled back to the UK. There was Howard Jones who, I recollected, was now doing extremely well running his own private equity firm in London. Our friendship had latterly disappeared under the weight of his success in relation to the fragility of mine, but we'd once been intimates, although I'd never cracked his inner circle of high-flying friends.

I looked on his website. There he was, right at the top of what looked like quite a lulu of a company. I dialled his line and was slightly startled to hear his voice, but not as startled as he was to hear mine. Presumably he'd been so immersed in the theology of making a fast buck that he'd forgotten I existed. After brief 'how are yous' I told him why I was calling. He didn't mind. In fact, the more I spoke the more interested he became. Eventually he rose to the occasion and revealed that he was having great difficulty finding a suitable person to head his Japanese energy research team. He said if I knew anyone who might fit the bill, he would be able to offer a substantial remuneration package. I said I'd have a think.

I got straight to work. It took me a week and a hundred phone calls to track down the right man. He was an English bloke working as a senior energy analyst at a bank in Tokyo and was looking to come back to the UK. *Voila!*

I called Howard and he was delighted. Because of the time difference I wasn't able to get hold of my man in Tokyo till the following day, but when I did he told me that Howard's private equity firm had beaten me to it and had already spoken to him. I was slightly miffed that they'd gone directly to him without even asking me for his number and called Howard to see what was happening. It turned out his firm was sending a director over to Tokyo to interview the candidate and that my services would no longer be required. Thanks a lot! All that work for nothing.

I spoke to Pete Divis about it at lunchtime.

"I'm afraid that's what's called 'being kept out of the loop', old boy," he remarked, stating the obvious with casual empathy.

"But what's my paltry fee to a company the size of his?"

"Nothing," Pete replied, stoically. "It doesn't matter if they're all on The Sunday Times puke list or a million pounds better off every time they blink, they still don't want to share the cookie jar if they can help it, especially with a pissy little headhunter. They've got their McMansions with their gravel driveways, their koi carp in the pond, their villas in Tuscany and their children at the finest schools in the land. D'you think they're going to allow you free access to the great ZiL lane of life? No way! They're OK; you're not OK, and that's the way they want to keep it. Law of the jungle, innit? Our type doesn't get to breed. It's natural selection: ensuring that greedy wankers inherit the earth, destroy it, then hand it back to its rightful owner: nature again! That's how evolution works."

"But he was a close friend in Hongkong," I lamented pitifully, bypassing Pete's restive ramblings on the meaning of life.

"That was then. You could have fucked each other for all he cares. Leave him in his aspiration kennel. Life goes on," Pete concluded, adamantly.

Elspeth called that evening. She was sniffing around for clues about my drink intake, as usual.

"I've been going to AA," I said, truthfully.

"Via half a dozen pubs," she countered.

"Says who?" I objected.

"Says me."

"No; apart from you, I pressed. "Who's been gossiping?"

"Everyone," she spat, as she slammed down the phone.

I mentioned the conversation to the counsellor the next time we met and asked if she had been talking to Elspeth.

"James, we have a confidentiality agreement," she said, reproachfully. "Nothing we discuss ever leaves the building."

Who was it then? Elvis? Certainly no one from work: they needed treatment more than I did. What about my flatmate? No. It wasn't his style, and besides he wasn't interested in my business. Which left only one person.

I called Jane. She said she and Elspeth had been in contact a couple of times. That did it. There it was; there was the leak. I didn't need a snitch in my life. Snitches get stitches. Jane had to go. The relationship was already on life support, but this time I would call the shots. Double shots.

Chapter 12: Exploration

So that was that. I was on my lonesome again with only Mr Radio and Mrs Television for company, but at least I could resume my drinking routine without intrusion. Jane was pretty cool. She understood the situation, although I heard via mutual friends that she was pretty relieved to be shot of me. It had been a relationship for which I had been ill-equipped. I was also informed through another grapevine that Elspeth had almost broken into hives now that her human spy camera had been taken away, but I knew it would be only a matter of time before she started rootling around for an alternative. I wanted an alternative to Jane too, for different reasons, but I knew it wouldn't be easy. Not with my stunted social life and questionable circumstances. I had appreciated Jane's company and was adrift without it. People didn't just grow on trees but they could be found in the jungle - and what was London if not that?

I pondered these thoughts on many solitary evenings as I presented my reclusive meals-for-one to the microwave for cremation before reaching for the inevitable magnum of discount screw top and descending into my private well of self-pity.

So where to start in the jungle? I decided to vary my routine of going for drinks after work and instead started to explore the shadowy guild of wine bars nearer home. I soon became bolder and ventured out towards Piccadilly and Mayfair, aware that the stakes were higher and the company more curious. One night I passed a snuggery behind Half Moon Street that had previously escaped my notice. I stopped and peered through the window. It was dark, quiet and louche: perfect for a bit of stranger danger. I went in and sat at one of the several unoccupied candlelit tables. A waiter came and asked what I'd like. I ordered a bottle of house white and two glasses, as if I were waiting for a friend. I feigned interest in a theatre brochure that happened to be on the next door vacant table while the waiter went away. I glimpsed at the few stragglers at the bar. They all seemed to know each other and were talking in muted, convivial tones. The waiter returned with the bottle and glasses just as a shapely brunette emerged from the group at the bar. The waiter asked if I'd like to try the wine. I told him, nicely, just to fill my glass. The brunette approached my table as the waiter was leaving.

"Going to the theatre?" she asked.

"I don't think so," I answered, a little surprised. "Why, may I ask? Do I look particularly theatre-bound?"

"Not necessarily, but you're reading my theatre guide," she attested, with a coquettish flutter.

"I'm sorry," I said, not feeling sorry at all. "It didn't look the sort of thing that belonged to anyone. Why? Are you going to the theatre?"

"In theory. Are you waiting for someone?" she asked, looking at the spare glass.

"In theory," I replied, wondering how best to play things. "Would you care to join me while our various hypotheses decide whether they're going to prove themselves?"

"Are you sure?" she queried, confidently. Of course I was.

"Certainly," I said, standing up to offer her a chair. "Are you an out-of-towner? They seem to be the only ones who go to the theatre these days."

"By the coach load, but no... I'm not a hick from the sticks. This is my local; I live just round the corner," she said, as she sat down. "What about you?"

And thus we started to chat. I poured her some wine. Her name was Ginny. I put her at around thirty-five. She was attractive and easy-going. She asked what I did. I told her I was a headhunter but didn't elaborate. It was boring. It was a non-job anyway, like most jobs. I handed her a business card as if to validate my spartan credentials and asked in turn what she did. She giggled evasively and then, with self-effacing coyness, confessed that she was a 'woman of leisure'. The candlelight played on her face, casting her features in an almost Mediterranean richness, but it was to the orientation of her not inconsiderable chest alignment that my gaze kept drifting. I ordered another bottle. She listened and laughed at my nonsense, and if her conversation was a little harmless, her loveliness far out-shone anything I had to offer.

"Neither of our theories seem to have materialised!" she observed tipsily as we came to the end of our second bottle.

"And there isn't a hypothesis in sight!" I empathised, wondering what to do next. "Shall we have another drink?"

"I don't think I can handle any more," she said, reasonably, "but you're welcome to come back for a nightcap at my place, if you want."

If you want? That was very reasonable.

She did indeed live just round the corner. Her flat was cosy and if the furnishings were a trifle 'Readers' Wives', at least her drinks cupboard was as well stocked as her chest was well stacked. She poured a pair of large brandies and sat invitingly on the blissfully small sofa, shoes off, fingers playing with an errant curl in her lustrous mane. I joined her and we continued weaving our magic, and then stopped. We kissed: lips, necks, lobes, our mouths no longer instruments of tawdry conversation. She drew back and looked at me.

"Breakfast?" she quizzed, eyebrows at arch.

I couldn't speak. She took my hand and led me silently to the bedroom. She disappeared to the en suite. I undid my tie and sat on the bed. I looked around. It was more boutique than boudoir, with a hundred recently dry-cleaned cocktail outfits suspended at the ready in polythened eagerness. She returned shortly, wearing a negligee ensemble, the likes of which I'd only ever seen playfully displayed in certain types of mail-order catalogues. She lit a scented candle by the bedside, evoking our initial encounter, only this time she looked even more entrancing. She unbuttoned my shirt and opened her negligee a fraction. She was wearing a brown lace bra. Brown hair, brown bra, and, by the flickering light, brown skin. I undid my belt, but before I could go any further she pushed me back and climbed astride me, breasts bursting with elastic anticipation, as nipples the size of riot shields peeked their pink areolae over the tops of their lacework parapets.

"You like my bra, don't you?" she cooed. "Do you like my tits? Would you like some bra sex? Or would you like some booby sex? Why don't you suck my nipples through my lovely bra?"

I nearly fainted as she brushed her décolletage pitilessly across my soundless lips.

"Suck and fuck; suck and fuck. It's nice, isn't it? Sucking my boobs through my lovely bra. My nipples are getting really hard. Tee hee!"

They weren't the only things that were getting really hard. She tore my trousers off with almost paedophilic urgency. She was in a hurry. I was in a hurry. I entered her plump wetness without encountering even a vestige of vulval resistance. We were a perfect fit. She started to rock on top of me, still breastfeeding me through her bra.

"Suck and fuck. Suck and fuck... inch by inch... it's a cinch! Yes. That's good. Yes... that's very good, isn't it?"

She sat up. Her bra had two ridiculous wet blobs where I'd been sucking her dugs with the ferocity of a smoking beagle.

She unhooked herself and let her glorious orbs spill out in all their pendent majesty. She leant her face close to mine. I took in her cologne, her warm breath, pregnant with the dew of honey-scented pheromones. It was too much. It was parking warden time. Or Radio 4. Or wildlife programmes. Lion chases zebra. Zebra zigs. Lion zags. Lion leaps. Zebra bucks. Lion lunges again. Zebra struggles and then gives up. Lion gorges. The zebra is still alive. *The zebra is still fucking alive!* Don't say the word 'fucking'! Bastard! Bastard! Bastard! Don't say the word *'Bastard'!* Back to wildlife. Documentaries. Television. Television advertisements. Chocolate biscuits. Washing-up liquid. Rubber gloves. *Oh no!* It was too late. I exploded with the force of ten megatons, practically bucking Ginny off like the zebra and the lion. Fuck. Fuck, fuck, fuck, *fuckkk* that was good! Another wave of pheromones hit me, this time my own. Ginny moaned to a melodramatic, juddering climax and slumped. I'd never felt so relaxed. My head flopped to one side. All I could remember was Ginny blowing out the candle and whispering "Good boy" into my ear. And then I tumbled into the deepest sleep, ever.

I woke up the next morning smiling. I stretched, pleased with my previous night's mastery, but I had the thirst of Tantalus. That last brandy had been a killer. It was getting light. I looked over at madam. She was dead to the world, mouth agape and eyeliner smudges all over her face. I felt a duvet twinge coming on, but I desperately needed something to drink. I got out of bed slowly, so not to disturb her. It was cold. I looked for something to put on and with hung-over logic, teetered over to a cupboard in search of a dressing gown. I opened a door but all it contained was some riding clobber, so I grabbed one of the thousand or so party dresses and wrapped it, still in its cellophane, around myself before proceeding, Ghandi-style, into the drawing room.

There were a few things I'd missed in the preceding night's excitement, in particular the photographs on the walls. They were everywhere, and all of Ginny. Ginny in furs, Ginny in boots, Ginny in a wetsuit, Ginny in a corset and bustier, all showcasing exactly the same impish smile she'd deployed when fate had so capriciously entwined our paths the night before. I went to the kitchen and inspected the fridge. There were just two bottles of champagne and a carton of orange juice. I grabbed the juice and drank it straight from the spout. It had gone off a bit, but I didn't mind. It was cold. I looked out of the window and rubbed my half-awake penis and by association thought about the night before. Bra sex. Booby sex. I shook my head. That girl was quite something. It was the best night I'd had in a long time. There was something almost professional about her technique... whoa! There was something *very* professional about her technique. Wait a minute. No! Surely not? She couldn't be?

I put the juice down and replayed the previous night's events, frame by frame. The theatre brochure: it wasn't hers. It was just sitting there; it was a freebie. She said she was a 'woman of leisure'. Or would 'pleasure' have been more apposite? And the flat: smack in the middle of Whore Central. What was that about? And her negligee and her *lovely bra*? Bra sex? New one on me. Did Elspeth do bra sex? Did the Queen? And the stage-managed orgasm and 'inch by inch'? And 'Good boy'? What was that about? Was I a john? A patsy? Moving on: the hunting garb. Did that include a riding crop? She didn't look the horsey type. Not in Pimpsville, W2. God knows what was in the other cupboards. Rubber wear? A policewoman's uniform? And the pictures on the wall, the scented candle, the amply stocked drinks cupboard... what was going on?

I went back to the drawing room and sat on the sofa wondering whether I was jumping to the wrong conclusions. There was a phone on the side table with an address book by it. I picked up the address book and started to flick through it idly, without thinking. An Arab name caught my eye. And another. And another. Then a Russian name. And another. All men. Were all her friends foreign gentlemen? All living in hotels nearby? And why the ticks by their names? Sometimes one; sometimes two; sometimes twenty? That did it. That tore it. Why, oh, why, hadn't I spotted it the night before? It was so obvious what she was. I had been pissed, but that wasn't the reason. I had been flattered. My ego had overruled my instinct and common sense. Well, what the Hell was I doing in that bar in the first place? I'd known I was looking for trouble. All that rhythmic delirium had been a charade. Whatever. There was nothing I could do about it now. Or could I? I had been conned. How much did I owe her? I only had £40 on me and I was damned if I was going to give her my credit card details. And who knew what I'd caught off her? Fucking AIDS nest. I hadn't used a contraceptive. I'd been riding bareback. Had she? Her condition was definitely 'willing'. She must've lubed up in the bathroom before we'd got down to business. And it was business. Unless, of course, I conned her back. For that I needed to get away without disturbing her. Pity. My early morning glory had now grown into an unmanageable wisteria. Normally duvet brain triumphed over head brain, but this time money was at stake. Heaven would have to wait. As would breakfast.

I tiptoed into the bedroom, gathered my stuff and dressed *vitement* in the drawing room. I slipped out of the flat without a creek and stepped into the crisp dawn air to find a taxi home.

I ran a bath when I got back and popped open a beer from the fridge. I was disappointed. And there was I, thinking I'd been such a dude! It had been an experience, but I wouldn't be going to *that* bar for a while. I wouldn't be going to *anywhere* like that for a while. It was a pity. I'd miss her astonishing tank-buster tits, real or otherwise, but I needed something different; a change of scene, a holiday perhaps. It had been so long since I'd been out of the country all my wanderlust mojo had completely disappeared. As had my passport.

I went to work but couldn't get my head around doing anything sensible. I swanned around the shops at lunchtime and pressed my nose against the travel agent's window next to the office. I checked to see if they had any special deals on offer. There were several. The nearest exotic package involved going up and down the Nile in a rust bucket for a week, which was quite cheap. It looked it. The itinerary gave a premonition of evenings spent enduring endless belly dancing, conjuring tricks and appropriately themed fancy dress parties, all thinly veiled as cultural enlightenment, but it was the stopovers that made me shudder. Visions of lobstered proletarians fighting off hordes of wife-bartering black marketeers came to mind, all for their five minutes of Lawrence as they meandered the backstreets, gaffer-taped to camels as syphilitic as the guides that led them. I took down the details and returned to the office.

"Don't do it," Pete warned me sternly as I sat down at my desk. "I went once and it was a disaster. Lor', love a duck. The knotted hankie brigade was there in full force! Plenty of geezers at Giza, I'm telling you! Fucking wailing music everywhere: talk about fish and Cheops! I managed to pick up a stomach bug halfway through. That holiday wasn't so much the riddle of the Sphinx as the dribble of the sphincter! Never again. You should try Goa if you want some proper trashy fun and sun."

I'd been to Goa before and had enjoyed it. It wasn't a bad idea. Any deal worth doing once was worth doing twice. I liked India. It was one of few countries where I felt really tall. The phone interrupted my reverie. Pete picked it up.

"It's for you," he said. "Says she's called Virginia Giordano."

I didn't know anyone called that. I picked up the line. Shit! It was Ginny from the previous night. Of course! Like an idiot I'd given her my business card. Mediterranean subtlety, my foot...she was flippin' Italian!

"Doncaster actually," she corrected, grumpily. "Or at least that's where Mum's from."

She was pissed off, but not for the reasons I was expecting. She was hurt that I hadn't stayed to say 'goodbye'. I felt a ripple of shame. I was pretty sure I knew what she did for a living, but that didn't make her a lesser person. Although she'd denied it, she had a job and from my impressions she was pretty good at it. I just wondered where I fitted in with her tart-with-a-heart routine. I mumbled my apologies and suggested we meet a few days later. She seemed a bit happier, and so was I.

We went out a couple of times after that but never truly recovered the frisson of our first encounter. Something wasn't right: it wasn't real. Ginny soon got my measure. It wasn't long before she realised that I wasn't quite the ticket out to wherever it was she wanted to go and, to be honest, I found her a bit ground crew, but we kept in touch.

Autumn rolled into winter and before I knew it, it was December. Graham Ruddock called to remind me about the Hongkong gathering he'd mentioned to me at the birthday party in Roehampton. It was being held at one of the private members' clubs in Pall Mall the following week. There was no way out. I had accepted and was expected, although I didn't really want to go. Expats thought they were so 'it'. They weren't. I'd been to similar things before and found them not to my taste; everyone was established, married or a godparent to the other's child. Collectively they were the walking dead. But Graham had been so conciliatory it had been difficult to say 'no', and in the vague hope that it might be good for business I confirmed my acceptance with anaemic good cheer.

The day came all too soon. I entered the main vestibule and was directed by a flunkey to a marbled stairwell that led to the function rooms. The cold echo of footsteps on stone reminded me of a different institution, probably built around the same time, possibly by the same architect, that I'd known all too well for twelve years of my life. In terms of clubs, this was infinitely more lordly than its distinctly lowbrow golfing equivalent in Roehampton. The portraiture was older, darker. They had no truck for the foolish moustache here. Here the full Darwinian beard ruled with brutish displeasure. There was a sign pointing to the 'Old Faithfuls' event that was being held in 'The Elgar Suite'. Yech. They'd let in a moustache.

Most of the party were already there. They turned and looked at me strangely as I entered the room. I felt as welcome as a Rastafarian with a shank, until Graham came forward and greeted me. He started to introduce me to the others, a few of whose names and faces stirred some recollection. The last was Tim Ball, to whom the others seemed to defer, who appeared to be in charge of proceedings. I'd know him from across a crowded room in Hongkong when he was working for the Swire Group. He'd been quite funky back then but now he was grown-up. He was chairman of the Baltic Exchange or something and wore his eminence like a mink stole. He didn't know who the fuck I was. There was no one from the Pan Asian for me to fall back on. There never was at this sort of thing. They seldom ventured outside their own cantonment, so they didn't count. Fortunately there was no sign of Howard Jones, my fee-dodging irritant. He had better things to do with his time, but someone who didn't was Henry Mercer who'd always been so obsequious when I'd known him as a toothy peon at Schroders Investment Bank. I'd never taken to him. He used to suck up to me like a dentist's spit-tube, but I'd hated him with the power of a thousand suns. I thought he was common: one of the low on whom assurance sits as the silk hat on a Harlem burlesque queen. He was now a director at Credit Suisse First Boston and more coolly disposed towards me than before, but the teeth were much the same.

I felt more at ease after a few glasses of champagne and had begun to loosen up by the time lunch was served. I found myself sitting rather joylessly between Henry Mercer and Mark Harbour, another former Hongkong acquaintance, but one with whom I'd also been at school. Neither looked particularly thrilled at being placed next to me, and I was not going to change that. I decided Henry Mercer would be the softer target, so it was on him that I first trained my aim.

"So, Henry, how's it going?" I opened, as the waiters started placing the first course in front of us.

"Ask me in February," he whispered, conspiratorially.

"Why? What happens in February?" I asked, lowering my voice to match his. I knew exactly what was happening in February. My job, after all, was to know which bank paid what bonus and when.

"Bonus time!" he purred.

"Fabulous!" I chorused, barely able to contain my excitement.

"I expect I'll get my full whack," he resumed, now speaking in more normal tones. "God knows, I deserve it, but you can never tell in this game, can you, Mallet?"

He would have known perfectly well that I wasn't part of the bonus script.

"No, you never can, Henry," I echoed, respectfully. I was getting comfortable. I was limbering up.

"Obviously there's a lot at stake; it's important to keep in front, if you know where I'm coming from" he added.

"I know exactly where you're coming from, Henry. And indeed, where you are going."

Now I'd found what I was I was looking for. It was time to pounce.

"I can help, if you want," I continued.

What do you mean?" he demanded.

"It happens to all of us at some point in our lives," I sighed.

"What on earth are you talking about?"

"I assume you're experiencing a spot of financial botheration, la?"

"Good Lord, no!" he guffawed, heartily. "That's the least of my worries, even if I do have more than half a dozen mouths to feed, one way or another."

"But you've only got one," I said, staring intently at the flecks of spittle now accumulating in the corners of his mouth.

"No, you tit! I meant my wife, my children, the housekeeper, the nanny, the groundsmen…"

"Groundsmen?"

"Well, fifteen acres of prime Essex parkland doesn't just look after itself."

"Why?" I persisted, objectively. "Do you live in a park?"

"Certainly not!" he yelped. "Pringles Court is one of the finest listed properties in the county, I'll have you know."

"Listed?" I queried. "Is that the same as being condemned? Is it listing?"

"No, it's *not*," he replied sourly, seeming disinclined to elaborate.

We picked at our food for a minute.

"And then there's the townhouse in Wandsworth," he carried on.

"Townhouse?" I enquired, attentively. "Is that like a house in a town?"

"Put it this way, Mallet, it's got seven bedrooms," he said, suddenly sounding as if he regretted bringing up the subject.

"Seven? That's nice. Do you take in lodgers? I do," I said, helpfully, trying to find some common ground.

"No, Mallet, I don't," he replied coldly, perhaps suspecting at last that I was taking the piss. "I think you're deliberately missing the point."

"And what is the point, Henry?" I asked, rounding on him as a waiter took away our plates.

"The point is, Mallet, I have expensive tastes that have to be met in order to live the sort of lifestyle a flyweight like you could only dream of."

"You poor thing," I grieved. "I thank God I was blessed with low standards."

Flyweight? That was nice.

Happily at that moment Henry's mobile started to make a commotion. He looked at the incoming number accusingly.

"Bloody office!" he muttered, bad-temperedly. "Why can't they make their own decisions? They can't leave me alone for five minutes!"

"You should try one of these," I said, proudly presenting my 1998 Nokia. "It's got an 'off' button."

"Look, Mallet," he said, just short of blowing his stack. "I don't know what you're playing at, but I don't like it."

"I'm so sorry, but I don't think the use of mobile phones is permitted in the club," I said, looking up at the waiter as he served the next course.

"That is correct, sir," he responded primly, as he dumped a triplet of potato croquettes on my plate. "It's against club rules."

Henry looked drained. I could see he didn't want to play anymore. He hadn't taken to me. In fact, he hadn't asked me one single thing about *my* life. Perhaps he thought I was an idiot. I let him go. It was time to focus my attention on Mark Harbour. It was his turn.

Mark had been two years above me at St Dweeb's College some three decades earlier, a detail that he never allowed to be lost on me whenever we met. However, on this occasion he seemed disinclined to engage in any badinage about shared memories, so instead I started to make a house out of the beans that I had left on my plate. I asked Mark if I could have some of his to complete the effect, but he told me to 'fuck off'. He'd been like that at school.

The table was too wide for me to talk to anyone on the other side. Nobody was interested anyway, so I concentrated on getting drunk. The waiter was scrupulously slow about refilling my glass, but just as I was thinking about disappearing into the ether, Tim Ball, in his capacity as titular tit-in-chief, stood up to make a short speech about himself. He then proposed a salutation to the health of the Hongkong stock market and sat down again.

The procedure signalled the close of ceremonies, but not before we were offered coffee and liqueurs. I ordered a brandy, which prompted me to think of the night I'd spent with Ginny Giordano and the pointlessness of it all, and then it was time to go. I thanked Graham

Ruddock, without any intention of seeming disingenuous, for inviting me to such a select occasion, nodded to one or two of the others and then made myself scarce.

It was only 2:30 and I wasn't nearly drunk enough. For a modicum of pomp and circumstance it had been a reasonable eighty pounds-worth, although I wasn't sure I'd succeeded in cementing any concrete relationships. It was too early to go home and I didn't fancy going back to work, so I bought a newspaper and headed for the nearest pub. Once inside I ordered a pint, found a chair and took comfort from reading a news item with the unsurprising revelation that the entire cabinet in office was on the take, before turning to a disturbing article about the rivers of blood that were now the foaming streets of London, but it was the travel section at the back of the paper that really caught my eye. There was a feature on Goa, praising its good value and weather. I knew the beach where they'd taken the accompanying photograph. That was it. That was my message from God. Pete Divis was right. Damn the Nile! Goa was where it was at! For me it was more than just a holiday. I had been kept under glass for more than twelve years; it was time to break out and do the cha-cha-cha. I resolved to go to the travel agent by the office the very next day.

I went to bed that night pissed at last and happy. I'd made a decision! I checked the internet at work the following morning for deals to India before going to the travel agent. There were thousands of them. There had been an inconsequential outbreak of plague in Delhi a few months before that had scared off half the tourist trade to Goa. I scuttled down to the travel agent and booked a three week break over Christmas and the New Year for less than £500. They were giving it away! And for a nominal service charge they would fix me up with a new passport and look after the visa for India. All I needed was a couple of photographs, a cholera jab, and I'd be on my way. I couldn't wait to tell Elspeth. There would be no silly 'Love-your-brooch-Mum,' conversation for me that Christmas; no silly gas-inducing food, and no silly television. It would be curried turkey for one! I would be safe, far away on a beach with a bottle or three, even if I did have to forego the tradition of the impositional Christmas present from Elspeth. She used to give me golf lessons or exercise contraptions. Why? Did I look unfit? One year, by way of a change, she'd given me a trouser press while I'd been in prison. I'd found it immensely difficult to live down, although it didn't stop people wanting to borrow it the whole time.

Back in the office I presented Fred with my holiday agenda. He didn't have a problem. It was going to be the quiet period anyway, but I noticed Craig taking a certain interest in what we were discussing and then talking to Fred after I'd returned to my desk. It was only when I went back to the travel agent to confirm my reservation that I realised what was going on. The snake! When Craig heard how little my arrangements were costing me, he'd asked Fred if he too could take a holiday break. Not only had he booked the same deal as the one I was on, but he'd convinced the booking clerk, who he knew from the pub, that we'd be travelling together and sharing the same room.

"Relax, dude," was his response when I confronted him. "It saves a ton for both of us on single room supplements. I'll find my own space when we get there."

A few days before I was due to leave I received a call from Mick Burton, a *bon vivant* with whom I'd once shared a flat when we were youths, asking me to a party that evening. Mick had become a feature on the micro-celebrity circuit and was known for his eclectic gatherings. I willingly accepted. He said the theme was 'fetish' and I could bring a friend, if I wanted. I immediately thought of Ginny Giordano and her line in exotic nightwear. She would be the perfect accompaniment! I was concerned that she might have other commitments at such short notice, but when I told her who our host was and the theme for the evening, she jumped at it on the spot. I asked her if she had anything that I could wear. She said she had 'just the ticket'.

Ginny arrived at my flat looking fabulous. She was wearing practically her own weight in lipgloss and some super-porno eyeshadow. Under her fur coat she had a black leatherette thong and a matching peek-a-boo top, fishnets and a pair of thigh-length boots. For my requirements, she'd dipped into her 'toy cupboard' and come up with a gimp mask, a whip and a red satin posing pouch. ("Hey - how do I look in these bad boys?!!") We looked superb. Ginny put her fur back on and I grabbed my longest, warmest overcoat as we pranced off happily to the party.

Mick greeted us at the door and told us to leave our coats in the bedroom. Ginny made some adjustments to her finery and straightened my posing pouch. We made quite an entrance. Ginny looked the consummate dominatrix and I her lurking sidekick. Everyone cheered and then quietened down. We mingled and chatted with the other guests who all looked very Christmassy. Out of the corner of my mask I saw Christine Hale talking to Chantal Davidson. They were giggling and pointing at us. Something was wrong. I looked around. Ginny and I seemed to be the only ones dressed to thrill. I took Mick to one side.

"Mick: I thought you said the dress code was 'fetish'."

"No, you plank! I said 'festive'," he replied, hardly able to contain his laughter.

Oh no! How *embarrassing*! Not Christine's Curse again? Not with her in the same room, surely? That was against club rules.

We didn't stay long. Ginny put her fur on as quickly as I took my mask off. She did *not* get the joke.

"You twunt!" she screamed, once we were out of the building. "You deliberately went out of your way to make me look like a complete slut."

"I didn't do anything deliberately," I moaned, woefully.

"This might be your warped, stupid idea of getting one up on me," she bawled, unrelentingly, "but mark my words, James Mallet, you are a dead man."

"Honey: I'm really sorry," I snivelled, to no avail. "It was a mistake. How do you think I felt?"

"I don't care how you fucking felt," she shrieked, now beginning to sob. "You had that fucking mask, at least. But I know how you'll be feeling once my Russian friends have finished with you. You'll be sipping your dinner through a straw; I hope you like hospital food."

"I quite like hospital radio," I remarked reflectively, perhaps missing the point.

"You little worm!" she screeched, for the last time. "You should be ashamed of being born. Now go and fuck yourself."

"I normally do," I murmured, unassumingly.

I had nothing more to say. I could tell she was cross. In fact she was incandescent, but she'd run out of things to shout. Instead she coughed, hoiked up a greenie, rolled it carefully around her tongue, before flobbing it elegantly straight into my face. Class. She'd always been stylish. I let it rest there without saying anything. That just made her catatonic. She mouthed voicelessly a word that looked like 'aerosol', but might have been something else, then stomped off, not so elegantly, into the night leaving me wondering what to do about the whip and gimp mask. I watched her as she disappeared and wiped my face. I was quite pleased I was going on holiday.

Chapter 13: Protrusion

Craig was waiting for me at the airport. He was wearing a sun hat. He'd done his research. The plane was late, so we opened our duty free in the departure lounge and got fried. We eventually slithered on to the aircraft, inebriation undetected, and slept till we were halfway over the Gulf of Oman whereupon Craig told me he had a confession: he was carrying roughly half an ounce of hash which he was now having second thoughts about bringing through customs at the other end. It seemed a shame to waste it, so we ate it.

By the time the plane landed in Goa, we were flying. It was midnight. I glanced through a 'Welcome to Goa' leaflet while we waited for our luggage. Apart from some religious festivals there didn't seem to be much happening, which was fine by me. Our luggage eventually flopped onto the baggage carousel and much as we begged to be strip-searched, the customs wallahs were having none of it. They wanted to go home. We left the building dejectedly and tumbled into the back of the awaiting tour bus. The bus jerked to a start and headed towards the hotel district. Craig was keen to make friends with anyone who happened to be within vomiting distance, while I tried to focus what was left of my single vision on the murky scenery passing by.

Then the most magical thing in the world materialised at the front of the bus. It was an apparition of Aphrodite. Her face was a picture of smouldering cool, surveying her new ill-assorted charges of excursionists, backpackers and lager louts, as a primary teacher might contemplate her brood of unruly six year-olds. She was our SunWorld rep. She spoke.

"Good evening ladies and gentlemen. Welcome to Goa! My name is Angelita de Souza and I will be your guide for the short journey to your hotel destination. Please listen while I tell you a few tips and precautions you should take to make your visit as pleasant as possible."

That voice! The honeyed sing-song rose above the low rumble of the bus. Everyone was transfixed, none more so than I. She continued to drivel on, but I was too pissed to take it all in. Something about not drinking the tap water; not encouraging beggars; being wary of hustlers. The composure of her delivery made us all look such plebs. We were.

"And so, in conclusion, I wish you a most enjoyable stay in Goa and I hope to see you back again very soon!"

She'd see me again very soon. She smiled a million sunbeams and took her seat behind the driver. There was an empty place next to her. My mind went into involuntary overdrive. As if in a trance, I automatically decamped from my seat and walked towards the front of the bus. All eyes were on me. I had no idea what I was doing. I needn't have worried.

"Excuse me, Miss de Souza, but is this space free?" I enquired. "It's a bit bumpy at the back and I tend to get travel sickness."

It wasn't my voice. They weren't my words.

She looked up. Her face was like her name. A little angel.

"Of course, sir. I'm so sorry you feel unwell."

No! No! No! How could I? I sat down. My mind was a complete blank.

"I like your neck chain," I spouted, surveying the crucifix nestling shyly in the suggestion of her cleavage. "Are you a Catholic?"

"Why, yes, sir, it is the principal religion of Goa," she articulated, in a voice made out of nougat. "Why sir, are you?"

"Very similar," I white-lied. "I'm an Anglo-Catholic, but you mustn't call me 'sir', Miss de Souza. My name is James... James Mallet."

I offered her my hand.

"Thank you, Mr James," she said accepting my clammy claw into her soft, unsuspecting palm. "And my name is Angelita."

"I know," I said knowingly, feeling a return to my old daft self. "It's a lovely name."

"You're very kind, Mr James," she said, oblivious to my lowbrow puffery. "But can you tell a little about the Anglo-Catholic faith? I am most interested."

Oh, no! I wasn't even sure that it existed. I regurgitated some half-digested pap from my schooldays about the Reformation. Angelita seemed to evaluate every nuance as I laboured on and I absorbed every message emanating from her searching, ink-black eyes. So serious; so cute. I felt an overwhelming sense of trust. I stopped yabbering. I didn't know what I was talking about anyway.

"That was most informative, Mr James," she remarked thoughtfully, her face radiating a sense of joyous, sublime discovery. "It is good to know our beliefs are so alike."

Perhaps.

There was a lull in our conversation and then I remembered the 'Welcome to Goa' leaflet I'd briefly browsed through while I was waiting by the baggage carousel at the airport.

"I'm very interested to see the Basilica of Bom Jesus. Do you know where I can find it?" I enquired, innocuously.

Stop it! Stop it! Stop it!

"Oh, yes, Mr James. It's in Old Goa Town," she correctly informed me. "You are here at a very good time because the Mass of Saint Francis Xavier is being held this Wednesday."

Just as the 'Welcome to Goa' leaflet had said!

"How fortunate," I remarked, beginning to hate myself. "I shall ask my hotel the best way to get there."

Shut up! Shut up! Shut up!

"There is no need to do that, Mr James. I am taking the day off for the ceremony. You can come with me if you don't mind riding on my two-wheeler."

Two-wheeler?

"Angelita, that's most kind but I mustn't impose on your day off. I shall pay for a guide to show me around, but perhaps we could meet for lunch or tea afterwards?"

"No," she insisted. "I will pick you up from your hotel. It will be difficult to meet otherwise. You won't need to pay me anything. I will collect you from your reception desk at eleven o' clock. Please wear some long trousers."

It was a pity I hadn't brought the gimp mask.

Craig and I decanted ourselves from the bus at our hotel. Angelita accompanied me to the lobby, said goodnight graciously and assured me of her punctuality for our Wednesday adventure. A bellhop showed us to our room and we crashed on our beds without bothering to unpack our bags.

I awoke first. It was Sunday. I got up and staggered towards the minibar. There was some mineral water and two small of bottles of Kingfisher beer. I sank one of the beers without thinking and opened the other to establish tenure before Craig woke up. I wandered into the bathroom and looked in the mirror. I looked a wreck. I showered, lit a cigarette and then guzzled the remaining bottle. I pulled back a shutter an inch and peeked outside. The light of the brochure-blue sky hurt, but it was beautiful and the recent monsoons had left an Elysian paradise in their wake. Little people went about their business below. An ox and cart passed by with an infant using a twig as flail. This was India! I was back in the land of upset stomachs and narrow-gauge loo paper! This was home.

Craig stirred and opened an eye.

"What time is it?" he asked groggily, interrupting my blissful reverie.

"About Margarita-thirty," I replied, without looking at my watch.

"That dope was a bit of a mistake," he remarked, hauling himself upright.

"It worked," I reflected, with a shrug.

"It worked on you for sure," he noted. "You were going tonto with that Indian tart last night."

"She wasn't a tart, she was a respectable woman," I reproved.

"She was a child, for God's sake, James," he countered. "Your socks are older than she is."

"She was our tour guide," I reminded him. "I was only asking her about the locality."

"As if," he cried, raising himself out of bed. "You were off your face. You should be ashamed of yourself."

"Whatever," I sighed, losing interest in his reprimands. "She's showing me the sights on Wednesday."

"It won't be the only thing she'll be showing you, if you have your way," he retorted, scathingly.

He had a shower and then we went downstairs. We'd missed breakfast, so we headed towards the bar and ordered two bottles of beer.

"So what's there to do here?" he asked, as he poured out his drink.

"Nothing," I informed him, knowledgeably. "Just change some money and float around. That's all I did last time."

"Great! I travel four thousand miles for *nothing*?"

"Nothing is the best option here, Craig" I continued, philosophically. "But don't worry. Something always turns up."

"I'll get some dope," he said, despondently.

"Be careful," I cautioned. "Things can go wrong here. Just occasionally."

We changed some money with the concierge and wandered onto the main road. We were two hundred yards from the beach. Some children followed, bugging us for money, but we were too stoned from the night before to be annoyed. We walked towards the beach.

"It's pretty, I'll grant you that," Craig noted, approvingly. "Where do we eat?"

I motioned to a cluster of beach shacks close by. We sat at one and ordered a couple of omelettes and some more beers.

Craig leaned back, lit a cigarette and looked at the sea.

"I could get used to this. But for three weeks?"

"Craig," I said, starting to explain again, "this is India. You don't have to look for funny things to happen... they just do... small things at first, like a goat up a tree or a street trader who can quote Shakespeare word-for-word, but they *will* come."

Just then three or four small faces appeared, trying to sell us some trinkets, as a man strolled casually by with a painted elephant on a lead.

"I see what you mean," said Craig, looking slightly more convinced. "It's like Blackpool with elephants!"

We finished our omelettes and asked for some more drinks as other holiday-makers started to wander in. They were a mixed bunch of retirees and young proletarians. That's what I liked about Goa: it had no class. We stayed for a bit, letting the friendly pie-dogs sniff our ankles and then asked for the bill. It was less than £5. We decided to go back to the hotel for a swim to cool off. The hotel had a small, well-kept garden and a poolside bar. It was very civilised. Craig wanted to explore the local environs but I was happier with a book and a sunlounger near the bar.

"What's it about?" Craig asked, picking up the book.

"It's about a middle-aged alcoholic who can't get laid."

"But that's all of us!" he decried, plaintively.

I pointed him in the direction of the nearest town and started to read my book. I couldn't concentrate. My mind kept drifting off, mainly to thoughts of Angelita. She'd been friendly enough, but had she just been extending politeness to a tourist? I couldn't be sure. Courtship or courtesy? If it was courtesy she was certainly exceeding her remit. I'd been so zonked I'd almost forgotten what she looked like, except that she was pretty. Pretty and forthcoming. I hadn't had those words in the same sentence for a while. Not since being a convicted criminal with an acute propensity for alcohol, but she didn't need to know that. And what if it was courtship? What then? With this pleasing dilemma I rolled over on my sunlounger and went to sleep.

Craig came back in the evening bearing a few battle scars. He'd hired a scooter and fallen over a number of times before he'd got the hang of it. He was deliriously happy. He'd bought a whole bag of what he called 'party clothes'.

"I love this place, man," he said, fizzing like a nine year old on a sugar rush. "I bought all this crap for less than twenty quid!" he said, pointing to the heap on his bed. I looked at it.

"You wuz robbed," I said, unsportingly. "It ain't worth a fiver. Never buy anything on your first day. You need to get a feel for the prices before you commit."

"It's only twenty quid, for crying out loud!" he said, bringing things into perspective. "And I need this stuff *now*!"

Next morning I let him go off and play with his motorbike while I had a go at getting reacquainted with the area on foot. I noticed that Craig was in no particular hurry to vacate what I considered to be 'my room', but I didn't mind. He was turning out to be an amusing travelling companion. What didn't work in the office often worked outside, and vice versa.

I was pleasantly surprised to see that nothing calamitous had changed to the townscape since my previous visit. The houses and shacks now had satellite dishes bolted onto their roofs, but actual development had been relatively restrained. Many of the shops and restaurants were much as I remembered them and the market was selling the same old tat as ever. At least they'd started stocking Duracells instead of the ridiculous 'Black Cat' batteries they had before. The prices, less surprisingly, had gone upwards, but so had sterling against the rupee, leaving *real* prices nicely unchanged for the passing tourist.

I beer-hopped between bars for most of the morning, chatting occasionally to other like-minded holiday soaks, and then stopped to look at some of the shops. In the afternoon I walked the two miles along the dusty Baga road back to the hotel. It was hot, quiet and far away from London. It was better than home.

Craig returned in the evening again with his now customary exuberance, carrying various bits of detritus he had bought in the course of his meanderings, but he had one thing he particularly wanted to show me. He produced a small round turd out of his pocket.

"Lovely," I remarked sarcastically, knowing it had to be something hallucinogenic. "What is it?"

"This, my friend, is something very special," Craig declared, grandly.

"It looks it," I scoffed, derisively. "Go on: tell me."

"This," he continued, proudly, "is not Junior Disprin. According to the local street pharmacist, it's the finest opium available in the district. It will make you believe in God and Unicorns."

"Super," I said, still unimpressed. "What do you do with it? I clean left my crack pipe back at home, officer."

"No, you tit. You eat it, just as we did with dope on the aeroplane. Only this stuff will take you to Pluto," Craig explained, excitedly.

"Well, what are we waiting for?"

"Easy cowboy," he said, looking at me sternly. "We'll put on our space suits tomorrow, on the beach, where everything's nice and the living's easy."

We dined together under the stars at another restaurant near the beach. There were Christmas lights in the trees and some driftwood bonfires flickering along the shoreline. The moon was full and the waves rolled lethargically into the sand. My thoughts turned to Angelita again. What on earth were we going to talk about? How long could or should I pretend to have any religious convictions? My absence of any opinion of the subject made it seem all the more sacrilegious. Fuck religion; what about sex?

"Are you hoping for a groping with that Indian bird on Wednesday?" Craig enquired, practically reading my mind to the closest neuron.

"Sure," I said, snapping out of my contemplations. "Otherwise I don't know what else we'll have in common."

"You'll think of something," Craig assured me, with the luxury of not having to be there himself. "I've heard you're good at getting women."

"No, I'm good at getting women *pissed*," I emphasised, firmly. "I'm no gynaecologist, whatever anyone's said, and I have a sneaky feeling this one doesn't drink. But give me a pretty girl with low self-esteem issues, and I am Uncle Sigmund."

The next day we were up in time for breakfast.

"Don't eat too much," Craig cautioned. "We don't want all this nasty wholesome food getting in the way of the real *plat du jour*."

We went back to the bedroom and he retrieved the opium ball from behind his cupboard. He cut off a wedge and handed it to me.

"Down the hatch!" he ordered, passing me a beer to wash it down and then repeating the process himself.

"Not too little and not too much! We'll just have a mild buzz for a couple of hours and then we can lie back and take in the real show!"

We strolled up and down the beach for a while. Craig was proving to be a bit of a diamond and I castigated myself for thinking ill of him before. My legs started to feel heavy, so we headed towards the nearest beach shack and ordered some drinks. Craig looked completely blissed, but then his eyes started to go weird.

"James: I think I might go back to the hotel before the main feature cranks up," he said, getting up unevenly. "The run-time is usually about three hours. You'll be fine on your own, unless you want to come back now. There won't be scary monsters either way."

I was feeling too relaxed to move, so I wished him well and waved goodbye. I took the precaution of relocating to a shady table away from the bar area before I became totally rooted to the spot, and settled down to watch some children kick a ball about on the beach. I felt at peace and safe. The opium was taking hold: I was about to enter The Theatre of the Absurd. I didn't have a care. I was miles away from England; I was miles away from anywhere, but thinking of England reminded me of the journey I would normally be taking into work, and the film posters along the walls of the Underground. I wondered why Sandra Botox kept making the same film over and over again and whether she was really George Hamilton in drag and why Julia Roberts stomped rather than walked in her movies and why Robert Redford could only really do Robert Redford and how Michael Caine still found work and why I hated Richard Curtis even more than Tony Blair but not as much as Julian Fellows or Coldplay, because they so darn successful or because they were creepoids I could not, at that point, explain. And Mel Gibson: why? And Tobey Maguire: please explain. Ditto James McAvoy. And Bill Nighy. And Michael Palin. And Ashton Kutcher. WTF? And wasn't Laura Dern a wee mumsy to be playing lead roles? What happened? And hadn't Harry Potter been done in The Worst Witch and why was Joanna Lumley's voice so tremulous and what was Christian Bale about and whether *Das Boot*, however good, was just das little bit too long and whether Churchill and Goering were related or, indeed, the same person and whether Gary Newman's friends really were electric and why dictionaries always opened at 'Renfrew' and wouldn't it be too awful if the Skype camera on my computer was on all day for the whole world to see and whether Orwell was twenty years too early, or Napoleon half a century too late and how Toffler was bang on the money and whether ugly couples enjoyed sex? I liked this drug. It could go wherever I wanted it to go. I was Captain of my soul. Debunk or bunk? Like why did policemen, from constable to commissioner, all sound the same? And archbishops. I thought about the dark side and whether Hitler had vision and Bin Laden a point, or if Alan Titchmarch and June Whitfield were the incarnation of all things evil and the breakdown of society as we knew it and why white lavatory paper always made me want to commit suicide, but it was getting too heavy, so I decided to return to the middle ground.

A waiter came to see if I was OK, but I told him not to worry. The children were still playing on the beach. I thought about Christine and questioned why I still obsessed about her and her damned, infernal curse despite the fact that she was just a pout on two legs, and then I started to laugh. I wondered why my life was just a conveyor belt of futile relationships and false starts which seemed pre-programmed to die the minute they started, just as life was pre-ordained to end from the moment of conception, and why my attachment to alcohol was the only one I'd ever really trusted and why it was as much to me as spinach was to Popeye.

I looked at my watch. It was intermission time. I needed a pee. I got up relatively easily but it took me twenty minutes to wee because the opium had seized my bladder, but it didn't matter. Someone had taken my chair by the time I got back but I didn't mind. I sat somewhere else and played with a dog's ear for half an hour before the dog got bored and sniffled off somewhere else. The kids had stopped playing football. The sun was coming down and the light was dancing playfully on the waves. A pretty fruit seller sold me a mango. I let her keep the change and looked at the mango for an hour. It was too beautiful to eat. It was starting to get chilly. I had to get my shit together. I would have hated Angelita to have thought I was a complete stoner tomorrow.

I asked the waiter for the bill and stood up. I was ten feet tall! The ground was miles away! I walked quite steadily out of the bar and shifted gear. I climbed a sand dune like a Jeep Cherokee and made for the path back to the hotel. I was taller than everyone else I passed but they didn't seem to care, and then I realised I wasn't tall at all; I was levitating! I arrived back at the hotel and regarded the swimming pool. If I could walk across it, it would prove that I was either Jesus Christ or that Jesus was a stoner. I decided not to put the matter to the test. It would be a project for another time. I made my way to the bedroom. Craig wasn't there. He must've gone for a *trip* on his motorbike. The opium had been an interesting diversion even if it was all rubbish. I did a swallow dive onto the bed and slept. And slept.

I woke up at six but I didn't know whether it was morning or evening. Or what day it was. Shit! Had I missed Angelita? Craig was in the other bed, fast asleep. I got up and looked out of the window. It was morning. Dawn was just breaking. Craig was dead to the world, but at least he wasn't dead. I got dressed to go down and find out whether I was on the right day. It was OK. It was Wednesday. I went to the beach to watch the fishermen land their catch. The nets weren't as full as they used to be. I looked at the trawler fleets in the distance against the deep blue early-morning sky. A fellow dawn beachcomber in a sombrero caught my gaze.

"Some of those bastards have dragnets five miles long between each ship. These little blighters haven't got a chance," he said, looking at the matchwood skiffs on the shore.

I walked back to the hotel, had a shower and shaved. I was still feeling a bit trippy and half-hoped that Angelita wouldn't turn up. But somehow I knew she would.

She was there at eleven on the hour. It didn't seem like the same woman, but I wasn't on the same drugs. This was Venus in blue jeans. She looked more gamine in her T-shirt, more teasing; more ingénue. We talked shyly at first, but once we started discussing our intended pilgrimage we loosened up.

"Come," she said taking control and leading me to her scooter. It had tassels on the handlebars and religious stickers on the windshield. A gypsy bike! On one side was painted 'The Spirit of Babu'.

"Who's Babu?" I enquired, grateful of another conversational opening.

"Babu's my father's nickname," she answered proprietorially, either of her father or the nickname. "He gave me the bike for my twenty-first birthday."

It looked brand new. Craig was right. She was a child. She kick-started and revved the engine in one coordinated movement. I scrabbled aboard the pillion seat. We zoomed off down the track and joined the main road. She drove like a demon but perhaps, I wondered fleetingly, there was another motive other than speed of transport. I tried to maintain a dignified physical distance by gripping the back panniers.

"Don't be stupid, James, you can hold on to me; I won't bite," she shouted over her shoulder as I was practically catapulted out of my skeleton going over a particularly large pothole. At least she'd stopped calling me 'Mr James'. I primly placed one hand on her waist.

"Is this allowed in India?" I cried. "Doesn't it look a bit odd, having a fat white man clinging on to a young brown woman at ninety miles an hour?"

"I don't care!" she yelled through the wind.

We made it to Old Goa town in one piece and Angelita parked the bike near the Basilica. It was a bubbling broth of human disarray. Wall-eyed men and waddling women heaved together towards the Basilica's entrance. Angelita left me to go and look for a better way in. She wouldn't lose me. I was the only crouton in this particular soup.

I needed a drink badly. I saw a beverage stall and prayed there'd be some beer on offer. There was better. There was a whole stack of 'Holy Wine' half-bottles, each retailing at a very reasonable forty five rupees. I bought one immediately and as an afterthought procured a can of Coke for Angelita. I lovingly inspected the bottle's 18% label and then necked back the contents in one. I handed the empty back to the vendor with an appreciative burp. Angelita reappeared and took me by the arm. Bit forward.

We joined the shortest queue she'd been able to find but it was still Hell. Angelita looked vaguely embarrassed by her fellow citizens' frenzied pushing and suggested we sit on the grass a little further off to hear proceedings over the public address system, along with the slightly saner believers. We sat down and listened. It was pretty tedious. I didn't want to be doing this for the rest of the holiday on the off chance of a wet kiss, but I needn't have worried. Angelita started sniggering as the speakers began to squawk a discordant descant.

"This is hopeless! I'm sorry, James, this is just so *Indian*! Why don't we say three Hail Marys and fuck off somewhere for lunch?"

Fuck off?! Bit rude. Was I hearing correctly? At the Basilica of Bom Jesus? In India? I stared at her in disbelief.

"James, we're allowed to swear in India! We have the internet, satellite and attitude too. We're not the ones who had the Dark Ages, you know. Come!"

She may have been a child but she knew her own mind. I followed her back to her bike. She kick-started it again with her usual aplomb, spurning the electric ignition.

"Why do you do it like that?" I asked.

"Because I can. You try," she said cutting off the engine.

I couldn't do it. She was a strong little thing.

We shot off down the road, swerving past wandering pedestrians and ambling street sellers hawking their silly glow-in-the-dark Jesus statues. For safety's sake I clung closer to Angelita and in the process developed the biggest erection ever created. It was peeping over my belt buckle by the time we arrived at the restaurant in the nearby capital of Panjim. Alas, to my chagrin, I'd also sprung a wet patch the size of Lake Tahoe above the pocket area of my Debenhams Casual Clubs. *How embarrassing!*

I hurriedly untucked my shirt to cover up and walked stiffly towards our table before carefully sitting down.

The restaurant was more of a café and didn't sell any alcohol. I didn't mind too much as I was still quite pissed from the Holy Wine and Angelita was also proving to be a captivating diversion. We chatted as if we'd known each other forever. Our contrasts were our strengths. Everything we said to each other seemed fascinating. She knew a lot of people at the restaurant. They appeared to be workmates. She introduced me proudly as her 'friend'. It suddenly dawned on my why she'd brought me there; it was to show me off! Of all people! The food wasn't marvellous. I picked at what little chicken there was in the curry but I was too engrossed to be hungry.

We wandered around Panjim afterwards. Angelita seemed to be familiar with everyone on the street. She put her arm possessively through mine as if I was hers. A warning bell repealed my erection. It was too easy. This didn't happen in England. Not to me. Not these days. I wasn't accustomed to it.

It was time to go home. Angelita drove back to the hotel, more sedately this time, but my erection was becoming a nuisance again. I hopped off her bike and tried awkwardly to hide my protrusion. Angelita stood back and considered it thoughtfully for a moment.

"Not bad!" she commended, as if she knew a thing or two about male arousal, and then laughed.

"Not fair!" I riposted, trying to think of an appropriate diversion. "How about supper?"

She became serious for a minute and said she had a commitment to cook for her family that evening. Then she had a thought.

"But come, please. I can pick you up. I don't live far away. And I need something big to stir the pot!"

I gave her a double take. Was I hearing properly again? But delightful as she was, I wasn't quite ready to meet her family. I'd had a little too much India for one day; I'd had enough. I didn't put it to her quite like that, but made my excuses and instead suggested we meet the following evening if she was free. She was.

I went up to my room with mixed feelings. While it was lovely to have the attention of someone so young and vivacious, it brought with it responsibilities that were not normally part of the holiday package deal. This wasn't Thailand. Older tourists didn't hang around with younger locals *here*. It could only mean one thing. Angelita was playing for higher stakes. If this was the case, then why not? Maybe she was *the one*. Maybe I was. Maybe this was the hand of God that I'd spent so long avoiding. I re-thought the implications. How could a twenty-one year old Indian girl who'd never left her own country hope to survive in an environment as cold, impersonal and bigoted as my social plot in London? Plus, how long would it be before she realised that she'd landed an alcoholic boob with a murder rap around his neck? Or, alternatively, how long could I, as an alcoholic boob, last in India with nothing to do but drink the local coffin varnish all day?

Craig and I had supper in the little hotel restaurant by the pool. The garden was nicely lit and smelled of jasmine, but I was still in a funny mood. Craig picked up on it and knew pretty well what it was about.

"James, you came here for a holiday, not a lifestyle change. Buy the woman a frock, then fuck her to bits and be done with it. I don't suppose you'd be the first."

"That's not fair and it wouldn't be fair if I did, if it was ever on the menu, that is, " I said, half in unction and half in self-doubt.

"But you'd like to," he said, cutting across my tweeness.

"Oh Hell, yes, man. She had me dripping like a fucked fridge when I was sitting next to her on the back of her bike, but that's not the point," I said, hoping my vernacular would put paid to his angle of questioning.

"The point being?" he persisted.

"The point being," I said, beginning to lose the will to rationalise, "as things stand, I think I might have to be aware Miss de Souza's marital expectations should anything conjugal occur between us."

If that hadn't bamboozled him into submission, it certainly shut him up. We'd finished supper anyway. Craig wanted to go off to a rave at a spot further down the coast and I wanted to go to bed, so we said goodnight.

I spent the next day casing the locale for somewhere that would hit the right note with Angelita that evening, while keeping an eye out for something suitable to buy her for Christmas, which was now only two days away.

Angelita was outside the hotel at seven, now Athena in crinoline. She was indeed, a goddess. I had an enormous erection.

"I see the elephant is up to its tricks again," she remarked, uncritically.

"I'm sorry, Angelita... the flesh is weak..."

"There's nothing weak about that!" she cut in, upping her tone an octave.

We'd only known each other properly for thirty-six hours, but it might as well have been thirty-six months. We walked the few hundred yards to the restaurant I'd found, our hands occasionally brushing together. I'd eventually gone for a Chinese bistro nearby called The Fuzzy Duck, which I subsequently found was *the* fashionable nightspot of the moment, in Goan terms. We sat at a table on the verandah, looked at our menus, chose what we wanted and plunged headlong into the magical pool of requited admiration. We stayed till closing time and then went for a walk along the beach, this time hand in hand. I had to kiss her. Our mouths locked like angry dogs. She pressed her pelvis against my willing bunion. I wanted to explode. She was eating my mouth, but I knew she wanted to eat something else. So did I, but just then I spotted two Indian lads monitoring our progress with devilish interest from behind a sand dune.

"Angelita! Cool it! We've got company."

We disentwined. The moment was broken, but only just. We walked back to her motorbike in a state of electric seizure. Friends are electric! My legs had turned to jelly and Angelita looked utterly annihilated. We kissed again outside the hotel but I untangled myself before we got into more trouble. I knew exactly what I'd be doing with myself once I was alone in the bedroom and I needed to get there fast.

"Tomorrow night," I croaked, not as a question.

"Tomorrow night," she gasped.

"Same time?"

"Yes, but I want you to meet my family."

"Are you out to lunch? We'll do that another time, surely?"

"I can't. We're having a little pre-Christmas party. It was arranged before we met. Please come. Craig can come too. We can go *triple-wheeling!*"

Oh, great! All three of us rammed up against each other on one motorbike. I could just imagine introducing myself with a woody the size of a Christmas tree and a sack fuller than Santa's, unless, of course, I got Craig to sit in the middle to act as a human prophylactic. I knew he had a function!

I kissed Angelita chastely goodnight on the cheek, held the moment... and quickly scuttled upstairs to relax the man's way, alone.

Craig and I were ready outside the hotel at seven the following evening. I'd tried my best to smarten up but Craig looked most strange in his new clothes. Angelita picked us up and the three of us proceeded aboard the bike in a curiously dignified manner back to her village. We entered the somewhat disappointing de Souza household and Angelita introduced us to the dozen or so guests, ending with her brother and parents. Everyone was friendly and none more welcoming than her small family. I had a brief glimpse round. The de Souzas were almost horse-and-cart poor. The furniture was threadbare and such decorations as there were looked as though they'd been picked up from the beach.

Angelita elaborately presented Craig and me with some local whisky and a soda siphon. What luxury! I struck up a conversation with her father who seemed unaware or unconcerned about my intentions towards his daughter. Like a lot of Indians, he had a natural tendency to over-enunciate, and this together with the local idiomatic style made him sound stiffer than Baden-Powell on a cold day. I then had a chat with her brother who had an MBA from the local university and was into platform software. We didn't talk for long. Craig was regaling the rest of the group with interesting stories about all the drugs he'd recently taken. Angelita's mother went off and came back with a platter of revolting Indian sweetmeats. I had another drink and started to enjoy myself. Underneath our Western ways, neither Craig nor I was nearly as informed as the other people present, yet they hung on our every word and asked our opinion on everything, as if we were oracles. I went for a pee. There was a bucket of water by the loo. They weren't on mains water but at least the electricity meant I could see what I was doing. I went for a nose around the house. It didn't take long. As far as I could tell Angelita shared a room with her brother. That and her parents' room, the kitchen, bathroom and drawing room, was it, which was fine. But they were the educated middle class; the professional echelon; *the haves.*

After a decent interval Craig and I decided it was time to make our excuses and leave. The other guests took our cue and we all wished each other a Merry Christmas. Craig and I were happy to look for a taxi but Angelita wouldn't hear of it and insisted on driving us back to the hotel. Her brother wanted to come too, so Craig had a lift on his bike and I had Angelita to myself. We were all a bit pissed but we made it back to the hotel, giggling like idiots. I invited our new friends in for a drink. There was a cluster of chippy Scousers smoking spliffs at the bar who didn't seem to appreciate our brand of cheer, so we went to the pool, rolled up our jeans and dangled our feet in the water. It was simple, innocent enjoyment, away from the William Davidsons and the Howard Joneses and the Henry Mercers and all the other mice of no consequence who seemed out to bugger up my life. Me? A flyweight? Bah! It didn't seem such a bad idea now to marry Angelita, start a family in India and kiss goodbye to the toilet that my country had become. But there again, family aside, I'd also have to kiss goodbye to all the good guys like Wally, Peregrine and Pete Divis. What to do?

Angelita and I spent Christmas Day together. Beyond going to mass, Christmas was business as usual as far as the rest of Goa was concerned. We beached, we swam ("Last one in's a kipper!"), talked, ate and laughed. Angelita was great. I was great. I was living the dream. It was heaven with strawberries. Had I, at last, found *my* girl from Ipanema?

We slept with each other early on New Year's morning. Repeatedly. It was no big deal. *Hot zigadee!* It was a *fantastic* deal. That wasn't in the brochure! No sooner had we finished, than we'd start again. ('If I brush my teeth, can we have another go?!')

Angelita drove sheepishly back to her parents in her frock from the dance we'd been to the night before. She hadn't been a virgin or I wouldn't have done it. Or so I told myself. She wasn't a child in that respect. It wasn't her first time at the rodeo by any stretch, which led me to wonder how this squared with her strong religious convictions, but Angelita saw no paradox. Conviction and compliance were words that did not necessarily have to be used in the same breath as far as she was concerned. She wasn't alone.

Craig moved to alternative lodgings, leaving Angelita and me to our own devices. We caught our bare reflection in the mirror one day.

"You're so white," she said, as if the thought had only just occurred to her.

"And you are so brown," I responded, admiringly.

We met for lunch near her office nearly every day and spent our evenings together. But time was running out. We discussed what we might do next. We thought we believed that anything was possible. I told her ours was not just like any shipboard romance. But I didn't tell her it was still, at heart, a fantasy.

The day came when Craig and I had to go. Angelita came with us on the tour bus back to the airport. Craig left us alone at the departure gate. We held each other close.

"You will come back?"

"Of course. Soon."

"Otherwise it will just be like any shipboard romance."

"It won't be."

"Keep in touch."

"I will."

"The world is your oyster: I am your pearl."

"I know."

I entered the aeroplane and wiped away, walrus-style, what could have been a tear.

Chapter 14: Consultation

I saw my empty seat next to Craig and sat down beside him. I looked out of the window as the plane took off. Of course I couldn't see her. I felt as miserable as a horse on a rainy day. Craig quickly asked the stewardess for two double gin and tonics when the plane levelled off. After she'd returned with our drinks, he looked at me and proposed a toast.

"Here's to a great holiday," he saluted, as we chinked glasses.

"Yes, it was good," I agreed reflectively, raising my glass to my lips. "And it doesn't make going home any easier."

Craig knew exactly what I meant but he was in no mood for mawkishness.

"Look, James, I'll give it to you straight. In Goa you're Donald Trump. In London you're Donald Duck... which will become increasingly apparent to Angelita if you ever bring her over. I'm not saying she's just after your money, such as it is, and I'm sure she loves you more than processed sugar, but however honourable both your intentions may be, she'll soon find out a few things about you that might not make for cosy sleeping."

"Yes, of course," I said, straightening myself in my seat. "I'll have to address those issues when I get home, probably by letter."

"OK," he continued. "Then there's the age agenda. You'll either be dead or approaching checkout by the time Angelita reaches a certain maturity, which may be sooner than you think. That's not going to be much fun for her. Or for you, I suspect."

"Thank you for your cheering advice, Craig," I said, not enjoying his tone. "Angelita and I have discussed all that. If the worst comes to the worst, she'll be well provided for."

"She will, will she?" he queried, cynically. "And what about the cultural divide? I'm of the mind that East is East and West is West."

"That's half the fun, isn't it?" I questioned, trying to think laterally. "Nobody cares where people come from nowadays, surely? The world's now more of an ethnic melting pot than ever before. Anyway, the cultural divide is infinitely easier to cross than the class boundaries that prevail in our petty, rank-obsessed commissariat that laughingly calls itself 'Great Britain'."

"You try explaining *that* to your parents," he admonished. "Or your highfalutin' friends. The men won't have a problem; they wouldn't mind a bit of chocolate on their biscuit themselves, given half the chance. It's the wives who won't get the joke. Not on their back croquet lawn."

"That's something we'll both have to consider. We would just have to deal with each difficulty as it comes. I think our feelings are strong enough to cope," I said, beginning to have my doubts.

"James, feelings are not instructions and optimism is not a durable strategy," he contended. "What you're talking about is attraction, and that doesn't always come with a lifetime guarantee. Angelita's not going to be a little fox forever. And little foxes have a nasty habit of changing into mean vixens."

"Point taken," I said, with rising irritation. "But you're looking at everything through a dead dog's arse. I'm looking more hopefully - at partnership and a way out of my pathetic, lonely existence. I'm looking at an act of faith in the future, because I sure as Hell don't possess either at the moment. You might see it as misplaced optimism but I see it as a tenable risk; a viable investment, if you like."

"Investment?" he cried, despairingly. "In a depreciating asset? Who are you kidding? She's not going to be cute forever and then what'll you be left with? How long before the darling from Darjeeling becomes the eyesore from Mysore? Women age faster than cars – that's a fact."

"*And men don't?* " I cried back, in disbelief. "Are we spared this inconvenience, Craig? Is this a *fact*? It's utter nonsense. Have you never known a woman's love?"

"What's love got to do with it?" he retorted, seemingly aware of any inanity. "Particularly in your case. She'll go off quicker than a lemon meringue; the pretty ones always do. They flower just long enough to be pollinated, and then they wilt. Besides, what are your *real* reasons anyway? Vanity? Self-affirmation? Self-indulgence? Or that ultimate killer: remorse? Or are you just buying into youth... or puberty, more like? Is this your Nabokov moment? Is that what's hooked you? Whatever it is James, I'd seriously re-examine your motives before you live to regret them."

"Now you're getting at me from all sides," I objected. "On one hand you're saying Angelita'll drop me like a red hot brick once she finds out I'm a career alcoholic from Planet Loser, and on the other you're saying I'm going to throw her out like a used condom when she develops any normal semblance of maturity. I can't win."

"Neither of you can; you're a hardened scumbag and she's scarcely out of the egg. I can't understand how you, of all people, can attach so much significance to what was essentially a fairly routine holiday fling. End of. Out of the context of a holiday, where can it go?

What'll she do in the UK? What *can* she do? Have lots of babies? On your money? Make lots of new friends? With your lot? I don't think so. Be real, James: it can't win. Besides, marriage is for grown-ups, and breeding without a struggle is the preserve of the very rich or, ironically, the very poor. You are neither. Someone like you is more likely to be killed by a terrorist than ever tie the knot. Your genitals, IMO, are for recreation, not procreation... fulfilment without commitment. What's not to like?"

If Craig had wanted to dash my dreams, he couldn't have done a better job. I felt decidedly bummed out for the rest of the journey.

January was never a nice month to start the year, particularly when accompanied by the heap of bills I had waiting for me inside the front door when I got home. The service charge for the maintenance work on the building was about to wipe me out, just when things weren't too peachy in the office either. The financial cupboard was looking very bare. I was beginning to regret the expense of going on holiday, however paltry.

While I spent every waking moment thinking of what to do about Angelita, the more I thought about bringing our lives together, the more Craig's stark words started to resonate. Broodingly, I considered who I could turn to for proper advice.

I hadn't seen much of Wally Barker or Peregrine Blücher since I'd moved companies the previous summer and wondered whether either would be on for a heart-to-heart, reminding myself that nothing bores a married man more than a single man's problems.

I deliberated which of the two would act as the better sounding board. I concluded that Wally had quite enough on his plate without listening to my woes. Peregrine, on the other hand, was more sanguine about personal matters and was, I thought, better versed in the field of human frailty. He was the man to call. I picked up the phone. He said he'd meet me at The White Sock at lunchtime.

He was there when I arrived. I noticed a small bottle of mineral water by his glass. I bought a beer and sat down opposite.

"You look well, for a change," he remarked unflatteringly, referring I assumed to my fading holiday flush. "Tell me about your trip."

I told him about the holiday, Craig and the drugs we'd taken, but for the most part my reminiscences centred on Angelita and my doubts about the situation we now found ourselves in.

"Greek brandy," he murmured, almost under his breath.

"Greek what?" I queried.

"Greek brandy," he repeated, impassively. "Something that seems immensely pleasurable on holiday, but not quite so hot when you bring it back home."

"I wish it were that simple," I said, ruefully. "I haven't brought anything back yet so I don't know. That's part of the problem."

"Are you sure your urges aren't part of the problem?" he queried, bluntly. "I have a feeling your objectives may be baser than you realise."

"These aren't just urges, Peregrine," I objected, affronted but adding as an afterthought, "although I wouldn't kick it out of bed for eating Doritos."

"All right then, let's look at the ethical ingredient," he continued donnishly, ignoring my frivolity. "Don't you think you're taking advantage of a child of the third world, who, by the very design of her circumstances, is bound to look up to you with an exaggerated estimation of what you actually are. Do think you that's fair, James?"

"It's not about that, Peregrine," I said, wretchedly, trying to avoid both questions. "It just seems that this is a gift from God I'd be an ass to pass up."

"Or not," he interjected, sternly. "As far I can as see, you're blowing out of all proportion what should have been a passing holiday moment into something that simply isn't compatible with your lot in life; you're trying to incorporate fantasy into reality. I'm saying you can't; not in your situation. Either way, you shouldn't just sit on it. You owe it to the poor girl to indicate your intentions. Either piss or get off the pot."

"The trouble is," I said, again slightly side-stepping the issue, "if Angelita does come over for a dummy run, her family will expect something conclusive to follow that doesn't involve the classification 'dummy', which slightly puts Angelita on the spot and makes difficulties for me."

"Well, you'll have to factor that in with the other stuff on your plate," Peregrine persevered.

"Such as what?" I quizzed, wanting him to be specific.

"Logistics and practical considerations, for instance. A bird may love a fish, but where would they live? Have you considered the resources you'll need to get hitched and start a family? Or thought of what sort of job Angelita might be able to find? Or would she be entirely dependent on you? Apart from a winsome smile, is there anything else she can bring to the table? Can you afford to keep a family in a style commensurate with your own upbringing? I know from painful experience the meter starts running from day one. That little bundle of financial joy you've got stashed under your mattress will be no match for the bundle of joy above it. It's not for nothing that 'diaper' is 'repaid' spelt backwards."

"That's more or less what my colleague Craig said, if not quite so eloquently," I observed, sullenly. "Match my own upbringing, huh? The middle class dilemma or the discreet smarm of the bourgeoisie? Look at me! I'm down to bogeys on toast as we speak. I'm so broke I soon won't even be able to afford table salt."

"Then I rest my case."

He got up to get me a beer and another bottle of mineral water for himself.

"Not drinking, Peregrine?" I asked.

"Not today. I haven't for quite a while," he stated, plainly.

"Why on earth not?" I demanded accusingly, as if he was completely letting down the side.

"It wasn't doing me any good," he replied, quietly. "Something had to go. It was either my job and family or the booze. So I decided it was time to show Mr Bottle the door and keep what was left of my life for me. Perhaps it's something you should consider if you're thinking of structuring a new existence around somebody you obviously care about, very much."

"I consider it the whole time," I said, sharply. "As you may know, I've been on an alcohol reform program, so I'm keeping an eye on it."

"Not good enough," he declared, austerely.

"Don't you start," I muttered. "Anyway I wasn't drinking in particularly large scoops in India."

"Only because you were smacked off of your nut on drugs half the time," he remarked, testily.

"It wasn't quite as bad as that," I protested. "But I am aware that I have a drinking situation."

"Still not good enough."

"Oh, for God's sake! I'm trying my best," I moaned, plaintively.

"I don't see much evidence. Trying is not the same as doing, James. The only way out for the likes of you and me is to be rid of the whole nonsense or it will just get worse. Whether this state of affairs has come about from your actions in the past, your dissatisfaction with the present or your concern for the future, you need help... you can't do it your own. Very few people can. I would seriously advise you to consider going back to AA before it's too late."

"Do you go?" I asked, trying to steer myself away from being the central point.

"Yes," he said, regarding me full on. "Only once a week now, just to remind myself about the shit I left behind. You see, it's not about stopping; it's about staying stopped. And as such I won't knock it."

We finished our drinks glumly and got up to leave. I thanked him gruffly for his advice and we went our separate ways. I felt abandoned and wondered what path our friendship could possibly follow now that he'd changed direction. And so much for providing a sanguine opinion. He'd been completely negative. Negative, negative.

It was with these thoughts I made my way back to the office, head bowed against the weather, when I accidentally banged into some dork with a Bluetooth strapped to his ear.

"Hey! Watch where you're going, buddy!" the dork shouted, without any express hostility. I knew that voice. It was Sven Gläzner, a jolly German who liked to pretend he was American. We'd worked together at the then-named Parker Barrow Brothers. We'd liked each other but unsurprisingly, given my subsequent custodial circumstances, we'd lost contact. He looked closely at me.

"James, you shithead! What were ya doin'? Trying to mug me?" he bawled, good-naturedly.

"Sven, you dicksplash! How ya goin'? You still at Barrow?" I asked, having a stab at being American myself.

"Nah. Just finished as it happens. Sixteen years was enough. I had a good run but it was time to move on. I'm starting at Dresden Commercial Bank International down on Lombard Street in a coupla weeks. I've just signed the papers. I'm gonna be head of sales, hah! What about you buddy? What are you up to these days?"

"I'm working for a small headhunting outfit just down the road; only vanilla fixed income stuff. It's not exactly astrophysics," I answered, humbly.

"Hey, maybe I could use you. I need to make a few changes at Dresden Commercial, so I'll be looking for new people just like that. If you know of the sort who are top shelf and looking for a change, give me a call in two weeks," he said, handing me one of his new business cards.

Sven Gläzner
Head of Sales
DCB International
(*Member*: Dresden Commercial Bank Group)

"Listen, buddy, I've gotta jam," Sven said, knocking me out of my stupefaction. "I'm already running late for my next meeting. Two weeks – right? I'll buy you lunch."

With that he turned and disappeared into the crowd. I looked at his card again. Well indeed! What an amazing coincidence! If we hadn't been passing at that very moment it would never have been. Chaos or fate, I wasn't going to let the opportunity slide through my fingers. Two weeks. That gave me a head start.

I slipped back into the office without fanfare and had a think. I had a vague recollection that Sven fancied himself as a bit of a ladies' man. He liked pretty things. I found a bond directory and leafed through it, looking for likely victims. I was still a bit out of touch with who did what, but my finger froze abruptly over a name I recognised under the Citigroup page. Theresa Batomata was a Japanese-American girl I'd once taken out on a date, to no effect. She'd be a woman now. I wondered if she'd remember me.

Things were now OK at home. My flatmate and I had declared an undiscussed truce whereby we were never in the same room at the same time, which worked well for both of us. He'd recently acquired a new girlfriend which added to his subtraction as he spent most of his evenings away, leaving me free to roam senselessly about the flat, bottle in hand, mooning over my predicament with Angelita. It was on one such evening, just as I was about to unscrew the cap of my second bottle of Liebfrau, that the phone went. It was Richard Hartley. My heart sank. I'd put The Pan Asian to the back of my mind ever since I'd embarked on my holiday to Goa and, apart from their ubiquitous advertising, had almost forgotten my part in Richard's corporate sleuthing.

After a short exchange of banter he came to the point.

"James, The Bank's new headquarters are nearly finished. All the departments are moving to their allocated spaces and my task is nearly done."

I detected a trace of chagrin his voice.

"Congratulations," I said, neutrally. "Do you know what you're doing next?"

"Yes. Leonard Fawcett called me into his office last week."

"Good news?" I asked, ignoring his downbeat tone. I never felt particularly sorry for anyone with a proper job.

"Not really," he answered, dourly. "How does 'Assistant Manager, Valletta Main Office, Malta,' strike you?"

"Not bad," I said, envious of anyone who had the chance of a change of scene.

"Not bad!" Richard snorted, disdainfully. "It's a fucking insult! It's not even a sideways transfer! They won't even trust me with my own branch, for Christ's sake! I managed to get the new building done three months ahead of schedule, on budget, with no fuss, and this is the thanks I get."

"Well, you won't die of ulcers," I said, trying to look on the bright side.

"That's what Leonard Fawcett said," Richard retorted, angrily. "He said I'd done a good job and this was The Bank's way of rewarding me: a cushy number in Malta until I reached retirement. That's not my idea of a reward."

"Did you say as much?" I asked, knowing that Richard didn't usually mince his words.

"Of course I did, and this is where it got strange: I told him I didn't want to be side-lined to some dot on the right-hand corner of the Med, and he told me that was what I could expect if I consorted with ex-Bank low-life such as you."

"He never!" I said, taken aback but oddly chuffed.

"I'm sure he was just fobbing me off with the first trivial notion that entered his skull. You were the last thing we'd spoken about before, but it seemed such a bizarre remark to make in the circumstances."

"Leonard and I never quite saw eye to eye from when we had to share that house together in Saudi," I said, thinking back. "But we didn't quarrel or hate each other anymore than was normal in such situations. He regarded me as a pretentious prick and I just thought he was a bit of an oik – perfect Bank material! We made no bones about either opinion and that was that, as far as I was aware."

"Not for him, apparently, because he went on to say that he hoped you'd put your Bank days behind and, as far as he was concerned, you were no longer 'Bank news'."

"Charming!" I said. "I don't see why I should forget a dozen quite important years of my life."

"I think he might have been referring to the other dozen quite important years of your life," Richard suggested, quietly.

"So that's what's making me so interesting. I'm box office poison!" I exclaimed, almost with pride.

"Whatever," Richard said, obviously wanting to steer the conversation back to the main track. "Apropos of nothing, I'm entitled, at Bank expense, to one official farewell party before I set off for Malta and I wondered if you'd like to come."

"You're shittin' me! Richard, you really are the gift that keeps on giving!" I whooped, eagerly. "I can't think of anything more invigorating than an official Bank farewell party!"

"I knew you'd be touched! They've given me the hospitality suite on the 42nd floor of the new building. Some of the brass will turn up, but not that many, I'm sure. The rest I'm allowed to invite myself, so naturally I thought of you. Can I count you in?"

"You betcha!" I cried, gleefully. "I can't think of a more fabulously inappropriate guest!"

"My sentiments entirely!" he rejoined. "And hopefully our friend Leonard Fawcett will be making an appearance, so you can catch up on old times!"

"Oh, I can't wait! I *promise* I'll be on best behaviour."

"I know I can always rely on you for that," he cooed, indulgently. "I'll tell you the details when they give me a date."

That wasn't the only invitation I received that week. For reasons best known to those involved, I received an e-mail request to attend a charity event the following Monday. It gave me an illusion of popularity, at least. It was a champagne reception at a swanky goods emporium in the West End between 6.30 and 8.00 pm. The charity at stake was Homeless Concern, which was no concern of mine, and carried a £25 entrance spank. Although champagne was not my preferred weapon of choice, I reckoned if I put my head to it I could drink £25 worth in the allotted time. It was, after all, for charity.

I spent the weekend on my own again. My flatmate had disappeared with his girlfriend to the big blue yonder, leaving me at liberty to investigate the significance of a dodgy DVD that had come attached to the latest copy of *Sluts 'n' Butts* magazine that I'd purchased from Mr Patel's Local Literary Experience earlier in the week.

I resolved to make an occasion of the occasion, so I headed down to Insanesbury's to buy a bottle of Bulgarian wine substitute and some animal remains to toss in the zapper for supper. I passed the other desultory Saturday evening shoppers: some often oddly mismatched couples, he older and English, she miniature and Oriental, neither looking quite so happy under the stark strip lighting of a British supermarket as their kitchen photographs would have them, rolling as they were, somewhere in some glorious honeymoon surf, ten or so years before. *Oh, pot noir*, I deliberated, thinking of Angelita as I made my way towards the ready meals section. I was just checking the ingredients of a box of in-store brand minimum 8% meat content spaghetti bolognaise from their Lonely Bachelor selection (good, but not a patch on Waitmore's Billy No-Mates range), when a face I vaguely registered hovered into view from behind the mixed olives and tofu enclosure. It was Roger Staples, the present incumbent Chairman of The Pan Asian Bank. 'Present' was the operative word. What luck! This was a gift I was not going to pass on.

"Hello, sir!" I hailed, deferentially, hoping he wouldn't notice the half dozen boxes of Wet Wipes on special I'd surreptitiously slipped into my trolley a few moments earlier.

He didn't recognise me. How hurtful! We'd once been co-signatories of a Pan Asian subsidiary I'd had to look after in the dim and distant past.

"James Mallet," I said, putting my hand forward. He took it hesitantly. At that moment an immaculately coiffed woman appeared by his side.

"Mrs Staples?" I ventured, as politely as possible.

"*Lady* Staples," she corrected pointedly, looking at me as if I'd just pleasured a mongoose.

I'd selectively forgotten that Roger Staples, or rather Sir Roger Staples, had been knighted the previous year for 'services to the financial industry', having just transferred fourteen thousand call-centre jobs to India and put The Pan Asian at the forefront of the sub-prime mortgage market in America, not to mention relocating the entire head office operation from its comfortable premises in the City to the dire panopticon of Docklands. He was also Leonard Fawcett's boss.

I apologised to Lady Staples for my oversight and congratulated them both on their elevated status.

"What with the new headquarters in the Canary Islands," I oozed, ingratiatingly, "it must have been quite a year for you, Sir Roger."

"Canary Wharf, James," he redressed stiffly, putting me to rights.

"Oh, different thing altogether! I laughed, affably.

"Do you work for The Bank?" Lady Staples enquired, tentatively.

"Good God, no!" I replied, with continued joviality. "I used to, but I got out as soon as I could. All the plum jobs seemed to go to the lads with unplummy voices. There was absolutely no point being socio-economic group A1 and being sent to, say, the Solomon Islands; it was a complete waste of being posh. That's why all the good people left."

"But I went to Weybridge," Sir Roger protested, woundedly.

"Never heard of it," I said, dismissively. "Sounds like a car factory!"

They moved on quite quickly. I decided to go for a Chicken and Tuna pasta bake, which was very reasonably priced, given its almighty 13% minimum meat content.

I returned to the flat basking in the glow of my insubordination to Sir Roger, made even more cowardly by the fact he'd always been perfectly pleasant to me, and anyhow I'd left the organisation over twenty years before. I loved supermarkets. They had to be the greatest levellers in the world. Like cocktail parties.

I took out the suspect DVD that had come with the porno mag. It was 'Busty Housewives II'. I drew the curtains and made myself comfortable. A naked woman was making the usual odd noises by herself on a tatty brown sofa. She wasn't particularly busty. A nude man with a prick the size of a loofah appeared from nowhere and started wanking in front of her. I watched for a bit but I wasn't in the mood. He eventually came, but it was a waste of a money shot as he completely missed the tart and garnished the draylon instead. What a divan young man!

The DVD got stuck and froze before the next skit had a chance to get going, so I got up to attack the Bulgarian wine liquid, marvelling to myself about how wonderful life wasn't. I tried to drink myself into a mellow state of mind but the more I drank the more restless, irritable and discontented I became. My thoughts turned, inevitably, to Angelita and I imagined how different things would be if she'd been with me right there and then.

I put the pasta melange into the microwave and flicked on the TV. There was a blue light procedural on Five with some policemen nosing around in a dark basement with their torches and some upper class slappers talking about clothes on Six. I found a Bond film on another channel. Judi Dentures was acting her arse off. I went back to the kitchen and punched the wall. The microwave pinged to comedic effect.

Monday arrived and with it the charity reception. I got there at 6:30 p.m. sharp, mindful of my £25 drinking objective. I felt a bit foolish at the start as I was the only guest and had to project a prolonged and thoughtful interest onto the one or two exhibits on display before the room started to fill up, but at least I had a monopoly on the Monopole.

One of the first to arrive after me was Fiona Buchanan-Dunlop, a polo-playing Sloane whom I'd admired from a distance since before my prison days. Time had treated her kindly. With her salon-perfect barnet swept into girlish ringlets, she still retained the patina of a *Penthouse* centrefold. From 1986. I sidled up to her with no particular agenda, except the relief of having someone I vaguely knew to talk to. She didn't appear to remember me but I ploughed on regardless and asked her about her equestrian activities. She rambled on about the cost of horse-ownership and mentioned that she'd just had to replace her old horse trailer. I said I'd heard that her box was a bit worn out. She looked at me oddly and drifted off speak to an elderly gentleman selling raffle tickets. I hated competition. I continued my swoop for more drinks and found that by forming a pincer movement between the various incoming guests, I was able to corral a waiter into repeatedly giving me two glasses of champagne at any one time, with relative ease.

To my delight there appeared to be a dearth of men. I saw two women talking to each other. I downed one of the glasses of fizz and handed the empty to a passing waiter. I had another look at the two women and decided I was sufficiently anaesthetised to interrupt their conversation. They turned towards me as I made my approach. Neither was in the first flush of youth, but one of them, certainly the prettier of the two, had a definite *je ne sais quoi*. She had been vacuum-packed into the slinkiest pink and turquoise catsuit affair, with a gold lion's head buckle in the middle. These, together with her five inch killer heels, made her look wonderfully costumed for a benefit event in aid of the homeless. Her friend seemed small and rodent-like next to such magnificence. She was wearing a black gymslip over her bony frame which did her no favours, although she looked pleased with the effect. I halted precariously in front of them. They looked at me expectantly.

"Good evening, girls!" I said, instantly regretting my form of address. "Can I join you for a moment? I was feeling a bit beached over there on my own."

"Beached? Awash more like!" Catwoman remarked, with what could have passed for an indulgent smile.

"Is it that obvious?" I said, taken aback but willing to play to her comment. "May I introduce myself and ask your names?"

"You can if you get us another drink," Ratgirl snarled, show-casing her sharp little incisors against her painted lips.

"Of course," I said, mildly irked by Ratgirl's terms of business, but relieved to find a lithesome waitress half their age close by to serve us.

"My name's James... James Mallet," I started, once the waitress had finished ministering to our requirements. "Now may I ask you who you two are?"

Catwoman pounced first.

"Certainly Mr Mallet! I'm Emma Behr and this is my friend..." Her voice trailed off. We looked at each other curiously, as if we'd met before but didn't know where. I examined her face. The thin latticework of lines around her swimming-pool blue eyes and her rich but greying hair could not disguise that at her zenith, maybe twenty years earlier, she must have been quite something. Perhaps she was even lovelier now than before, exuding as she did a certain warmth in her faded glory that, like a pressed flower, may have eluded her when younger. I slowly took her hand and shook it gently, but Ratgirl was becoming irritated by my awe-struck manner.

"And I'm Beryl Holmes-Smith," she asserted. I quickly decoupled my hand from Emma's and grasped Ratgirl firmly by her prehensile claw.

"How do you do, Beryl?" I said, stiffly. "I take it you two are familiar friends."

"You can take it how you like," Emma brushed aside, resuming the lead. "But how about you, Mr Mallet? What's your function?"

"My function? To get totally drunk, of course," I said, thinking inanity was the best, if only card I had to play. "What's yours?"

"I wouldn't say it's to get totally drunk," she giggled, tellingly. "But I do like a party."

Beryl looked unmoved by our exchange and didn't seem inclined to join in, but nor would she leave us alone. It didn't matter. I had broken the ice with Emma, which was a welcome plus for an otherwise unremarkable evening. We had a few more drinks as they came by and the girls soon joined me on my inebriated cloud.

The waiters ceased serving on time and started encouraging people to leave. The girls suggested we resume our drinking elsewhere, but I sensed something expensive about them that made me hold back. I had done very well, alcoholically, and decided to bolt while I was still in one piece. The girls weren't taking 'no' for an answer, but the more they pushed, the more inclined I was to think what they really wanted was a stooge to stand them drinks for the rest of the night. They gave up in the end, but not before I'd obtained their numbers on the premise that we would continue the ritual another time. Beryl's number was, of course, a formality but Emma's was a triumph.

I let them drift off into the night in search of fun and stood my turn at the queue for my coat. I looked at the phone numbers. Emma's had the same area prefix as mine. That was handy! Maybe there could be life without Angelita. Emma would be a welcome diversion, at the very least.

What was not such a welcome diversion was seeing Christine Hale, also in the coat queue. I wasn't too put out this late in the day. It was the sort of corny event she would turn up to, if someone else was paying, but I couldn't see anyone with her.

"Hi, James!" she called, as she noisily barged up the line to join me. "It was so good catching you at Mick Burton's party before Christmas. You looked incredible in that mask! Just like a murderer, in fact!"

"Christine, must you talk quite so loudly?" I shushed.

"It's OK, James!" she said, breezily ignoring my request. "And who was that girl you were with at the party? I could tell she was no shrinking violet! One or two guys said she's into advertising… in telephone boxes. Is that right?"

Now was not the moment to explain the mix-up with the fancy dress theme. Mercifully we had reached the front of the queue.

"That one over there," I said to the attendant, hurriedly pointing out my coat.

"How much does a street treat cost these days?" Christine persisted, piercingly.

I wasn't playing.

"Never mind," she continued, disappointed. "I'm sure she was worth every penny!"

"Thank you, Christine," I said tersely, as I grabbed the coat. "Always a delight when we meet."

"Not leaving a tip?" she cried, as I hastily made for the exit, then seeing no reaction shouted, "'Bye, James! Looking for a pay and spray again? There's a spank-bank just around the corner if you want one!"

I wasn't humiliated. I was just worn out by Christine's ability to get under my skin and get one over me every time we chanced upon each other. What was it with that girl? What had I done those two decades ago to warrant such vitriol every time we met? And what was it about her that kept my pilot light of anger so aflame? I didn't have an answer to either question, but I did have a hankering for another drink. A proper one this time. I was feeling decidedly 'restless, irritable and discontent'.

I caught the tube and wove my way back to the flat. Except for Christine's curtain call there had been ample reward for the £25 forfeit, although I felt a bit strange. I wasn't drunk, but my legs seemed to be. I nearly fell over a couple of times, which was strange. I fixed myself a large whisky when I got home and thought nothing more of it.

I called Theresa Batomata, the woman I wanted to target for Sven Gläzner's job openings at Dresden Commercial Bank at her Citigroup office the following day. She remembered me. I furtively implied that I was working on Dresden Commercial Bank's behalf and was looking for top-quality candidates to enhance their London operations. She wasn't able to talk at will at that moment, but said she could see me after work to discuss the matter at greater length.

We met at a bar outside her office. She hadn't changed much. She was still pretty, married now, but had much the same get-up-and-go attitude as when we'd first become acquainted, many years ago. I told her as much as I knew about the Dresden Commercial Bank deal.

"It sounds interesting," she said, as my hopes started to rise. "But not to me."

My shoulders sagged a little, but only for a moment.

"However, I do know people who'd have a look, if the price was right. And they're good people. Take my little sister Deidre for one; she's in the market and looking for a change. It's the perfect time. Bonuses have been paid; some people are happy, some aren't. If there's a more responsible position with more money you should talk to her, but it's got to be bulletproof and no bullshit, do you understand? Nothing cutesy or your arse will be toast – OK?"

She gave me her sister's number. I thanked her with fawning gratitude.

"That's all right," she said, less guardedly. "I'll try to put together some other ideas. Let's see how this one goes with my little sister, but be discreet."

Richard Hartley called to give me the date for his leaving party at the new Pan Asian Bank headquarters the following month. Things were looking up. Things were happening. I phoned Emma Behr to see if she was free to go out to supper sometime. As I expected she didn't live far away and we agreed to meet at a restaurant close by. We had a good evening and drank too much. The bill was a bit of a parking ticket, but it was the only way in. It turned out she'd been widowed a few years before. Her husband had been a Swiss businessman who'd left her and their offspring sufficiently well provided for that she didn't need to worry about money, but she was bored. We went back to her flat for a nightcap and what I hoped would be a bit more, but that didn't happen. I could look but I couldn't touch. She had children and a 'B'-list lifestyle I couldn't match. I didn't mind too much. For once I was happy just to look.

Chapter 15: Contrition

I held Sven Gläzner to his proposal that we should meet for lunch to discuss his staffing situation and called him soon after he started work at Dresden Commercial Bank, or DCBI as he preferred, not far from my own office. He told me about his game plan and the parameters of his hiring strategy. He was pleased that I'd done some research in advance and let me put forward some suggestions. I mentioned Theresa Batomata's little sister Deidre to him, as an *hors d'oeuvre* at the junior end, and an Italian fellow I'd been talking to as a main course at the meatier end. Sven was open to both recommendations and gave me the go-ahead to set the wheels in motion for him to interview them.

I met the two candidates separately soon afterwards. Both were amenable. Deidre was cheerful and willing, whereas the Italian was a bit dour but a heavier hitter. They passed their interviews and by the end of the month I had an efficient production line of useful applicants going in to see DCBI. Sven was happy and I responded in kind by taking him to a few strip joints, which he appreciated. At last I was able to see capitalism at work, from the inside. At last I was playing a true part in it: I was a pimp, in every sense.

The evening of Richard Hartley's farewell party at the new Pan Asian Bank building in Canary Wharf soon arrived. It was a Saturday and, but for the small flicker of activity as people arrived for the party, the entire zone was as dead as the moon above it. For practical as well as cosmetic reasons I had decided to hire a car and driver for the occasion, but my sense of self-importance was soon pricked.

A car as big as a whale drove past my rented Nissan before turning into the junction leading to the new PABS headquarters and pulling up in front of me at the main entrance. Either it, or its PABS number plates seemed immediately to arouse the doorman's confusion and he leapt to open its rear door with a demented curtsey as the thing came to a halt. Much to my annoyance, Leonard Fawcett emerged with a shit-eating scowl and his elegant Indian wife by his side. The doorman saluted with the precision recoil of a Glock 33. Leonard nodded a terse acknowledgement and led his wife through the entrance. Leonard had chubbed out quite a bit since I'd last seen him, but he wasn't fat. Before he was tall; now he was big. Very big. His charabanc sped away into the night, leaving the doorman to ignore my own arrival. I let myself ignominiously out of the car as my driver sat quietly rolling a cigarette in the front.

I gave the Fawcetts a wide berth and hid behind a statue of a blob as they made their way to the express lift for the hospitality suite on the 42nd floor. (Why are they always on the 42nd?) Once they'd disappeared I came out of hiding and made my way to the reception desk. I was given a security pass the size of a prize rosette and directed towards the lift. I ripped the pass off once I was out of sight and pressed the button for the 42nd. I looked at the departmental directory etched on the granite wall and waited. It was like a hall of remembrance. It went on and on. And I'd been part of it once, not that many people would remember me now.

The lift door opened just as a couple appeared beside me. I let them go in first. Their expressions matched the granite.

"Thank you," said the man. He was American.

I pressed level 42. It was the only button.

"Bank?" he asked.

"Was," I replied. "I used to work with Richard. I'm James Mallet."

I offered my hand. He took it. His grip was vice-like. It was like being clasped by a prosthetic clamp.

"Norman Tranvic," he said. "Securities and Investment Department," then added, almost as an afterthought, "and this is my wife, Adele."

I took her hand just as the blood flow was returning to mine. She looked a bit of a dumpster and judging from the cursory nature of his introduction, her husband thought likewise. I should have recognised Norman's face from the press coverage he'd received since he'd joined PABS a few months before. He had been brought in at vast expense from Goldbergs to give a much needed shot of chutzpah into the PABS's flagging capital markets division. There had been quite a commotion at the time about the Pan Asian at last breaking with tradition and hiring from outside. That together with its recent bid for pole position in the American sub-prime market had made Norman Tranvic a very serious member of The Bank's pecking order indeed. And the highest paid, although for reasons best known to The Bank, he hadn't been made a main board director.

The lift made its journey too swiftly for us to take the conversation further. A security guard waved us towards the function rooms where Richard's party was taking place. I was surprised that the Tranvics were going to such a lowly event.

"Richard was very helpful with assisting my department's move to these new premises," Norman Tranvic explained, sensing my disconnect.

Richard was at the front of the foyer, greeting his guests as they came in.

"Norman... Adele! How nice of you to come!" he exclaimed, deliriously. If he'd been a dog his tail could have knocked over the Venus de Milo. "And James! What a delight! Have you met Norman and Adele Tran..."

His voice trailed off as he watched the Tranvics make a bee-line straight towards the crowd.

"We introduced ourselves," I said, feeling slightly wretched for him. His wife, Patty, was doing her bit circulating around the throng, but he cut a lonely dash now as the rest of the room buzzed along without him. It was as if he was hosting his own wake.

"I hate this sort of thing," he said, wiping a bead of sweat from his brow.

"It goes with the job," I commiserated. "Anyway it will probably be your last big gig for quite a while."

"That's true," he sniffed, relaxing a little. "I can't see management beating a path to Valletta three years hence when I'm finally thrown off Bank property for the last time."

"Talking of management," I said, looking at all the suits, "I thought you said you weren't expecting much royalty tonight."

"Well, that's what I thought," he said, looking round. "But you know how Bank people operate: they feed off each other because they haven't got a social life outside in the real world. That or there wasn't anything on telly tonight. One thing's for sure... these people aren't all here just for me."

Another cluster of guests arrived for Richard to attend to, so I moved into the main reception room. I hardly knew anyone. The Bank had got too big. Most of the men were wearing PABS logo ties and I even spotted a few PABS scarves wrapped round the throats of some of the womenfolk. It was Saturday night, for crying out loud! For my part, it was like being in a class reunion at a school I'd never attended.

Eventually I spotted a lone civilian. It was Richard's sister Cheryl, looking bored. I hadn't seen her since leaving The Bank. She'd always been sceptical of PABS shtick, so we'd inevitably bonded. I crept up behind and whispered "Cunt" gently into her ear.

"James, you old poo stain! Thank God there's someone here with a pulse at last!" she cried out, whirling round, not too worried about her volume control. "I don't know why Richard insists on dragging me out to these bloody things. He hates them more than I do. Moral support, I assume. Fat chance! I've got nothing in common with these stiffs. What kind of fresh Hell is this? All they talk about is the bloody Bank and who's been promoted or left behind. Honestly, there's more life in a morgue than this overpriced ice bucket. Do you still smoke?"

"Of course," I replied, indignantly.

"Oh, good!" she said, cheering up. "Fancy a lungster? It'll give us a chance to get away from this concrete filing cabinet and do some catching up."

We headed for the lift, made our way to ground zero and lit our cigarettes under the moonlit silhouette of the new building. I asked her about her life and told her a little about mine.

"Do you miss The Bank?" she asked, out of the blue.

"Occasionally." I weighed up the reasons why. "While I was in it I couldn't wait to get out, but I'd be the first to admit I miss the security of working for a large organisation."

"What security?" she snorted, contemptuously. "You never know where they're going to send you. You never have any say in anything and nowadays they'd just as soon fire you at the end of an assignment as come up with a sensible alternative. Just look at Richard."

"He wasn't fired," I remonstrated.

"He might just as well have been as far as he's concerned," she grunted, cooling down a bit. "You know what he's like. I don't think Assistant Manager, Valletta Main Office is Richard's idea of a meaningful existence; to him it's more like corporate burial"

"He's still got the protection of a two-thirds final salary pension to look forward to in three years' time."

"Protection is its own form of prison."

I blew a smoke ring.

"It's the sort of prison I would quite welcome at the moment," I said, thinking of my personal lack of future provision.

We finished our cigarettes and stamped the butts into the ground. Cheryl suggested going to a pub, if we could find one, but I hadn't hired a car and driver just for that. I tried to convince her of our social obligations.

"Think of Richard. You did mention moral support," I reasoned.

"Bollocks," she said, following me reluctantly. "I'd rather bleed to death in a warm bath. You and I don't work for The Bank, therefore we're not part of it, and if we're not part of it we might as well not exist as far as that lot are concerned. I don't need to suck that kind of dick."

She had a point but nevertheless stomped petulantly into the reception in front of me. We became separated as Cheryl went to look for Richard and I went in search of a drink. Just as I was casting about for a waiter I caught the Fawcetts wandering between two groups. Leonard's face fell when he saw me.

"Mallet? I didn't expect to see you here. What an unpleasant surprise," he sniped, I hoped in jest. "I thought I warned Richard not to associate with people like you. I'm shocked that you got through security. We don't normally allow convicted felons on Bank property."

"Hush, Leonard! Must you be so rude?" his wife chided, with an apologetic glance to me.

I knew Leonard's wife was a doctor and that they had met when he was manager of the PABS office in Mumbai.

"Don't waste your sympathy, Rania," Leonard growled.

"I'm so sorry about him, Mr Mallet," she persisted, ignoring her husband. "He has the manners of a guttersnipe."

"Do call me James, please, Dr Fawcett," I urged, gratefully.

"And I'm Rania," she said, offering her delicate, nut-brown hand. "I think I've heard Leonard mention your name before."

"You bet you have," he muttered, rolling his eyes heavenwards. "As if being in Saudi Arabia wasn't enough, I had to put up with this amoeba for the better part of two years. It was enough to turn a man to drink, which is no mean feat in a place like Saudi."

"You made enough of the stuff to fill a lake, as I recall," I said, thinking that I might be touching on a nicely sore point given his current standing in the company. "Besides, I thought we had quite a good time."

"Good time?" Leonard cried, in disbelief. "You were the most puffed up little prick that walked God's earth; living with you was tantamount to purgatory!"

"I'm sorry to hear that," I said, unrepentantly.

"You were stuck up and useless," he emphasised, straying I thought beyond the boundaries of normal banter. I didn't mind.

"I think it might be good to put things in perspective, Leonard," I said, trying to rein in his fervour. "You were suited to living overseas and I wasn't; you liked working for The Bank and I didn't."

"Well what did you expect?" he challenged. "If you join The Pan Asian Bank's overseas division, there's a fair chance that you'll end up working overseas for The Pan Asian Bank, right?"

"That's all very well, Leonard," I said, beginning to rise to his derision. "But I wasn't expecting to be working and having to cohabit with people like you. Sure, I was making a living, but I was living a lie. That's why I left: it wasn't a normal life. By the way, do you still call the lavatory 'the toilet'?"

"Oh, fuck off Mallet," he said, dismissing my attempt at social one-upmanship. "If you were 'normal life', you'd come level with a sea urchin."

"Stop it Leonard!" Rania Fawcett commanded, firmly. "Why are you always so confrontational? Pipe down, for goodness' sake."

"All right," he acquiesced reluctantly, as he turned to lead her away. "Let's move on. I need to talk to Norman."

"Talking of Norman," I said, gently, "isn't it strange giving orders to a man who's on four times your salary?"

Leonard stopped in his tracks, his face suddenly going puce.

"Yes, I'm looking into that," he said, with a faraway gaze. "Come on, Rania. I'm fed up with talking to this insect."

"Insect?" I enquired, brightly. "First I was an amoeba, then a sea urchin, now I'm an insect! Nature or nurture?   Do I see evolution? This is flattery indeed! Especially from a reptile of your stature!"

"Darling, you talk to Norman Tranvic; I know you'll want some privacy. I need to speak to James about something, nothing to do with The Bank," Rania pronounced, to Leonard's annoyance. And my surprise.

"Suit yourself," he said, and left us to it.

"I'm so sorry, James," she reiterated, as Leonard disappeared from view. "Leonard's been under quite a lot of pressure recently. It's not an excuse, but it may be a reason. He's been snarling at everyone who's come within biting distance. Part of the problem is he's now so senior he can get away with it; there's no one who stands up to him, except the Chairman and the Chief Executive Officer.   And me, sometimes."

I looked at her and smiled.

"Then he's in good hands – sometimes," I said, feeling considerably calmer now that Leonard had disappeared. "I know you both met in Mumbai, but beyond that I don't know the circumstances."

"There was nothing wildly exciting about our courtship," Rania started, also regaining her composure in Leonard's absence. "The Bank doctor referred Leonard to me when he was in Mumbai. I specialise in liver function. Leonard had contracted hepatitis while working in the Middle East and was sent to see me when it started bothering him again in India. He saw me a couple of times and we liked each other. He started inviting me to occasional functions when he needed a bit of local respectability by his side. I was there, and before we knew it, we were an item. Very dull really, but I've had the opportunity to see some places I wouldn't normally have gone to and I've been able to continue working wherever we've been sent. There's never been any shortage of business for me, especially amongst the expatriates and Bank personnel, both past and present. That's what I wanted to talk to you about."

I gave her a sideways glance. She was looking straight at me.

"James, do you drink?"

"A bit," I mumbled, coyly.

"I thought so," she said, staring me right in the face.

"Why do you ask?" I queried, defensively.

"Your eyes look jaundiced," she remarked. "You might like to get yourself checked. Have a blood test. You may have a vitamin deficiency; B1 probably. I suggest you contact your GP or give me a call if you want to talk about it."

"Thanks, Rania," I mumbled, awkwardly. "I might have a problem. I'm on an alcohol reduction regime at the moment, but I can't say it's having much effect."

"They seldom do. Not for your sort. I've seen a lot of people like you die of this contemptible disease. Take the expatriate staff: they drop like flies. The Bank doesn't seem to care; cuts down on pensions, I expect."

"Alcoholism and The Bank aren't exactly strangers to each other," I remarked, reflectively. "But it's everywhere else you look as well."

"Comfort in numbers?" Rania queried, looking at me closely again.

"Only cold comfort, I suppose."

"And that's all you'll get if you don't seek proper help," she remonstrated.

"I'll call my GP. For some reason my legs have been playing up recently. I nearly fell over a couple of times the other day and I wasn't even particularly drunk..."

"Sounds like peripheral neuropathy to me. Call me if you need a second opinion. Leonard's secretary knows how to get hold of me."

"Thanks. I appreciate your concern."

"I think you deserve it. You lived with Leonard for two years!"

We both smiled. We talked about India for a while. I told her about Angelita and the predicament I was now facing.

"That could be tricky," she deduced. "It was OK for me. I had The Bank to fall back on. It has its own internal society with hundreds of mixed marriages, so it was no big deal for me moving here, but for a young Goan girl on her own who's never left India before... now that's a different story."

"That's rather what I was thinking," I said, glad of her insight.

"Listen James," she said, as if suddenly remembering where she was, "I'd better catch up with Leonard or he'll be even more impossible, but you will keep in touch? I'd like to know how you're getting on."

With that she disappeared to join her husband and the growing coterie of fawning courtiers around him.

What an excellent woman! Utterly wasted on Leonard, I thought to myself, but I suspected she'd known what she was letting herself in for. A rich husband for one thing. I hung around a bit longer and had a few more drinks to justify the cost of the journey. I spoke to a few PABS ties, but they were either thrusting young bucks too stupid to know their own unimportance, or timid oldsters too frightened to be anything other than pleasant for fear of losing their jobs. I'd booked the car for four hours round trip and my time was nearly up. I said my goodbyes and thank-yous to Richard and Patty and blew a kiss across the room at Cheryl as I exited towards the lift.

The driver dropped me back home. I tipped him sufficiently and climbed the stairs to my flat. But for my brush with Leonard, the evening had been like my tip to the driver: sufficient. It was good seeing Cheryl again, and Rania Fawcett was lovely, if a little direct. I felt a twinge of guilt as I poured myself a large Scotch, but it tasted delicious. At least my legs had behaved themselves for the duration, but I made a mental note to look up 'peripheral neuropathy' on the computer when I got into the office on Monday. I shivered as I finished my drink and got up to pour another. My legs were starting to go.

I hit the computer first thing that week and looked up 'peripheral neuropathy'. I clicked my way through the various websites. I didn't particularly like what I saw: 'The most common form mainly affects the feet and legs... muscle weakness... twitching... tingling... loss of sensation... loss of balance and co-ordination...' That was me. '... bladder dysfunction (e.g. incontinence) and sexual dysfunction...' Not me, surely? Not yet, please! I moved on to the causes. 'Vitamin deficiencies and alcoholism... alcoholic neuropathy... dizziness, fainting...blah, blah, blah... cutting back on alcohol... nerve damage... complications... decreased self-esteem... alcoholism... alcohol... alcoholism...'

Wonderful; just wonderful. Couldn't a man enjoy himself once in a while? I stared at the screen and rubbed my chin, wondering where I stood - if I stood - in terms of damage already done, or portents of things to come. Description or prediction? Confused, I grabbed my jacket and marched out of the office in search of an early morning off-licence. I didn't have to look far.

I returned to the office feeling refreshed. I gave Richard a ring to thank him for the party and wished him well in Malta. I was sorry that he was going, but I hoped his new job might bring an end to his theorising about The Bank's dark side, if there was one.

"It's a good time to let that one go, don't you think?" I proposed just before we signed off.

"You can, if you want," he replied, testily. "But the facts speak for themselves. On another level, one thing I do know is that you haven't gone off radar as far as Leonard Fawcett's concerned. I don't know what you said to him at my party but you rattled his cage quite convincingly. I spoke to him later and I can't say he's your number one fan."

"*Quelle catastrophe!*" I squealed, delighted. "What can he do? Post me as tea boy to PABS Huddersfield?"

Emma Behr, my new drinking friend and latter-day object of wishful thinking called a few days later to ask if I could escort her to a wedding reception that coming Saturday. I was 'Mr Invitations'! The reception was being held at a boutique hotel in Knightsbridge, just a mile down the road. I knew for sure I wouldn't be doing anything else, and willingly agreed to act as her chaperone. I said I'd drop in on her and we'd take a taxi together to the hotel.

Annoyingly the party wasn't due to start till later in the afternoon, which meant staying a long time sober. I gave up at around lunchtime and opened a bottle of wine. It didn't last very long, so I opened another.

I was swaying slightly as I made my way over to Emma's and vaguely regretted confronting the second bottle. Fortunately Emma had made considerable inroads into a bottle of champagne herself, so I helped her finish what was left and we lurched in affectionate unison out of her flat to find a cab.

We arrived there in no time, dumped our coats at the cloakroom and made our way past the lobby to the main reception area. Emma seemed to know a lot of people. They were her world. I wasn't in the mood to be introduced so I teetered towards a quiet bar behind the lobby and bought a drink on my own. Eventually I plucked up the courage to re-enter the party. I wandered, slightly out of my box, between the various guests and tried to drink myself back to sobriety. I spent an hour making indifferent small talk to complete strangers before silence was called and the speeches began.

Although I had met the nuptial couple once or twice before, the family guests meant nothing to me. I felt remote and uninvolved. I was uncomfortable and regretted coming. I wasn't a proper guest and, while it was not a large event, I couldn't see Emma anywhere. I didn't care. She'd probably found another tippler to tattle with.

The speeches ended and a small four-piece band struck a short marital refrain before launching into its orchestral version of 'Save All Your Kisses For Me'. It was far too early for dancing. As I could hardly put one foot in front of the other I decided to do the decent thing and vanish before I caused any injuries. Some other people were also leaving and once again I found myself standing in a queue to get my coat. It was moving at the customary snail's pace. I heard a voice behind me that I recognised. I looked round. It was Russell Crouch, the prominent newspaper editor and broadcaster, with a sultry, telegenic lady friend. He had an early slot on a London radio station, a programme called *Russell's Bustle* that I liked listening to. I wanted to say something nice. I turned to introduce myself.

"Hello! You don't know me, but I know you! I listen to *Russell's Bustle* nearly every morning. It's very good."

He thanked me. We stood in awkward silence. The queue really wasn't moving very quickly. Somebody had to say *something!*

"It's an excellent show," I said, repeating the point I'd just made.

"Thank you," he said again.

"No, you really are *the* moral compass," I reiterated, in all sincerity. His chest swelled a button as his lady friend looked on indulgently.

Silence again. Now what? Why wouldn't he say anything? I began to panic, but my intoxication took care of everything.

"Unfortunately," I continued, ponderingly, "you tend to start your broadcast at about the same time in the morning as I start to masturbate, and I always have to switch you off just as you're getting interesting."

Why on earth did I say that? If it was a joke it had fallen desperately flat, and to cap it all, I had to add: "So I wondered if there'd be any chance that you could start your programme a little earlier or, perhaps, a little later?"

Shut up! Shut up! Shut up!

They looked at me askance, Russell in total bewilderment and his companion in utter disgust.

"I'll see what I can do," he replied, meekly.

I turned back, my ears smouldering under the embers of my self-inflicted embarrassment, and started to examine my cloakroom ticket as if it were a Fabergé egg. Mercifully it was soon my turn at the front of the queue. I grabbed my coat and ran, avoiding any further eye contact with the beleaguered couple.

I jumped on a bus, sat down and breathed a sigh of relief. Was the episode a case of Christine's Curse or simply another example of my drunken idiocy? It didn't matter, as long as I was going home.

Emma called the next morning.

"What happened to you?" she demanded.

"I'm sorry." I said, repentantly. "I needed to go home. I didn't see you; I was a bit pissed."

"You can say that again," she remarked, unsympathetically. "I bumped into Russell Crouch and his girlfriend, just as they were leaving and they asked who you were."

"So?" I said, trying to sound unconcerned.

"Russell told me what you'd said to him."

"Oh, that!" I said, laughing. "It was quite funny. He looked a bit shocked!"

"Shocked?" Emma fumed. "He was disgusted. It was pathetic. Russell Crouch is a very close friend of mine and bitch-slapping him with stupid comments reflects pretty badly on me."

"I'm sorry," I repeated, pitifully. "I'd obviously had a bit too much to drink."

"A bit!" she spluttered. "You were completely off your face before you started. That wasn't cool, James. I'll admit I was a bit merry myself, but this was a special occasion and I specifically asked if I could bring you as my partner. And so what did you do? You let me down. Other people kept asking me how I knew you and whether you were OK. You could hardly stand up. It was demeaning. I like a drink, but you were dreadful. You've got to do something about yourself, James. You can't go around like that."

I felt slightly remorseful as I made my way to the office that Monday. Emma didn't get upset easily, but this time I'd clearly gone too far. However there were other things I had to think about. Angelita's letters were becoming less loving and more demanding with each post. Gone were the days when I'd get an erection just looking at her handwriting; now it only made me sad. She wanted answers. She said unless she heard some indication of a positive response, she'd assume the whole thing was 'one big fat "no"'. Also I was trying to get as many people as possible in front of Sven Gläzner before he filled his quota at DCBI by other means. To add to it all, Elspeth had started to put pressure on me to attend rehab or a detox centre at least, but I couldn't go *now*. I had too much on my plate. Perturbed, I gave Wally Barker a call. Perhaps, I reasoned, he might provide some solace in place of Peregrine's recent, less than cathartic consultation. Wally mentioned a quiet pub near his office.

He was well into his first pint by the time I got there. He ordered one for me and we stayed at the bar undisturbed.

"So James, I can't imagine you called to talk to me about work," he assumed, correctly. "So what's up?"

I mentioned various issues I was having with Elspeth, Emma Behr and other things that were on my mind, all of which, I said, were secondary to the painful quandary of what to do about Angelita.

"Ah, Peregrine did mention that you were having a spot of confusion on that front," Wally said distractedly, looking more interested in the formation of froth on his beer than any froth concerning my personal life, but was polite enough to ask, "And is it coming to crunch time, by any chance?"

"Or not," I responded, dully. "You don't mind playing father confessor for a few moments, do you?"

"Delighted to be of service," he said, looking anything but, "although I'm slightly out of touch on matters romantic; I've been married far too long, I'm afraid."

"That's exactly why I called you," I said, quickening up. "You know a thing or two about matrimony and fatherhood, or you should. I wondered how it works, for you, in a nutshell."

"Bottom line?"

"Whatever you've got," I answered, aware that there was a danger that he might drone on a bit.

"Logistically, it's a nightmare," he began. "Especially with children, who you've got to look upon as cost centres, which should come as no surprise."

"Go on," I coaxed.

"To the uninitiated, and by that I mean you, I expect the whole process looks to be fraught with difficulties, and up to a point that's often the case," he continued, "but everyone seems to be perfectly capable of overcoming them, and I don't see why you should be the exception."

I waited while he collected his thoughts.

"It depends on what you want. If you're a man of normal means and character, it's financially crippling and emotionally draining, all of which will go completely unacknowledged by those who benefit from your hard graft. However," he said, drawing breath for a split second, "if you cut your cloth accordingly, you might just get away with it."

"It doesn't sound much like fun," I ventured, despondently.

"It isn't. Well, not all the time," Wally affirmed. "But on the odd occasion that things go right, then there is no finer feeling a man could wish for. And in your case, if you're prepared to wander around in Economy Class, marriage needn't be expensive. The State's there to educate, medicate and adjudicate, and as long as your expectations don't go any further than consigning your life to sitting in front of a telly the size of a ping-pong table in a house the size of an egg box, having your weekly treat at The Little Chef and taking the family for the fortnight's annual torture in Port Grimbo or Alicante, then that world is yours. But that's it. If, however, you wish to go Business Class, then you have to be prepared to pay more."

He left it there, enigmatically.

"Have you finished?" I asked, disappointedly.

"I could go on, like I normally do, but you're a grown man; you already know what it's all about as much as I do. There's nothing to know really; it's completely open to chance. When you think of all the things that could go wrong, matrimony, parenthood and the inevitable sexual Saharas that follow would seem very foolish undertakings, but that's never stopped anyone. Also, you've got to consider the alternatives. Do you want to spend the rest of your life in your current state? Are you happy travelling alone?"

"However I travel, it'll have to be Economy for me," I remarked, balefully.

"And what difference does it make, really? You can still drink in Economy."

"That's another problem," I said, now growing utterly depressed.

"It will be if you don't get me another pint," Wally chided.

I smiled and signalled to the barman.

I came away from my meeting with Wally as confused as I was after last seeing Peregrine, but my confusion was exacerbated a few days later by another call from Emma. Once again she wanted me to escort her to an event with which I had only tenuous connections, but this time it was as if she were exacting a penance for my crimes of the previous weekend. The order, for that effectively was what it was, was to accompany her to her son's Third Eleven hockey match on the coming Saturday afternoon at his school just outside London, against my own alma mater, St Dweeb's College.

I could have thought of several things I would rather have done, but in the spirit of absolution, I accepted.

"Bring a hip flask!" she barked, with the double standards of an experienced drinker. "And make it a big one! It might be cold out there."

Any excuse would do.

We drove the short distance and drew up by some playing fields where various matches were taking place. Her son's game had already started. It was a bit boring. Neither side was good enough to warrant much excitement, and the boys kept bumping into each other or missing the ball. There were a few parents in small groups by the touchline, good-naturedly cheering things on. They were happy, young and rich. The Bentley Mulsannes and Porsche Cayenne Wankmasters parked nearby said it all. It was a world I could allude to as an old boy, but not as a parent. Craig's assessment of my procreative situation was unnervingly accurate: only the fortunate and the unfortunate could afford children. There was no middle road. Not for me.

A man trussed up in a greatcoat and trilby was marching up and down the touchline bellowing: "Come on, Dweeby! Possession, Dweeby! Oh for God's sake Dweeby!"

St Dweeb's had never been called 'Dweeby' in my day. Perhaps he was a first-time buyer. Whatever, it was a milieu to which I was almost relieved to no longer belong. Emma's child joined us at half-time. He was a good kid and willingly accepted a swig from my hip flask when no one was looking. We got together again at the end of the match. The teams congratulated each other and then started boasting about their parents' cars. Not that the situation was ever likely to happen, but if it did, I was fucked if I was going to spunk thirty-five big ones against the wall year after year for that kind of shit: it was rip-off for which there would be no thanks. Fuck Business Class. Fuck Economy. I'd walk if I had to. And walk I did.

Chapter 16: Aggression

So I bit the bullet and Angelita bit the dust. She wasn't happy. Not only had I managed to turn her heart to carbon, but I'd also utterly ransacked her belief in mankind, certainly of the paler variety. Perhaps I'd been aware from the start that we were only kidding ourselves that there was any mileage in the affair, but it was the trip to Emma's son's school that really did it. It confirmed what I should have known all along: that matrimony and parenthood, especially of the sort that was on display that afternoon, were, for me, spiritually and financially out of the question. Not that I was obliged do either on the same scale as the Behr family, but it did provide a convenient, if entirely self-vindicating grounds for not being able to entertain the concept of matrimony, by simply not being in a position to provide what was required. Whether my motives were excusable or born out of contrived self-justification, once I'd made the decision, I stuck to it almost like an act of excommunication. I sent Angelita a pathetic letter of explanation by express post and then did nothing. I didn't pick up the phone at home for a month. Instead I sat tearlessly by the answering machine, listening to her messages washing over my abstract contrition as I stared blankly into space. We had been impulsive. It had been fun and fanciful but it was, unfortunately, a *folie à deux* and now the time had come for foreclosure. Or so I thought.

Things were OK at work except that business with Sven Gläzner and DCBI was running dry. Sven had more or less filled his hiring requirements. There was a limit to how many people he could take. Suddenly my cash cow lacked take. What would replace it was not immediately apparent, but a casual conversation I'd had two months previously became an earnest discussion the next, and before I knew it I had the makings of a different, more serious business proposition that was henceforth unimaginatively referred to as 'the deal', or even 'the big deal'. It didn't matter; we knew what we were referring to. It evolved into something far larger and more muscular than anything I'd done for Sven. This wasn't about moving just one heavy hitter. It was about moving an entire department of heavy hitters. My part in it had been small but nonetheless fundamental in getting the project off the ground. Without my involvement nothing would have happened. By a sheer fluke I was able to make use of one of the few contacts I still had in the Far East to access the levers that made the whole monster move; a point that was lost on some of my colleagues, I was later to find.

In the interim, between trying to eke out other means of doing business, I idly whiled away the office hours by amusing myself on the internet. I grazed through various want ads and dogging sites before I stumbled across what appeared to be a bona fide dating page that promised, for a modest fee, to relieve the subscriber of his or her immediate loneliness. As my liaison with Angelita was now a thing of the past, I felt no shame as I submitted my bank details and a cropped, finer, younger likeness of myself to the cyber-intermediary. Once my submission had been accepted, the computer proceeded to ask my particulars and preferences. Before long it returned with a shortlist of a dozen or so matches, of which I selected six of the most promising. I now had to wait for their consent to get in contact. After a while I received assent from four would-be participants. I had kept my criteria dainty and I was pleasantly surprised by the quality of the respondents. From their photographs, if they were their photographs, they appeared perfectly presentable. I pushed the copy button, numbered the printouts in order of preference and placed them in a file for further consideration.

My drinking at this time was much the same, although the effects were becoming increasingly bizarre. I started to get dizzy spells, and the symptoms of peripheral neuropathy that I had so recently read about with interest were now manifesting themselves with alarming regularity. Occasionally I attempted going cold turkey by not having any drink in the flat, knowing full well that I'd chicken out in good time to get to the off-licence. On one occasion, however, I left it too late and failed to reach the shop in time by five minutes.

I spent a fretful night writhing around and by morning was a dribbling wreck. I only just managed to put my clothes on and hobble, like a freak, out to the supermarket before I went into spasm. I fumbled in my pockets for some change to buy half a bottle of Scotch and staggered towards the photo-booth across the arcade. Once in I ripped the curtain shut and collapsed onto the swivel seat. I was barely able to put the bottle to my lips without spilling it over my clothes, but on the third attempt I managed to get some liquid down and eventually stopped shaking. That was close! I caught my reflection in the self-take machine. I looked insane. I pulled myself up, put the bottle in my pocket and made my way back to the flat in a straight line.

I ran a bath and got in with the bottle close to hand. It had been an unpleasant experience and one I vowed never to repeat. From then on

I resolved always to keep a spare bottle concealed about the premises. Just in case.

I entered the office quite calmly a bit later. The big deal had started to take on some proper definition and provided a welcome diversion from my drinking difficulties. That was the problem: as long as I felt safely within lurching distance of a bottle or had a distraction to occupy my mind, I was fine. But this was not always the case. As the deal started to take shape, a little more was expected of me - including working all hours or schmoozing various punters late into the night.

Working outside office hours had never been one of my passions, but because of the deal I was obliged, one evening, to remain upright and sober in order to meet one of the principals whose participation in the project was pivotal to its success. After two paltry beers and three gruelling hours of persuasion, I finally managed to convince him of the wisdom of moving to another company for double the money. I went home relieved, but thirsty. It was late. Nothing was open, but I wasn't too worried. I had my secret stash somewhere in the flat. Or so I thought. I couldn't find it. I looked in the last possible designated location, behind the bread bin, but there was nothing. I froze. There was nowhere else to look. In vain I tore open every cupboard and drawer in the kitchen, knowing it would be to no avail. As an alcoholic I knew I would have obsessed about replacing the errant bottle if I'd drunk it by mistake. So where had it gone? I knew my flatmate wouldn't have nabbed it; it wasn't his style. And besides, he was hardly in the flat anymore now that he was ensconced with his new girlfriend.

Then with a sickening thud I thought of Elspeth. She had keys to the flat... but even she couldn't have been that devious, surely? That she was the most likely suspect became all the more horribly imaginable, but at that moment the who or why wasn't important. What was important was to import something to drink before I went spare, but short of taking a taxi to a nightclub where I'd probably be denied entry, there was nothing I could do. At least I knew what to expect.

I dragged my feet to the bedroom and made a fruitless attempt to see if I could elicit a few drops of something from my collection of hip flasks, but they were all empty. I went to the medicine cabinet in the bathroom and found two old codeine tablets in a pill bottle. I chewed them to try to get a maximum tongue hit, but they were useless and tasted vile. With the dread of the condemned, I climbed into bed, switched off the light and cursed myself to sleep.

As sure as God made little green apples I awoke up with alcoholics' false dawn and started to sweat. It was four o' clock. What could I do? Call an ambulance? I waited till six, counting every minute, my heart pounding like a battery of howitzers on the Kaiser's birthday. Each minute seemed like an hour. I couldn't take any more. In blind panic I grabbed the phone and, with hands shaking like a water diviner's on flood alert, punched out Emma Behr's number.

She wasn't thrilled to hear from me.

"What is it?" she demanded, groggily.

"It's bad, honey," I croaked. "I've got chronic alcohol withdrawal. Can you help?"

"How?" she gasped, resentfully.

"Please... please come round with some booze... something strong... I'm about to shake myself to bits."

"I don't think I've got anything. I drank it all last night."

"You must have *something*," I cried desperately. "Some cooking sherry or some... Greek brandy?"

"I'll see if I can find anything in the children's rooms."

"Please don't leave it too long, Emma. Dispense with the make-up ritual, if you can," I pleaded. "I'm in a Hell of a state."

She took fifteen minutes. It felt like fifteen years. She had a bottle of gin with two inches still in it. I prayed it was enough.

"You look like you've just been dug up," she rasped, appalled.

"Thanks," I rasped back.

She held the bottle up to the early morning light.

"I hope this'll do; it was all I could find."

"It'll be... fine," I spluttered, gratefully. "Just help me get it down my throat."

Emma held me still and slowly applied the bottle to my lips. I was shaking like a lectern at a Parkinson's convention, but the relief far outweighed any humiliation. I started to calm down after the first two hits.

"Thanks," I said again, rubbing away a tear.

Emma didn't say anything. She looked shocked as she handed me the bottle, to finish unaided

"Coffee?" I suggested guiltily, as I hauled myself up.

"OK."

We went to the kitchen. My shaking had nearly stopped. I put the kettle on, poured the rest of the gin into a tumbler and lit a cigarette with a slight shiver. Emma said nothing. Her silence did the talking.

"I know," I said, fatalistically. "You told me... I've got to see someone about it."

"Oh really? Is that so? You shit me not, Sherlock," Emma scoffed, snapping out of her reticence. "I've never seen anything like it. James, you idiot, you looked as though you were about to kick. And I've seen that before," she added, referring, I assumed, to her late husband.

"I'll go to see the GP this time. She's nice. She knows what to do," I said, draining the last of my glass.

"She'd better," Emma cautioned, looking at me sharply again, "or I may not be quite so neighbourly next time..."

I'm sorry about that," I said, sheepishly.

"You should be," she admonished. "Now I've got nothing to drink."

Of course I didn't see my GP. Not immediately, anyway. But I did get out the computer dating dossier in the office once I felt sufficiently recovered to face the opposition. I looked at the first composite. Victoria Smedley. Age: 33, blah, blah, blah. I looked up her link, typed out a few words of salutation and asked when would be convenient to talk. I received a response shortly afterwards, saying she could talk at lunchtime. I called her at one. She sounded brusque but willing, so I asked her if she'd like to meet. She took the lead.

"I'm out this week, but I can do next Tuesday," she asserted, as if she was quite the mutt's nuts.

"Sure," I said, benignly. "Is there anything particular you'd like to do?"

"There is actually," she replied, with continued self-assurance. "I've been given tickets to the Spring Exhibition at the Royal Academy which I don't want to miss. Are you up for that?"

"Oh, yes!" I answered, slavishly. "I love tickets!"

We met at a wine bar close to the Academy after work. Victoria was as good as the picture in her composite, but judging from the undisguised disgust on her face, I perhaps wasn't quite up to mine. She told me more about herself. Although she was pretty enough, there was something definitely unfeminine about her. She played golf. She was a poker champ too and drove a Harley. She also had a black belt in Karate and ran motivation courses for aspiration-deficient executives in need of stimulus. Short of smoking a pipe, she couldn't have been more masculine.

She wasn't particularly interested in how I passed my time of day, which was fine by me as I had nothing to match her lifestyle. The more she spoke, the more I wished the sofa where we were sitting would swallow me up. Or her. I'd had a few drinks beforehand to get me in the mood, but nothing had prepared me for this. *Brusque?* She was a complete ball-breaker!

She decided when it was time to make our way to the Academy. The exhibition was being held in the main gallery on the first floor beyond the central staircase. There were plenty of people, but no one I instantly recognised. Victoria had no such problem and almost immediately spotted Lord Dale, an ignoble noble who'd been quite a feature in the press of late. He'd bought his title through the usual channels but had come unstuck when he'd been caught going a bribe too far by the media. He had been bound over to keep the peace for a while, but his title, if not his reputation, had remained intact. He and Victoria seemed to be on familiar terms.

"Oh, my God – it's Dale!" she shrieked in a voice that could've sunk the *Bismarck*, as she scuttled across the floor to meet him.

"Not 'God' yet, Victoria; 'Lord' will have to do for the time being!" he responded, jovially.

Yech.

Victoria didn't seem inclined to introduce me, so I drifted off with the £10 catalogue I'd felt obliged to purchase on the way in, and inspected my new surroundings. The exhibition was sponsored by Simon Mulam Securities, a seemingly innocuous brokerage house that had recently been held responsible for ramping elements of the soft commodities market across the globe, much to the cost of the general consumer. I had known the co-founders, Toby Cater and David Hobson vaguely in my former capacity as a bond trader and had, even then, had my doubts about their moral rectitude. I needn't have bothered. It had done them no harm. They both looked perfectly happy, glad-handing the affluent effluent trickling through the entrance door, David working the room like a President, now no longer sleek, yet possessing the nimble familiarity of the assured fat cat that he'd become. At least the little prick had lost his hair.

A waiter offered me a glass of fake-o, closely followed by a waitress presenting a plate of canapés. I opted for a smoked oyster aboard a yellow cracker, thanked her and continued to look around. This was my kind of town, as long as Christine Hale wasn't around, but someone who did catch my eye was Tim Crawley-More who'd attended St Dweeb's at the same time as me and whom I'd once counted as a friend. He'd gone on to establish a successful chain of hair salons and had distanced our acquaintance as they had prospered. I'd heard he'd subsequently developed his own chemical romance and adopted demons similar to mine, albeit in powdered form. His businesses had gone to pot as he'd gone to something stronger, and he definitely was no longer the Renaissance man I'd seen profiled in various glossy magazines a few years before. He looked haggard, and his brocade jacket that once would have created quite a stir now made him look like a jerk. I buried my nose back in my brochure. If he didn't want to know me when he was on the way up, I certainly didn't want to know him on the way down. We had too much in common.

Whether it was the feeling of relief at getting away from Victoria or the effects of the smoked oyster canapé, but whatever it was I suddenly needed to go to the loo in a hurry. I asked a commissionaire for directions and was pointed towards a door at the other end of the reception room. It was occupied. I waited outside, trying not to look desperate. I heard a flush and some minutes later an old bag emerged smugly from the smog. I looked in. It was tiny, added to which the old cow had swiped practically all the shit tickets. There wasn't enough left for the job in hand. It wouldn't do. Not if I was going for the big one. I lunged for the exit, practically knocking Lord Dale off his perch as Victoria talked animatedly to a man who looked as if he ate people. They must have been too busy comparing technique or etiquette because Victoria hardly batted an eyelid as I pushed past. I couldn't see any signs of life or lavatories, so I ricocheted, Parkour-style down the main stairs and shot out of the building like a speeding bullet. What a party pooper!

I sprinted to the nearest tube, cursing myself just as it was too late to turn back to the wine bar. There were only four stops to Alphabet Street, but it didn't prevent me from wanting to drop the whole load there and then, so I had to concentrate. It was a question of mind over matter. Dark matter. I got to Alphabet Street and pirouetted back to the flat. *Don't check the post now, idiot!* I charged up the stairs, made a nonsense of the keys, but burst into the lavatory just in time.

Dodgy oyster or narrow escape, something odd was definitely happening to my internal organs. Thirty years on the treadmill of alcoholism had finally caught up with me. I couldn't take it anymore. I could countenance the peripheral neuropathic aspect of the problem, but incontinence was another subject. I spoke to Peregrine Blücher about it the next day, more in triumph than in shame, but he wasn't impressed.

"It'll occur more often," he cautioned, humourlessly. "You may not find it quite so amusing if it becomes a regular event, which may well happen the way you're going. It's your body's way of saying it's had enough; it can't cope anymore with the constant abuse. It's time you started to live in the solution, not the problem. I suggest you go for help before it's too late."

I put the phone down, duly chastened and resolved to call my GP the next day to make an appointment. But I wasn't through with Victoria. Not yet.

I decided to send her an e-mail to thank her for the previous evening's indulgence, more out of a desire to irritate than ingratiate.

>*Hi Victoria! Thank you so much for last night. It was very civilised and great meeting you. I'm sorry I didn't have the opportunity to say goodbye to you properly but I had an emergency call and had to skedaddle. Talking of opportunities, it would be great to have another chance to get together. Would you like to meet again?*

I got an answer two minutes later.

>*No.*

Good. I wrote back:

>*Oh, well, it was worth a try! Pity, because I thought you were terrific and had loads of interesting stuff to say. With your glamour and understated approach, you'll have no problems finding 'Mr Right'. My only regret is that I am not that man, but I wish you well and appreciate your time.*
Yours, James x.

I clicked the 'send' icon and smiled, safe in the knowledge that any derision would be lost on her. Cunt.

I pulled out the sheet of paper with all her particulars from the dating file and gazed at it thoughtfully as I slipped a stick of gum into my mouth. The picture was good and the details were all present and correct. I gave it one last lingering look, chuckled a bit, folded it and put it into my breast pocket. I had a peep at the three remaining possibilities in the dossier, sighed and put them back in the drawer. I'd had enough excitement for one week, but I knew I'd have to move soon before some other arseholes got to them first.

Pete Divis tapped me on the shoulder a little later and asked if I'd like to go for a drink. He had been quiet for several weeks and we hadn't spoken at any length for a while. I willingly assented, so we grabbed our jackets and left the office. I started to cross the road to our usual watering hole, but Pete grabbed my arm before I'd taken two steps.

"Not that one, James," he said, quietly. "If you don't mind, I'd like to go to somewhere where the others won't be around."

"Sure," I said, a little surprised. Pete normally loved a crowd. "Anything wrong?"

"I'll tell you when we get to where I've got in mind," he said, steering me down a side alley.

I saw an old phone box we were passing and asked him if we could stop for a moment. He looked at me oddly.

I went into the kiosk, took Victoria's details out of my pocket and quickly scribbled on the page, 'Hand: £20. Blow: £40. Straight: £60. Anal: £80. No condoms required', underlined her phone number and stuck it up with the gum I'd been chewing next to the 'New in Town' tart tags wedged between the glass and the defunct phone apparatus. Pete peered inside.

"Isn't that just a little piece of terrific!" he commended, slapping me on the back. "Something to offend everyone! Now she'll meet some really nice people... she'll love the disused phone box crowd – they're such fun!"

"Do I get a gold star?" I trilled. "You never know, she might find the love of her life! I like to think of myself as helping others; you know the sort guy I am."

"I sure do, James," he enthused. "Cheeky but never blue... but I don't think Victoria will be darkening your door for a while! Pity, she looks quite tasty."

"Tasty? We mixed about as well as wine and toothpaste!"

We arrived at Pete's pub, got our drinks and sat down.

"So?" I said, wondering why he'd got me on my own. "What's it all about?"

"It's all about me," he answered, phlegmatically.

"OK. And what does that entail?" I asked, relieved that I wasn't the reason for his secrecy.

"It entails my departure from the firm, old bean."

"What?" I spluttered in disbelief. "But you are the firm. Well, part of the furniture at least."

"I know," Pete agreed. "But my time has come. I've been here for a long time, given our type of business. I could've stayed longer, but I haven't been able to cut it for quite a while now."

"We all have our ups and downs," I reasoned, not wanting him to leave.

"I know. But the boss and I came to the conclusion that it would be best for both of us to have a change. For me that means starting afresh at another company, and for him it means branching out to fill the void once I'm gone. It's not the end of the world, you know."

"I'm still sorry to hear you're off," I said, thinking that without Pete in the office there'd be nobody I could completely rely on.

"You don't need to be," he responded, calmly. "I have another job lined up. It's OK."

"I'm not talking about you, you tit!" I retorted, crossly. "I'm talking about *me*! Once you're gone I'll be on my own; I won't have an ally to act as general conciliator."

"That's true," he considered. "You'd better look out for that. You're going to have to look after that arse of yours once you're on your own."

"I can sense that already," I replied, despondently.

"I don't like what's happening to that deal you're all working on. It's too hot to handle; too many people are trying to muscle in, like dogs circling a bone," he observed, accurately. "You've done your part; without you there'd have been no deal in the first place. Make sure people remember that."

"That's going to be difficult without having you around to keep the mongrels off the meat. I could use a hand with Craig at the moment. I fear he may be up to his old tricks again; he's being far too helpful for someone with no apparent vested interest."

"It's not Craig you've got to worry about," Pete remarked, bleakly.

"Well who else then?"

"Fred. He's the one you've really got to look out for," Pete warned. "He'll find any excuse to block you. I can see it happening already. Mark my words: he will try to channel every last centavo he can into his own pocket with the gold lust of Cortés."

"OK, but where does Craig fit in the scam?" I asked, trying to follow his logic.

"As a smokescreen, perhaps," Pete suggested, plausibly. "Craig's expendable. At the moment he's doing Fred's dirty work. And when the time's right, you'll be expendable too."

His words made chilling sense. I had noticed that Fred had taken to ignoring me and not keeping me informed. His manner had become decidedly offhand. A pattern was beginning to emerge. It was all beginning to stack up.

I saw my GP that Friday and told her about my problem. She didn't seem particularly surprised or alarmed. She was cool. It was nothing she hadn't seen before. But she did say that I needed to do something about it soon. I knew that, but how and where? The alcohol reform program that Elspeth had made me attend had had precious little impact. The doctor proposed two options: detox or rehab. Detox involved, unsurprisingly, a detoxification programme but only required two weeks' residential treatment. Rehab was not dissimilar but needed a considerably longer time span, perhaps months. Months? Fuck that for *un jeu de soldats!* The detox was relatively simple to arrange, but the rehab presupposed a long waiting list. No contest! But the timing couldn't be worse. I could ill afford to be away from the office given the vulnerability of my position, but on the grounds that I had to do something, I took the detox. The doctor made a call. Due to a cancellation she told me she could get me into a hospital near Paddington the following weekend. I considered the possible consequences. It was better to do it sooner than later. I gave her an upward thumb.

I received the confirmation of admission the following week with some literature advising me what to take with me and what to expect. It seemed I no longer counted as far as Fred and Craig were concerned, and they could hardly conceal their rapture when I told them I had to go to hospital for two weeks. I didn't say why and they didn't care, as long as I was out of the way. I got the dating file out before I left. I e-mailed the three remaining respondents individually to say that I was going on a fortnight's business trip and would be in contact when I got back. Lucky things! Business trip? As if.

The detox centre was pants, but at least they kept me flaked-out on diazepam most of the time. Some of the other patients were a bit weird, but the two weeks floated by painlessly enough. I checked out with a clean bill of health after the two weeks, and headed for the nearest bar. I might have come away from the hospital detoxified, but my habit was thrilled to have me back.

Things in the office had carried on apace, but by now I'd almost been written out of the deal. As expected, Craig had continued to take an unhealthy interest in proceedings, despite not having any apparent stake in the affair. He'd appointed himself project manager and was in no hurry to relinquish the position just because I was back. His self-appointment appeared to have Fred's full blessing. He'd also usurped my function with my candidates and had made a point of meeting them several times during my spell away. It was obvious that I was being kept out of the loop again, but this time by the very company I worked for.

It didn't stop me from pursuing my romantic activities in the dating file as a diversion. I looked at item #2, Annette Wazebo, an attractive-looking Creole from Brentford, and gave her a call. She sounded friendly. She quite brazenly agreed to come to the flat one evening and I cooked supper while we chatted. She was nice and every bit as attractive as her photograph but I got the impression she expected something a little more than just supper if we were going to take things on to a higher plane. Like payment in one form or another. Not another one! Didn't anybody do a decent day's work anymore? I said I'd get in contact again as the evening drew to a close, but I didn't. The day I had to pay for it would be the day I'd give up.

Matters at work went from bad to dire. It was now so blatant that I was being cut out of the deal that Fred Armitage had given up any pretence of being civil and it was plain I was no longer welcome at the firm. I didn't exist. Then he became insufferable and I didn't want to exist. That was all I needed: another mouse of no consequence in the outside world, just out to make things unpleasant. Pete Divis had left. I had no one to back me. Instead I spent most of the time keeping out of harm's way by hiding in Pete's secret pub, which meant I'd often return to the office even more incapable of making business calls than before I'd gone out. It was a vicious circle. The more depressed I became, the more I drank. The more I drank, the greater the grounds were for my dismissal.

Events came to a head one afternoon when I returned from my beery hideaway feeling tired and worse for wear. I knew I was beyond doing anything sensible so I surfed the net for a while and, without meaning to, dozed off in my chair. I woke up about an hour later. The office was quiet and it appeared that my inertia had gone unnoticed. I still felt drunk. There was no point hanging around. I seized my jacket and slipped out undetected. The newsvendor was in particularly high spirits as he handed me the evening paper, and the tube wallah propping up the ticket machine at the underground cheerily doffed his cap as I passed through to the platform.

The train was busy but I managed to find a seat. I glanced at my paper, relieved that I'd left the office without attracting any comment, but after a few stops I became increasingly aware that I was being observed. I looked up from the paper. There was an attractive young woman staring straight at me. I ignored her watchful scrutiny and went back to my paper. Another stop came and went. I couldn't concentrate. I looked up again. The young woman was still gazing at me, this time with an amused smile. So the little vixen was playing, was she? I took her in.

She had a large rucksack by her side with a small Australian flag stitched on the flap. I assumed she was on the way to the airport. She was gorgeous. I smiled back. I'd always liked Australians, but this was strange. I regarded myself as average-looking and not the type to normally set a crowd alight, but there was nothing average about me today. I wondered what it was. I'd recently had a haircut which I didn't think had done me any favours, but obviously this woman thought otherwise. I turned the paper over to study the crossword. It was no good. I couldn't stop myself from looking up. She was at it again. Her eyes burned into mine with an intensity I'd never experienced before. What was I to do? Was this the girl of my dreams? Was this the answer to my prayers? Could *she* be the future Mrs Mallet?

I had two more stops to go before it was my turn to get off. If she was a backpacker on the way out of town then the matter was settled. There was no way I could casually ask her if she had time for a coffee. I couldn't persuade a complete stranger to change her life's plan on my account. Or could I? Then there was only one more stop left. I shifted uneasily in my seat and undid my tie. I felt cooler. I looked cooler. I could tell. The girl was either in love or giving me the biggest come-on in the world! I wasn't used to it. I couldn't handle it. I wasn't drunk enough. It wasn't the same as it had been with Angelita. The train came into my station. I got up. The woman was looking at me pleadingly. God, she was pretty. The doors opened. I got out. I turned round. The doors closed. She looked sadly at me through the glass. I looked sadly back. I'd botched it. The train pulled out of the station. I'd bottled out of the greatest opportunity of my life. Idiot. Again.

I hauled my sorry arse broken-heartedly towards the station lift, but I wasn't broken-hearted for long. The lift doors opened at ground level. Another beautiful woman was standing there. She looked at me casually, and then gave me a double-take. She lit up. She looked excited. She couldn't take her eyes off me! I knew she knew that I knew. I was having a good hair day! She disappeared into the lift as I got out. I didn't care. There were plenty more like her around. Knock 'em dead, kiddo!

I strutted back to the flat, quite the big banana in the pink pyjama. It was a good day to be good-looking. At last I was being seen for what I was: a fun, attractive, lovely guy! No more the schmuck with no luck for me! Not while I was on beauty duty! I smiled at everyone I passed. They all smiled back brightly. Everybody wanted a little piece of me! I felt like a jewellery shop on *Kristallnacht*! I arrived at the flat, unlocked the door and went to the bedroom. I didn't know what all the fuss was about, but I was about to find out. I threw my keys on the bed and took off my tie. OK, big boy, let's check it out! I entered the bathroom, pulled the light cord and looked in the mirror. I jumped out of my skin. *Holy fucksticks*! My face was covered in marker-pen rubbish. My so-called 'colleagues' had stencilled spectacles, devils' horns, a moustache and goatee beard all over my pretty little dial. The little shit monkeys. It was all smudged now. This, together with my red, bloated, alcohol-soused nose, just made the picture. I went to the drawing room, sat on the sofa and quietly started to weep.

The fact that Fred Armitage had allowed my fellow workers to deface my face while I was caught snoozing on the job illustrated the low level of regard he had for me. He didn't give a damn. I must have passed over a thousand people on the way home that afternoon. *How embarrassing!*

I went into the office the next day, inflamed rather than humiliated, and said to the assembled few in a voice as quiet as a prayer: "Never, ever trespass on my face again."

Someone sniggered but shut up when no one else joined in. For once I'd caused the office to become silent.

But there was one person who took no heed of my change of tune. Something happened a few days later that was much more interesting. To me at least. I was sitting quietly, idly perhaps, late one afternoon just as most people had left the office when I overheard Craig on the phone to one of my candidates. He was arranging a meeting and finalising one or two points. He hung up, looking pleased as he jotted down some notes. I gave a stage cough. He didn't look up. That was it. I'd had enough. He was talking to *my* candidate over *my* head as if it was now all his deal.

"Craig," I said, gently, "you do know that was one of my candidates you were talking to, don't you?"

"So?" he challenged, defensively. "It's not doing any harm."

"I know," I accepted, "but you're doing so without my permission. I have sourced these candidates from my contact base, of which you have no part. I want you to remember that."

"That's balls!" he roared. "Who do you think put this whole thing together while you were out having your liver re-sprayed? We all know why you went away."

"Craig, they are still my candidates, not yours," I insisted, firmly.

"That's crap," he shouted, throwing his pen down in fury.

Lather or lava?

"It's not, I'm afraid," I said, softening my tone, sensing trouble.

"The fact is, James, you have been incapable of doing anything for the last two months," he said, lowering his voice a decibel. "You're either drunk or fast asleep; your candidates have got no time for you. *That's* why I'm dealing with them."

"Thank you, Craig," I pressed on. "You've just said it. You just said 'your candidates'. That's the point. They're my candidates, no matter what you do. I just wanted to remind you; you know the rules."

"You ungrateful sod!" he erupted, rising threateningly from his chair. "You may have come up with the seeds but I was the one who watered them."

"Craig, I'm sure we can agree to come to some sort of an arrangement," I said, starting to get worried.

"Dead fucking right we can," he retorted, drawing himself up to full height.

"But it will have to be on my terms," I parried weakly, feebly attempting to take a stand.

He hesitated momentarily, as if to assess what I was implying. Then I had a thought. In that split second I had an epiphany. Maybe I could make something of the situation. Yes. Now was the opportunity. Now was the time for a complete volte-face.

"Are you gonna bark all day, little doggie or are you gonna bite?" I snarled, as annoyingly as possible.

"You cunt!" he shrieked, regaining his resolve and starting to advance towards me.

"That's *Mister* Cunt, to you," I goaded.

"You'll be picking your teeth out of your shit with a broken arm by the time I'm finished with you," he railed, now only a matter of feet away.

"Sure I will, *Mary*," I said, egging him on defiantly.

That was it. There was no going back. He'd gone beyond his point of no return. He hit me. And it felt like a kiss.

Chapter 17: Obfuscation

That was it. I was back. It didn't hurt. I wasn't upset. Quite the opposite: I had witnesses. It was a toehold rather than a stranglehold, however it did mean that I wasn't quite so expendable. Not to the boss. Not now. Not without a hitch. Craig immediately realised his mistake. I got up, wiped my mouth and saw some blood. It was just what I needed and just enough of it.

"I'm sorry James... I'm so, so sorry," Craig spluttered, disjointedly. "I didn't mean to... I don't know what happened..."

I didn't say anything. I switched off my computer, picked up my jacket and turned to leave.

"James... James... can't we sort this out?" he snivelled. "Where... where are you going?"

"Liverpool Street," I replied, indifferently.

Tube station? Or police station? Both were only five minutes away. Craig's face fell.

"James, please don't... it's just that... " he continued to whimper, before straightening up. "Look they're your candidates, so it's your money, right? I was only trying to help... please... James?"

I glanced pointedly at the two other co-workers who happened still to be present. It was unfortunate that the main protagonist, Fred Armitage, wasn't there to mark the spectacle himself, but the others would do. One of them actually liked me and neither was particularly crazy about Craig.

I left the office with my jacket slung coolly over one shoulder, Jimmy Dean-style. I wiped my mouth again and smeared the blood over my shirt. My lip only had the tiniest nick but it was bleeding like a broken hymen. I saw the police station and smiled. Do it. I went in nervously. The duty sergeant looked up from his newspaper.

"I'd like to report an assault," I said, looking sorry for myself.

"I see, sir. Will you be pressing charges?"

"That depends. Can I just file a complaint for the record for the time being?" I asked, distractedly.

"Not unless you intend to press charges, sir."

"What would you suggest?" I questioned, pointing to my mouth.

"I'd sleep on it, sir. See how you feel about it in the morning."

"That may prove uncomfortable, but I'll abide by your advice," I said, ending, I hoped, on a conciliatory note. "Thank you, officer. You've been most helpful."

News travelled fast. There was a commotion as I entered the office the next day. Neither Craig nor Fred was there, but everyone else was. My lip had swollen up nicely.

"What happened?" Fred's secretary asked, anxiously.

"Craig gave me a bunch of fives," I answered casually, as if he'd given me a bunch of flowers.

Now I had the rest of the office in on the gig. I waited till eleven. There was still no sign of Craig or Fred. It was time for a drink. I sauntered to the pub across the road and ordered a beer. They'd know where to find me. I'd told Fred's secretary where I was going. I didn't have to wait long for company. Craig came running in, looking even more agitated than when I'd left him the evening before. Fred must have sent him over. He'd really gone through the mangle. Fred had obviously given him the third degree. He looked as if he was hanging by a thread. He dragged himself through the same forlorn routine. I was more talkative this time.

"James... James..." he wheedled.

"What the fuck did you think you were doing?" I snapped.

"James... I've been under a lot of pressure recently. I don't know what's going on..."

"So you threatened to kick seven different colours of shit out of me and hit me instead?"

"James, it was a ..."

"Shut your noise, Craig. Is this the sort of person I was quite happy to let gatecrash my holiday to Goa? I think you have a bit of explaining to do. Like why the fuck were you sticking your nose into my business in the first place?"

"James... you don't understand... I'm no longer on contract like you... I'm an employee."

I stopped for an instant and considered the implications. There were more than met the ear.

"When did that happen?" I barked, sharply.

"When the deal started to look interesting."

"Why wasn't I told?" I demanded, imperiously.

"Because it was a *Fred and me* thing. It wasn't anybody else's business. Besides he told me not to tell anyone."

"And that made it OK for you both to shaft me?"

"I don't know, James. I was paid by Fred to do as I was told."

"To stuff me?"

"Listen, I'm really sorry, James, but yesterday changed all that. Fred knows you went to the police."

"How come?"

"I followed you out of the office. I wasn't tailing you; I was going that direction anyway, but I saw you go into the police station."

"That was handy for you."

"And I assume you reported me?"

"I might have," I acknowledged, inscrutably.

"Which means, if you press charges, Fred will probably have to fire me," Craig blathered on.

"He could fire both of us if he wanted and keep all the money. That is, *if* the deal ever comes off," I observed, scathingly.

"That's the point: he knows if he does something too dramatic, he'll have a fight on his hands. With you, breach of contract, and constructive dismissal with me. Either would have a high chance of blowing the whole caboodle out of the water long before the payola starts cranking out the moola, which would rather defeat the object, *n'est ce pas?*

"Un petit peu," I concurred. "But as I seem to be the last person to be informed, would you mind advising me where we stand now?"

"If you drop charges, I'll keep my job and you'll keep your commission."

"Which is how it should have been all along, if you hadn't had your cock-ring rammed hard up Fred's arse the whole time."

"Look, James, if you want to cut up rough, talk to Fred. But if you don't, and we all just act as if everything's hunky-dory, you'll get your cut, I'll get my salary and Fred, as usual, will get the rest."

"How much is your salary?" I challenged, not trusting any particular aspect of the arrangement one jot.

"James, I can't tell you *that.*"

"It's important, Craig."

"Not very much, James; you know what Fred's like."

"I was just interested to know what the market rate for a piece of shit was these days."

"Don't, James. I'm not complicit in this one anymore."

"But you'll admit that you *were.*"

"Who knows? I don't know what goes through Fred's head these days or whether I'm still part of it even. It's not something I can account for."

"Well, you go back and tell him that as long as I get my full percentage, he can do what he likes with the rest."

"Thanks, James. I'll tell him," he said, appearing relieved.

I watched him waddle across the road back to the office, and finished my pint in thought.

It didn't come as a total surprise that my stipulation had a negative effect on Fred. Just when I thought things couldn't get any worse, there were new lows; new depths. Fred knew that I knew that he was a complete scumbag. He hardly spoke to me, but even deep in sulk knew he had to put on a modicum of civility while the cash cauldron simmered gently in the background. I on the other hand had to go through the motions of pretending to work on other projects that might further enrich him, but it wasn't easy.

Once Fred had grown tired of his silent vigil, he became more audacious, contradicting everything I said and objecting to anything I happened to be doing. What a horrid little place the company had become. Business was already hard enough to come by and Fred wasn't helping. The smaller banks that had been our bread and butter were being squeezed out of the market as spiralling compliance costs and the growing paucity of business made their operations untenable. This left just a handful of self-contained global monoliths that seemed disinclined to discuss their staffing requirements with a nincompoop on the periphery like me. Attempts to try the Japanese were equally luckless. They had either packed their bags or amalgamated into the three or four consortium banks that remained and even these were finding it difficult to compete now that their home economy was no longer quite the force it once was.

All of which didn't stop me from glancing at my dating folder from time to time and maintaining a flat-screen flirtation with the two remaining internet intimates on file. I eventually had the gumption to join up with respondent #3, Tina 38, who described her agenda as 'WLTM suitor for love and commitment and able to offer same in return'. Yech. I called her and we agreed to meet at a wine bar we knew off the King's Road.

She was an hour late, which I could deal with, but it would have been nice if she had called or texted to let me know what was going on. She was as attractive as her image in the dossier, liked a drink and seemed jolly enough. She worked for the managing director of Allied Swiss Bank, to which she attached great importance, so we talked about that for a while and drank a fair bit. I got the impression that she thought I was OK; nothing special, but acceptable. I felt the same about her, but like so many she was very much a woman who defined herself by her job. We eventually left the bar, slightly the worse for wear, leaning against each other as we walked towards a crossroads in search of transport. My legs had started to go but I managed to steer Tina towards a lamp post on the corner which I casually leant against to prop myself up. We kissed while we waited. She was all right; a bit of a job hero, but a smokey-jokey type and otherwise reasonable.

A taxi stopped. I let Tina have first dibs with the cab without suggesting that we share a ride home or that she come back to my place. I was too drunk to take the evening further, and so, by the look of her, was Tina. But things boded well for the future; at least she was affectionate, which was more than could be said for my other recent e-mail experiments. If the subject matter of our conversation had been somewhat monotone in content, she was still worth another call, if she was up for it. It was high time that I found a more tangible outlet for my romantic passions than my burgeoning magazine collection.

I hailed the next taxi home and just made it to the flat by crawling up the stairs on all fours. The detox treatment had been a waste of time. It was pathetic. No it wasn't: I was pathetic. I crashed onto the bed, tried kicking off my shoes, gave up and went to sleep fully clothed. I awoke the next morning feeling as if I had scabies. I had spots before my eyes. I made a cup of coffee, doused it with a large shot of Scotch and ran the bath. I got in and savoured my concoction contentedly as I re-evaluated the previous evening's encounter. My elation at the prospect of forging any future liaison with Tina was mildly tempered by a sense of foreboding that all I'd found was yet another drinking companion, which was not what I needed. I had plenty of those already. I would have to think.

I got out of the bath and made myself ready for the office. I had been remiss in not keeping in contact with Sven Gläzner at DCBI. I knew he wouldn't have any work for me, but perhaps I could get him out for a drink, for old time's sake. Drink, drink, drink. I brushed my teeth and ran a comb through my hair. I still saw spots in front of my eyes. I thought about having another two fingers of whisky to dispel the illusion, but I was beginning to reek of the stuff. I straightened my tie and made for the front door. I opened it and pressed the stairway time-switch light on. Fuck! There was a body on the landing! I reeled back into the flat and slammed the door. Who was it? Tina? What did she want? Not much, judging by her condition. My heart started to race. Then my head joined in. It couldn't be a corpse. It had to be my DTs. But they'd never been like this before.

Gingerly I opened the door again and peeped out. The time switch light had gone out, but whatever it was, it was still there. I could clearly discern the outline, so it wasn't my DTs. Was it a corpse? Was it a Mafioso-style warning from The Pan Asian Bank for Richard and me to lay off with our snooping, before they got *really* heavy? Or was Fred Armitage trying to say something? He wasn't exactly my number one fan. Nor was Craig. No matter what the circumstances, I had a horrible sense of *déjà vu*. The atrocity I'd committed twelve years before had involved the same stairwell and the same state of alcoholic anxiety as I was experiencing now. And neither instance was an apparition.

"Anything wrong?" a disembodied voice enquired, quietly from behind.

I jumped out of my skin. It was my flatmate in his dressing gown, looking for all the world like Marley's ghost.

"There's something outside," I gasped, quivering.

He poked his head round the door.

"It's the rubbish. I put it out last night," he remarked, calmly.

He put the time switch light back on. Of course it was! It was just a black plastic bin liner full of refuse that had fallen on its side. How was I to know? He'd never touched the rubbish before, and besides I hadn't seen him for nearly two weeks. Fucking freak!

I breathed a sigh of relief.

"Sorry. I thought it was something else," I muttered.

I strolled into the office as if I hadn't a care and immediately set about looking for the Alcoholics Anonymous website on the computer. I tapped in 'The Twelve Steps' and peered round nervously. Nobody was looking. Why should they? I clicked on the search icon. The screen blinked to life. I studied the list from the top.

'Step 1: We admitted we were powerless over alcohol – that our lives had become unmanageable.'

I had been told by those who knew that until the first step had been fully digested and understood, there was little point in tackling the other eleven. I had no problem admitting I was powerless over alcohol and that my life had become unmanageable, but I just didn't think that there was anything that could be done about it. For me a life without alcohol was unthinkable, unimaginable, and well-nigh improbable. Much as I hated being addicted and dependent on drink, it was my *raison d'être*; my definition; my motivation; my aspiration. It was the route I'd chosen and I was going to stick with it, come rain or shine. Or was it chosen?

I looked up from the computer. Fred was staring at me, looking as shifty as a Kennedy. I clicked off the website and smiled pleasantly.

"Can I help you?" I asked politely, hoping to head him off with a pre-emptive strike.

"I was wondering what was happening with Sven Gläzner at DCBI," he said reflectively, as if the idea had just occurred to him.

Bullshit. He was sizing up the pros and cons of keeping me on in relation to the gains of getting rid of me.

"Funny you should mention that," I chirped, airily. "I was just thinking about him this morning. I'll give him a call."

I picked up the phone and dialled.

"Sven?" I enquired.

"This is he," came the hokey response.

"Oh, grow a pair, Sven! It's only me – James, remember?" I chided, derisively. "And you're German, not American, or have you forgotten? Any chance of wheeling you out for a drink sometime?"

"Not now, James. I can't do anything at the moment," he said, lowering his voice. "Things are pretty rough round here; we might even have to start laying people off."

"I'm sorry to hear that, Sven," I said, with genuine regret. "You've been a good friend and customer. Let me know if I can help any of the casualties or if you'd like a break and take in a show sometime."

"Thanks, James," he said, sounding grateful. "I'll let you know on both fronts, but entertainment, I'm afraid, is going to have to take a rest for a while."

He phoned off. It didn't sound good. Fred was looking at me expectantly.

"He said there's giong to be a change of emphasis at DCBI, away from cash to a more derivative-driven business model," I lied, hoping Fred wouldn't understand what I was talking about. I didn't. "Once that's sorted out he wants to get together with me to discuss his hiring strategy."

Fred eyed me doubtfully. He didn't know whether to buy me or not. What I didn't want him to know, was that my run of luck with Sven was all but over. I was now just a one-note concerto with the big deal as the only audible chord. I needed to diversify, but how? I was getting precious few leads or referrals from the others in the firm now that Pete Divis had left. I suspected Fred was behind that. I was trapped. Maybe I'd have to leave the company, with or without the big deal in the bag.

I spent the afternoon compiling a list of recruitment companies to write to. Why not? I had many years' banking experience; one and a half years' recruitment exposure... and a twelve-year gap in my CV from when I'd been in the slammer. Who could resist me? I gave Pete Divis a call on his mobile when there was nobody important around, and asked how he was getting on. He'd started a few weeks before at his new recruitment company but said he was finding it tough and wasn't in a position at that moment to put me forward for an interview at his firm. He did however have a contact, a certain Mr Heimann, who'd seen him at one of the larger headhunting companies, but hadn't actually offered Pete a job.

"It's a start," Pete prompted, as he gave me the contact number. "And the very fact that the geezer deigned to see me would imply that the company's looking for people. Give him a call; it'll be good practice and what harm can come of it?"

I resolved not to call the euphoniously named Mr Heimann immediately. I needed to think my approach through properly; I would only have one chance and I wanted it to be in private with my CV on hand, but only if required. Instead I decided to give Tina a shout, just to be friendly and perhaps sound her out for another date. She wasn't exactly congenial.

"Don't call me in the office," she hissed.

"Why not?" I whispered back.

"I never take personal calls at work," she remonstrated, breathlessly.

"I do. Is your job more important than mine?" I asked, without irony.

"I can't talk now," she replied, putting my question to one side. "I'll call you tonight."

She hung up. Bitch! Why did women take their jobs so seriously? It was only a job, for fuck's sake. She did call me at home later. She apologised for her manner earlier, but said she had her rules.

"Don't worry," I said, understandingly. "I've got a lot of people who don't want to talk to me at the moment."

"Don't be like that, James," she said, gently. "It's got nothing to do with being a goody-goody; it's just that I can't afford to muck around. Allied Swiss is a very important bank."

"So's The Pan Asian, and I was management. That didn't make me '007, Licensed to Insult'," I said, fractiously.

"James, you don't get it. This is the way I operate. Business is business and my social life doesn't cross into it," she said, sounding a bit cross herself.

"If two minutes of Allied Swiss's time is more important than mine, then so be it," I said, self-righteously.

"Stop it, James!" she protested. "We had a real laugh last night. I thought you were fun. I'd love to see you again, but not if you're going to get at me for trying to do my job properly. We hardly know each other. Don't you think it's a little early in the day to have an argument?"

She had a point. I let it go. I'd made my point. We agreed to meet the following week at my flat and I'd cook supper. For me it was cheaper than going out and if we drank enough who knew what would happen?

It did happen. At least Tina didn't beat about the bush and it was good to find that she adopted the same businesslike approach to what was necessary in my bedroom. Her tits tasted of Marlboros. She wasn't such a bad lass, although once again she'd been inordinately late because of work. At least this time she'd called to tell me. She also said she'd help me make my CV and its very short list of achievements look as nice as possible, which was paradoxical as that was supposed to be *my* job. I handed over a rough draft for her to type out in her lunch hour, if she had one.

Elspeth was up to her old tricks again. This time she wasn't taking 'no' for an answer. The detox treatment had quite plainly had no effect and when, a few weeks later, I was rushed by ambulance to a nearby Accident and Emergency unit following a blackout after a particularly heavy drinking session, Elspeth was there with a pen and twelve-week rehab form for me to sign. It was only because it was Thursday, when I knew she had her hallowed weekly bridge fix, that I was able to malinger just long enough in the seclusion of the emergency room for her to finally give up waiting, four hours later, and go home. I was off work for two days, but by then it had got to the point where my non-attendance was welcomed throughout the office.

Tina and I got together again soon after. She had my CV nicely formatted, but I couldn't believe it when she kept me waiting for an hour again at another wine bar we were due to meet at. I'd felt more than a prat just sitting there. I had to be pleasant when she eventually arrived because of the CV, but I was getting tired of her life-sapping conversation about her job. I found it difficult to maintain a sense of proportion with someone who put her work so far above everything else.

She finally went too far when I'd organised some tickets to go to a film together. She called while I was waiting at a pub next to the cinema to say she was behind with an office assignment, but would be with me shortly. I waited and waited, until it was too late to sell the tickets back to anyone in the queue. There was no queue. The film had started a lifetime ago. I went home without calling her. She finally caught up with me back at the flat, just as I was about to go to bed. I buzzed her in. She rushed up the stairs.

"James, I'm sorry," she gasped, breathlessly. "If work has to be done, it has to be done. You know what Martin's like."

Martin was her boss. Why are they always called 'Martin'? I'd had a few drinks by then and was not in a forgiving mood.

"Listen, Tina," I began. "That's three strikes. You're not long on manners, are you? In fact you're about as reliable as a Filipino ferry. I'm not an Allied Swiss employee and I'm not on their payroll, but through you they seem remarkably profligate in wasting my time. I'm fed up with stress-heads in finance. You say it's a big bank. So what? Look at Barings. Look what happened to them. They fucked up. They all do in the end."

"Perhaps," she responded, sounding unconvinced. "But while Allied Swiss are ahead, I'm going to give them one hundred percent of whatever they want."

"Fine, but not on my account. I despise them," I retorted.

"James, I'm only trying to do a decent day's work," she pleaded. "I'm not much good for anything else. It's the only chance I've got and Allied Swiss has given it to me. I'm not going to throw that away for some stupid film."

"Tina," I began, building up a head of steam, "you said under your wants and desires in your computer profile, 'WLTM suitor for love and commitment and able to offer same in return'. Well, you've got all that with Allied Swiss Bank. You don't need me and I'm not looking for the 'good attendance medal' type either. You can give your favourite teddy bear and your dying breath to Allied Swiss for all I care, but you can't expect me to hang around your small, disappointing life on the off-chance that you *might* be able to fit me in around *their* schedule."

Tina went quiet. A tear trickled down the side of her cheek. She opened her bag and silently handed me an envelope. I opened it and looked at the contents. There was a newer, even smarter version of my CV, together with a copy on disk. I looked at her again.

"That's why I was delayed," she said, in what sounded like a mixture of mumpish justification and self-pity.

I wanted to say something but I was too slow off the mark. She'd snapped her bag shut and was already halfway to the front door. I heard the door slam. I felt a complete heel. So much for my head of steam; it had utterly evaporated. I glanced again at the CV. Hang on, I thought, it couldn't have taken *that* long to change the font and run off a disk. Whatever the cause, the effect was that we never saw each other again.

The twelve year gap in my already threadbare CV looked just plain silly. I mulled over the problem at work the next morning and came to the conclusion that my only chance of ever finding an alternative place of employment would be via a recommendation or a referral. As a recommendation was unlikely to be forthcoming at that moment, I decided to treat Pete Divis's contact, the mellifluous Mr Heimann at the larger headhunting firm, as a referral. I called him shortly after noon when most of my colleagues had piled over to the pub opposite. He was slightly befuddled by my approach and had no recall of Pete when I explained how I'd come across his name. Undaunted, I gave him a brief rundown of my experience and managed to strong-arm him into agreeing to see me one lunchtime the following week. We decided Wednesday would be a good day.

It was nearly summer. Spring had gone in a dazed instant. The big deal, however, was in no such hurry. It was still creaking along at its own pace. In theory everyone was in agreement, but in practice this simply wasn't so. There was always a niggle that needed to be seen to, or a clarification about who was being paid what before everybody could proceed to the next stage. Despite our fracas, Craig was still very much driving my car and I had to take the back seat while he busied himself on my behalf. I had no choice. Fred saw to it that I wasn't involved in or informed of what was going on. Recently I had taken to going into the office at absurdly early hours in the morning in order to photocopy various files and reports in case I had to abandon ship *rapidement*. After I'd done the necessary, I would disappear faraway for a coffee or something stronger if I could find it, before re-entering the premises at the normal time. There were no CCTVs or time devices recording my movements that I was aware of, but I was probably fooling no one. If I had had the smarts I could have downloaded the whole lot on to a single disk, but I knew there was a firewall in the computer that would have given the game away. Perhaps I was paranoid but, I reasoned to myself, I was learning that paranoia was healthy when it came to dealing with Fred Armitage.

I slipped out of the office the next Wednesday in good time to be with Mr Heimann at the 'larger headhunting company', taking in a schooner of aroma-less dry sherry at a gay pub nearby.

The company had its own office building in St James's. They weren't 'larger'; they were 'big'. I'd known the firm for many years from when I'd been a more tradable commodity. They'd put me into

Conmax Securities just before the crash of '87. A stoat with a roach-clip moustache and goatee came into the reception area. He was about my age. It was Heimann. He took a look at me as he was showing me into his office and I could tell he wasn't interested. I wasn't surprised. I'd cut my nose on a banister while falling down the stairs when I was drunk a few days before, and the bandage now made me look like a criminal.

He indicated to a chair and we sat down. I handed him a copy of my CV. I had tried to conceal the missing twelve years in my job history by artfully having my details spread over two pages, the twelve years magically disappearing when flipping from the first page to the second, and the staple attaching the two pages placed in such a way that it obscured the dates at the top of the second page. He paused out of politeness to look at it briefly and mercifully never got beyond the first page. Instead he lighted upon the fact that I'd gone to St Dweeb's. He quickly mentioned that he had his two sons there in a tone that seemed to emphasise that he was in a position to afford it. I noticed a greatcoat hanging behind the door that rang a vague bell. I wondered whether he'd been the man I'd seen frothing at the mouth on the touchline of Emma Behr's son's hockey match earlier that spring term. I doubted it, although he too had all the attributes of a first-time buyer.

We chatted for a bit. I mentioned that his company had helped me find a job at Conmax Securities a while ago. He had another glimpse at my CV and put it on his desk. He thought for a moment and then spoke.

"Mr Mallet," he began, "as a company we are always pleased to maintain ties with our former candidates and keep abreast of their progress, but regarding our own hiring requirements, we tend to look to the MBA, or at least the CFA end of the scale before we consider any selection."

"That's a shame for you," I said.

"In what respect, Mr Mallet?" he quizzed, looking slightly puzzled.

"Because MBAs are only put on this earth to talk to other MBAs," I replied, sullenly. I didn't care. He'd already told me there wasn't a job for me.

"That's not true, Mr Mallet," he said, going on the attack. "You've only got to look at the sort of people who are prepared to undertake the hard work required of an MBA program; without exception they're studious, ambitious and eager to improve. The MBA credential is a widely applicable qualification that has been tremendously beneficial to the commercial world."

"Has it?" I enquired doubtfully. "It hasn't done the American car industries any favours and they've been the greatest exponents of the MBA ethos."

"Well, we're really more interested in banking and finance in this instance, Mr Mallet" he asserted, touchily.

"And they're different?" I hit back. "Are they immune to market forces?"

"Of course not. That's not what I said, Mr Mallet," he objected, starting to get narked.

"Good!" I declared, malevolently. "Because there are a few cracks in the financial wall that will take more than a couple of MBAs to paper over. MBAs didn't exist fifty years ago. They're a Hallmark invention, like Mother's Day or Father's Day. They're an entirely arbitrary qualification. They're not like a legal or medical proficiency or, say, a commercial pilot's licence yet everyone seems to behave as if they're magic wands: they've created their own market. Like actuaries... just look at them! Give them a shifting demographic and they wouldn't know one end of the Phillips curve from the other. Or the Institute of Directors. What about them? What have they added to the world, beyond their own self-interest?"

"That's enough, Mr Mallet!" He'd lost it. "I'm sure most people would disagree with you, and besides these are the yardsticks that the world goes by. We have to sort the sheep from the goats."

"I wonder what happens to the goats," I said, suddenly taking an interest in his lower lip garden.

He glanced at my CV again, uncomfortably.

"Are you married, Mr Mallet? It doesn't mention it in your particulars."

"No. I have a microwave."

"What about languages? Any French? Or Spanish, perhaps?" he asked timidly, getting desperate.

"There is no need for peasant languages in the society I keep, Mr Heimann," I informed him, sternly, "but I expect you know them all."

"I think we'll leave it there, shall we?" he suggested, suddenly looking a bit frazzled.

We got up and shook hands stiffly.

"Let me give you my card," he said, opening a desk drawer. "We're always on the lookout for good people – if you know of any."

I looked at it.

Paul Heimann MBA
Actuary
and member of
The Institute of Directors.

And the air of a council planning clerk. I practically creased myself once I got outside. Of course I'd cheated. I'd looked up his profile on his company website before going to the interview, but that didn't make it any less funny. Not to me, it didn't. I had to share it with someone. I called Wally Barker and told him all about putting Mr Heimann to rights over his MBA obsession.

"Excellent!" he effused, with the luxury of an Oxford double first under his belt. "It's ridiculous: people solemnly pay to sit in some breezeblock university in Lausanne for a year and hey presto suddenly they feel entitled to triple their last salary! MBAs are like titles: you go out and buy them; they're not gentlemanly. Elocution lessons would be much more beneficial. I mean, have you ever heard of anyone who's actually failed an MBA?"

With that Wally had to go, so we left it there.

My recent attempts to find romantic compatibility via the computer had left me with a sense of scepticism about electronic matchmaking. So it was with a heavy heart and a sense of an expedition feebly abandoned that I consigned the details of Penny Gibbs, 'Age: 43; Interests: canoeing and canoodling (!!)' to the waste bin of what would never be. However, if my data-dating darlings had left me feeling somewhat jaded, it was simple human neighbourliness that was to prove that romance, of a sort, was not dead but merely hiding just around the corner.

It had become Emma Behr's wont, or in this instance folly, to ask me at short notice to make up numbers at her various dinner parties whenever she was short of a guest. I wasn't feeling madly inspired by the time she summoned me to supper on this occasion, as I was just in the middle of a bottle of Latvian screw top and already quite mellow when she called. However, as she had come to the rescue in my hour of need so recently I felt beholden to comply with her subpoena.

I wasn't expecting an outrageously exciting group, and my expectations were amply met. The men looked a bit wet, and aside from Emma the only woman who appeared vaguely enticing was so taken with herself that there didn't seem to be room to manoeuvre. Instead I spoke to a plainer but more approachable guest called

Monica, a Canadian who'd also been invited as a last-minute shoe-in. She was a loss adjuster and had lived in the UK for several years.

There were ten of us in all and the evening initially passed away pleasantly enough. I was probably not alone in becoming a little drunk, but I was alone in becoming belligerent. One of the men had to leave early as he had a plane to catch the next morning. The conversation turned to our own travel experiences after he'd left, and the woman who was up herself took the floor.

"I had an amazing thing happen to me last month when I was going to New York," she announced to the remaining ensemble. "This guy came up to me while I was queuing at check-in and said he'd get me upgraded to first if I sat next to him."

"He wanted your cunt," I muttered moodily to myself. No one heard.

"So I sat with him in first and we talked," she went on. "We had some champagne, ate great food and then when we got to New York he had this fabulous limo waiting to take us into town. He said there was no way he was letting me stay in the hotel where I was booked and instead ordered me a suite at The Pierre on Fifth where he was staying!"

"He wanted your cunt," I mumbled again, under my breath.

"Well it only turns out he's got an even bigger suite a couple of doors down the hall and he sends me the biggest bunch of roses I had ever seen in my entire life!" she shrieked, exuberantly.

"He wanted your cunt," I murmured, still unnoticed.

"So then he takes me to *the* most expensive restaurant on Park Avenue, orders a bottle of Krug and a bottle of Petrus '74 to go with the lobster that *I chose* from the tank!" she continued, whipping herself into a frenzy.

"He wanted your cunt," I said, upping the volume to an almost audible whisper.

"And then the next day he takes me to Saks and buys me the most darling Balmain outfit – for the opera we're going to that evening – balcony seats, of course!" she whooped, almost on the brink of going multiple.

"He wanted your cunt," I repeated, still sotto voce but loud enough to register.

Emma gave a confused double take.

"But get this;" the woman gabbled on, obliviously, "before we make off for the opera, we're having drinks in his suite – champagne, of course, except this time it's Bollinger '88 and he produces this box from Tiffany's with the most exquisite three string freshwater pearl necklace in the world – to go with my new dress, *naturellement!*"

"He so definitely wanted your cunt!" I said conversationally, throwing caution to the wind. Suddenly everyone realised what I'd been muttering.

"Shut up, James," Emma barked, irritably. "I want to hear what happened. What *did* happen?"

"He had to go to Chicago the next day and I had to check out of the hotel," the women replied, wistfully.

"Was that it?" Emma enquired, anxiously. "Did you ever hear from him again?"

"Not exactly," the woman replied, bashfully. "But he was very nice."

"And he got what he wanted," I extrapolated helpfully, putting the matter, to my mind, to rest.

The evening ended on a slightly subdued note. Emma held me back as the other guests were about to go.

"James, I want a word with you," she said as she waved the last person off. I knew I was in trouble.

She closed the door and turned to address me.

"James, all I'm going to say is, *that* word is going to get you into deep confrontation one day."

How right she was, as events were later to prove.

"I'm sorry Emma," I said, feeling suitably chastened. "It always comes out when I'm a bit juiced up. That woman didn't help; it comes out like a truth drug the moment I get a whiff of any Billy Bullshit. It's a bit like Tourette's syndrome... but it's such a good word... and it breaks the ice at parties."

"Well it doesn't cut any ice at mine, nor anyone else's for that matter. That's not how polite company operates," she admonished. "Now go!"

I walked into the night, humbled and depressed, again.

To my surprise there was a figure leaning against a car a few yards further along in the dark. It was Monica, the Canadian woman, of all people.

"Hello, James," she said, cheerfully. "Did Emma give you a bit of stick?"

"Some," I said, glad of her upbeat tone, but at a loss as to what she was doing there.

"I'm not surprised, but you hit the nail on the head," she remarked, approvingly.

"In what way?" I asked, searching for some positive ratification for my behaviour.

"You proved your point," she announced, straightening herself up. "Rich boys like pretty girls and pretty girls like rich boys. Nature doesn't fool around looking decorative just for sake of it."

"I'm glad you saw it that way," I said, as we started to walk down the road together, adding hazily, "Dexter's Law."

"Dexter's what?" she enquired, distractedly.

"Mike Dexter, an old acquaintance. He mentioned it to me shortly before I went to pri..." I trailed off, just in time. Now was not the right time to mention my nefarious past. There never really was a right time.

"To where?" she pressed.

"To Princeton. I was sent there by my company for a six week course on financial engineering," I lied, hurriedly. "But Mike Dexter's Law Number One was 'There's nothing that cunt likes more than money. And money *loves* cunt'."

Phew. That was close. A diversion at least.

"Delightful. I dread to think what Mr Dexter's other laws were," Monica censured, a little sanctimoniously.

"I don't think there were any others," I prattled on, relieved. "He seemed to think Law Number One was enough to explain the mysteries of life."

"However as we in the real world know, it's not quite that simple," she declared, learnedly. "Compromises have to be made, but most people still have a price. We're all whores, one way or another."

"Although I'll admit in my case crudity tends to devalue candour," I said, in reference to my recent use of language.

We came to a road junction.

"It's getting late," she said, looking at me obliquely. "I've got to go this way."

"And I've got to go that way," I said, still wondering why she'd hung back as I started to move in the other direction.

"James, wait: I'll give you my card," she said, reaching into her bag. "Give me a call if you want."

All was explained. She passed me her card without another word. I looked at it as she turned to go the other way. How strange. She wasn't quite what I was looking for, but the moment had left me feeling pleasantly bewildered. I watched her as she walked away. Nice butt though, I thought to myself. On second impression, she was quite a sassy little thing.

Chapter 18: Disintegration

Summer segued unobtrusively into autumn and life trudged on in its now customary colourless custom with the big deal as ever, neither closer or further from fruition. If there were any personal storms gathering, they were content, for the time being, merely to manifest themselves as ill winds. Dresden Commercial Bank, amid rumours that it was about to be taken over by a rival Teuton institution, had had a change of heart about its commitment to its London operation and decided to fire almost everyone on the dealing floor, including Sven Gläzner and Amy Batamato. It was a sad for day both of them as, to a slightly lesser extent, it was for me. DCBI had been my only regular performing account, even if it had gone cold in recent times.

Teresa Batamato was less than sanguine about her little sister's plight when she called a few days later.

"James, I thought I told you 'no funny stuff' when I originally gave you Amy's number, and now this happens. She'd hardly been there nine months. That's not going to do wonders for a girl's track record, is it?"

"Teresa, I don't think I can be called totally to account for DCBI's sudden sea change," I said, I thought with some justification.

"No, but you can be called to account for branding DCBI a blue chip company to Amy," she hit back, angrily.

"I thought it was," I appealed, with wounded honesty.

"Blue chip? Chip fat, more like. They were useless!" she rallied. "They couldn't settle any of Amy's trades, not that she was able to do many without being messed about. The research was non-existent and there was zero support. It was embarrassing! All her clients gave up in the end; she lost the lot. They won't come back."

"I'm sorry," I said, feeling genuine remorse. "I'll try to get her in somewhere else."

"Oh, no, you won't!" Teresa remonstrated, fiercely. "I'm not letting you anywhere near her! I don't care if she goes off to help starving children in Cambodia as long as she's a million miles from you. You stay away from her, you hear?"

Sven Gläzner was a little more pragmatic when we spoke. I asked him if there was anything I could do to help.

"I dunno, James. I thought I saw some trouble coming, but I had no idea it was going to be this bad. It kinda takes away your faith in the system. I guess I was sold a rinky-dink and passed it on to everyone else I hired. Now I'm the one who's toxic waste. No one's going to take me on in a hurry after this shit."

"No country for old Sven?" I suggested, hating myself the second I'd said it.

"I suppose it's time I reassessed my priorities in life, whatever they are," he carried on, regardless.

"You gave me a break, Sven. I won't forget that. I'll call you if I hear of anything," I said unconvincingly, feeling now was not the time to mention Cambodia. Or taking in a show.

The big deal was being a big pain. Whether it was the client or one of the other protagonists who were playing up I never knew, such was Fred Armitage's determination to keep me out of the picture. But I found another source of solace in an unlicensed newsagent run by a wily Pathan, who sold Alcopops and bravely named lagers from a fridge at the back. Then I would sit in an overgrown thicket in a graveyard nearby for as long as was decently possible, just to keep out of Fred's hair. At home I no longer bothered with beer or wine if I could help it. I couldn't see the point. I either had whisky or, if I was feeling saintly, whisky with a dash of water. I was now falling over with such regularity that I was practically on first name terms with half the medics at the Chelsea A & E.

With Sven no longer in play and the big deal in a near permanent state of permafrost, I was beginning to run out of money. Things weren't helped by my flatmate upping sticks and vacating the flat without so much as a week's notice. Either he'd had enough or he reckoned there wasn't much point paying me any rent now that he was spending all his time at his girlfriend's flat. There was no way I was going to be able to pay for a lease extension. I had a lurking notion that the property market was getting a bit toppy and wondered whether now might be as good a time as any to sell. I could then buy something more modest or rent somewhere for a while. I heard that a smaller flat, slightly further down the road was being sold by a woman I vaguely knew. I found her number and called her to see if this was the case. She said it was, so I ran the suggestion that if we to came to a private understanding we could cut out the external fees. She saw my logic and agreed a time to view.

The flat was perfect. Although it was smaller by a bedroom and a bathroom than mine, it had a good feel. There was a separate storeroom which would come in handy should I decide to let the place out and disappear on an Elspeth-free gin and tonic bender round the world with some of the money left over from the exchange of contracts.

I had a few drinks at home before going over to the other flat and was feeling quite relaxed by the time I got there. Mrs Little Flat opened a bottle of wine once she'd finished showing me around, and we sat down to discuss numbers. She was bespectacled, probably of pensionable age, but there was a pleasing tenor about her. In the warm glow of the table lamp by the sofa where she was sitting, she looked strangely beguiling.

We chatted casually about the local property scene for a while. If she knew anything about my less than perfect past, she didn't show it. She wanted me on side. If we could do a private sale, she would save thousands in estate agents' commission. She rose to refill my glass. I clocked her considerable, if mottled cleavage as she bent over. She wasn't showing off, surely? Or was she? Exhibition or invitation? My genitalia stirred in sympathetic speculation at either prospect.

She sat down again, her bosoms heaving slightly after all the exertion. They were all I could think of. I was fixated. They were all that I wanted: a dirty great pair of fat, sloppy old tits slapping against my stubbly chops as I buried my face deep into her ever-swelling chest. My erection was starting to become unmanageable, as it nosed its way hungrily through the seamy labyrinth of my Y-fronts, faster than a snake through weeds. I crossed my legs.

"Of course Foxtons are very good, but I like the man at Winkworth... what's his name...?" she burbled, as my tumescence assumed agonising dimensions against the portal of my fly zip.

"Someone told me that Douglas & Gordon are very good, but of course I'd rather deal directly, especially with someone who I know and trust," she warbled on, idiotically.

Shut up, you old bag! Shut the fuck up! Fuck, fuck, fuck! Oh, no! My thingie had gone all sticky.

"And I could deduct fixtures and fittings off the price to keep you within the lower stamp tax band."

Shut up! Shut up! Shut up! I took a large gulp of wine.

"The curtains are very good. They keep the light out in the summer and keep the heat in, in the winter..."

Oh, for Christ's sake! I wanted to explode. All it would take was two quick strokes through my trouser pockets with a diversionary cough and I could finish the job in seconds.

"The carpets are in quite good condition, but they need to be professionally cleaned to really bring them up nicely..."

So would my underpants if I didn't think of something quickly.

"Would you mind if I sat next to you?"

Silence. Who said that? Shit! It was me. It was my voice. Fuck! There was no going back now.

"Sorry, I don't think I heard what you were saying," Mrs Little Flat remarked, one eyebrow lost forever.

"I said, 'Would you mind if I chat next to you?'" I falsified, to little effect. The damage was done.

More silence. Oh, dear. *How embarrassing!* If I could turn back time!

Mrs Little Flat looked utterly perplexed, as she slowly latched on to what I might or might not be insinuating. She peered at me over her demi-lunettes, more in disbelief than shock, and then slowly, sadly, shook her head.

"I'm so sorry... my words might have been misconstrued... I think I've had a bit too much to drink," I stammered, unconvincingly.

My erection, as if by magic, quickly made itself disappear. It had left town without saying so much as a 'fare-thee-well' and was now hiding in the dense undergrowth of my pubic plumage, like the dastardly coward I had come to loathe and distrust.

Mrs Little Flat showed me warily to the door.

"I hope this doesn't jeopardise what we've discussed," I mumbled, hopelessly. "I'll call you tomorrow, if that's OK?"

She closed the door firmly behind me and triple-bolted it noisily. I skulked off into the night with my ignoble tail well between my legs. What a chump I was. Maybe it was time to turn myself in. But where?

Paradoxically I received a call out of the blue the very next day from Monica, the Canadian loss adjuster woman I'd encountered at Emma Behr's dinner party from what was now a fortnight ago. I'd kept her business card but I'd been unable to summon the energy to get in contact and had let the moment pass. But Monica hadn't, which was odd as the North American loss adjuster type didn't normally take to me. In the absence of any move on my part she'd asked Emma for my number and was phoning to ask me to a private view at an art gallery that evening in the West End. Not more art? I didn't know what to say. I didn't want anything to start between us. I wasn't in the mood, and yet I was flattered that she'd called. It didn't happen much these days. I had to make a decision.

"Sure. I can meet you there after work," I proposed, denying her any suggestion that we might go there *together*.

"I've asked Emma if she wants to come too," she added, as if to legitimise the invitation with another *fun* person.

It was also, I suspected rightly, Monica's idea of initiating and reciprocating hospitality. It didn't cost anything and required little effort on her part.

I arrived casually late. Monica greeted me excitedly, her eyes feverishly devouring every move and body signal that I unwittingly happened to make. I remained polite but distant. Emma Behr appeared soon afterwards with her friend Beryl Holmes, the Ratgirl who'd been with her the first time we'd met. That's what I liked about private views: they were open to the public. At least the pair provided a momentary diversion for me to go in search of a drink, although I'd taken the precaution of packing a hip flask in case the catering situation wasn't up to standard.

I spotted a waiter with a tray of champagne and made a beeline. Just as I scooped up my flute's worth a woman with a similar calling carelessly knocked my arm, causing me to spill some of my drink. She offered no apology.

"Vot eez zat?" she demanded, waving at the remaining contents of my glass to the waiter.

"Champagne, madam," he replied.

"Vot sort?" she questioned, imperiously.

The waiter looked back towards the bar area.

"Moët et Chandon, I believe, madam," he answered.

"I only drink Cristsal," she informed him snootily, as if he should have known, and promptly selected a glass of orange juice, thus disproving her point.

I was impressed. I looked at her. Her features were so flawless, so utterly ovate, that they bordered on the bland: eyes without a face.

The waiter moved on, leaving us alone. I tried to think of something to say.

"I take it you're not from these shores," I remarked, delicately.

"Vot you not sure?" she queried, going slightly off topic.

"No: I was saying I didn't think you were originally from England," I explained.

"I'm from Poland," she muttered, already sounding bored.

"Oh, how nice. But you live in London?" I ventured, deferentially.

"Yes. I live in the most fashionable street in Acton," she declared, without irony.

"Isn't that a contradiction in terms?" I chided, good-humouredly.

"There are no turns. I live on a straight road," she made clear, looking at me as if I was a moron.

I was getting nowhere in a hurry. I took her in again. She had a body that must have been developed by NASA. She was manufactured for sex. Commercial sex of sorts, of course, not relationship sex, or not with me at least. She was nicely turned out, in a summery dress that accentuated her proportions magnificently. But it was the clashing peach lipstick and mauve mascara that made me nearly cream my jeans.

"What do you do, work-wise?" I asked, clutching at anything to keep in the conversation.

"I vork vor important fashion house in Sloane Street," she replied, haughtily. *Ergo* a shop assistant, I thought to myself.

"Well, thank goodness for that," I said, getting desperate. She wasn't making it easy.

Then, just as I was about to give up, she sparked to life.

"Vot you do?"

"I vork vor a firm of headhunters," I said, in unintentionally cloning her voice.

"You not vork vor bank?" she demanded.

"No, but I vork *for* banks," I explained, hoping I wasn't confusing her.

"Why four banks?" she probed, looking utterly perplexed.

"No not four banks, for banks," I clarified, breaking into a sweat.

"I don't believe," she asserted, dismissively. She was losing interest. And I was losing the will to live.

I looked round and saw Monica giving me the evils with almost erotic hostility.

"Would you excuse me?" I asked the Polish woman, with unnecessary courtliness. She gazed at me blankly. I looked into her eyes again. I couldn't detect much of an intellectual hinterland. The reel was turning but the projectionist was dead.

I put my glass down and headed for the exit. Phew! It was good to be outside. I spotted an alleyway a few doors down and ducked out of sight. I reached for my hip flask. The Polish woman had given me the heebie-jeebies. I unscrewed the top of the hip flask and chucked back half the contents in one gulp. That was better. I replaced the cap, returned the flask to my pocket and re-entered the gallery. Monica was waiting.

"Oh, Hello!" I said, with prickly effervescence. "This is nice, isn't it?"

"Isn't it just," Monica acknowledged coolly, before going in for the kill. "Was that woman a friend of yours?"

"No," I said, truthfully. "She just happened to be there."

"Oh," she commented, affecting only a passing interest. "So do you like the exhibits?"

"Yours or hers?" I replied jokingly, surveying the general artistic mishmash. "Are they all by the same person?"

"I don't think so," she reflected, pondering the sanity of my question.

"Monica," I put forward, casting about for another means of escape, "would you mind if I left you for a moment? I need to find the loo."

The only lavatory was downstairs in the basement, as was the other half of the exhibition. I locked the door behind me, took the hip flask out of my pocket and sank the remaining half right on the spot. I might have quenched my thirst now, but what was I going to do about Monica? I couldn't stay in the loo forever. I pulled the chain without peeing, washed my hands and re-entered the downstairs display area. I looked at some paintings. There was nowhere to hide. There were no other exits. The only way was up. A conversation nearby diverted my attention. I turned round. It was Rick Cooper, the popster lead singer with the messiah complex hairdo from Simply Ill-Bred, talking, so it seemed, to his business partner. What luck! A diversion indeed! The alcohol was now pumping nicely through my veins. I could do anything. I was bored with the paintings and had a compulsion to introduce myself. The compulsion had to be obeyed.

"Wotcha, Rick!" I blurted abruptly, right in the middle of their conversation.

The business partner-type looked at me as if I was an idiot.

"Love your stuff, man!" I blathered on, obliviously. "I listen to 'Bunny's Too White to Section' the whole time, man! It's massive, man!"

"Thank you," Rick allowed, quietly. He didn't look too annoyed. He was used to it. He just looked a little sad. His face seemed to say, 'What is this sound coming out of the red-faced man's mouth?'

I read the hint.

"Sorry, man. Just had to say it!" I squeaked, retreating towards the stairs. "Keep up the good work, man!"

Not again?! It was *so embarrassing!* I wanted to regress into a sperm. I was such a dickhead. What was I thinking? That a few atoms of his success might rub off on me? Why couldn't I just shut up? Or put a cork in it? I was out of my mind. My brain wouldn't do what it was told. It did as it wanted. I had no control.

I saw Emma and Beryl chatting at the top of the stairs. Thank God! I started to climb up, snaffling a drink off a waiter on his way down. I joined them.

"I was just saying to Emma, it's my turn to have a dinner party. What do you think, James?" Beryl asked, as if my opinion ever counted.

"I'm sure it's my turn to do something," I mumbled. "I never do anything."

"James, you're a boy!" Emma oozed, maternally. "You're not expected to do anything. Just smile and buy the drinks."

"Whatever... but don't talk about dinner parties right now," I said, seeing Monica advancing towards us.

"Are you all right?" Monica quizzed me, with a concerned frown.

I didn't know then, but it was a question I would soon tire of.

"I'm fine," I said, trying to pay her no attention.

But I wasn't fine. I felt decidedly ill. I hadn't eaten all day and the hip flask was taking its toll. I hoovered my champagne in one to prove to myself, as much as the others, that nothing was wrong. It was a mistake. I immediately felt über-queasy.

"Excuse me, everybody," I said, making another dash for the exit. I made it to the little alleyway just in time and puked. And puked. But I wasn't puking food. It was blood. I heard steps behind me and a voice.

"James... are you all right?"

Oh God. It was Monica.

"What does it look like?" I replied, biliously.

"I'll look after you," she answered, ominously.

"I'll be OK," I insisted unconvincingly, as I started to retch again.

"I'll get a taxi," she said with maidish urgency, as if my continued existence depended on it. At that moment it did.

She came back a few minutes later.

"I've got one, poppet," she said, lending me a steadying hand.

Poppet? Yech.

She guided me towards the waiting cab.

"He'll be all right," she assured the driver, who was looking at me dubiously.

I lay on the seat. The window was open. The skyline swept by. I felt a bit better. Just very tired. I closed my eyes. I needed to get home. I opened my eyes again. We were going in the wrong direction. Where were we going? Not another A&E unit? Monica told me not to worry. Too exhausted to think, I fell asleep.

"Come on, poppet!"

Not again? We were outside her flat. The driver helped me out. Monica paid him and then manhandled me into a lift. The next moment I was in her flat and about to black out.

I awoke the following morning in a strange bed. I looked around. Monica was beside me, still asleep. I didn't feel too bad, all things considered, but my mouth was as dry as dust. I must have puked out five pints of liquid. I rose slowly out of bed, careful not to disturb Monica. I was wearing pyjamas. Pyjamas? How did that happen? I headed for the kitchen. It was new and shiny. Not like mine. She had a double fridge. The bitch was minted! I looked in. There was loads of girls' stuff; health juices and low-fat pudding pots. Then I saw what I was looking for, just behind the lo-cal soya milk. Four small tins of lager. Carlsbergs. A good breakfast beer perhaps, but not quite strong enough for the kick inside. Typical woman. She wouldn't have known any better. They would have to do. I stretched through and broke a tin off from the pack. I pulled the ring and slowly reached for another one.

I wandered into the drawing room, had a slug from the can and burped loudly. I looked around. There was a reproduction painting of a cart in a ditch on the drawing room wall and some preposterous union jack cushions scattered on the sofa. I found a cartoon in the loo of some cats and dogs peeing against a wall. Very amusing. It was a nice flat, but something was missing. I glanced about. I couldn't quite nail it. And then it hit me. Apart from a boring thinky publication left casually on the coffee table, there was no literature, anywhere. No books, no newspapers, no magazines, not even any junk mail in a wastepaper basket. The place was infecund; it was incapable of propagating any literary progeny. Was this the product of a tidy mind or an empty life? Or were they same thing? I heard some rustling in the bedroom. My belch must have woken the kraken.

Monica appeared in a white towelling dressing gown. She looked quite becoming, until she opened her mouth.

"Are you all right, pet?"

It was too early for politesse, but there was no place for profundities either.

"I'm better, thank you," I replied stiffly, then relaxed. "And thanks for helping me last night. I don't know what came over me."

"I do," she remarked, without reproach. "Don't worry, I'll look after you."

No, not again? Was this *Play Misty for Me* or *Misery*?

She came a little closer. She pulled me towards her. I buried my face in her hair. I caught the slight scent of her previous night's shampoo.

"I love the smell of balsam in the morning," I murmured, softly. "It smells like... victory."

She didn't register.

"I think we've got a lot of work to do, don't you?" she teased, drawing me in tighter.

My penis inclined in agreement and politely raised its hat.

No! No! No! Not now, *please!*

"What do you mean?" I asked, as my stupid penis started to rear its ugly head over my pyjamas.

God, how I hated that thing.

"I mean you've been a very naughty boy for a very long time," she taunted, strengthening her grip, python-like.

"What's it to you?" I questioned, panicked as my pyjama bottoms turned mainsail.

"Nothing, perhaps. But I know something that might help. Oh, look what we've got here!" she giggled, glancing down. "I wonder what it is!"

She led me back to the bedroom. Bitch! There was nothing I could do. Not with a spine of a jellyfish and my pyjama display flapping like a spinnaker in a force ten. I was all at sea.

I regretted everything the second we'd finished. "Don't do the slime if you can't do the time," an Australian friend had once advised me. I knew there would be a problem. Not that anything had been bad or disappointing. In fact, it was quite the opposite. The momentary release from everyday cares was cathartic, to say the least. There hadn't been such relief since Mafeking! That was the problem. If I wanted any more of this sort of comfort, I'd be locked in. Monica knew what she was doing, but why? I was subsequently told by a mutual friend that Monica had arrived from Canada several years before, looking for her 'dook'. She'd had little success but had mistakenly alighted on me as a possible candidate because of my association with Emma Behr, who she regarded as part of the 'smart set'. In her haste to assimilate she'd adopted various incongruous Anglicisms like 'pet', 'poppet' and 'rotter' and was under the impression that she'd now found someone genuinely 'English'. She had, but then again so was Jack the Ripper, probably. To her credit she was sexy, kind and accomplished. There was absolutely nothing wrong with her, except I wasn't of the mind for an emotional Helvetica. There seemed no point sacrificing autonomy for a contrived relationship.

So there was my dilemma. Should I count my blessings or walk away a free, but lonely man? Had I reached the age and stage where the options were limited, and accept that chance without choice was the only thing on the menu? Had life's musical chairs finally ended and was I the only one left standing? And wasn't it just providence, as was so often the case, that the one woman on the planet who saw any value in me was the one woman I didn't want? What value did she see? It was obvious I weren't no 'dook'. What did she *really* want? She was a lovely woman; the sort you could take home to your parents. And leave there.

But I gave in. I was in no state to fight. For a time Monica and I led a cosseted, if slightly boring co-existence, mainly at weekends, eating microwaved slop in front of the TV, watching late night reruns of *Father Turd* and *Jonathan Crack*. Our social life, such as it was, mainly consisted of occasional forays to private views and Monica's company's corporate events, neither of which afforded me much excitement unless I was totally trashed, but sufficed for Monica. For her, a drunk me was better than a no me. Or so I thought, because little did I know that Monica had forged a dialogue, indeed a close association, with my own darling sister, and every pixilated move I made was being monitored and collected for onward transmission to Elspeth's information cell as evidence for the prosecution. Monica loved it. It meant she was part of a secret; she belonged to something at last. She'd finally found her very own Peyton Place. Now I knew what she wanted.

This culminated one evening when Monica and I were in bed enjoying the benefits of each other's company, when by a complete freak of nature I accidentally farted and, sad to relate, followed through on to her leg. Peregrine Blucher's words of warning about alcohol-induced incontinence rang a horrible bell.

"You rotter!" she cried, good-naturedly as she got out of bed to clean herself off and I rolled over to go to sleep. Was there nothing I could do to put her off? The incident, however, did not go unreported and a few days later I received an unexpected visit from Elspeth. This time she *really* meant business. Unfortunately I was mortally pissed.

"Right, I've had enough. You're going to rehab," she announced, her face looking like a spanked arse.

"Oh, no, I'm not!" I contested, resolutely.

"There's a car waiting outside," she retorted,

"That's what you think," I said, taking another swig of grog straight from the neck.

"You're going, James, whether you like it or not!" she howled.

"Well, I don't like it, so I won't. Who the fuck do you think you are anyway?" I demanded angrily, and to my mind justifiably.

"A sister who's pretty fed up with your lack of consideration for me, our parents, and everyone else you happen to come in contact with!" she screeched, as her milk of human kindness quickly started to curdle.

"And I'm fed up with your postcode-sized arse, but I don't make a song and dance about it," I said, unkindly. "You should have surgery. It's a fucking disgrace. It's the only thing a man sees when he looks at you."

"Shut up. Pack your bags and bring your cheque book. And your passport," she ordered, wattle at full throttle.

"My passport?" I quizzed, in disbelief.

"Yes, you're off to Spain," she explained, tight-lipped. "It's not expensive. The change will do you good and it's only for six weeks."

"Six weeks?" I mewled, confounded. "I've got the biggest fucking deal of my life on my hands and you just march in and... "

"I've called your office," she cut in, looking particularly pleased with herself "They know what's going on. I have their full support and they've agreed it's in your best interests."

"I bet they have!" I howled. "That deal's worth millions and if I'm not there they ain't going to pay me a dime."

"That's a risk you'll have to take," she said, looking at me triumphantly. "Consequences, James. It's your life that's at stake here; money doesn't enter into it."

"You fucking bitch!" I screamed. "You just don't get it. You've never had to earn a proper living: you fucked everything with a wallet till you got to the top of the heap and just sat at home eating chocolates ever since."

"That's bullshit, and you know it," she asserted. "Most of my boyfriends were flat broke. Just because I happened to marry a man with a modicum of financial sanity doesn't make me a gold-digger. We lead an ordinary life and we both put in decent day's work. Secure? Perhaps. Ostentatious? Definitely not. Just because I'm generous with my time over you and put a few things in your fridge from time to time doesn't make me a bad person. Do you get it? And I hate chocolate."

"Well it certainly doesn't show!" I shouted unkindly and in the event, unwisely.

"We're done here, James," she whipped back, irrevocably. "Pack your stuff. You're out of here in five minutes."

"Listen you cunt..."

That did it. She came at me and socked me. I dropped like a stone. Well, I never! The old buzzard! She got me fair and square on the kisser! It was the surprise of it all and being pissed that floored me, rather than the actual force of the blow. I could have done something, but I didn't want a fight. Not with a woman. That had got me into trouble once before.

I got up from the floor. Elspeth was now on her mobile talking to the driver. Nice. I staggered to the bedroom. There was somebody there. It was Monica. She was packing my stuff. Judas! I'd never been sure of her. She smiled up at me timidly.

"Are you all right, poppet?"

"Oh, shut up, Monica. What is this? The fucking *Truman Show*?" I spat, contemptuously. Except it wasn't contempt. She wasn't worth it; she didn't count.

The driver was coming up the stairs, except he wasn't just the driver; he was the managing director of the rehab company. How pony. They must have been desperate for business. He was a big lad. I wasn't going to put up a fight. Not after Elspeth. If I couldn't take her on, I certainly wasn't going to put up my dukes for this lunk. He spoke.

"Come on, James. It'll be fine. You'll be with people who'll become friends... real friends... people who'll know what you're up against. They'll know how you feel."

He seemed alright.

Spain was rubbish and cost a fortune. A fortune I didn't have. It was like going on holiday with people I didn't know or particularly like for that matter, *and* having nothing to drink. Why Spain? Elspeth had found it on the internet and in her wisdom reckoned that it would be the best place for me to spend six weeks away from alcohol. Away from home. They had the AA twelve step program. It was tedious and I didn't get it. I made one or two friends towards the end, but it was probably because they were glad I was going. They all had tattoos and most were in for smack 'n' crack. I wasn't on their wavelength.

I got drunk on the way back. Monica was waiting for me at the airport. Shit.

"Are you all right popp... "

"I'm fine," I cut short. "Don't you dare say anything to Nurse Ratched back at Temperance Control in Arndale or I'll kill you. I've been sober for six weeks. I'm in charge now, so don't go mouthing off that I had a few perkers to celebrate on the way back, you understand?"

Things were weird when I went back to work a few days later. There was a surreal silence whenever I entered a room. I took Craig to one side one day when no one was around.

"What's going on with the big deal?" I asked.

"It looks as though it's going through, but I don't know when," he answered shiftily.

"How do you know it's going through?" I pressed.

"Everyone's signed the contract," he replied, looking over his shoulder.

"Are you sure?"

"Sure I'm sure," he reiterated. "They must be starting soon. Fred's already spending money as if it's going out of fashion. He's bought a new car."

"What sort?"

"A Mercedes SLK," he whispered, as if divulging state secrets.

"When did *he* take up hairdressing?" I asked, facetiously.

"He's got it parked round the back," Craig persisted, my frippery obviously frittered fruitlessly on his cloth ears. "He doesn't want anyone to know, but it's easy to spot; it's got personalised number plates."

"Like what?" I retorted, not so quietly. "Let me guess... Fred Armitage? How about 'FA 2U'?"

"Ha-ha," Craig laughed, without smiling. "He's been spending on other things too."

"Like what?" I demanded angrily, but with slightly waning interest.

"Russian hookers; the gee-gees: the usual stuff people like him get up to when they think they're cashed-up," Craig responded, sensing my annoyance. But I wasn't quite finished.

"Have you been paid?" I cross-examined, trying to think ahead.

"Of course not. The client hasn't sent the cheque through yet. They won't till everyone starts working, but it can't be long. It's all been agreed."

I tried my best to avoid annoying Fred, but short of shooting myself there wasn't much I could do to appease him. I was at his mercy. If he gave me the flick, that would be it; I'd get nothing. He had total power. Being away for six weeks hadn't exactly helped my case and was further proof, if proof were needed, that I'd been alcoholically neutered for most of the negotiations.

So I waited. I tried to see as little of Monica as possible. I had the odd drink on my own, but on the whole I was pretty good. A few people suggested I should go to at least some AA meetings as a form of after-sales service, but I'd just had six weeks of the stuff rammed down my throat and didn't need any more. Or so I told myself. Whatever I did, I had to make sure that Monica was totally unaware of any drink intake, however small. Anything to the contrary would, inevitably, get back to Elspeth.

Beryl Holmes, Emma Behr's Ratwoman friend, followed up her threat of having a dinner party and called to invite me.

"Do you want to bring Monica?" she asked, accommodatingly.

"Do you mind if I don't?" I replied. "But don't let me stop you from asking someone in her place."

"Let me have a think," she deliberated for a moment. "I might have someone who'll do."

"Do I know who?" I asked.

"Not yet," Beryl answered. "But you trust me, don't you?"

"Of course," I affirmed, without any intended sincerity.

The evening came. It was Saturday. In terms of alcohol I'd managed to keep my purdah dry for most of the day, but by nightfall I'd fallen into a state of irritation. I bought a bottle of so-so wine to bring with me. If I couldn't drink, I was damned if I was going to bring anything decent.

I knocked on Beryl's door and held my breath. It was the first occasion since going to Spain that I'd have to sit for any length of time and watch other people drink. Other recent social occasions had been tolerable because they'd been drinks parties or pub gatherings, where I could escape if necessary. Tonight I'd have to endure a minimum of three hours. I wondered who the mystery someone was that Beryl had lined up. Not Christine Hale, I prayed. I wasn't in the mood.

Beryl answered the door.

"James! How's Mr Abstemious?" she trilled.

"Wishing he wasn't," I answered tersely, but pretending to share the joke.

I hung my coat in the hall. Beryl had a pretty mews house neatly tucked away in a backwater of Pimlico which she insisted on referring to as 'Belgravia'. The other guests were already there. They looked up as I came in except one, a woman who had her elegant back to me as she chatted to a man opposite. There were eight of us, including inevitably Emma Behr. Beryl heralded my entrance with a flourish.

"And this, everybody," she announced with unwarranted enthusiasm, "is James Mallet!"

The woman with the handsome back stopped talking and turned round. My heart missed a beat. It was Fiona Fellon, a former fixture of my fantasies who curiously had taken to visiting me during the early stages of my prison confinement. She'd stopped visiting, almost as suddenly as she'd started and we hadn't seen or spoken to each other since. I'd subsequently been told that she wasn't particularly disposed towards male company, which made her visits all the more strange. But they stopped when she found a new girlfriend.

Beryl set about introducing me formally. There was a chap with a cravat who seemed to be Beryl's other half; then a slightly over-boisterous banker who, judging from his possessive behaviour, appeared to have appointed himself as Emma's object of attention for the evening; and a boring-looking couple from Wandsworth. Then there was Fiona.

"Hello James," she said, with an impish smile, as if she knew that I knew and it didn't matter anyway.

"Fiona," I said, slightly at a loss. "What a delight!"

Emma Behr needed no introduction, but even she looked a bit miffed by what was apparently Beryl's pairing of Fiona with me.

"James, let's get something *refreshing* for you to drink," Beryl offered firmly. "Come and have a look in the fridge."

I got the impression that she'd prepped everyone about my drinking situation. We went to the kitchen. I took advantage of having Beryl on her own.

"Bezza," I opened, chummily, "is Fiona the mystery surprise that we were working towards?"

"Well it's not *me*, silly!" she said, not taking me nearly seriously enough. "Why? Anything wrong?"

"Only that she's a les... " I lowered my voice "...a carpet muncher."

"A what?" Beryl quizzed, looking utterly confused.

"Prefers taco to sausage; a gusset nuzzler; a todger dodger... " I was starting to run out euphemisms "...prefers oysters to snails; a skirt lifter; off solids; someone who drinks from the other cup."

"I don't know what you're talking about," Beryl said, beginning to look cross.

"She's a *fucking lesbian*!" I hissed, exhausted by my attempts at discretion.

"I don't know what she is at the moment," Beryl remarked, calming down. "And I don't think she does either, but she was the only person I could get who was free this evening."

She handed me a Diet Coke and we went back to the drawing room. I spoke to the boring couple for a while. He worked for a fund management company and she had her hands full with the children. Beryl announced that supper was ready. We went through an alcove into the dining area and squeezed into our places around the table. I found myself sitting next to Fiona. The first course looked nice. The Diet Coke in front of me, didn't. I tried to engage Fiona in some arbitrary conversation about what she'd been up to since we'd last met, but everything I said came out sideways. I couldn't relax. Not without a proper drink. I felt crap and she looked great. It wasn't worth bothering. I could smell my own BO. The pheromones of fear. My mouth was as dry as my reservoir of ideas of what to talk about. I'd never had these problems when I was drinking.

Beryl took the first course plates away and then placed a casserole in the centre of the table for the second. She placed another can of Coke by my glass. She had gone to a lot of effort. Emma's slightly over-boisterous beau, if he was her beau, started talking to Fiona. I tried to join in but he wasn't having it; he was cock-blocking me like an elephant in musk, pulling faces and theatrical winks for Fiona's entertainment. He was confident. He could be. He had Emma to fall back on. Fiona looked on, amused but not saying much. I started talking to Boring man's wife. She spoke glowingly about life in Wandsworth and the children's schools nearby. It sounded like living Hell. I glanced surreptitiously at my watch. It was nearly ten o' clock. I had to do at least another hour. I could try to work on Fiona, but dyke or not, I wasn't in her league. Besides boisterous banker-wanker was doing such a good job of cutting me out, I couldn't get a word in edgeways or any ways.

The main course was done.

"I haven't got any pudding, everyone," Beryl announced, "so you'll have to make do with cheese and biscuits, or there's fruit if you want. Anyone for port or brandy?"

Bitch. Cravatboy and Mr Wandsworth started talking about the political situation in Africa and one by one people joined in. Except for me. I didn't know what was going on. I didn't care. It was just another mess. The conversation began to get serious. I felt as if I was the only man at the United Nations without a headset. More Diet Coke. It was 10.30.

Banker-bore took it upon himself to change the subject. He was in charge of the table. He was in charge of the world. It was joke time. He had a really good one. Or so he said.

"Powerful Pierre... the famous French fighter pilot?"

I'd heard it at prep school, and it was crap then. I didn't say anything. He seemed to have the long version. It went on and on. Everyone listened obligingly with expectant smiles. I went into rigor. At last he arrived at the punchline.

"... because I am Powerful Pierre, the famous French fighter pilot, and I always go down in flames!!"

Everyone laughed. Banker-canker sat back, basking in the glory of a good joke well told. He might have been a banker, but he wasn't investment grade.

"That's outrageous!" Beryl cooed, indulgently.

"It was very clever," Boring man's wife said, looking confused.

Fiona retained her composure.

So you want a joke, I thought to myself. I'll tell you a joke. It was my turn to be the gag-meister.

"I've got one!" I chirruped, brightly.

All eyes were on me.

"How do you get a nun pregnant?"

Beryl raised an eyebrow, quizzically. Nobody knew.

"Fuck her!" I announced, triumphantly.

Silence. Gun beat spear.

"What should you do when you come across an elephant?"

Not a sound.

"Wipe it off - hah!"

Total quiet.

"Wait! Wait! Wait! I've got another one," I cried, enthusiastically. "Why do women have vaginas?"

Silence, again.

"Because if they didn't no one would talk to them!" I rejoiced, jubilantly.

No reaction. Banker-ranker stepped in.

"Steady on, James. Don't you think that's a bit *orf.*"

"One more! One more! *Please!*" I insisted, playfully.

"How do you get a queer to fuck a woman?"

Really stunned silence.

"Try shoving some shit up her cu..."

"Right, that's enough," Banker-anchor interrupted, furiously. "I think it's time you left, you vile little man. Get out! Out! Out!"

Boring man and Cravatboy joined in the clamour.

"Out! Out! Out!"

"I'll get your coat," Beryl harrumphed, as cross as two sticks.

I got up in disbelief. It was only a joke. They'd gone thermo! Boring man's wife was now wailing and flapping her arms like a headless turd. They were all like wasps in a jar! Except Fiona Fellon. She was too cool for that sort of thing. I sloped off ignominiously into the hallway.

"Can't I even have a pee?" I asked feebly, as Beryl bundled me out of the front door.

"No, you can't, James. Just go!" she shouted, throwing my coat out after me and banging the door shut.

Well that was clever. I looked at my watch. It was 10.45. I'd nearly done three hours. I'd slightly fucked things up with Fiona Fellon, even though she'd taken no part in the final hiatus, and, if I wasn't mistaken, even looked vaguely sympathetic, if not a little amused by my predicament. I still needed a pee. The cold night air didn't help. Reluctantly and morosely, I hailed a taxi home.

"I told you that word would get you into trouble," Emma Behr remonstrated, when she called me the next day. "Just because it's there doesn't mean you have to say it."

"Yeah…well…" I mumbled, lost for words.

"The least you can do is send Beryl some flowers," she continued. "You wrecked her evening."

Fuck flowers! I called Beryl to apologise. She hung up when she heard my voice. Cunt.

I was the first one in the office that Monday. The post fell through the flap. I picked it up. There was a letter from the client on the big deal. Their logo was on the envelope. I fiddled with it, assessing the contents. There wasn't much. It wasn't even a letter. Then I felt a paperclip. Bingo! It had to be the cheque and a compliment slip. It couldn't be anything else. At last! I put it at the bottom with the rest of the post on Fred's desk.

Fred's secretary was next in. She picked the post up from the desk and took it into her office. I watched her as she opened each letter. Her face lit up at the last one. It was the cheque! I went into her office. She showed it to me gleefully. I'd never seen anything quite so beautiful or perfect. Or so big. But I wasn't there yet. The cheque wasn't made out to me.

The others started to drift in, but not Fred. I waited. The suspense was too much. I went back to the secretary's office. The cheque was sitting there, on her desk, but face down now.

"Fred's late," I noted, rather more in question than statement.

"He's not coming in today," she said, unflappably.

"What?!" I cried.

"Wife problems," she explained.

Big wife problems if he wasn't coming in, today of all days. Unless he was up to something.

"What's happening to the cheque?" I asked, affecting nonchalance.

"I'll pay it in," she said, as if it was just petty cash.

"And my share?" I prompted, increasingly less sure of my ground.

"I'll write you another cheque," she replied, all offhand.

"You're a signatory!" I gasped, incredulously.

"Sure, always have been," she asserted, looking at me as if I was stupid. "Fred's just given me the go-ahead, although he wasn't too happy about me showing you the main cheque, for some reason."

"Well, there's a thing," I said, neutrally. I wasn't going to cause any ripples at this stage.

I teetered back to my desk. I said nothing. I couldn't believe it. After all that! I looked in my drawer for my untarnished paying-in book. I slipped it into my breast pocket and stayed put.

The secretary came out of her office and handed me an envelope without fanfare. Nobody noticed. Perhaps that was the idea. I opened the envelope and looked inside. There was my cheque. It was a lot, but not the full amount. I went back to her office and closed the door behind me.

"It's not the right amount," I said, calmly.

"It's what Fred told me to write out," she responded, once again, impassively.

"Show me the counterfoil," I said, firmly. "I want to see the breakdown."

"I can't," she said, stonily.

"Why not? The numbers don't make any sense," I pumped, no longer worried about making any ripples.

"I've shredded it," she hit back.

"I don't believe you," I countered.

"Fred told me to. It's routine." she replied, unflinching.

"Bullshit," I said tersely, stating the obvious.

"Talk to him tomorrow if you've got a problem," she retorted, with clinical detachment.

Another bitch. I left the room quietly. Shit. I needed to get to the nub of the matter there and then. If I couldn't browbeat the secretary into giving me details of the breakdown, I'd have no chance with Fred. I wouldn't even try. I looked around. Craig was eating a sandwich. He knew nothing. I spirited myself out of the office and headed for the bank. I handed the cheque and paying-in book over to the cashier. She stamped both and handed me back the book without batting an eyelid. Why should she? It's what she did all day, every day. But what she didn't know was that now I could pay for my lease extension. Which would double the value of my flat. But that was my story. And the story wasn't over. Yet.

Chapter 19: Consternation

I wasn't going to confront Fred until the cheque cleared, if I was going to confront him at all. The cheque cleared. I considered the best means of approach. Diplomacy was no longer an option. There was quite a lot of money at stake, but I didn't want to be hostile. I wasn't good at it. Not in these circumstances. So I mentioned it to him quietly. Pete Divis's prediction that Fred would exercise all possible excuses to pare back my commission proved correct, but came as no surprise. Fred deployed, amicably at first, every mutant form of mumbo-jumbo to explain his maths, which simply didn't add up. But without proof of the breakdown, there was nothing I could do. When I eventually summoned the gumption to challenge him, he blithely brushed aside my objections, as if they were mere quibbles that had no place in the general scheme of things. I tried to point out that without my connections and knowledge of the business, there wouldn't have been a general scheme of things in the first place.

"There really wasn't any need to have two negotiators on just one project," he said, dismissively. "In the end, it simply came down to a case of less is more. Besides, Craig told me that on the one occasion that you were expected to turn up to try to convince the key candidate of the wisdom of moving to the new firm, you were so pissed that you nearly blew the whole deal. So I had to take you off the case. Judging from the state you were in the next morning, I considered it would be in the firm's best interests to hand the matter over to Craig immediately."

"For your information," I recalled, bringing to his attention a major flaw in his argument, "I saw the candidate on a Friday night. The next day was Saturday. I don't go to the office on Saturdays. Nor, I suspect, do you. I would also like to add that it was I, not Craig, who successfully managed to induce my candidate and all the other candidates to jump ship, the reason being that I had the right contacts and know-how. Anyway it wasn't so much what I did or didn't do that provided the magic spark to make the deal possible, it was who I knew. That was the magic ingredient and none of you had it. I want you to remember that, Fred."

He looked at me impassively, as if I hadn't spoken. The unblinking obsidian eyes had won the day again. He wasn't going to budge. People were funny like that. People were funny with money. Less is more? What was that about? Less for me, more for Fred, as far as I could see.

Fred's version of events was even less convincing to Craig, who for several days had been blissfully unaware that the client had already settled our fee. He turned a whiter shade of pale when he got wind of it, but he went deep purple when he discovered that Fred had no intention of paying him an extra penny for his endeavours. In fact, he went ballistic and stormed out of the office, never to return. He caught me a little later as I was *en jet* to the pub for my eleven o' clock sharpener.

"Why the fuck didn't you tell me about the cheque?" he snarled.

"I thought you had a 'Fred and you thing' going," I parroted witheringly, wondering whether he'd remember his own words.

"You're a cunt, Mallet," he fulminated, perhaps understandably. "I was as much a part of the deal as anyone else. Who do you think covered for you when you were at your rehab... sorry, your 'adult education' centre in Spain?"

"I have no idea," I answered, as best I could. "No one told me what was going on, least of all you. It would seem to be a case of *tant pis,* wouldn't you say?"

"You absolute shit!" he exploded. "Without me nothing would have got done and Fred would have fired you months ago."

"I wouldn't know," I countered, temperately. "Perhaps if you'd been more forthcoming with the facts rather than your fist, things would have been different."

"That's cheap!" he seethed, continuing his tirade. "You know the sort of pressure I was under. Cut me some slack, for Christ's sake!"

"Why should I?" I reasoned. "You never cut any for me."

"James: can't you see where I'm coming from?" he implored. "I'm not going back to that office. I'm through with Fred, and if you had any sense, you would be too. *Now* is the time for us to present a united front."

"I don't think that's likely," I said, objectively. "Apart from going on holiday together, we've never had a united anything."

"I carried you, James," he said, reverting to type. "You have a great big cheque and I have nothing. Doesn't that strike you as being out of whack?"

"Not particularly," I replied, trying to distance myself from the question yet knowing full well that something was up. "You were a paid employee: that was *your* deal."

"That's not the point," he said, beginning to flounder.

"So cut to the cheese, Craig. What is it exactly that you want?"

"A couple of grand," he proposed, with a telltale hint of desperation.

"Forget it," I said, off-handedly. "You're not on my payroll."

"I'm not on Fred's now, either," he put in, despondently.

"That's not my problem," I pointed out, coldly.

"But it could be to your benefit if you want me on side, should you take any action against Fred," he pointed out, perceptively, for him.

"Craig, are you expecting me to pay for your whoredom at this late stage of the game?" I demanded, affecting indignation.

"It might keep me focused, should you ever need me," he said, seemingly more in proposal than as a veiled threat.

"I'm not doing two grand," I countered.

"One?"

"No, the money's all tied up," I lied. "I can only do cash. Five hundred is all the machine will do, then I'm out."

"It's not enough," he grunted.

"It's five hundred more than you deserve," I said, going on the attack. "I gave you five grand for doing the square root of fuck all on the Barrow Brothers' deal."

"That was ages ago," he whined, irrelevantly.

"The principle still holds. The fact is, my money always ends up in your pocket; it's never the other way round."

Craig went quiet. We went to a cash machine. I keyed in my number. The machine spat out the money.

"That means you stay off my back, right?" I cautioned, handing him the freshly delivered cash.

"Sure, James," he whimpered, defeated. "I suppose I should thank you. It's more than Fred's ever done for me. This at least should get me over to Goa. I need a break after this shit."

"You do what you've got to do, Craig," I said, giving him a benign pat on the shoulder. "And I'll do what I've got to do, which might involve you at a later date, as long as you've got the necessary balls to face up to Fred."

"I'll be there all right," he snivelled. "Anything to get one back off that slime bucket."

"I'm sure I can depend on you, Craig," I said, allowing myself some harmless sarcasm. "Always have; always will."

I watched him walk away. Goa didn't seem such a bad idea. Christmas wasn't so far away. Graham Ruddock hadn't invited me to the Old Faithfuls reunion lunch this year, thankfully. There would be no socialising for me here. Not if I wasn't going to be around anyway! I could do without the family; the silly conversations and the endless TV. And then there was Monica. I could do without her too. With the deal now in the bag I could afford to think about other things, like

Angelita and whether there was any point in trying to pick up where we'd left off. It was a nice idea, I thought wistfully, but perhaps it was better not to put it to the test.

I pretended to do some work for the next couple of days. I tried to avoid Fred as best I could but he caught me one lunchtime on my own.

"You were talking to Craig after he left the office the other day," he remarked casually, as if he was just shooting the breeze. "What did he want?"

"Money," I replied, as if I was made of the stuff.

"Did you give him any?" he asked, with just a hint of concern.

"Sure."

"Why?" Fred queried, looking at me as if I'd lost all sense of perspective.

"To get him off my back," I retorted. "And yours for that matter."

"I don't need you to protect me," he shot back, sourly. "You're an idiot. You didn't need to give him anything."

"No, I didn't," I willingly agreed. "But I did. I'm funny like that. It's called 'decency', Fred."

"Are you trying to say something, James?" he rounded on me. "Because if you are, I don't like it. Any more crap like that and you'll be showing people round Thorpe Park in a silly hat for a living, d'you understand?"

"Entirely, Fred," I apologised, "but you must be confusing me with someone who gives a massive shit."

I could be very brave when I had nothing to lose especially now the cheque had cleared, and besides I needed to show a little abrasion to keep Fred interested. He didn't like losing. If I showed a bit of attitude, he'd want to show me who was boss. He wouldn't be able to do that if I wasn't around to be at the receiving end. Stupid fuck; he was going to have to wait me out, but I needed to stay on if I was to have any chance of finding a way to recoup the balance he owed me. I would go when I was ready. I'd already had some informal advice from a solicitor. He'd told me there was nothing much I could do. It was my word against Fred's. He said my contract wasn't worth the paper. If I tried taking Fred to court the case would be long, messy and expensive, for both parties, and Fred had plenty more firepower than I, so I was shafted. I should have left there and then, but I was in no hurry; it wasn't as if I had anywhere else to go. Also my presence seemed to have a disquieting effect on Fred. That gave me great pleasure. It was my turn to be difficult. It was something I was good at.

I started going to work early again, but for a different covert objective this time. I needed evidence if I were to prove Fred's misappropriation of my full share of the commission on the big deal. It was unfortunate that on one of these dawn raids I sustained a paper cut while I was sifting through some semi-confidential files I'd found in an unlocked drawer by Fred's desk. There was blood everywhere! It seemed even the most basic espionage was beyond me. I had to shred the soiled documentation to cover my tracks and the prospect of wandering around with my finger sticking out like a sore thumb while Fred rummaged around for his missing, now shredded and bloodstained paperwork left me no choice. I had to leave. Now.

Although there was no moral imperative to say goodbye, I would've liked to have left with a flourish, but it would have been impolitic to have lingered one moment longer. There was very little more that I could achieve and I had achieved very little. I had a holdall on hand, handily tucked away at the back of a cupboard, 'specially for this occasion. I took away some essential items and personal effects, but otherwise left my desk undisturbed. I didn't want Fred to know about my evacuation. Not immediately. There was no harm in keeping him guessing.

I grabbed the bag and made my exit. I would post the keys back through the box in due course. I needed a drink, either to celebrate or to calm my nerves, but it was far too early to find anything alcoholic for purchase. Fortunately my hip flask had returned to being a regular component of my office battledress. I headed towards a coffee bar off the main drag, ordered a cup of hot chocolate, anointed it with a jig from the hip flask and sat back comfortably to contemplate my situation.

I rethought my immediate plans. Christmas was now dangerously close. It really would be sacrilege to spend it with the family. It would be so much nicer to spend it in Goa, but that brought me back to the question of whether Angelita would be quite so pleased to see me again. There was only one way to find out. It was time to get the dust off my passport. I resolved to call the travel agent who'd organised my previous Christmas sortie to Goa the year before and check out the availability to do likewise this year.

I also had to consider my financial circumstances. Large though the payout from the big deal had been, the taxman and the cost of my lease extension would eat most of it, leaving me with zip. Unless I found a job that offered a reasonable stipend for my services, I would have to sell the flat. At least it would come with a respectable lease. I felt in my waters that the employment market was about to take a dive, so the chance of finding anything with a salary sufficient to pay for any but the most basic outgoings seemed unlikely. I knew a local estate agent I could talk to. I'd give him a call when I got home. Liberty, after all, came with its responsibilities.

The estate agent didn't think there'd be much business activity given the time of year, but did say that he had one customer who might be interested. I went over to his office in the afternoon to hand him over a spare set of keys. He knew the flat. I said he could have carte blanche to show it to anyone, anytime; it was ready to view.

I spent the next morning checking out schedules to Goa. I made a provisional booking for one week either side of Christmas with the travel agent. It was expensive, being the peak holiday period and no there being imminent threat of plague this time, but it would be worth every penny if it removed me from the excruciation of the season at home. The fact that my inner alcoholic was jumping with joy at the prospect of two weeks uninterrupted cheap drinking was beside the point. It would simply be a case of Elspeth: nil; inner alcoholic: 15. Just the thought of it made me thirsty. There wasn't an abundance of booze around the flat. I had been trying to keep stocks down to a minimum in order to allay any suspicions that Monica might have harboured about me going back to my old ways. I grabbed my coat and headed for the off-licence.

There was no point mucking about. Wine wasn't going to do it. It was a whisky day. I reached for a bottle of 'Old Fraud' and a packet of peanuts. I was travelling first class today! I passed Mr Patel's Local Literature Experience on the route back. Providence or self-knowledge? I went in and surveyed Mr Patel's latest offerings. He always had an amusing selection. I brushed past the scat and spanko stuff and headed for the general interest section. I scanned the racks and decided to go for *Asian Spreaders* and *Danish Bungholes*. I normally set my limit to one magazine per visit but today was a two magazine occasion. It was going to be party time with my new friends! I hadn't self-dated properly for months. My half-hearted attempts at sobriety had left my libido in a confused state. Now was the time to rectify matters and take the issue with a tissue in hand.

I headed straight for the bedroom when I got back and flopped on the bed. I opened the whisky and took a couple of slugs. I retrieved a few magazines from my library for old time's sake and opened the copy of *Asian Spreaders*. There was a letter from the publisher inside the front cover, another Russian oligarch who'd taken over huge swathes of the British porn industry who signed himself off as

'Noscho Olfees'. I perused the contents. Talk to the hand! The flat-chested cutie in the centre gate was no match for the slapper-titted piece of MILF in the 'In Your Dweams' section at the back. I had another two gulps from the bottle and got down to work. It was quick. It was magnificent. I saluted my sense of well-being with another mouthful of hooch and fell into a deep, contented coma.

The phone rang a few hours later. It was the estate agent, sounding none too pleased. I looked at my watch. It was late afternoon.

"Well, that wasn't very clever," he growled.

"What wasn't?" I asked, in genuine bewilderment.

"Me coming into your bedroom with a client while you were out sparko under half a ton of stroke mags and a field of tissue pansies stuck to your duvet."

How embarrassing! Except I wasn't embarrassed.

"*Wankus interuptus*?" I quizzed.

"More *in medias masturbationes*, actually," he informed me, in all seriousness.

"Sorry about that: part of my five-a-day - ha!" I chirruped back, cheerfully. "The sword never sleeps in my hand! What did the punter think of the flat?"

"Not much," he snarled back, sullenly. "Something must've put him off. I thought you said the flat was 'ready to view'."

"It was," I said, defensively. "But I wasn't, unfortunately."

"I think we'd better make it 'viewing by appointment' from now on," he advised, sternly.

"Probably a good idea," I agreed jauntily, adding, "and perhaps we'll have better luck next time."

"If there is a next time."

"Don't be such a wuss. The market's roaring, surely?" I queried, buoyantly.

"It is not roaring; it's overheating. And it's going to blow up any day now, as are many things, I fear. The little pricks who think they're in control can never see an investment bubble until it bursts in their face, but I'm telling you: there will be blood."

He hung up. I scratched my chin and wondered.

I confirmed my travel plans to Goa. The family accepted with weary resignation that once again I wouldn't be on hand for Christmas. I didn't tell them about *my* resignation. I'd save that for later. I suspected they didn't care. Nothing surprised them anymore. Not with me. They'd given up. I knew the routine for getting to Goa by now. Jabs, visa, malaria pills and a floppy hat; I just needed to add some cash, collect my ticket and I'd be on my way to paradise. Or so I thought.

I arrived pathologically early at the airport, Luton this time, so early that the check-in desk hadn't opened. I bought a newspaper, treated myself to an Egg McToilet and coffee, found a seat and humanised the coffee with the contents of my hipflask. I looked at the paper. There was a TV supplement with the Christmas schedules. I glanced at all the dreck I'd be missing. What was so supreme about *The Bourne Supremacy* that it warranted top billing on terrestrial for Christmas Eve? They must have shown it a million times before. Was *The Great Escape* so great that it had to be aired every Christmas Day afternoon, year in, year out? And was *As Good as it Gets* on Boxing Day, as good as it got? I looked at the other stuff. *The Blair Witch Project; Nightmare on Elm Street; The Hills Have Eyes; Saw II; Dr Who and the Daleks.* Why had they chosen the birth of Our Lord as a time to celebrate such evil things? Surely there was more to Christmas. Not much. And what was it about the flippin' *Hunt for Red October* and *Bridget Jones' Diary* that warranted them being repeated every flippin' day?

I turned to the business section and was immediately struck by the headline:

PABS says bad loans will take years to fix

Now that was top billing! I read on.

The Pan Asian Banking System announced yesterday that it would take at least five years to fix its portfolio of bad loans in the US as the meltdown in the sub-prime mortgage industry continued to gather pace. Investors were assured that PABS was tackling the problems that prompted the bank to increase its bad debt provision by 36% to $10.6bn last year. PABS executive director Leonard Fawcett said that he would take responsibility for putting things right. 'The buck stops at my door,' he said. Loans in the final quarter were souring at the astonishing rate of $51 million a day.

There was an archive photo of Leonard surrounded by a dozen grinning chimpanzees wearing PABS lapel badges.

I put the paper down. Souring at the rate of $51 million a day? No wonder Leonard had been a tad sour himself when we'd met at Richard Hartley's farewell party a few months earlier. Interesting.

And as far 'The buck stops at my door,' I suspected the buck might have other ideas.

I finished my coffee and went for a wander round the shops, mindful that I didn't need anything. It didn't prevent me from buying an overpriced shaving mirror that glowed in the dark. I stopped at a magazine rack and proceeded to purchase enough printed matter to build a papyrus boat, if I'd wanted to. I made my way back to the main concourse. The check-in desk for my flight was now open but I noted with dismay that there was now a long queue snaking to the front. I joined the back and forlornly flicked through some of my newly acquired literature, looking on at the threadbare column of travellers casually reporting to the 'Premier Club' queue for the same flight in the next door aisle. My queue inched forward, bag by bag. What did it matter? Eventually I was close to the front. I heard a voice I thought I recognised approaching the 'Premier Club' desk. I looked up from my magazine. *Let joy be unconfined*! It was Leonard Fawcett and Rania! And, shucks, I'd just been reading about him! The unrelenting Venn diagram of coincidence had struck once more. I just had to say 'Hello'.

"Not you again?" Leonard sighed in torment.

"Don't worry Leonard, we won't be sitting together," I said, pointing to the 'Standard Club' sign above my check-in desk.

"Thank God for that!"

"Stop it, Leonard!" his wife implored, agitated.

"Dr Fawcett, how nice to see you again," I said in greeting.

"My name is Rania, or had you forgotten?" she said, coquettishly. "Are you in good health?"

I didn't mind the question, coming from her.

"Sort of," I replied, elusively. "Are you going to Goa on business or pleasure?"

"Both," Leonard shot, abruptly.

"Sort of," Rania chipped in, bashfully.

"Staying somewhere nice?" I asked.

"The Royal Coronet De Luxe in South Goa," she answered, unassumingly. "And you?"

"A small *pension* near 'The Fuzzy Duck' in North Goa," I responded with equal modesty.

They looked at me blankly.

"So we won't be seeing you," Leonard said, as if putting an end to our exchange.

"Probably not," I said, casting a rueful glance towards his wife. "But I'll see you in the departure lounge before we go."

"Not if I see you first," Leonard retorted, as he handed their tickets and passports to their check-in clerk, only just sparing my sensibilities with a wry smile. "We'll be in the 'Premier Club' lounge."

Pity, I thought, as they were cleared to go through to security. I wanted to ask him a thing or two. There were still some loose ends about PABS I hoped he might help to tie up. Smug bastard. 'Premium Club' lounge. It was a poxy charter airline, for goodness' sake, flying out of Luton, not flippin' El Dorado International. A clerk asked me to put my luggage on the scales.

The security check took even longer this time because some toe-rag had tried to blow his and everyone else's bollocks apart half way over the Atlantic a month before, but at least it meant I was still in sight of the Fawcetts who were having the same problem. Eventually they passed through. I wasn't far behind. They didn't go immediately to the 'Premier Club' lounge. Instead they headed for the duty-free area. By the time I caught up with them Rania was in the cosmetics section and Leonard was inspecting bottles in the liquor department. Great! I could have him all to myself, albeit briefly.

"See you made the papers today," I remarked cheerfully as I ambled, happenchance in his direction.

"What of it?" he snapped.

"Nothing," I said, affecting an air of nonchalant, unconcerned indifference. "Although those numbers they mentioned about the sub-prime market were quite something: looks as though the candles cost more than the cake!"

"Your point being?" he challenged.

"There is no point," I said, backing off a bit. "Except that I think it's extremely brave of you to volunteer such phrases as 'The buck stops at my door'."

He looked at me unsurely, unable to decide whether I was being deferential or just taking the mick.

"All in a day's work," he said, giving me the benefit of the doubt. "It's something we have to deal with and I have elected to handle it."

"Well, good luck," I said, as if I were taking my cue to end the conversation.

But I wasn't entirely finished. I only had a few sentences to play with, but there was one last nugget of information I wanted to prise out of him.

"The Bank has weathered many storms... wars... communist and nationalist insurgencies... not to mention discredit, closer to home," I continued, abstractedly. "Events surrounding Thorn Bay, for example and what's Alec Dunhill's peerage all about? Are the two connected?"

I'd done it! I'd popped the question. But the reward for my guile was non-existent. Leonard did not look happy. He'd rumbled my ruse.

"No," he answered, coldly. "There is no scandal associated with Lord Dunhill or any of his parliamentary appointments."

That was all he said. He walked away without saying anything else. *Appointments?* Were there more to come? I watched him as he joined Rania and led her towards the 'Premier Club' lounge. Was that it? Damn! What a wasted opportunity. I bought a bottle of aftershave for myself, perhaps in a subconscious attempt to prepare myself for any meeting I might have with Angelita, and then went to the departure area to wait for the flight to be called.

The flight out wasn't nearly as much fun as it had been the last time with Craig. I ordered too many drinks and bought too much unnecessary crap from the catalogue at the arse end of the in-flight magazine, ostensibly for Angelita, but insensibly because I was drunk.

She wasn't at the airport. She might have been promoted or switched over to other duties. Instead there was an over-zealous customs official who looked as though he was itching to give me a 'cavity search', until I farted rather loudly which seemed to put him off the scent. I turned round, as if looking for an errant foley artist. The customs officer quickly waved me on in *horror*. I was quite pleased. I'd been baking that fart in the aeroplane for hours.

I was staying in the same hotel as before, but nothing was quite the same. What was once picturesque now seemed seedy. The former quaintness now looked cheap and tawdry. The staff, who'd previously seemed so obliging, were now surly, and the Christmas decorations that had once added a naïve charm were, quite frankly, ridiculous. The place was a dump.

I got up early on the first morning and went for a stroll on the beach. There were no fishermen now. There were no trawlers on the horizon. They'd done their job. They'd gone home. They'd fished the sea dry. I walked back to the hotel. Nothing looked nice. The views meant nothing. It wasn't my country. Everything was just poor, gaudy and shabby. Yesterday's *fantastique* had become today's *diabolique*.

I got hold of Angelita at her office later. She didn't seem particularly thrilled or surprised to hear me.

"I'm here," I said, neutrally.

"I know," she said, listlessly. "One of my colleagues saw you at the airport."

"Can I see you?" I asked.

"I'd rather you didn't," she replied, stonily.

"There are one or two things I'd like to explain."

"I'm not interested.".

"Just once?" I begged.

"I'm on call for the next two nights," she said, opening up a little. "I could meet you after work on Tuesday, if you insist, but it must be brief."

"Can you do a quick supper?" I proposed, feeling mildly relieved. She paused for a moment.

"I can see you at Lobo's in Calangute at seven o'clock, but that's all," she said, neither confirming nor denying me the pleasure of a supper arrangement.

"That's good of you," I said, humbly. "I'll be there."

I had two days to fill before our rendezvous. I wandered between the bars and the beach shacks, trying not to get too trashed, and spent the afternoons looking at stuff I didn't need to buy, just to while away the time.

Tuesday came. I took a motorbike taxi for the short journey to Calangute. I knew Lobo's well. Angelita and I had had a few meals there in happier times the year previously. I ordered a drink and waited. She was late. It reminded me of Tina, although this time I was more concerned. She arrived after about half an hour.

"I'm sorry," she said, as she sat down.

She didn't look it. She looked pissed off. What was I to expect?

"It's OK," I mumbled, hoarsely. "I'm the one who should be saying sorry."

I'd forgotten how pretty she was, even if she looked as though she'd been sucking lemons for a week.

"Why didn't you return my calls?" she asked quietly, ignoring my bootlicking. She wasn't wasting any time.

"I didn't know what to say," I replied, hopelessly but honestly.

"So you treated me like shit, instead," she snorted, with rising contempt.

"I was confused," I professed, trying to steer her away from her negative mantras. "It wasn't an easy year for me."

"How do you think mine was? Never mind the heartache, I was a complete laughing stock. Even the taxi drivers were taunting me for screwing a white man and ever thinking I might marry him. It was horrible."

"I can imagine," I said, picturing the scene. "It was a risk we took, we both knew that. But it wasn't like winning a contest. I'm no prize. That was the problem. I knew I would be a disappointment. I thought would be just too difficult, for both of us."

"So you left me just dangling? You didn't feel any sense of obligation to let me know what was going through your mind or listen to my thoughts on the matter?"

"Look," I said, desperately, "I said I'm sorry. I can't do anything more than that. It happened; I can't pretend otherwise."

"'Sorry' didn't put Humpy Dumpty back together again," she muttered, surprising me with her knowledge of British nursery heritage.

"I know, but the important thing is, where do we stand now?"

Angelita paused for a moment and then looked at me in utter disbelief.

"Where we stand *now*?" she quizzed, absolutely stupefied. "Are you crazy? We stand nowhere. What do you think I am? A toy? I'm not your holiday whore, you know."

"Of course you're not," I backtracked, hastily. "I would like to think that our attraction was mutual, without a price tag either way. I was just enquiring about your present feelings towards me."

A waiter approached our table and stood by expectantly. I asked for some drinks and said we'd have a look at the menu. Angelita was quiet.

"You still haven't answered my question," I coaxed, gently.

"James, you're a deluded fool," she observed, concisely. "You didn't expect me to spend the rest of my life waiting by the telephone just for you, did you? No, siree. I got the hint fast enough. One man showed some common decency, though; stood by me while others laughed, and in time we fell in love. Things went well and we're now happily engaged to be married, I'm very pleased to say."

"You didn't hang around," I grumbled.

"What did you expect?" she chided, almost good-naturedly. "I'm going to be twenty-three in a few months' time. That's a good age for a girl to marry in India. I certainly didn't want to leave it much longer. You blew your chance, James: I'm not blowing mine."

She reached for her handbag and took out a photograph. She passed it to me. I looked at it. It was an Indian geezer with a moustache.

"He's called Evan," she said, proudly. "He comes from a good family."

"I'm very happy for you," I remarked, sarkily.

"Good," she said, unconcerned by my shrewish undertones. "I'm very happy too. I know I am lucky."

The waiter came back with our drinks and asked if we were ready to order some food.

"James, I'm not eating," Angelita announced. "I've got to go. Evan's expecting me. I don't want to keep him waiting. I think you and I have done all the talking we need."

The waiter caught the vibe and withdrew to another table. She got up to leave.

"Goodbye, James and good luck," she said, her expression bordering on pity. "Enjoy your holiday but don't try to break any more hearts for the fun of it. India's the wrong place for that sort of thing."

She turned to go. I watched as she walked away. She was in control. There was nothing toy-like about her composure. It was quite the opposite. It was pure, unadorned poise. I'd forgotten to bring the offerings I'd brought for her on the plane, which was perhaps just as well. A charter airline teddy probably wasn't going to do it. Not tonight.

I felt sorry for the waiter and tipped him for the meal we never had and finished my drink. I went back to the hotel via a liquor store and bought a litre of local whisky and two packets of stale cigarettes. I had a feeling I was going to be in for a long night.

I paced the bedroom, smoking and drinking, wrestling with what could have been, till the early-morning heat started to beat through the thin print window curtains. I opened them an inch, sighed and went to bed.

I woke up at around midday. I didn't feel great. I had a shower and put on a pair of shorts and a T-shirt. I went down to the beach and once again walked along the shore until I reached one of the beach shacks that Craig and I had frequented the year before. I couldn't face anything to eat, so I ordered two bottles of beer and made myself comfortable on a sun-lounger. I skulled one of the beers, pulled a towel over my head and put the other bottle close to hand. I let the sun ooze the whisky from my pores, gulped the other beer and drifted into a state of semi-consciousness. It was Christmas Eve. Things weren't so bad. Maybe I was better off without Angelita. Or Monica. Or Tina. Fuck 'em.

My reverie didn't last long. Reveries seldom did in India. Just as I felt myself falling into an almost pharmaceutical sense of bliss, a shadow darkened the pink bedroom of my closed eyelids.

"You want mango... papaya?"

Super. That was all I needed: a frigging fruit seller. It was a young girl. The sing-song continued.

"You want banana... jackfruit?"

"No! Go away! *Purlease!*"

"You want saffron...?"

"Oh, for fuck's sake!" I snorted, ripping the towel off my face and sitting up with a jolt. And then I stopped. With the sun above, this beatific vision, this apparition of junk jewellery and flowing rags, stood there and smiled.

"Happy Clistmas, Mr Tourist!"

She was about twelve.

"What do you want, you little *rapscallion*?"

"You like saffron, Mr Tourist? It's Clistmas!"

"No, I don't like saffron, you little git. Now fuck off!"

Her face fell. So did my heart.

"It's Clistmas," she said, looking down at her little bare toes.

"Oh, wank me with a boxing glove," I said, rolling my eyes to no one. "How much is it?"

"Two hundred!"

"Come off it! For saffron? I could buy a new liver for that!"

"One hundred!"

"I don't even want it!"

"Fifty! Fifty! You pay fifty! It's Clistmas!"

"Shut up, you little scrote!" I said, yielding like a sap. "I'll do a hundred, dammit. Now leave me alone!"

Her face lit up like a firework. It was worth every paisa. Not even the flash above Hiroshima could have matched it for brilliance. Then she became serious. This was business. I took out a one-hundred-rupee note and handed it to her. She looked at it, turned, and without stopping to say 'thank you' or 'goodbye', skipped down the beach, screaming: "It's Clistmas! It's Clistmas! It's Clistmas!"

I smiled and lay back on the sun-lounger. I had done the right thing. And there was a God to witness it.

I got up a little later and returned the bottles to the bar. The barman looked surprised and gazed at me. He recognised me from the year before.

"Your friend come here," he informed me.

What friend? I didn't have any. Angelita, perhaps?

"Who? When?" I prodded, feeling mildly curious.

"Mister Craig. Two days ago. He's living near Candolim village."

"Living?"

"Yes. At the Robert's Hotel. He was with a woman."

Craig must have beaten me to Goa by quite a while if he was *with a woman*. He didn't have a *woman* in London. He was hardly on the agenda as one of the people I wanted to see, but he was better than nothing. I walked back to the hotel and made up my mind to try to find him the next day. It would give me an objective and would be a nice surprise for him. A bit like a Christmas present.

I hired a motorbike in the morning and asked directions to Robert's Hotel. Christmas or not, everything was open as usual again. I drove through Candolin village, past the Aguda prison, till I saw a rusty signpost pointing down a dirt track to 'Robert's Hotel'. Some hotel. It made mine look like the Ritz. It was a ten-room hovel and nobody was in. I went round to the back and found an old-timer, perhaps the owner or the handyman, peeing into a watering can.

"Good for wegetables," he explained, with a knowing grin. I asked him if he knew 'Mr Craig'. He shook his thingie, zipped up and then waved in the general direction of the beach. I wished him 'Melly Clistmas' and walked down a scrub-strewn path towards the seashore. There weren't so many shacks or people about as there were on my part of the coast and I soon found Craig, sitting in the shade by a bar. He had a girl with him. He seemed pleasantly surprised to see me at first. He introduced me to the girl, invited me to sit down and called the barman for a beer. I told him that I too, in the end, had split from Fred Armitage's outfit.

"Best thing for it," he said, as the waiter put a bottle down in front of me. "It was about time you pulled yourself out of that tomb. And so you came out here to do a 'geographical'?"

"A 'geographical'?" I probed, knowing exactly what he was getting at.

"Sure. Pretending to go on holiday, when all you really want to do is to get totally pancaked where no one can see you."

"Oh, this?" I said, bashfully raising my beer bottle. "I'm not as bad as I used to be."

"You shouldn't be bad at all!" he remonstrated, tartly. "And you weren't popping out for just a cream soda the last time I saw you."

"I still drink, but not so much now," I said, trying to justify myself.

"You know that's a no-no," he said, knowingly. "You sip, you slip; you booze, you lose."

"How come you're so well acquainted with the subject?" I demanded, huffily.

"I had my own fondnesses not so long ago, remember?" Craig reminded me, referring, I assumed, to his drug attachment. "I had to make a determined effort to stop."

"And yet you still drink," I observed, stating the obvious.

"Yes, but alcohol was never my Achilles heel. I don't have a problem with it; I can still function. I don't need someone to carry me through. Unlike you James," he said, pointedly.

"Are you getting at something again, Craig?"

"I am actually. I had to look after three aspects of your life, James, as you might know by now. I had to broker the big deal when you weren't up to par, which was most of the time. I also had to act as mediator on your behalf whenever Fred felt like firing you, which was practically all the time too. Finally I had to keep your sister under control whenever she wanted to get you sectioned, which again was practically all the time."

"My sister?" I cried, incredulously.

"Yup," he affirmed. "Fred didn't want to know of course, so when your sister first called to say she was taking you off to rehab, he naturally passed the phone over to me. I put her in the frame about Spain. I know the guy who runs it. We used to hang with all the other class 'A' mob around Notting Hill."

"No wonder the place was so full of junkies," I remarked, spitefully.

"That didn't matter. They follow a similar twelve-step program."

"It was still crap," I countered, bitterly. "It was a waste of time and money."

"It's not a magic wand, you know, James," he, reproved. "There has to be some degree of cooperation along the line for it to work properly. 'Easy does it' doesn't mean you do fuck all. Anyway, your sister asked me to keep an eye on you when you returned, and to report on your state of progress, which I did."

"*Et tu, Brute?*" I cried.

"Then fall, Caesar!" he matched. "Except you didn't. You had me to prop you up, not that you were in any condition to be aware of it. I busted my chops looking after you on all fronts, James, and quite frankly five hundred quid doesn't quite float my boat."

The girl got up from her chair. I looked at her. She was nice.

"I'm going for a swim; I'll see you guys later," she said, wisely leaving us to get on with things.

"Look," I said, turning back to Craig, "I'm sensing an impasse here. You cannot expect me to agree to you retroactively taxing me on income which you were doing your darndest to prevent me from earning in the first place."

I paused.

"Fred was your employer," I resumed, "and as he helped himself to over eighty percent of the take, it is to him that you should turn for redress, not me. Can't you see? I'm not your man."

"I still say you're an ungrateful sod," he persisted.

"Say what you like," I retaliated. "I gave you the money to get out here. I don't see much gratitude for that. Did you meet your lady friend here? She seems pretty cool."

"Yes," he muttered, reluctant to be drawn into a diversion. "About two weeks ago. She's a bit of a spunk, isn't she? What about you? Are you getting it back together with Angelita?"

"Not exactly," I said, evasively. "In fact, not at all. We met for a drink but she more or less told me to piss off. She didn't want to see me. She was just being polite. She's got someone else on the boil, a local lad. They're engaged, so my sweet nothings came to sweet nothing."

"Oh, well," he remarked, gazing out to sea. "It would seem to be a case of *tant pis*, wouldn't you say?"

I soon left, feeling depressed. Craig had someone else to play with. He was settled and didn't need me around. He was going to stay in Goa for a while. He had nothing to go back to in the UK. Nor had I, except for some bills. I drove back towards Candolim and stopped to look at the Aguda prison, wondering what sort of Christmas all the misfits and petty 'street pharmacists' were having of it. Not much call for a trouser press there I thought, recalling Elspeth's Christmas present to me during my own incarceration. I shivered and continued my journey back to the hotel.

I tried to change my return flight the following day so that I could leave a week earlier, but I had no success. It was the time of year. The flights were full and people seldom broke ranks with their charter schedules. I didn't want to stay. There was nothing for me. The sun-baked merriment of the other holidaymakers that had seemed so engaging the year before was now just annoying. The working class cackle reverberating amid the clink of empty bottles, the half-chewed remains of bombed-out post-Yuletide whoopee and the dregs of the devil's advocaat did little to dispel my mood of remorse. This, and a new undercurrent of unease permeating the general atmosphere as a result of the sudden influx of rowdy Russian tourists taking over the resorts, lent an aura of noisy menace on even the sunniest days.

My afternoon meanderings around the shops were to no purpose. Experience had taught me that what looked bright and shiny under a blue sky seldom travelled well or survived the scrutiny of a dull winter's day at home. So I continued my daily alcoholic safari from bar to shack to restaurant and back to bar again, carrying books I'd never read, thinking of Angelita, my flat, my future and back to Angelita again. At last the final day arrived. I couldn't wait to go. The inebriated babble of pissed revellers, the inconsequential chat of idiotically happy couples and the banter of gobby oldsters and all the other stringvestites held no comfort now.

I spent the last day alone in a dusty watering hole set back from the main road, reading trashy airport magazines left by other travelling folk, and drank. I bought half a bottle of local hooch on the way back to the hotel, just enough to see me through the night. I didn't want much. I had an early start the following day. The pickup bus was due at 5.00 a.m., and besides I needed to think about preparing myself for some sort of alcoholic self-control when I got home. I had my last meal at the restaurant downstairs, together with a relatively modest two glasses of wine, then went to the reception desk to settle the bar bills and retrieve my passport from my allotted strongbox. I couldn't be arsed to pack what little stuff I had when I got back to the bedroom later. I'd do it in the morning. I set the alarm for 4.30 a.m., lay on the bed, put the liquor bottle near the pillow and drifted off to sleep.

There was a loud banging on my door. I woke with a start. I looked at the clock. It was 5:30. Shit! Like a tit I'd shoved the thing to 'quiet' and missed the signal. I leapt out of bed, accidentally knocking the bottle by the pillow onto the floor. It smashed. I wasn't. Oh, thank you, Mr God. There was nothing I could do. I opened the door. It was the bellhop.

"The bus already leave, Mr James," he announced, cheerfully.

"How nice of you to wake me up *after* the event," I remarked, grimly.

There was no way I'd find a taxi at that time of the morning. I had to be at the airport at seven. I was fucked.

"Don't worry, Mr James," the bellhop started to assure me, brightly. "My brother can take you to the airport. He wait downstairs."

The little turds. They'd deliberately let the bus go without me so they could hold me to ransom with a ride to the airport.

"How much?" I asked as nicely as possible, trying to suppress my obvious misgivings.

"Nine hundred; cheap – la?" he declared, magnanimously.

In other words, a thousand, or double the normal rate. It was still cheap. At least I'd get there.

"Cheap? It's a miracle, as are you and your brother," I eulogised, encouragingly. "We need to leave in ten minutes, but I have to have a shower first and then I need to pack quickly."

My heart was pounding with the abruptness of events. I was thirsty too. I checked the fridge minibar. There was nothing there. Bastards. They must have emptied it the second I'd cleared my bill at the reception. Typical India. I got into the shower. It felt good. I let some water trickle into my mouth. It tasted weird. I spat it out. I was damned if I was going to be struck down with some creepy disease at this stage of the game. I got out of the shower, dried my face and went back into the bedroom. The little tyke had cleared up all the mess on the floor and packed my gear! Typical India. There was just my passport and wallet on the table and his choice of my travelling clothes on the bed. The little beauty!

The bellhop picked up my bags and started towards the lobby. I was now really thirsty. I left the room key on the reception desk and looked around.

"Is there anywhere I can get a drink?" I asked the bellhop, desperately. The grill was drawn over the bar. "What about the kitchen?"

"Kitchen closed till mess boy come," the bellhop replied. "We buy something at the airport."

Obviously he was coming too! The car was outside. The road was clear. There wasn't a soul about. Or a shop open. Every corner we turned and every crossroad we passed I prayed there would be a stall or a store with a light on, but there was nothing. The driver was hitting the road like a loon. We were making good time but I was going mad. Then I realised the problem. This was no ordinary thirst. This wasn't a case of mere dehydration; I was in a state of alcoholic withdrawal. There was nothing I could do. Or so I thought. Then I remembered the aftershave in my wash-bag. I scrabbled through my luggage and grabbed it. The bloody thing was an atomiser. Where was a screw-top in my hour of need? I started furiously to pump the nozzle onto my tongue. It was disgusting. The bellhop looked at me aghast.

"No, Mr James! You kill yourself!" he cried, as he tried to wrestle the aftershave out of my grasp.

"You dork! Can't you see I'm dying?!" I screamed back.

"Mr James, we only ten minutes from airport," he gasped, as he finally managed to wrangle the bottle off me.

"There'd better be some alcohol," I shouted.

"It's too early to drink, Mr James," he protested.

"You wouldn't understand: it's never too early to drink where I come from," I barked, as he hurled the aftershave bottle belligerently out of the car window.

My tongue was now so thick I thought I was going to choke. We made it onto the airport road. I could see the lights of the control tower against the dawn in the distance. I exhaled a breath of relief. We drew up to the departure entrance. I gave the boys their money, thoughtfully tipping them with a half-empty bottle of leftover tanning lotion. They fussed around my bags.

"Find me a drink, for Christ's sake!" I choked.

There was nothing open. One of the boys spotted an itinerant ice cream salesman across the other side of the concourse but he'd be no use, unless he happened to be selling crème de menthe frappés. Most of the other passengers had gone on through to emigration. I stumbled towards the check-in. The woman took my ticket and passport. I lobbed my bags onto the scales unsteadily. She glanced at my face. There was someone behind her. It was my friend, the over-zealous customs official who'd wanted to bugger me on the way in, two weeks earlier. His eyes lit up. My head started to spin. I turned around. There were four people looking at me. I squinted and tried to focus. I couldn't believe it. There they were: Angelita, Craig, and of all people Leonard and Rania Fawcett. What the Hell were they all doing there, or was I hallucinating? I started to tremble. This had to be the DTs.

I turned back to the check-in woman. The over-zealous customs maniac had my bags. He was tearing at the contents like a hungry dog. I looked back at the group to see if they were still there. They were. Why? Angelita was no fan of mine and nor was Craig the last time we spoke. Nor was Leonard Fawcett. My tremors went into full spasm. The customs wallah ripped back the zip of the other bag. Checking bags *before* leaving the country? He flipped open the top and started to go bananas. I looked back at the group again. Then it hit me like a Mack truck. Of course! It was so obvious! The bellhop packing my bags; the Fawcetts being there on business, *sort of*, it was all part of a plan. It was a plant. It was Christine's Curse at its finest!

In almost pornographic slo-mo, the customs 'nana pulled out a brown packet from the middle of the bag and started to wave it about victoriously, like a Dervish whirling a severed head. Drugs. Of course it was. Ten years in Aguda jail. Minimum. Great. Another prison. Angelita would get her vengeance. Craig would get his revenge. Leonard Fawcett would continue to proceed up the ziggurat without having a runt like me around to cramp his stylus. And I would get my long-overdue come-uppance.

Now it was the departure hall's turn to start spinning. The group ran towards me, led, ironically, by Craig - Cyrene to my Nazarene - but too late. The customs psycho was shouting hysterically and Angelita was squawking like a seagull protecting its young. I couldn't take anymore. I stumbled forward. Something hit my face. It wasn't Craig this time. It was the floor.

Chapter 20: Restitution

Marvellous. This was all I needed. This was better than life itself; to come round, with the vision of Leonard Fawcett looming over me with a bottle of vodka in his hand and his wife Rania at his side carefully taking my pulse. I was in a room, on a bed.

"He's OK!" I heard Rania Fawcett announce. "He's coming to."

"What happened?" I asked, groggily.

"You fainted," Rania answered, matter-of-factly. "Sort of."

"Sort of?" I queried, rubbing my face.

"You had what appears to have been an alcohol-related seizure that led you to have a short blackout," she explained. "In the absence of any Librium, Leonard's got some vodka if you need something to calm yourself down."

"Doctor's orders?" I quizzed incredulously, but not ungratefully.

"Luckily for you, I happen to be an expert in this particular condition. Don't drink it if you don't need it."

"I need it all right," I said, suddenly panicked by the prospect of my life source being taken away.

Leonard passed me the bottle. I sat up, took a slug and looked around.

"Could someone tell me where we are exactly?" I enquired, gingerly, as I wiped my mouth.

"Sure," Rania granted, letting go of my wrist. "We're in a small emergency room off the departure lounge and we're due to board the aircraft in about half an hour. Fortunately for you I am allowed, in my capacity as your self-appointed physician and subject to your being airworthy, to act as escort and ensure your safe passage back to the UK. After that I must refer you to a specialist the moment we land. I can help you with that, but in the meantime you'll be travelling with us."

"In Premier Class?" I questioned, still in shock.

"At no extra cost," Leonard chipped in, glibly.

I tried to piece together events immediately prior to my losing consciousness. I recalled the energetic customs official ripping into my bag like a dog with an old cushion.

"What happened about the drugs?" I asked, uncertainly.

"What drugs?" Rania queried, looking suspicious.

"The drugs that you or your lot planted in my suitcase," I said, accusingly.

"You mean the stuff in the brown packet?" Rania enquired, looking utterly perplexed.

"Yes! The plant, you idiot!" I snapped, suddenly thinking I'd never spoken to a PABS executive director's wife like that before.

"It was a plant," she conceded, reluctantly. "Sort of."

"Can we cut out this 'sort of' crap!" I cried, exasperated. "What was in the fucking packet?"

"Well, it *was* a sort of plant," Leonard intervened. "If you call dried saffron a plant, that is, but it was the stuff that the fruit sellers peddle on the beach, that's all. The customs man thought it was some form of medication you carried around in case of emergencies. He thought you were having an epileptic fit. He was rather embarrassed when he opened it."

"*He* was embarrassed!" I exclaimed.

Angelita flounced into the room at that moment, looking very official. She was relieved to see that I was alive, at least.

"That's settled, then," she said, with brisk efficiency.

"What now?" I groaned, becoming tired of my own questions.

"I've got you sitting all together!" she declared, triumphantly.

"Hang on," I said, looking at Rania and Angelita together. "How come you know each other? And where does Craig fit in exactly?"

Angelita took the lead.

"It's my job now to look after VIPs and 'Premier Club' passengers," she explained, proudly. "I was escorting Mr and Dr Fawcett to the check-in when I saw Craig seeing his girlfriend off back to the UK. I stopped and said 'Hello', when you appeared, looking worse for wear. I knew something was really wrong when I saw your eyes rolling around everywhere and the difficulty you were having putting your baggage on the scales. We all ran to your assistance, but you'd already keeled over by the time we got to you. Fortunately Mr Fawcett was able to calm the customs official down with a nice five hundred rupee note and we were practically given a guard of honour to the first-aid room here. Craig took off back to his hotel as he was no longer part of the fun, but he wished you well. So thanks to Mr Fawcett's financial foresight, Dr Fawcett's presence of mind and my knowledge of airport procedure, you, by the grace of God, are about to be on your way home."

I got off the bed unsteadily. Angelita helped me stand up. We walked out of the room to the departure lounge together.

"You be careful, James," she whispered, warningly. "Do what Dr Fawcett says. She has a good plan for you. Take her advice; you need to get fixed."

"Fascinating," I said, wondering what I had coming to me.

"Be serious, James," she implored.

"Angelita," I said, seizing the open window for redemption, "I am really sorry for what did or didn't happen between us. As you can see I'm not in much of a position to look after myself, let alone anyone else. I really didn't mean to hurt you."

"I understand," she assured me. "You don't have to worry about that anymore. Just get better. I know now why you had to let me go."

So there I was, not exactly feeling my best, wedged in a seat between a disgruntled director of The Pan Asian Bank and his eloquent, but somewhat sermonising wife. For nine hours. One consolation was that I had a drink in front of me, which was having a restorative effect.

"I feel immensely stupid about this," I confessed awkwardly to Leonard as Rania got up, ostensibly to talk to someone she knew on the plane.

"It's OK," he replied, sounding equally uncomfortable. "I'll admit this part of the venture wasn't entirely my idea, but Rania normally gets her way when it comes to other people's welfare. Quite frankly, I'd rather have left you sleeping it off at the back of the kite."

"Now why doesn't that surprise me, Leonard?" I asked, levelling up to him. "You haven't been exactly sociable since we first clapped eyes on each other at Richard Hartley's farewell drinks."

"Oh, it goes way before that," he declared, in what I hoped was jest, though his face said otherwise.

"That's nice," I said, disconsolately.

"Look," he went on to explain, "we were colleagues and that was fine, but apart from that we were never really friends in the true sense, were we?"

"I thought there might have been some vestiges of friendship that would have seen us through," I sighed.

"On your part perhaps," he remarked, unflinchingly. "But business is business. Once you'd left The Bank and ceased to be a colleague, well, what was the point?"

"Obviously you're a busy man," I said, inspecting his suntan respectfully, "but that doesn't mean you have to be rude."

"Doesn't it?" he challenged. "Being nice doesn't seem to have got you very far. Besides, I'm not rude, just honest. I don't have time to be nice for the sake of it. There are more important things on my plate to attend to."

"It's nice to be important," I put in, turning to look at him. "But it's important to be nice."

"Oh, cry me a river, for fuck's sake," he wailed, barely able to contain his irritation.

"It's not a river you or your company should be crying about," I said, opportunistically. "It's a bay you should be more concerned with... Thorn Bay."

His face became bloodless.

"Not that old chestnut again," he balked. "That was cancelled due to lack of interest years ago."

"How convenient for The Bank," I noted, hoping that I wasn't sounding too lippy. "It's no wonder no one wants to talk about it now."

"Let's get things into perspective. This wasn't some Whitewater whitewash or a gorefest on the scale of the Mai Lai Massacre. Can't you see: this was not a hill to die for. This was Hongkong, not Hollywood. Nobody outside gave a pig's arse about the bloody thing."

"But The Bank's not just in Hongkong anymore; it's a little bigger these days," I observed, understating the obvious. "Doesn't that make it slightly more interesting?"

"I doubt it. Who cares? Besides, before you really start to go 'Holy Joe' on yourself, why don't you consider your own role in it all?"

"In what sense and context?" I demanded, somewhat taken aback.

"How about Joy Wathen: Jakarta 1983?" he interrogated, knowingly.

"What about her?" I challenged, now totally baffled.

"You tell me," Leonard replied. "Or would you like me to tell you a thing or two?"

I shrugged my shoulders. I couldn't believe what I was hearing. What had Joy Wathen's existence twenty-five years ago got to do with a main board director of The Pan Asian Banking System, travelling at 35,000 feet on a fine January morning?

Leonard took my reticence for acceptance that he should proceed.

"Joy was employed as a junior counter clerk at the PABS Jakarta main office in March 1980. Nothing odd about that, except she was employed under the direct orders of our Chairman, which was unusual to say the least for such a humble position in a relatively unimportant part of The Bank's operations. That is, if you didn't know who Joy Wathen's real father was."

He paused, more I thought for composure than dramatic effect.

"Go on," I coaxed, becoming interested, despite myself.

"OK," he said reluctantly, as if loath to divulge any more information. "Well, as you really don't seem to know, she was only the illegitimate and much-favoured daughter of the President of Indonesia, wasn't she?"

"You're shittin' me!" I yowled, incredulously.

"Allegedly, apparently, supposedly; there were no DNA tests back then, but they had everything else. She was only supposed to be at The Bank as an intern on a temporary basis, but she stayed on and nobody could get rid of her."

"She never mentioned it; no one mentioned it. I was told her father was an important customer, but I didn't know he was that important," I said, still reeling from the revelation.

"It wasn't general knowledge; that was the deal. Her adoptive father was a Bank customer, not President Sukarno, but he was an important client nonetheless. He was one of Sukarno's henchmen."

I did a little arithmetic. It didn't compute.

"Hang on a minute. Do you mean President Suharto, perhaps?" I queried, without wishing to appear pedantic.

"Suharto, Sukarno, Sudoku, Subbuteo... one of 'em," Leonard said, getting annoyed, if not a little flustered. "But the fact was she'd been running round the branch for three years, screwing any senior member of staff and helping herself to petty cash whenever the mood took her. There was nothing anyone could do about it. Officially she was no one, but unofficially she was unsackable. To have done so would have meant a high risk of The Bank's licence to operate in Indonesia being revoked. That's how the country functioned. It wasn't going to happen, unless of course she was caught red-handed by an official third party... like, say, the Internal Audit Department. Which she was, by you, you daft prick, but you didn't report the fiddle because you were too busy fiddling with her!"

"Ah, I was told you knew about that," I remarked, warming to the subject.

"Of course. It all came out."

"So I assume it was you who attached the mystery addendum on the matter to my personnel file," I adduced, tentatively.

"For posterity's sake, a while ago," Leonard confessed. "You see, you don't realise how significant your non-disclosure was at the time. When the truth about Joy eventually came out, along with a whole list of other misdemeanors, it was too late. A case of stable doors and horses. But I still don't think you get it."

"No, I don't, quite frankly," I admitted. "It seems much ado about nothing."

"OK," he said again, "For conjecture's sake I'll tell you what probably would have happened if you'd reported Miss Wathen's misconduct at the proper time. First: she would have been summarily dismissed; there was no other procedural option. Secondly: there could have been a high chance of intervention on President Suharto's behalf. The Bank would have been caught between the devil and the deep blue sea, especially with everything being out in the open. It wouldn't have been able to climb down from a procedural decision. At the same time Suharto was used to getting his way and had precious little truck with foreign companies, whatever his daughter's employ. He would have relished mucking up The Bank's business in Indonesia or, more to the point, extracting a considerable forfeit to do otherwise. Don't forget the political climate at the time: we're talking 'Bribesville' here. Thirdly: having gone through its scandal phase, the matter would have been crying out for an international investigation, which would doubtless have revealed how Alec Dunhill was up to his tits in the Thorn Bay 'club', which itself was about to turn turtle in very muddy waters. Suharto was, despite his corporate xenophobia, a key member of 'the club' too; that was the connection, but he was a dictator so he could do what he liked, such is dictatorial hypocrisy. There's nothing new in that.

"The scope of the investigation would quite likely have forced Alec Dunhill and most of the PABS board to resign. This would have meant a new board being appointed with, by design, a safer directorate and a less flamboyant agenda, which in all probability would have stuck to the more plodding business of commercial banking instead of going the investment banking route and buying rubbish companies like The Stronghold Finance Corporation of New York. From a personal point of view it might have meant I'd got onto the board earlier and should've been in a considerably stronger position than I am now to make a bid for the top. Maybe *that's* why I'm a bit iffy whenever you see me."

"Leonard, this is a bit *Tontons Macoutes* for me. Don't you think it's all a little far-fetched?" I queried, thinking he'd gone completely bonkers.

"It's absurd," he acknowledged, "but *something* along those lines would have happened. Don't underestimate the importance of the missed opportunity in this incident. This was the Goldilocks Effect writ large. All the ducks were in a row, and it was the perfect chance to be shot of Alec Dunhill and his North American swashbucklers. Most people wanted The Bank to stick to what it was good at, namely good old-fashioned commercial banking in the Far East. It might have become *the* firebrand financial powerhouse of the area, ready to grasp one of the fastest growing economies in the world, as opposed to what it is now: a rather bland international wet lettuce. That's my opinion, anyway"

"I wonder,' I uttered, unconvinced. "Although they say a fish rots from the head down."

"A dead fish, James; just a dead fish," Leonard corrected. "And the Pan Asian ain't dead yet. Not by a long chalk line."

"Yet?" I questioned, having always assumed that his faith in The Bank was based on the eternal.

"Empires come and empires go," he replied, dispassionately. "It would be crass to think that The Bank is impervious to the ebb and flow of economic tides."

We grew quiet for a moment. I wondered where Rania had got to, but was glad to have the field clear to rake over some more dirt.

"Which still doesn't satisfy my curiosity about how Lord Dunhill escaped censure over Thorn Bay," I said awkwardly, still trying to milk it.

"Cool it, Serpico: rattle the cage much more and you'll kill the canary," Leonard snarled, agitated. "Your preoccupation with Alec Dunhill and The Thorn Bay Company may go unrewarded. The can of worms you're hoping to prise open is not stocked at this particular shop. I hate to disappoint you, but the Thorn Bay case and Lord Dunhill's elevation to the Upper House are unconnected. It wasn't as if his ennoblement would have created some sort of *cordon sanitaire* that would have precluded him from being brought to book in Hongkong. The case was closed. It was that simple and that was the end of it."

"But he effectively bought his position."

"He made a substantial donation to an ambient cause," Leonard conceded, "but it was a largely apolitical gesture."

"Hmm," I hummed, looking at him doubtfully. "Are you at liberty to expand?"

"In this instance, I don't see why not," he said, taking a sip from his drink at last. "It's quite straightforward. Lord Dunhill had always had an interest and expertise in environmental causes, and he was wealthy. He put the two together and established a charitable foundation that attracted funds from other wealthy individuals. In time he and the foundation became increasingly influential. When the regnant government decided they needed additional representation on the subject in the form of a benign voice rather than say, a battering ram, the House of Lords was the obvious instrument and they approached Alec Dunhill to be their man. Sir Alec, as he was then, took the view that even if he did dress, politically, more to the right than what was on offer, it was better to be a government appointee on the inside than just a trustee on the board of a charity on the outside, so in the name of the cause he took them up on their proposal. That was his only intention: to be the most effective he could be in the objectives he'd set for himself. Hate the game, James, not the player."

"Hate 'em both," I griped quietly, but audibly.

"Well let's face it: there are worse things than being a spokesperson for environmental affairs. It's all for the future good of humanity. So to answer your query: there is no query. You're out of step. Move on."

It was my turn to fall quiet. Rania was taking her time. I could have done with an interruption to lighten things up. I took a large gulp of my drink. Leonard had been succinct to the point of being presumptuous in quashing my qualms about Alec Dunhill and the Thorn Bay situation, but I thought there was still room for further discussion.

"That's quite a balls-up you've inherited at Stronghold," I remarked, reiterating the point I'd made just before we'd left for Goa, and the cleanup operation he would have to undertake.

"If I'm going to play lumberjack, I've got to handle my end of the log," he remarked, stolidly.

"What happens if you don't pull it off?"

"Fuck knows. The damn thing wasn't my idea," he bit back, alluding, I assumed, to the original PABS boardroom decision to acquire Stronghold a few years before.

"Whose ever it was, it was a pretty dumb one," I asserted, exploiting the moment. "You must have been part of the voting process?"

Leonard remained tight-lipped, saying nothing.

"You must have had a vote," I insisted. "You were there, weren't you?"

"The vote was held *in camera*," he revealed, eventually. "I'm not at liberty to divulge who voted for what in such circumstances."

"Whatever. It just strikes me as a funny way to bet the farm," I said, determined to push the point.

"It wasn't the farm," Leonard grunted, indignantly. "Just the barn, James. Just the barn."

He went quiet yet again and then, almost as an afterthought, sparked back to life.

"We're not alone, he began, abstractedly. "We're not the only bank that's screwed up in the US; we're just the first to admit it."

"Really?" I quizzed.

"Yes, really," he stated emphatically. "It's happening on both sides of the pond. There's a whole clusterfuck of trouble out there. It's all gone a bit Amstrad. Everyone's very confused and one way or another confidence – and by that I mean interbank liquidity - is totally up the creek... there's at least one major UK bank that's already looking decidedly rocky as we speak."

He shot me a knowing glance that was lost on me. I waited for him to say more, but he'd gone into thought. I had just one more thing I wanted to clear up, more out of curiosity than for the sake of fact-finding, but I didn't want to address the matter as a yet another question.

"Richard Hartley seemed a bit anti-chuffed with his recent posting," I remarked, randomly.

"Oh, 'im" Leonard muttered, as if Richard was minor irrelevance, which at that point he probably was. "I'm sensing a bit of mission-drift here... we didn't know where to put him. We couldn't give him a full branch... he was a bit wayward in his methods but he worked well under supervision and when Assistant Manager, Malta came up, I thought why not? It didn't help that he seemed to be on a macabre one-man crusade to expose the supposed black arts of his superiors. Society loves a whistle-blower but imagination, however vivid, is hardly the bedrock of reality. Richard was biting the hand that was feeding him – but for no reason or purpose. It was only because I pounced on the Malta idea that he escaped 'early retirement'.

Leonard lapsed back into silence. He wasn't going any further. I'd had a good run and got more or less as much as I could get. I'd gone as far as I could. There was no point in spoiling it. It really was time to move on.

As luck would have it Rania reappeared, sparing Leonard and me the ignominy of falling into a permanent Trappist silence.

"OK, James," she said, taking her seat again. "I've sorted a few things out."

Leonard looked away. The bastard! He'd known all along what was going on.

"Like what?" I asked, suspiciously.

"I've just spoken to your sister," Rania replied, evenly. "She's going to meet us at the airport and take you on from there."

"What?" I yelped in panic, not for the first time that day. "How did you even know I had a sister?"

"Simple: she was under 'next of kin' in your passport when I rescued it from the check-in girl at the airport," Rania explained, calmly. "I've been in the cockpit with the captain. He's radioed ahead for assistance when we get there. Your sister and I have agreed on a rehab facility in Luton that can take you on at short notice. It comes highly recommended. The captain's brother's been there. It's very effective, apparently."

"Don't I have any say in the matter?!" I whimpered, despondently. "And what about the money?"

"Best to keep quiet and not complain too much," Rania replied. "In these circumstances anyway. And I've checked... it's not so expensive."

"I don't care anymore," I said, feeling beaten. "I'm sick and tired of being sick and tired."

"That's no bad thing," she commiserated. "There's no point fighting it; there's no shame in surrendering to the winning side."

Yech. The times I'd heard that before. And the times I'd hear it again.

I needed to go to the loo. I undid my seat buckle and turned to Leonard.

"Will you excuse me?" I asked, humbly and contritely. "I have to go to the *toilet.*"

There was no Monica at the airport this time. Just Elspeth. We drove with our customary wordlessness to the rehab centre. It wasn't far, just on the other side of the town. I only had my holiday clothes with me. Luton. In January. This place wasn't going to be like the one in Spain. This one meant business. Or so Rania had said, and I had no reason to disbelieve her.

Luton's a town that's a bit down on its luck. It's just gone one chicken nugget too far. The town centre's a no-go zone after 8 p.m. and during the day the only shops that do any business are the pawnbrokers and Cash Converters, or 'Crack Converters' as they're called affectionately to much merriment in local quarters. Among the cafés and bus shelters everyone seems to be filling a form, either for social or disability benefits, indicating there's fuck all to do here and no work. And there are a thousand other Lutons, up and down the land.

The rehab centre's not much better, but I'm getting the hang of it. I've been here nearly three months now. I'm at the halfway stage between what they imaginatively call the primary and secondary treatments. If six months of the AA Twelve Step program doesn't put me off drink, surely Luton will. Rania was right: it's not too expensive, which is just as well for a six-month stretch. In fact, it's as cheap as chips and sometimes it shows. Most of the other 'clients', as we're called, are remand prisoners on drug busts, with crime raps as long as my arm, so I feel quite at home, really.

Of the other participants in this *tableau vivant*, I have heard very little, although Pete Divis visited me recently with some interesting news about Fred Armitage. It would appear that Mrs Armitage finally became fatigued by Fred's late-night Russian divertissements and, having made sure of her financial footing, kicked him gently in the balls and not so gently out of the house. I expect most of the money that Fred wheedled out of the big deal will end up in her bin, illustrating a point that money can be funny with people who are funny about money. As if that wasn't enough, to add to Fred's woes, most of the people who generated decent fees at his company upped and left, leaving him all on his lonesome. Which goes to show there must be some stock in the adage that if you wait by life's great river long enough, the bodies of your enemies will eventually float by. But so what? That's not in God's telescope, and anyway is not revenge a dish that best goes stale? Nevertheless it's a shame, as there was a time when I, among others, used to look up to Fred, but for now it would seem to be another case of *tant pis*.

Pete also told me of the sad demise of Martin Letts, the man who'd been responsible for introducing me to the headhunting business. He recently entered a charity fun run up Sca Fell and fell himself, halfway down, dead of a heart attack. Not much fun in that, but at least he died rich.

One of the benefits of my newly enforced sobriety, apart from giving me the wherewithal to say my piece, is that I've had the chance to reflect with a clear mind on what Leonard Fawcett and I discussed on the plane back from Goa. Some of what he said I have to accept as bona fide in the absence of any inside knowledge to the contrary, but some I simply have to take with a bag of salt. That Alec Dunhill received his peerage at the same time as giving massive donations to worthy causes may be a happy coincidence. That he wasn't called to account for his part in the Thorn Bay affair, I'm not so sure. Not in my mind anyway, although it would go to show how the system looks after its own, with a grip as vice-like as any wrestling hold, so no changes there. Also Leonard's comment that one major British bank was 'beginning to look decidedly rocky' turned out to be alarmingly true. Likewise his remarks about other banks skating on thin ice including I've since heard, my former employers at Barrow Brothers, over CMO default of all things! Let the bodies float by! It couldn't happen to a nicer bank.

As for the other stuff we discussed, who knows? I had no part in the world order. Why should I have? I am and was nothing. And yet, if I had reported the incident in Jakarta, or been taken to task for not doing so at the time, would that have led to a further investigation into the circumstances surrounding either of Joy Wathen's fathers' string-pulling? Would either's efforts to keep their not so spotless daughter in respectable employment have gone on to prove the darker side of Alec Dunhill's association with Thorn Bay? Perhaps. Perhaps not, but it might have drawn attention to the seamier side of The Pan Asian. An alert enquirer need only have scratched the surface to reveal that there was something a bit more substantial and untoward between the two companies. Such an insight might have hastened Alec Dunhill's retirement as Chairman of The Pan Asian and thenceforward altered the composition of the board of directors for years to come. Unlikely? Stranger things have happened. A board with a more selective attitude to systemic risk and a proper dynamic between its executive and non-executive members might have averted the gung-ho gluttony of later years that led to The Bank entering the American sub-prime market with such enthusiasm, by its acquisition of Stronghold.

To go one step further than Leonard Fawcett, this would have been more than an internal matter, in that if The Bank hadn't entered the sub-prime market with such abandon, its actions *pour encourager les autres* wouldn't have happened. Although PABS was by no means the trailblazer in the sector - there was no trail – its participation lent a certain credibility, if not indeed direction up the garden path, even if the path itself led, inexorably, to an abyss. Had this state of affairs been otherwise, would other banks in the UK, Europe and elsewhere have shown more restraint without the PABS example to mobilise them, and therefore have taken a closer and harder look at what they were letting themselves in for? And what would have happened then? Had they not been quite so hasty in augmenting the American sub-prime market, either as investors or participants, would worldwide economic meltdown have been averted? Would they have been less easily seduced by the puffery being peddled by the charlatans of the American mortgage market without The Pan Asian's precedent? Maybe. Maybe not.

Après moi le deluge! Or is this just a case of self-aggrandisement that often comes as part of the delusional grandiosity that makes for the alcoholic package? Even so, my part in the general scheme of things would appear to have been more pivotal than I was ever aware. Perhaps I wasn't such a flyweight after all, or am I straying into territory that belongs to Cleopatra's nose? It might be far-fetched, but how far? Me and my dick, eh? Anyway these things will doubtless be eclipsed in the universal conscious by even more calamitous events of the future, and become like everything else: a thing of the past.

Also published by Longcross Press:

The Companion to British History
by Professor Charles Arnold-Baker O.B.E. (Third Edition)

Seven Stories for Christmas
by Henry von Blumenthal